Bad Little Falls

ALSO BY PAUL DOIRON

Trespasser
The Poacher's Son

BAD LITTLE FALLS

Paul Doiron

MINOTAUR BOOKS
NEW YORK

This is a work of fiction. All of the characters, organizations, and events portrayed in this novel are either products of the author's imagination or are used fictitiously.

BAD LITTLE FALLS. Copyright © 2012 by Paul Doiron. All rights reserved. Printed in the United States of America. For information, address St. Martin's Press, 175 Fifth Avenue, New York, N.Y. 10010.

www.minotaurbooks.com

Library of Congress Cataloging-in-Publication Data

Doiron, Paul.
    Bad Little Falls : a novel / Paul Doiron.—1st ed.
        p. cm.
    ISBN 978-0-312-55848-2 (hardcover)
    ISBN 978-1-250-01091-9 (e-book)
    1. Game wardens—Fiction. 2. Murder—Investigation—Fiction. 3. Wilderness areas—Maine—Fiction. I. Title.
    PS3604.O37B33 2012
    813'.6—dc23

                                                                    2012007787

First Edition: August 2012

10 9 8 7 6 5 4 3 2 1

For Monica Wood

I thought she was probably a little crazy. It was all right if she was. I did not care what I was getting into.

—ERNEST HEMINGWAY, *A Farewell to Arms*

Bad Little Falls

I

The last time I saw Lucas Sewall, he left a school notebook under the passenger seat of my truck.

It was a curious document. The boy had drawn disturbing images on the covers—pictures of vampire women and giant owls with bloodstained beaks. The inside pages were crammed with his indecipherable handwriting, words so small you needed a magnifying glass to read them. There were maps labeled with cryptic directions to "lightning trees" and "old Injun caves" and hieroglyphs that might have been messages in secret code or just meaningless scribbles. With a compulsive liar like Lucas, you never knew whether you were dealing with fact or fiction.

The dated diary entries were especially hard to unravel. Between his other weird jottings, the kid had seemingly kept a careful record of the tragic events in Township Nineteen, as if he had anticipated that his eyewitness account might one day prove useful in a court of law. But who knows what was going on in that oversize head of his? In my short acquaintance with him, I learned Lucas Sewall was a deeply damaged child who believed in manipulating adults, settling scores, and tying up loose ends. Sometimes I wondered whether he didn't see the notebook as his last will and testament, with me in the role of executor.

The first entry was dated three nights before the fatal snowstorm:

FEBRUARY 12

Randle came around last night drunker than usual and made us leave the house again so he could get at his stash of drugs without us knowing where he'd hid them.

Ma didn't want to let him in, but Randle had the Glock he bought off that Mexican in Milbridge and said he'd use it this time if we didn't wait outside in the dooryard while he got his pills and powder.

We had trouble bringing Aunt Tammi down the ramp on account of her wheelchair not having good grippy-ness on the ice and snow.

Ma said we should at least wait inside the car, where we could run the blower, only she'd forgotten the keys on the kitchen table. That just made her more pissed off than she already was.

We could've waited in Randle's car except that Uncle Prester was passed out in the shotgun seat and he smelt like he'd puked himself, which wouldn't be the first time.

Randle was inside the house a long time, making shadows behind the curtains. When he came out, Ma said they were broken up forever and she didn't like him hiding his drugs in her house for the cops to find.

That got Randle all exercised. He said if she ever ratted on him, she'd be sorry, and he said that went double for the Boy Genius.

Randle didn't figure that I'd already found his stupid drugs stuffed behind the insulation in the sewing room . . . easiest place in the world to find, on account of the pink dust all over the floor.

He didn't know what I did to the pills, neither . . . and wasn't he in for a wicked surprise when someone swallowed one of them Oxycottons?

I would pay GOOD money to see Randle get his ass kicked.

As it happened, Lucas didn't have long to wait.

Two days later, his mother's ex-boyfriend was dead and his uncle Prester lay in a hospital bed with blackened claws where his fingers and toes had once been.

2

The zebra had frozen to death beneath a pine tree.

The animal lay on its side in a snowbank with its striped legs rigidly extended and its lips pulled back from its yellow teeth in a horsey grimace, as if, in its final moments on earth, it had grasped the punch line of some cosmic joke.

The owner of the game ranch had called the local veterinarian in a last-ditch effort to resuscitate the hypothermic zebra, and Doc Larrabee had brought me along because he needed a witness to back up this crazy story down at the Crawford Lake Club. It didn't matter that I was the new game warden in District 58 and a flatlander to boot.

Doc knelt in the snow beside the equine. He had removed his buckskin mitten and was rubbing his palm across the dead animal's thinly haired haunches. The frost melted beneath the warmth of his hand.

"You understand that a zebra is a creature of sub-Saharan Africa?" he asked Joe Brogan.

"Yeah," the ranch owner said sourly.

"It is well adapted to life on the equatorial savanna—as opposed to the boreal forest of Maine, I mean."

"I understand that!"

Brogan wore a beaver hat that might once have been fashionable on the streets of Saint Petersburg. His face was also furry. A single brown eyebrow extended across the bridge of his nose, and a luxuriant beard grew thickly down his throat before disappearing, like a shy animal, inside the collar of his wool shirt.

A small crowd of men had met us outside the gate of the Call of the Wild Guide Service and Game Ranch. They were big bearded men wearing camouflage parkas, synthetic snowmobile pants, and heavy pack boots. Now I could see their bulky silhouettes lurking in the shadows of the pines and smell their cigarettes drifting on the crisp February air. The ill will carrying downwind in my direction was as pungent as tobacco smoke.

The guides at Call of the Wild did some conventional outfitting in the fat spruce land outside the ranch's barbed wire—leading hunters in pursuit of deer, bear, coyote, and moose—but Brogan had built his business on a practice that animal rights activists termed "canned hunting." He owned miles of fenced timber, which he had stocked with the oddest menagerie of animals imaginable. The sign outside his gate advertised the services offered: RUSSIAN BOAR, BUFFALO HUNTS, RED STAG, ELK HUNTS, AND FALLOW DEER HUNTS.

The zebra hadn't survived long enough to make it onto the sign.

At Call of the Wild, hunters paid thousands of dollars to sit on thermal fanny warmers in protected tree stands and take potshots at exotic creatures. According to a strange loophole in Maine law, what happened on game ranches was generally not the concern of the Department of Inland Fisheries and Wildlife, for which I worked; rather, it was under the jurisdiction of the Department of Agriculture. The state basically viewed these places as farms and the foreign animals as livestock. In my mind, the entire setup was a disgrace and an embarrassment to sportsmen.

The Warden Service had just transferred me from midcoast Maine to the unpeopled hinterlands of Washington County. I'd gotten into some administrative trouble down south the previous spring and summer—not the first time for such things, and unlikely to be the last. My commanding officer never came right out and said I was being exiled to Siberia, but when you are reassigned to the easternmost county in the United States—a place known for its epidemic drug abuse, multigenerational unemployment, and long tradition of violent poaching—it's pretty clear your career isn't on the rise.

While Doc Larrabee examined the carcass, I documented the travesty with my Nikon.

"What are you taking pictures for?" Brogan asked.

"Souvenirs," I said.

Brogan and I had already locked antlers a week earlier. I'd issued a criminal summons to one of his coyote-hunting guides, a meathead named Billy Cronk, when one of his clients discharged a firearm within a hundred yards of a residence on posted property. Given the unemployment rate in these parts, losing your commercial guiding license was a pretty big deal. On the other hand, Cronk's customer could've killed the old woman who lived in that house, and in my book, that was an even bigger deal.

I glanced around at the cigarette-lit faces. "Where's Billy tonight?"

Brogan spat a brown stream of tobacco juice at my feet. "None of your fucking business."

My former supervisor had given me some advice before I was transferred to the boondocks. "Play it tough," Sgt. Kathy Frost had said. "When you're assigned to a new district, you need to come on strong, or people will think you're a pussy. Especially way Down East, where they eat wardens for breakfast."

Everywhere I'd gone for the past three weeks, people treated me like a leper.

Doc Larrabee was one of the lonely exceptions. Maybe he felt sorry for me, or maybe, as a recent widower living alone in an isolated farmhouse, he thought that hanging around with the hated new game warden would be the cure for midwinter boredom.

"Well, obviously the animal has expired," said Doc.

"Obviously," said Brogan.

"I would attribute the official cause of death to freezing its ass off."

Larrabee was a slope-shouldered man in his early sixties. He wore round eyeglasses, which were constantly fogging over, requiring him to wipe away the moisture with a handkerchief. For reasons I couldn't fathom, he wore an Amish-style beard: a fringe of hair along the jawbone, with no mustache to match. He was dressed in green coveralls and tall rubber boots fit for wading through all kinds of manure. His work as a large-animal veterinarian kept him busy in the outdoors—delivering breached foals and tending to sick cows—and he had the healthy glow of a person who breathes a lot of fresh air. On the drive over, he'd told me he was working on a book of his misadventures titled *All Creatures Sick and Smelly.*

"So that's it, then?" the ranch owner said.

"Unless you have a musk ox or a greater kudu you'd like me to examine."

Brogan moved the wad of tobacco in his mouth from one cheek to the other. "You're one hell of a comedian, Doc."

The veterinarian rose, stiff-kneed, to his feet. "I'm going to have to report this incident to the Animal Welfare Department, Joe," he said, no longer grinning.

Brogan narrowed his eyes beneath his hairy brow. "What for?"

"Aggravated cruelty to animals is a Class C crime," I said.

"I didn't know it was going to freeze to death."

"It's a zebra, Brogan," I said.

"We've got all kinds of animals here—African ones, too," he said. "They all handle the cold fine."

"Brogan," I said. "It's a zebra."

"The guy who sold it to me said it was hardy. He misrepresented the animal. He's the one you should be harassing."

"I'm sure the district attorney will agree," I said.

"Fuck you and your attitude," Brogan said.

I heard murmuring and snow crunching in the shadows around me. My right hand drifted toward the grip of my holstered .357 SIG SAUER.

Two years earlier, when I'd been a rookie fresh from the Maine Criminal Justice Academy and full of self-righteousness, I would have welcomed a confrontation with this jerkwad. But I had made strides in managing my anger, and besides, there was no urgency here: The zebra was dead. I would hand over my notes and photos to the Animal Welfare Department, and that would be the end of my involvement in Brogan's bad business.

Doc glanced at me and gestured in the direction of the gate, hundreds of yards away through thick snow and dense pines. "I'd say it's time for us to go, Warden."

"Gladly."

Brogan, of course, had to have the last word.

"Hey, Bowditch," he said. "You're not going to last long around here if you don't cut people some slack."

"I'll take it under advisement," I said.

When we got back to the road, I half expected to find my tires slashed, but no one had molested the vehicle in our absence. My "new" truck, a standard-issue green GMC Sierra, was actually older than the pickup I'd been assigned in Sennebec. It seemed like all of my equipment here was shabbier than what I'd been issued before. Maybe being given obsolescent gear was part of my punishment.

Doc Larrabee drew his shoulder belt tight across his chest. When he exhaled, I caught the sweet smell of bourbon on his breath. "Well, that episode was definitely one for my book," he said.

I started the engine and turned the wheel east, in the direction of Calais—pronounced *Callus* in this part of the world—on the Canadian border. "I can't believe that idiot brought a zebra to Maine."

The veterinarian rubbed his mittens together. "Joe's not as dumb as he looks. He's smart about looking after his own interests. And like most bullies, he has an eye for a person's weak spot. Those men who work for him are all terrified of pissing him off."

Doc's description of Brogan reminded me a lot of my own father. Jack Bowditch had always been the scariest guy in whatever town he'd happened to be living. Out in the sticks, where people live far from their neighbors and are leery of reporting misdeeds to the authorities out of fear of violent retribution, a reputation for ruthlessness can get a man most anything he wants.

"My new supervisor warned me about Brogan," I said.

"How is Sergeant Rivard?"

As big a prick as ever, I wanted to say.

Like me, Marc Rivard had been transferred from the affluent south to dirt-poor Washington County some time back, and he was still bitter about his circumstances. Unlike me, he had subsequently earned a promotion and was now in the position of off-loading his frustrations on the nine district wardens under his supervision.

"Sergeant Rivard has a unique approach to his job," I said.

Doc removed his glasses and wiped them with a snotty-looking handkerchief. "Do you mind if I ask you a personal question? Did you impregnate the commissioner's daughter or something? You must have pissed off some eminence down in Augusta to get stationed out here in the williwags."

I found it hard to believe Doc was truly ignorant of my notorious history. If he read the newspapers at all, he must have known about the manhunt for my father two years ago and he would have heard that I'd shot a murderer in self-defense back in Sennebec last March. Maybe he didn't realize how deeply I'd embarrassed the attorney general's office in the process. In the opinion of the new administration in Augusta, I had become a public-relations nightmare. And if Colonel Harkavy couldn't force me to resign, he could at least sweep me under the rug.

"It's a long story," I said.

"I'd enjoy hearing it sometime," Doc said. "I might be misreading your social calendar, but I'm guessing you don't get many dinner invitations. Why don't you come over tomorrow night and I'll cook you my widely praised coq au vin. After Helen died, I had to learn how to feed myself, and thanks to Julia Child, I became quite the French chef."

I didn't much feel like socializing these days, and the idea of eating dinner alone at this old man's house made me squirmy, I'm not ashamed to admit.

The veterinarian must have sensed my discomfort. "Maybe I'll invite Kendrick over, too," he said. "He's a professor down to the

University of Maine at Machias and runs the Primitive Ways survival camp. Kevin's a musher, a dogsled racer. He and his malamutes have raced in the Iditarod up in Alaska a couple of times and finished in the money. He's had a pretty unusual life and is something of a living legend around here. He knows these woods better than the local squirrels."

Kendrick's name was familiar to me. My friend, the retired chief warden pilot, Charley Stevens, had mentioned the professor as someone worth getting to know in my new district. My one consolation in being transferred Down East was that it moved me closer to Charley and his wife, Ora, who had recently purchased a house near Grand Lake Stream, an hour's drive north of my new base in Whitney.

I tried to put Doc off, but he was persistent.

By the time I dropped the veterinarian at his doorstep, we had agreed that I would join him for dinner the following evening.

I took my time driving home. It wasn't like I had anyone waiting for me in bed.

The moon was nearly full, so I paused for a while atop Breakneck Hill and gazed out across the snowy barrens, which extended as far as the eye could see. Washington County is the wild-blueberry capital of the world. During the never-ending winter, the rolling hills become covered with deep drifts of snow. In places, boulders jut up through the crust. At night, the slopes look almost like a lunar landscape, if you can imagine twisted pines on the moon and a looming cell tower blinking red above the Sea of Tranquillity.

I switched on the dome light and reached for the birthday card I'd tucked between the front seats. It had arrived in my mail that morning, just a week late. The picture showed a cartoon cat hugging a cartoon dog.

To a purrfect friend, it read.

Sarah had always given me ironic cards—the sappier the better—so why should it be any different now that our relationship was over? She'd handwritten a note in purple ink inside:

Dear Mike,

  I hope things are well and that you're enjoying the win-
ter Down East. Do you have any time to ski or ice fish?
How are Charley and Ora doing? I know it's not your way
to do something special for yourself, but it would make me
happy to think of you having some fun with friends today.
Life is busy here in D.C., but it's stimulating work and I'm
meeting lots of fascinating people. One of these days we
should catch up—it's been so long since we talked.

xoxo

S.

I didn't really want to speak with my ex-girlfriend. Sarah and I were finished forever as a couple, and probably finished as friends, no matter what her birthday card said. A year earlier, she had become pregnant with my child, a condition she had hidden from me until she miscarried. The fact that she had concealed her pregnancy proved that she would never overcome her doubts about my fitness to be a husband and father. We had broken up by mutual agreement over the summer, before I'd received my transfer to the North Pole. She was now living in Washington, D.C., working for the national office of the Head Start program. Sometimes I pictured her going out for drinks with people our own age—with *men* our own age—while I was stuck in the wilds of eastern Maine, fielding dinner invitations from elderly veterinarians.

I'd been struggling to find meaning in the sequence of events that had led me to this wasteland, but my prayers always seemed to disappear into the black void that stretched from horizon to horizon, and I never got any answers. All that was left to me was to accept my fate and do my job with as much dignity as I could muster.

Tonight, however, I found myself yearning to hear Sarah's voice, even though I knew that speaking with her would make me feel more lonely and not less. Two years earlier, when we were weathering a rough patch, I had convinced myself that I was a lone wolf by nature.

It was the reason why I had chosen the profession of game warden—because I secretly wanted a solitary life.

Now I knew better.

The moon was high and bright overhead when I arrived at my trailer on the outskirts of Whitney. I'd lived in my share of mobile homes as a child, and this one was better than most. The roof barely leaked, all but two of the electrical sockets worked, and a rolled towel pressed against the base of the door was enough to stop the snow from blowing in through the crack. My rented trailer was located down a dead-end road, far enough from the main drag that I could park my patrol truck out of sight—although every poacher, pill addict, and petty criminal within a hundred miles knew where I lived.

As I turned the truck into the plowed drive, the bright halogen bulbs swept across the front of the building. Something long and dark seemed to be affixed to the door. I couldn't tell for sure what the black thing was until I climbed the steps with my flashlight in hand.

The object was a coyote pelt. Whoever had killed the animal had done a poor job of skinning it, because the fur stank to the heavens. A tenpenny nail had been driven through the head into the hollow metal door.

There was a note written in block letters, large enough for me to read in the moonlight: "WELCOME TO THE NEIGHBORHOOD." It was signed, "GEORGE MAGOON."

The moon don't rotate, you know. All you ever see is the same side of it! There could be space aliens living up there in the shadows and we'd never know if they was planning to invade us.

Aunt Tammi don't believe me.

What do you think that Pink Floyd song means? I ask her.

She's knitting in her wheelchair. Which one, Lucas?

The one you're always playing. DARK SIDE OF THE MOON.

She says it don't mean anything. It's just a song.

We're all having dinner, Tammi, Uncle Prester, and me. Ma likes to eat at the table like we did when Gram and Gramp were alive and this was their house.

She always makes us say a prayer now, ever since she started going to those Don't Drink meetings.

About halfway through dinner, Randle comes by to get Uncle Prester.

Randle's got that scary new tattoo all over his face—the spiky one he got after Ma kicked him out before Christmas.

You don't have to go with him, Ma tells Prester.

Yeah I do, Prester says. He seems real sad about it, though.

Randle laughs and says they're just going coyote hunting is all.

Where's your dogs? I ask him. He used to have a pit bull, but they don't hunt.

Don't need any.

You using bait, then?

Nope.

So how you going to get them?

We call them in, he says. He does a sort of wolf call then, because he likes to scare Tammi and me.

After Randle and Prester leave, I say to Ma, They ain't going coyote hunting, are they?

She don't answer. She just keeps washing dishes.

They got some kind of big drug deal, don't they?

That gets her all worked up. Don't you have homework?

I already did it, I tell her.

Don't lie to me, Lucas.

She gives me that X-ray look. I can't understand how she figures things sometimes.

The curtains are rolled up in my room and the moon is shining in until I yank down the shade. I don't like seeing the full moon out my window. It reminds me of the White Owl.

3

W ho's George Magoon?" I asked Sgt. Kathy Frost.
I'd risen early to do push-ups, burpees, and planks, and I was standing in my boxer briefs, with the cell phone clamped to one sweaty ear. The windows inside the trailer were all frosted over, but I could tell from the ashen light that the day was shaping up to be a dark one. The sun had risen brightly at dawn, but menacing clouds were already rolling in from the northwest. The forecast called for snow.

I'd reached Kathy on the road. She was heading up north for a few days, towing her Ski-Doo Renegade on a trailer behind her patrol truck. The guys in Greenville needed some extra wardens to help work snowmobilers over the Presidents' Day weekend. There had been a fatality on Moosehead Lake five days earlier—too much booze, speed, and testosterone.

Kathy's voice was cutting in and out. Our connection wasn't great. "George who?"

"George Magoon. I checked the computer, but there's no one in the area with that name."

Kathy laughed. "I wouldn't think so."

"What do you mean?"

"George Magoon is a fictional character—like Robin Hood or Brer Rabbit. He was this wily poacher who was always outwitting the game wardens Down East. There are all kinds of tall tales about his exploits. Ask Rivard about them."

Kathy Frost wasn't just my former supervisor; she was the closest thing I had to a friend in the Warden Service, someone who had been a confidante to me during the tense days when my father was a fugitive in the North Woods. Kathy was also the most physically fit person I'd ever met. She was a tall, strong-limbed woman who wore her hair in a blondish bob and could bench-press her own weight. She routinely won triathlons without ever bothering to train for them.

"So you're saying that some jackass is pulling a prank on me?" I said.

"Just be glad he didn't nail a skunk to your door."

"What do you know about Brogan?"

"He's so dumb, he needs to unzip his fly to count to eleven."

I missed Kathy's warped sense of humor. I fancied myself a stoic, but the isolation of my new post seemed to be having an insidious effect upon me. The blank-eyed, unsmiling face I saw in the mirror each morning seemed to belong to one of those guys who sleeps under a bridge. Part of being a Maine game warden was being ready to move at a moment's notice. But the department's decision to transfer me out of Kathy's division (technically, I had volunteered) was an especially cruel blow.

There was static on the other end of the line. "You should talk to Rivard about that coyote," she said. "He might have some idea who the local jokers are."

"OK."

Rivard and I were scheduled to meet later that morning. My new sergeant had woken me at dawn, saying that he needed me to accompany him to a nearby school to confront some teenagers who might or might not have broken into several vacated summer cabins on the shores of Bog Pond.

"How you holding up down there, Grasshopper?" Kathy asked.

"Fine."

"Liar. You'll be all right once you get laid."

"Jesus, Kathy."

"We're breaking up here," she said before we finally lost the signal.

* * *

Washington County has lots of nicknames.

It's sometimes called the Bold Coast because of its wave-washed cliffs. Others refer to it as the Sunrise Coast because, as the easternmost stretch of land in the continental U.S. it is supposedly the first place to see the sunrise—provided there's no mist, rain, or snow, which is almost never. There are stony capes and islands here that see more fog than San Francisco or the entire Olympic Peninsula.

But the most common term people use to refer to Washington County is *Down East*.

In Maine, you might say that up is down. You travel *down* the coast from New Hampshire to New Brunswick—not up it—despite the fact that you're heading north the whole time. Down East is an old nautical term from the age of sail, when schooners sailed downwind from Boston, carrying passengers and rum to Maine's eastern ports and the Canadian Maritimes.

The windjammer trade might have blown south, but the contraband was still flowing freely in Washington County, although rum had largely been replaced by coffee brandy (Maine's unofficial state liquor), crystal meth, heroin, locally grown marijuana, and illegal prescription drugs, many of which were smuggled in from Canada. After the terrorist attacks of September 11, 2001, the border with New Brunswick had hardened. There were more checkpoints, more Immigration and Customs Enforcement (ICE) agents, more unmanned surveillance of the boundary woods and waters. Certainly there were more hassles for anyone who wished to drive from one nation to the other. None of these impediments seem to thwart smugglers.

By most measures, the state of Maine has the worst prescription-drug-abuse rates in America. The Maine Drug Enforcement Agency had given wardens a list of commonly abused medications, which included Dilaudid, Lorcet, Lortab, OxyContin, Percocet, Percodan, Tylox, Librium, Valium, Xanax, Adderall, Concerta, Vicodin, and Ritalin. Cross-border smuggling was only part of the problem. Addicts also forged prescriptions and conned multiple doctors into writing multiple scripts. They stole pills from the medicine cabinets of sick friends and relatives. Occasionally, some drugstore cowboy would even hold up an actual pharmacy. Painkillers were easy to obtain in Down East Maine—provided you had the money.

The problem was, nobody had any money. The street price for an Oxy 80—an eighty-milligram tablet of oxycodone—was eighty dollars. Very few jobs in depressed Washington County paid half that much for a day's work. As a result, burglaries and home invasions were epidemic. Aside from the drug dealers themselves, the only entrepreneurs thriving in my district were the backwoods fences who dealt in stolen electronics and Grandma's heirloom jewelry.

After I showered and shaved, I buttoned my uniform up over the thin ballistic vest I was required to wear each day. The uniform was olive-colored, like the fatigues worn by soldiers in Korea or Vietnam, with POLICE stenciled across the back. The trousers tucked into black combat boots. My P226 rode low on my gun belt, counterbalancing a holster containing Cap-Stun pepper spray. Every day I dressed like a man going to war.

I opened the fridge to see what I had for breakfast. Inside was a single blue can of Foster's, half an onion in a plastic bag, and a box of baking soda. I'd purchased the beer the night I'd moved in as a housewarming gift to myself but had decided against opening it. Toward the end of my relationship with Sarah, I'd been drinking way too much, and I worried that living alone, I might fall into bad habits. Seeing that can of Foster's every day and not opening it had become a personal test of will.

I was still studying my bare cupboards when Rivard's GMC pulled up to my trailer. He gave the horn a honk, scattering a flock of Bohemian waxwings from the crabapple tree across the right-of-way.

I zipped my parka and stepped outside into the barbarous cold. Instantly, my eyes began tearing up and my cheeks burned as if I'd been smacked in the face with a bag of ice.

I slid into the passenger seat. "Jesus, how cold is it?"

"Minus four."

As usual, he was wearing dark sunglasses despite the overcast sky.

Marc Rivard wasn't that much older than I was—I would have guessed thirty or thirty-one—but he seemed to have suffered an early onset of middle age. The black hair along his temples was edged with gray strands, and he had a developed a paunch, which bulged over the top of his gun belt. Rivard had grown up in a Franco-American household outside Lewiston, and his speech reminded me of my mom's French uncles and aunts. You didn't hear many people of my generation with that singsong accent.

"So where are we headed?" I asked.

"SAD seventy-seven," he said. "Whitney High School."

SAD stood for school administrative district, but the acronym seemed sadly fitting in this part of the state.

"And what are we doing, exactly?"

He pulled the truck out onto the road that led down to the coast. The asphalt was lined with five-foot-tall snowbanks. A week of sub-zero temperatures had hardened the drifts into rock-solid ice. If an ambulance came speeding along behind us, there would be no room to pull over, I realized.

"There's a kid I want to talk to named Barney Beal. My snitch says he's the one who broke into those cabins over on Bog Pond, the ones with satellite dishes."

"He was stealing TVs?"

"No, there's this microchip inside the relay that connects to the television. It goes for one hundred dollars a pop. It's small and easy to hide in your pocket. It's like stealing hundred-dollar bills."

"Why do you need me for this?"

When he turned his head, I saw my fun-house reflection staring back from the bronze lenses of his sunglasses. "What's with you and all the questions today?" he said. "It's more intimidating if there are two of us showing up in his classroom."

Rivard was in a foul mood again. He had gotten divorced and remarried the previous summer, and many of our "conversations" were long monologues by him on the inequities of the state's laws concerning alimony and child support. His new wife was already pregnant, too, but he didn't seem to see it so much as a blessing as another expense he couldn't afford.

He removed his hand from the wheel to sip coffee from an aluminum mug. It occurred to me this was yet another difference between my two sergeants. Kathy would never have come to my house without also bringing me a cup of coffee.

"Do you mind if we get some breakfast first?" I asked.

He glanced at the clock on the dashboard. "The McDonald's in Machias has a drive-through."

Ever since I'd moved to Whitney, I'd been in search of a regular breakfast joint. Back in my old district, I'd become a fixture at the Square Deal Diner. Just about every day, I'd stop in for a molasses doughnut and some good-natured ribbing from the owner, Dot Libby, or her plainspoken daughter, Ruth. They'd been among the first people to welcome me into what had started out as an unfriendly community. Over the course of the two years I'd spent in Sennebec, I'd formed an unexpected attachment to the restaurant. It surprised me, thinking about the Libbys, to feel such intense homesickness.

We drove along, listening to the fuzzy chatter on the police radio. I turned my head to take in the view.

The road into town was hardly beautiful. The snowbanks outside my window were black with soot and impacted grit. The bigger pines and birches had all been cut within the past fifty years, and so you were left with nothing but adolescent trees elbowing one another for sunlight. The scattered houses were a mix of rusty trailers, farmhouses with advanced cases of osteoporosis, and newer modular homes that looked like they had come out of the same cereal box. The residents tended to hang their laundry even in the dead of winter: faded bedsheets, spit-stained onesies, stretch pants, and a surprising amount of thong underwear.

Back on the midcoast, we'd had hidden pockets of poverty amid the splendid rows of summer cottages. Here, the poverty was proudly on display for the world to see. Whenever it snowed, everything would look pure and white again, but only for a few hours, until the first plow came along or the first pink panties got pinned to a clothesline.

After ten minutes of not conversing, I tried again. "So tell me about Joe Brogan."

"Kind of a dick—but his business is good for the local economy."

"I'm not a fan of game ranches."

"Yeah, well, they're legal, so you'd better get over it."

"What sorts of problems have you had with him and his guides?"

"One of his buffaloes got loose a year ago, and we spent a month looking for it in the woods. Freaked-out people kept calling us after it ran through their yards, asking us if there were bison in Maine. A guy finally shot it the first week of moose season, thinking it was an obese moose or something."

"What about Billy Cronk?" I asked.

"Good guide. Grew up in the woods. Are you still going to send that night hunting charge against him to the DA?"

Rivard had never told me to let the matter drop, but I could decode his sentiments easily enough. And the truth was that I was conflicted about the matter myself. Brogan might have been a jerk, but Cronk seemed like a decent guy, and the thought of ruining his life rubbed my ethics the wrong way. But Kathy had warned me against seeming soft. "I haven't decided yet."

"Well, it's your call." My sergeant took another sip of coffee. "That zebra thing is pretty crazy shit."

"It gets crazier," I said. "When I got home from Brogan's last night, there was a coyote skin nailed to my front door."

He didn't turn his head, but his mouth twitched. "No shit?"

"There was a note on it, saying, 'Welcome to the neighborhood.' It was signed, 'George Magoon.'"

"Probably kids," he said. "When we get to school, I'll show you the kinds of punks you're dealing with around here."

We rode the rest of the way in silence. Obviously Rivard would be no help in my search for this "George Magoon" character. Kathy had called it a prank, but the pelt had struck me more as a warning than a joke. Impaling it on my door was the kind of thing I could imagine Billy Cronk, or one of Brogan's other disgruntled guides, doing. It didn't seem like the stunt a random teenager would pull. Then again, Rivard knew the area better than I did.

Still, I had my doubts.

Uncle Prester didn't come home last night. That ain't the first time. Once we found him curled up asleep under the mailbox, drunk.

Ma's worried on account of how frigging cold it's been. She don't like him hanging around with Randle, neither.

If he tried sleeping outside again, he'd turn into one of them cavemen scientists dig out of glaciers.

Ma's late for work because she's worrying about Prester. Ma's a shift leader over to McDonald's.

I tell her I'm sick because I want to stay home and read that Ranger book Mrs. Greenlaw gave me, but Ma ain't buying it.

Once I pressed my head to the radiator to get it all hot and then told her I had a fever and she could feel my head to prove it.

She still didn't let me stay home.

Ma makes sure Tammi's all set in her wheelchair with the TV remote and everything. Sometimes I think she's lucky because she don't have to work or go to school or nothing. Then I think how much it must suck not being able to walk.

Outside, it's REAL cold. I'm worried it's going to snow again.

Mrs. Greenlaw says Maine was buried under a mile of ice during the last ice age. She says the glaciers crept down from Canada and nobody knows why. It just snowed and kept snowing for thousands and thousands of years.

I bet there were Abnormal Snowmen all over the place back then.

I seen one of their tracks one time in the woods behind the house. It looked like this . . .

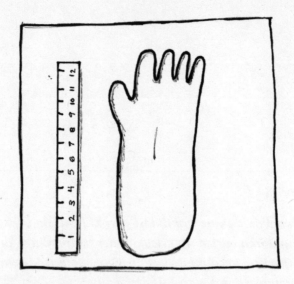

I told Ma what I seen, but she didn't believe me about that one, neither.

Maybe the Yeti got Prester.

4

After twenty minutes of frost heaves and potholes, Rivard and I found ourselves on the outskirts of Machias, the county seat and what passed for a metropolis in this part of the world, if you could even use the word *metropolis* to describe a place with a population that barely nudged two thousand.

Unlike many of my fellow wardens, I'd studied history rather than conservation law, and while the degree served no useful purpose in my current job, it made me see shadows of the past everywhere. I knew that the first naval battle of the Revolutionary War—nicknamed the "Lexington of the Seas"—had been fought at the entrance to Machias Bay in 1775. There was even a commemorative plaque down by the water. With crushing unemployment, a row of shuttered storefronts, and a rampant drug culture lurking behind locked doors, I couldn't blame the good people of Washington County for wanting to celebrate their past glory, such as it was.

Route 1 crossed the Machias River above Bad Little Falls, where a torrent of coffee-colored water—stained brown from pine needles—plunged down a steep terrace of granite shelves, dropping from one swirling pool to the next. It was so cold that the waterfall had partially frozen, forming a jagged crust of ice along the edges and a coating of rime on everything else from the frozen spray. Long icicles hung from the footbridge strung across the falls.

We passed the little university—a huddle of brick dorms and classrooms—on its lovely hillside, heading south along the Machias "strip."

The McDonald's was located in a mall across from the one and only grocery store. It advertised itself as a café, although I didn't understand what made it one. You couldn't order a McCroissant or anything. Several ring-billed gulls perched atop the roof, waiting to grab a dropped hash brown or whatever fried thing people ate at this hour of the morning.

There were five vehicles waiting in line at the drive-through. "Let's just go inside," I said.

Rivard groaned. "I knew this would happen."

Inside, a group of old men sat around a series of adjacent tables. Across the room, a group of old women sat similarly. In Machias, as in so many Maine towns, the neighborhood McDonald's doubled as the local senior center.

I waited for my turn to order and stepped to the counter.

"Good morning," said a young woman with an incandescent smile.

She was wearing the standard uniform—striped back smock, loose black pants, and a visor with the Golden Arches emblazoned on it—perhaps the least sexy outfit a woman could possibly wear. And yet she was undeniably attractive. She was short: scarcely five feet tall. Maybe a few years older than me. Her hair was chestnut-colored, although there were streaks of blond and red in there, too. She had cheekbones fit for a fashion model and a slight cleft in her chin. Her eyes were large and maple brown. Her name tag said JAMIE.

"What will you have?" Her voice was a bit rougher than that of most women her age.

I smiled back. "The usual."

She cocked an eyebrow at me. "I don't know what that is."

"You will."

She laughed and nodded, clearly an expert in deflecting flirtations. "Nice try," she said. "What can I get you?"

"An egg McMuffin and a large coffee with cream and sugar."

She punched the order into the computerized cash register and took my money with practiced efficiency. I watched her fill a cardboard cup with steaming coffee and then place a wrapped sandwich on a plastic tray. She didn't make eye contact again until she slid the tray across the counter at me and said, "Are you a forest ranger?"

I tapped the badge on my chest. "Game warden."

"My son's really into nature and stuff. He's reading this book about rangers that his teacher gave him."

I glanced down at her hand but didn't see a wedding ring. The mention of the boy seemed to be a yield signal, though. "Sometimes we do school visits," I said with a bit of a stammer. "We have a display we take around of antlers and furs we've confiscated from poachers. We'll have an exhibit at the Machias Blueberry Festival in the summer."

"I'll tell him," she said with another smile, this one more polite than come-hither. She looked over my shoulder at the next person in line, indicating I should move along.

Damn, though, she was pretty.

I carried my tray to the table where Rivard was hunched over his BlackBerry. He seemed totally preoccupied by whatever text message or e-mail he was reading. "Shit," he said.

"What?"

"The National Weather Service just issued a blizzard warning for tonight."

"I thought we were just supposed to get a few inches."

"Now it's a foot of snow, with sixty-mile-per-hour winds."

I thought about my soirée with Doc Larrabee, wondering if the revised forecast would be a legitimate excuse to cancel, then imagined the old widower slaving away in the kitchen in anticipation of his big dinner party. I peeled the waxed paper from the egg sandwich, took a bite, and again felt nostalgic for the home cooking at the Square Deal Diner in Sennebec.

In the plus column, this had to be the cleanest McDonald's I'd ever seen—not a crumb anywhere.

My chest hurt. I'd strained one of my pectoral muscles doing push-ups. I massaged the muscle through the Gore-Tex fabric of my parka. Lately I had begun to feel like a convict doing life in prison: Compulsive exercising and masturbation seemed to be the available leisure activities.

At the far end of the room, the door swung open, and I saw a few of the older customers stiffen in their seats.

Two men entered the restaurant. One was fairly short and wore a watch cap, a faded denim jacket, and baggy jeans: your garden-variety Washington County hoodlum. The other guy seemed to belong to another species: *Homo giganticus.* He was tall, with wavy brown locks, and was dressed in a distressed-leather jacket and black cargo pants. But what you noticed all the way across the room was the Maori-style tattoo on his face. The dark spiked pattern looked like permanent war paint.

The two men swaggered to the counter. From the angle at which I was sitting, I couldn't see the reaction of the woman at the register, but the older people at the end of the room began whispering to one another nervously, as if trouble were brewing, and I decided I'd better take a look for myself.

Rivard raised his eyes from his cell phone with surprise. "What's going on?"

"I'm not sure."

Before I could reach the front of the restaurant, the two men had reversed course and were being escorted out the door. The pretty young woman had the tattooed one firmly by the arm and was pulling him along, a look of utter mortification on her face. The shorter, shambling guy kept his head bowed, his eyes to the ground. As the other one passed me, though, he smiled wide, tapped his illustrated temple with two fingers in a kind of mocking salute, and said, "Top o' the mornin', Officer!"

The three of them exited through the double doors out into the frozen parking lot. They crossed the salted asphalt to a waiting Pontiac Grand Am. The smaller man slid immediately into the passenger seat, as if desperate to escape the wrath he knew was coming. The woman began shouting something—her words were lost through the glass walls and road noise—and shook a finger in the face of the tattooed man. He kept grinning from ear to ear.

Suddenly he thrust out a hand and lifted the McDonald's visor from her hair. He held it above her head, playing keep-away for a few seconds, before setting the visor down at a jaunty angle on his own skull. The woman snatched it away and stormed toward the restaurant's entrance, her hands balled into small fists at her sides.

Stepping aside as she came through the doors, I said, "Is everything OK, ma'am?"

But she refused to meet my eyes. "No, but I've got it under control."

The old folks looked at me with scared and confused eyes, but there was nothing I could think to do except return to the back booth, where Rivard sat scowling.

"What was that about?" he asked.

"I thought that woman might need help."

"If she's with Randall Cates, she definitely needs help," he said.

"You know that creep?"

"Everyone knows everyone around here," my sergeant said. "But that tattoo is kind of hard to mistake.'"

"What's his story?"

"Dealer," Rivard said. "Oxycodone, heroin, crack, meth. Anything and everything. The Maine Drug Enforcement Agency thinks he has somebody working for him across the border in New Brunswick. There's another rumor he's paying off someone inside the sheriff's office, which is total bullshit, if you ask me. Last year a girl died—a student here at the university. It's no secret who sold her the poison that killed her, but the DA couldn't connect the dots."

Looking through the frosted window, I could see the Grand Am still parked in its space, blue smoke rising from the tailpipe. I memorized the license plate: 766 AKG. I was wondering what the men were waiting for, when I saw Jamie emerge from behind the counter again, this time carrying a big paper bag and a tray with two coffees. She walked purposely out through the door and straight to the driver's side window. Two big hands reached out to accept the food and coffee.

Rivard followed my gaze. "You'd think those women would learn eventually, but they never do."

So my sergeant believed. But my own mother had escaped a youthful first marriage to a violent and abusive alcoholic, even if her later life in the suburbs didn't turn out to be the dream she'd imagined. I'd also seen Jamie's expression up close, and the look on her face hadn't been one of submission, but of defiance and rage.

On the way out the door, I noticed her smiling picture posted on the wall:

JAMIE SEWALL
EMPLOYEE OF THE MONTH

Mrs. Greenlaw gave me this book to read . . . NORTHWEST PAS-SAGE. It's pretty cool.

RANGER ORDERS

- *Have your musket clean as a whistle, hatchet scoured, sixty rounds powder and ball, and be ready to march at a minute's warning.*
- *When you're on the march, act the way you would if you were sneaking up on a deer.*
- *Don't sleep beyond dawn. Dawn is when the French and Indians attack.*
- *If somebody's trailing you, make a circle, come back onto your own tracks, and ambush the folks that aim to ambush you.*
- *Don't stand up when the enemy's coming against you. Kneel down. Hide behind a tree.*
- *Let the enemy come till he's almost close enough to touch. Then let him have it and jump out and finish him up with your hatchet.*

For my birthday I'm going to ask Ma for a hatchet.

5

A sign loomed ahead: WHITNEY HIGH SCHOOL. HOME OF THE WARRIORS.

It was a boxy two-story brick structure indistinguishable from a hundred school buildings around the state, except that the cars and trucks in the parking lot looked harder used than the vehicles kids drove in southern Maine. There were also a dozen or so snowmobiles parked in a line on the banked wall of ice. No teenagers had ever ridden Arctic Cats to my alma mater. It was yet another sign of the cultural rift between the suburban and rural parts of the state.

Schools always reminded me of Sarah, who'd been a teacher before she moved to D.C. If she had carried our baby to term, he or she would be two months old now, I realized. After Sarah miscarried, the doctor offered to tell us the sex of the fetus, but Sarah said she didn't want to know. She'd said it would make her too sad.

I'd wanted to know.

Rivard turned off the engine and hopped out of the truck without waiting for me. I followed him inside, down the greenly lit hall to the vice principal's office. From my best guess, Whitney High School must have received its last renovation during the Eisenhower administration. The tan lockers and scuffed linoleum floors would have looked at home on the set of the movie *Grease*.

The vice principal was a wiry young guy with a ponytail and round little glasses. His outfit—tweed jacket, blue jeans, openthroated hemp shirt—reminded me of a hippie teacher I'd had in elementary school in the backwoods of western Maine. Rivard introduced him to me as a Mr. Mandelbaum.

"I have to tell you I am very uncomfortable with this situation," he said. His forehead was furrowed, his eyes wary.

Rivard had turned his sunglasses around so they faced the back of his head, the way baseball players do. "We just want to ask him a few questions."

"If this is some sort of interrogation, I need to call Barney's parents. I won't allow you to question him without their consent. The children here have rights."

"You're blowing this way out of proportion," said Rivard. "We just think Beal can help us out with some information about a case we're investigating. It's a routine inquiry. All we want is five minutes."

I was fairly certain that my sergeant was misleading the vice principal. He'd told me he suspected Barney Beal of theft and drug dealing. The earlier discomfort I'd felt about this school visit returned as an itchy sensation along my torso.

Mandelbaum readjusted his glasses on his nose. "If any of your questions seem at all accusatory, I will cancel the interview. Understood?"

Rivard curled his lips like someone attempting a smile for a portrait photographer. "So where's Mr. Beal at the moment?"

"In America Two."

"Excuse me?" I said.

"Social studies," Mandelbaum explained. "If you wait right here, I'll go get him."

The vice principal carefully closed the door behind him as he left the office.

"You told Mandelbaum you weren't going to interrogate the kid," I said.

"Just let me handle this, will you?"

A moment later, the vice principal returned, followed by the Incredible Hulk's twin brother. "These wardens have a few questions for you, Barney," Mandelbaum said. "You don't have to answer anything that makes you uncomfortable."

Barney Beal had a brown flattop and painful-looking acne. He wore a sleeveless black T-shirt bearing the Teutonic logo of a heavy-metal band that had been popular in the rest of the country three decades ago. His eyes remained blank as he shambled into the room. Without waiting for directions, he took a seat in one of the three chairs arranged before the vice principal's desk, extended his legs, and folded his thick, pimpled arms across his chest. He had some sort of biblical verse tattooed on his forearm: Ezek. 23:30. How old did you have to be to get inked these days? I wondered.

Rivard stepped forward, so that he practically loomed over the boy. "I'm Sergeant Rivard and this is Warden Bowditch."

The invocation of my name caused the boy to turn in his chair and look me flat in the eyes. His pupils were tiny black dots.

"I'd appreciate your looking at me when I talk to you," Rivard said.

The kid paused just long enough to make the point that he was doing so because it suited him and not because it was a command.

The itching I was feeling started to burn. The *Scared Straight* approach had its uses, I supposed, but as a rule, I didn't believe in humiliating children, even gargantuan ones.

Standing beside me, Mandelbaum shifted his weight from one foot to the other, then back again. He could sense that, despite my sergeant's earlier assurances, something here wasn't on the up-and-up. He lowered his head, trying to catch the kid's almost catatonic gaze. "Are you sure you don't want me to call your folks, Barney?"

"No, suh."

"We've had some break-ins over at Bog Pond," Rivard said. "You know where that is?"

It was a lake in Township Nineteen, not far from Doc Larrabee's house, I realized.

"Yes, suh," said Barney Beal.

"You ever go snowmobiling over that way with your friends?" Rivard asked.

"I don't know. Maybe."

"We have witnesses who said they saw you riding your sled on the pond last Friday night. You and your friends."

"That sounds like an accusation," said Mandelbaum.

"It ain't illegal to go sleddin'," Beal said.

"But it is illegal to break into someone's cabin to steal the satellite TV chips," Rivard said. "We know it was you who broke into those camps, Beal."

Mandelbaum held up both of his narrow hands. "That's enough! Don't answer any more questions, Barney."

"We're talking about a Class D felony, Mr. Mandelbaum. That's punishable by a year in jail."

"In which case, Barney should have an attorney present, as well as his parents." The vice principal turned to the boy. "I apologize for bringing you in here. I never should have agreed to this conversation."

Beal raised his chin. "Can I go now?"

"Yes," I said, scratching the itchy place over my heart. "You can go back to class."

Beal lurched to his feet so abruptly, he kicked the chair over.

The boy reached down with his long arm and lifted it as it were made of balsa wood. He set the chair delicately into place. I made a note to myself, in case I ever encountered him again, that this teenager was as strong as the Hulk.

"We'll be watching you, Beal," Rivard said. "You won't know it, but we will."

For the first time, the faintest trace of a smile appeared on the boy's pimply face.

"Yes, suh," he said on his way out the door.

Mandelbaum waited until the boy was out of earshot before laying into us. "You lied to me," he said. "You came in here and you lied. You told me Barney wasn't a suspect in any crimes."

"Those weren't the exact words we used," Rivard said. "What I said was, we wanted him to help us out with some information."

"That's—sophistry! You have no right to bully my students. These are good kids here. Yes, some of them have some problems. There's poverty and addiction. But just because Barney Beal comes from a broken family—just because he has a tattoo—doesn't mean you can treat him like a thug. Not without evidence."

"How long have you worked here, Mr. Mandelbaum?" Rivard asked.

"This is my second year. Why?"

"That's what I thought."

"So because I'm not a Maine native, I'm a second-class citizen who will never understand this place?"

"Basically, yes."

"We apologize for the intrusion, Mr. Mandelbaum." I pulled my gloves from my coat pockets. "I'll be outside when you're ready to hit the road, Sergeant."

I could feel Rivard's eyes boring into my back as I left the room.

I'd never missed Kathy Frost so much in my life.

When I was in high school, I was the straightest of straight arrows. All my teachers adored me, and the football coach made me a team captain despite my limitations as a tight end and linebacker.

The only serious trouble I ever got into was a single fistfight. After school one day, I came across a kid who looked almost exactly like Barney Beal bullying a nerdy freshman, and I ordered him to knock it off. When the bully told me where I could shove my advice, I cold-cocked him in the nose. Our fight was long and vicious, and by the time the phys ed coach pulled us apart, we both needed stitches.

Afterward, the vice principal had confronted me in her plush office, not so much with anger as with hurt and disbelief. It was as if I had broken her heart in some way. I was such a great kid, she said. Out of what dark place had this violence suddenly come?

"I don't know," I said, lying.

The truth was that rage was twisted into my genetic code. It was my father's enduring birthright. Every day I fought to deny the existence of my simmering anger, to push it back inside my dark heart.

At the hospital, my mother looked at my fierce eyes and wounded

jaw with horror, fearful that I had begun some lycanthropic trans-
formation. Her greatest worry was that I was destined to become a
bloodthirsty creature like her ex-husband. After the divorce, she did
everything she could to keep me away from my dad. She'd moved
us from the North Woods to the Portland suburbs. She discouraged
me from talking to him on the phone. She even frowned on my own
hunting and fishing pursuits, worried I was becoming increasingly
like my old man.

My mother now spent her winters in Naples, Florida, and we
spoke less and less. My choice of a dangerous profession had seemingly confirmed her worst fears, and I think she fully expected that
some night the telephone would ring and it would be Colonel Harkavy, telling her that I had been shot in the head by a Down East
poacher. It was better not to think of me in that case, to pretend her
doomed son no longer existed, to protect herself from future grief.

I waited for Rivard in the frigid parking lot, literally blowing off
steam. Every shimmer of breath was visible in the air for several
seconds before being swept away on the breeze. If anything, the sky
looked even more ominous than when we'd arrived, but perhaps it
was just my miserable mood.

My sergeant didn't speak until we were on the road again. "You
could have backed me up in there."

"Mandelbaum was right. You lied to him."

"The guy's living in a dream world. Beal is the one who robbed
those cabins. Him and his buddies. Did you see his pupils? They
were microscopic. The kid was high on Oxy or God knows what."

"If you're so sure he's robbing cabins to buy drugs," I said, "you
should turn your evidence over to the sheriff's office or the Maine
Drug Enforcement Agency. It's their job to investigate that shit, not
ours."

Rivard kept his eyes on the road, but he rolled his head around
on his neck as if it were crimped. "I was trying to send that punk a
message."

"I think you failed, Marc."

He turned his head, and once again I was confronted by my distorted reflection in his sunglasses. The anger I saw in my features stopped me cold. I felt like Henry Jekyll looking into the face of his other self.

"You've got a lot to learn," Rivard said.

"So you keep telling me."

He flicked on the windshield wipers.

I'd been so consumed with my grievances that I hadn't noticed it was beginning to snow.

They sent us home early on account of the snow. Erick says there's a big blizzard coming. The Storm of the Century, he says.

On the bus I kept thinking about the White Owl, wondering if she'd come to my window like she did the last time it snowed.

The bus came around the corner and I saw Randle's new car in front of the house and I got a sick feeling in my stomach like I ate too much peanut brittle.

Ma's van was there, too—but she don't usually get home till after 2. That's when her shift ends.

Randle's always got some new car. This one's a black Grand Am.

After the bus left, I wondered if Randle and Prester shot a coyote like they said they was going to. I wondered if they had it in the back-seat.

All I did was look in the window!

Suddenly Randle came out the door, yelling F this and F that and telling me to get away from the car. His face was all weird and scary from his new tattoo.

He HIT me!

Right in the side of the head. I fell over and everything! My whole backpack spilled onto the ground. When I touched my head, there was BLOOD!

Ma came out screaming. Don't touch him! Leave him alone!

She ain't afraid of Randle. She gave him a shove, but he just pushed her into a snowbank. Then he called her the C word.

If you touch my son again, I'm gonna kill you! Ma said. I never seen her so mad.

F you, Jamie, Randle said. Come on, Prester.

Uncle P didn't even try to help us up or anything. He just did what Randle told him to do, same as always.

Randle peeled rubber all the way up the road.

Ma helped me pick up my stuff. I'll never let him hurt you again, Lucas, she told me.

I heard that one before.

She knew what I was thinking. I mean it this time, she said.

6

It scarcely seemed possible, but my day went downhill from there.

After Rivard dropped me at my trailer, I discovered that the baseboard heating had gone on the fritz. I checked the fuse box, but there were no spare fuses. That meant I would have to drive down to the hardware store in Machias before my pipes froze and burst. Either that or try heating the entire building with my propane stove.

I was lacing up my wet boots again when I remembered a dusty metal box under the kitchen sink. Inside were all sorts of orphan screws and random washers, along with a handful of new electrical fuses. I had to wait half an hour for the trailer to warm up again before I dared leave.

Out on the road, the visibility was already going to hell, and it wasn't even midday.

I'd decided to visit a gun shop—people in these parts tended to run them as home businesses—to ask the owner about "George Magoon," but I found the door padlocked and the barred windows dark. Instead, I drove over to Snake Lake to check ice-fishing licenses. As cold as it was, I expected a few fishermen to be sitting in the warmth of their brazier-heated shacks, enjoying hot coffee or more adult beverages. But all I found out on the ice was another ghost town. Everyone but me had the good sense to hunker down inside and wait out the storm.

On the drive home to Whitney, I passed a convoy of ancient

school buses inching along in the snow. The local kids were being sent home for the day. I decided to take a hint and do the same. I finished the paperwork I owed the Warden Service and watched the snowflakes fall from the tepid comfort of my trailer.

When I ventured out again for dinner, I found my personal vehicle—a 2005 Jeep Wrangler—hiding under a new white blanket. The storm had been gathering force all afternoon, and now with darkness descending, snow was both falling from the sky and being blown upward from the thickening drifts. I had outfitted my Jeep with new snow tires, but even with the studs digging into the snow-pack, I was reluctant to push my luck. Creeping along at twenty-five miles per hour made me feel like a daredevil.

After I crossed into Township Nineteen, it occurred to me that I should've brought a gift of some sort. I had always relied on Sarah to take care of my manners. At twenty-six, I still had no feel for even the most basic social graces.

Even going slowly, I almost drove past Doc's farm. His mailbox, already knocked off-kilter by a plow, sprang up like a ghostly apparition out of the frozen mist. I pressed the brake and felt the Jeep shudder and fishtail before it slid safely to a halt. When I looked again, the mailbox had disappeared into the gathering night. Peering through the flurries, I detected a fuzzy yellow glow on the hillside above me. It was Doc's porch light. I turned the wheel and headed up what I hoped was the driveway—the paved way was indistinguishable beneath the drifts—toward the beacon.

I didn't hear the dogs until I opened the door. Their cries were carried along on the howling wind, so that they seemed part of the storm itself. Larrabee had mentioned that he was also inviting his musher friend, Kendrick, to dinner, but I never imagined that the man would drive his sled here on a crappy night like this. I squinted into the side yard, where a few snow-laden fir trees were huddled against the cold, but I saw neither dogs nor sled. There was something eerie about that disembodied baying in the night.

I rapped hard on Doc's side door and waited, shivering, for my host to let me in. After an eternity, he appeared. "I thought we might need to send a Saint Bernard looking for you with a cask of brandy," he said.

"Sorry I'm late."

"The snow's supposed to stop later, so you should have a safer drive home."

"Not if it keeps blowing like this."

I stepped into the mudroom and stamped my boots to clean off the clumped snow. Doc had so many coats hanging from the hooks, there was no place for mine. After a moment, he realized my distress and said, "Let me take your parka. You can put on those moccasins, if you don't mind removing your wet boots."

I had never seen Doc without a coat, so this was my first gander at his spectacular belly. He looked as if he had swallowed a watermelon whole and it had lodged somewhere between his upper and lower intestines.

I sat down on a hardwood bench and began untying my laces. "Those must be Kendrick's dogs I heard."

"A storm like this is nothing to Kendrick. I think he's half polar bear."

A gray-snouted mutt came waddling on bad hips down the length of the hallway. Its tail swung slowly back and forth, and it held my gaze with two rheumy eyes. "Who's this?" I asked, scratching its chin.

"This is Duchess."

"How old is she?"

"Fourteen. Helen and I got her when she was just a puppy."

A call came from the interior. "Hey, Doc! Where's the hooch?"

"Excuse me," Doc said, and with that, he disappeared down the darkened hall. The dog followed like his four-legged footman.

The moccasins Larrabee had offered to me were high-topped, flat-soled, and fashioned from bleached deerskin. They looked Indian-made, which would have made sense. The Passamaquoddies owned reservation land that brushed up against the eastern edge of my district.

I found Doc and Kendrick in a dimly lit room at the end of the hall. With its hooked rugs, birch rocking chairs, and horsehair sofa, it had more of the the feel of an old-time sitting parlor than a modern living room. Doc had the woodstove cranking, but its efforts were in vain. The storm was pulling heat from the building through every crack and seam.

I seemed to have caught Kendrick declaiming in mid-speech.

> "There are strange things done in the midnight sun
>   By the men who moil for gold;
>   The Arctic trails have their secret tales
>   That would make your blood run cold;
>   The Northern Lights have seen queer sights,
>   But the queerest they ever did see
>   Was that night on the marge of Lake Lebarge
>   I cremated Sam McGee."

Kendrick paused and took a sip from a cocktail glass filled to the brim with amber liquid and ice. He was something to behold: a handsome brown-bearded man with wild, curling hair, dressed in a buckskin vest over a flannel shirt, and wool logger's pants that were rolled up at the cuffs, exposing a pair of long bare feet. How in the world were his toes not freezing?

Doc was holding an empty bottle. With his free hand, he gestured at his other guest. "Kevin can recite 'The Cremation of Sam McGee' from front to back. That and 'The Shooting of Dan McGrew.'"

"That's because I'm from Alaska, where it's mandatory you learn those poems in kindergarten." He leaned forward on the couch and extended his strong, calloused hand. "Kevin Kendrick."

"Mike Bowditch."

"Doc was just telling me about your frozen zebra. That's what prompted my little poetry recital. You might have tried defrosting it in a furnace, like they did with old Sam McGee."

"I don't think it would have helped."

Kendrick raised his glass and the ice clinked. "Maker's Mark?"

"I'll have a cup of coffee."

Larrabee left us alone while he went into the kitchen. I settled down in a rocker near enough to the fire to melt whatever ice had formed in my veins. The chair creaked alarmingly as I leaned back. Doc's elderly mutt plopped herself next to the woodstove with a heavy expulsion of breath.

"That's one old dog," I said.

"Doc's going to have to put her down one of these days, I'm afraid. She's riddled with tumors. It's the humane thing to do. But he can't bear another loss after Helen."

"I heard your dogs outside," I said. "They were really wailing."

"Those wimps just need some toughening up."

"How so?"

"A night like this focuses their attention," he said. "I've got fifty pounds of bricks on that sled to build their endurance. That's what I like about canines. Their bad behavior is correctable."

Unlike people? Charley Stevens had told me that Kendrick was a professor at the University of Maine at Machias. He had probably had his share of incorrigible students.

"Doc told me you've raced in the Iditarod," I said.

"Anchorage to Nome by dogsled, twice. But that was a long time ago, when I was young and foolish. Now I'm just middle-aged and foolish."

I would have estimated Kendrick's age as being somewhere between mine and Doc's, but exactly where he fell along the spectrum was hard to guess. People who spend a lot of time outdoors develop sun wrinkles and burst capillaries in their faces, making them look older than they actually are. But the professor had piercing eyes and an aquiline nose I suspected women found appealing.

As was my habit when I met a stranger, I let my gaze roam casually over him, looking for clues about his background and inner life. The buckskin vest looked handmade; I was guessing Kendrick had tanned it himself. Around his neck hung a necklace of three bear claws. When he leaned back on the sofa, I saw a big hunting knife in a sheath on his belt. His entire outfit seemed like a costume.

He crunched down hard on an ice cube. "Did you hurt your hand?"

"Excuse me?"

"You're rubbing your right thumb like it's giving you trouble."

I was unaware of doing this. "I broke a couple of bones last year, but they're mostly healed."

Doc Larrabee reappeared, carrying a tray with two cups of coffee and a new bottle of whiskey. He spilled a little whiskey over the rim of Kendrick's glass. "You sure you don't want a shot in yours?" he asked me.

I shook my head no and held the cup in both hands, warming them. Then I rocked back in my chair, looking at Kendrick. "Doc tells me you're a professor at the University of Machias. What do you teach?"

"Environmental studies," he said.

"I call Kendrick 'the Last of the Mountain Men,'" Doc said. "You wouldn't believe the crazy things he's done in his life—hiked the entire Appalachian Trail *barefoot,* paddled in a kayak he made himself out of sealskin from Nunavut to Greenland, discovered three new bird species in the Amazon, lived for six months with cannibals in Papua New Guinea—"

"The Asmat aren't cannibals anymore."

"The *New York Times* wrote a whole profile on him a few years back. Tell me, Kendrick, how many nights did that pretty reporter sleep in your wigwam?"

Kendrick didn't take the bait. "That story made me sound like some strange hermit or survivalist because I choose to live in the woods and practice primitive ways."

"That's the name of the survival school he teaches in the summer," Doc interjected. "Primitive Ways."

"It's not a 'survival school.' I teach basic wood skills—friction fire techniques, wildcrafting, tracking."

"You have to admit that you're something of a guru," said Doc.

"I'm just a teacher who wants his students to question their assumptions about the so-called superiority of the modern world."

I remembered the story Rivard had told me earlier that morning.

"Someone was telling me today that you had a drug overdose at your university last year."

Kendrick looked at me with a curious expression. There was something about his eyes that reminded me of a dog's: a copper color you rarely saw in human beings. "Trinity Raye."

"Did you know her?"

"Of course I did. It's a small school."

The sharpness of his response caused me to let the matter drop. We sat silently for a few moments, listening to the wind shake the clapboards and shutters. Out in the dark, one of Kendrick's own dogs was wailing like a lost soul in purgatory. Then a buzzer sounded in the kitchen.

"I believe dinner is ready to be served," said Doc.

At the table, Doc brought up the recent break-ins at Bog Pond. "You can't see the lake in the snow," he said, "but it's right at the bottom of the hill. Those are my neighbors who got robbed."

"Do you have any idea who might have done it?" I asked, remembering the contracted pupils of Barney Beal.

"Drug addicts," said Kendrick. "Every crime around here is drug-related these days. I used to believe in legalization." He didn't elaborate. "If you want to make yourself useful, you'll stop harassing good people like Bill Cronk and go after the real scumbags around here."

Something I'd said had darkened Kendrick's mood. I resolved to steer the conversation in what I hoped was a less controversial direction. "I forgot to tell you, Doc," I said. "After I dropped you off last night, guess what I found waiting for me at my house."

"A woman scorned?"

"A coyote skin nailed to my front door. There was a note with it welcoming me to the neighborhood, signed by someone who called himself 'George Magoon.'"

Doc raised his eyebrows. "Is that so?"

"I understand that George Magoon is a character out of local folklore," I said. "Sort of like Robin Hood."

"Oh, he was real enough," offered Kendrick. "Didn't they teach you about the Down East Game War of the 1880s? When the state of Maine rebranded it as 'poaching,' it consigned hundreds of poor people to near starvation."

"That's one interpretation of events," I said. "But I also know that two game wardens were gunned down in this vicinity in 1886 when they tried to seize a poacher's dog."

"There's a book about it," said Doc, rising shakily to his feet. "I'll loan you Helen's copy."

"Does this Magoon character have some connection to the murders of those wardens?" I asked Kendrick.

"No, that was probably Calvin Graves," he said. "Magoon never killed anyone. He preferred to use humor and embarrassment against his persecutors. Sort of like a nineteenth-century version of *The Monkey Wrench Gang.*"

The veterinarian returned from his office with a dog-eared green paperback titled *George Magoon and the Down East Game War.* On the cover was a pen and ink illustration of a group of men with guns standing beside a dead moose, which was suspended from a tree. "You're welcome to borrow this."

"Thanks, but I'm more concerned with the joker who nailed a coyote pelt to my door."

"I doubt he was joking," said Kendrick. "It sounds more like a warning to me."

"I agree with Kendrick," said Doc Larrabee, stroking his beard. "The Game War might seem like ancient history, but people around here have long memories. If you don't believe me, pay a visit to the little cemetery over in Wesley after the snow melts."

I stopped flipping through the book. "Why? What's there?"

Doc leaned his sharp elbows on the table. "The grave of Wilbur Day. He was one of Magoon's band of rascals. I remember hearing about his exploits when I moved to this neck of the woods. One day I decided to visit his grave myself. A rifle bullet was set carefully atop the headstone. Every time I've been back, I've found a new cartridge there, and every time it's made me thank God I'm not a Maine game warden."

I have a BIG cut on my head where Randle hit me. Ma put OINT-MENT on it before she tucked me into bed.

Do you think maybe someday Dad could teach me karate? I asked her.

She gave me the funniest look—like I just read her mind or something. Maybe someday, she said.

Dad is into mixed martial arts. He's an Ultimate Fighter. He's competed in octagons over in the Orient. I've seen him break a board with his fist . . . but it took a couple of tries.

Dad gave me a Bruce Lee poster for my room. It says DRAGON'S ROAR. I've never seen that DVD. But it looks pretty good from the poster.

He works over at the Shogun Karate Studio. I asked him once if he would give me lessons so I could kick the shit out of kids at school. He said that the purpose of karate ain't attacking people. It should only be used in self-defense, he said.

What a load! Who would want to be a mixed martial artist if you couldn't use your powers to beat people up? That's the whole point of karate!

Try to forget about Randle, Ma said. She kissed my head before she closed the door.

Outside, the wind is really howling.

I forgot about the snowstorm. I'm worried SHE is going to come to my window again.

7

E very few minutes, a gust would come charging by the house, and you would have sworn it was a freight train from the way it rattled the windows and shook the pictures on the walls. I was both dreading the drive back to my trailer and eager to start out on my inevitable journey. If I had waited for Doc Larrabee to stop with the coffee and folklore, I would have been there all night. After a while I gave a false yawn and stretched my arms over my head. "I guess it's about time for me to head home. In this storm, it should only take three or four hours."

"You sure you don't want another cup for the road?"

"My bladder will burst if I do."

"How about you, Kendrick? I've got a collection of Helen's cordials begging to be opened."

Between them, the two men had already polished off the last of the Maker's Mark as well as a bottle of Cabernet Sauvignon. Doc had increasingly come to resemble Rudolph the Red-Nosed Reindeer, but Kendrick displayed no visible signs of intoxication. Even if he was a bit impaired, I figured his dogs knew the way home.

"Good luck catching your prankster," he said in a not-unfriendly tone of voice.

Doc Larrabee followed me to the chilly mudroom and waited patiently while I laced up my boots. For the first time, I noticed that he was wearing thin little slippers, which made me think of Ebenezer Scrooge waiting for his ghosts on the night before Christmas.

"Careful out there," he said. "It's not a fit night out for man nor beast."

"I suspect the beasts know better than to venture out into a blizzard."

He shook my gloved hand with drunken formality and opened the door for me. A gust of wind caught it and snapped it open. The tipsy veterinarian grappled with the knob to regain control.

Snow was swirling like white smoke in the porch light and billowing from all directions. The sheer force of it made my eyes water. I had misjudged the storm. This one was the real deal.

My Jeep had burrowed deep into a snowbank. At first I had trouble waking it. The engine grumbled for a while before it turned over.

I turned the wheel and swung around through a windblown drift. I tried the high beams and the low beams and decided there was no appreciable difference between the two. Eventually I found my way back to the road and turned west, headed for Whitney. My hyperbolic estimation of the time it would take to get there—three or four hours—might not be out of line, I decided.

I could understand why my friend Charley Stevens had wanted me to meet Kendrick. If even half his exploits were true, he definitely deserved a profile in the *New York Times*. And if he knew the wilds as well as I suspected, then he might prove useful to me down the line. Still, something about the self-styled mountain man rubbed me the wrong way: His confidence seemed to border on monomania.

I hadn't seen much of Charley and his wife, Ora, over the previous months. They'd been forced to leave their beloved cabin in western Maine when a real estate developer bought the land out from under them. Ora had written a lovely note to offer me consolation after Sarah moved to D.C., and she promised to invite me to dinner at their new home, but so far, that hadn't happened. Every few weeks I'd get a call from Charley, who wanted to chew over some gristle of news, but he often seemed preoccupied by issues he wouldn't discuss, and I had the good manners not to ask what was troubling him.

I'd never made friends all that easily. After the evening at Doc's, it was safe to say that dinner parties with veterinarians and dogsledders would not become the basis of a satisfying new social life, either.

Everyone has heard the old saying that the Eskimos, or Inuit, have umpteen different words for snow. The idea is that they live closer to their environment than we do and thus have not lost the ability to differentiate among the multitudinous forms freezing precipitation can take. Where we see snow, the Inuit see subtleties.

This charming legend, like most charming legends, is false. The Inuit have just about as many words for snow as do English speakers; they just tend to combine their terms in certain ways to add specificity to their meteorological conditions.

I have no doubt, however, that the Inuit recognize the difference a few degrees in temperature can make in shaping a snowflake. Warmer weather means wetter snow. Wet snow is heavy; its weight shatters tree branches. It clings to power lines and brings them crashing down. On the road, it turns to slush and sends tractionless cars skipping into ditches. Wet snow melts quickly in your hair and runs down the back of your neck. It follows you into your house by riding in the treads of your boots and leaves puddles to mark its passage. I know this because, like the Inuit, I live mostly outdoors in the winter.

Because of the low-pressure front pushing down from Canada, the snow that was falling in the road was not wet, but in fact very dry. The wind whipped it around like white sand in a white desert, forming metamorphic dunes and ridges that changed shape while I watched. Dry snow carries its own dangers. It clings to nothing, not even itself, and is so light it can be stirred by the faintest breeze, turning a black night blindingly white. Weightless, it resists plowing and shoveling. It covers your tracks in the woods, making it easier for you to get lost, and because dry snow is the harbinger of subzero temperatures, it makes losing your way a potentially life-threatening mistake.

I'd been on the road for fifteen minutes or so when my cell phone rang in my coat pocket. The number on the display told me that the caller was Larrabee.

"Doc? What's wrong?"

"My neighbor Ben Sprague just called. He and his wife, Doris, just had someone show up at their door, frozen solid. They want me to come over and have a look at the guy. It sounds like he's in rough shape. Would you mind heading back this way? I'm in no condition to drive."

"Where's Kendrick?"

"He's going to head over to the Spragues' on his dogsled."

"I'll be there as soon as I can."

"It sounds like that poor fellow is in rough shape," Doc said again for emphasis.

Without a second thought, I did a slow U-turn and began creeping through the blizzard to Doc's farmhouse.

I found him at the foot of his drive, bundled up from head to toe, with only the tip of his nose and his fogged-over eyeglasses exposed. He wore an Elmer Fudd–style hunting hat with the flaps buttoned under his chin, and he'd wrapped a scarf tightly around his mouth and beard. He was toting his black doctor's bag again. I wondered what medicine or instruments a veterinarian might possess to treat a human being for frostbite and hypothermia.

He climbed in beside me, set his leather bag on his knees, and pulled the safety belt tight across his chest. "The Bog Pond Road is up here on your right," he said. "Look for the tall mailbox."

The tall mailbox? Soon enough, I saw a candy-striped pole sticking up from a snowbank. Nine feet up in the air, a mailbox was balanced on top of it. The words AIR MAIL were painted on the side—someone's idea of a real knee-slapper.

The Bog Pond Road was in considerably worse shape than the main drag. You would have believed it had been months since a plow truck last visited. The snow was piled above the headlights of my Jeep, yet somehow we managed to push through the drifts without getting stuck.

We passed a darkened trailer that seemed to have been abandoned for the winter, then another ranch house with boarded-up windows.

"What's that noise?" asked Doc.

"Where?"

The raging wind was so loud, I almost didn't hear the snowmobile. A single yellow light, like a bouncing lantern, showed in the dark ahead of us. While we watched, it grew larger and larger, brighter and brighter. Some fool was riding his sled straight down the middle of the road.

"Can't he see us?" asked Doc.

I let up on the gas and engaged the clutch. The Jeep crunched to a halt.

The snowmobile seemed to be accelerating as it drew nearer.

Larrabee pushed himself back against the seat and straightened his arms against the dash. "That idiot is playing chicken!"

I clenched my molars, but at the last possible moment, the snowmobile veered off to our right, narrowly missing a row of spruces that ran down the hill. I caught a glimpse of a goblin-green sled with a person dressed in the same color snowmobile suit. Then the rider disappeared into the darkness behind us.

"Who the hell was that?" said Doc.

Unbidden, the face of Barney Beal popped into my head. "I don't know," I said, "but he's going to wrap himself around a tree if he keeps that shit up."

I put the Jeep into gear. The wheels spun and the vehicle began to shake like a dog just emerging from a cold lake. We were going nowhere fast.

"The Spragues live at the bottom of this hill, not far from the Bog Stream bridge," Doc said. "We can walk there."

While Larrabee waited, I grabbed a few supplies. I pulled a halogen headlamp over my Gore-Tex cap. I dumped ice-fishing tip-ups out of an ash pack basket. I found a wool blanket and a wilderness first-aid kit.

When I looked up with the dancing beam of the headlamp, I saw

Doc hurrying down the road in the dark. The liquor in his system had already done a number on his judgment.

"Hold up, Doc!"

I pulled the straps of the wooden pack basket over my arms and retrieved my snowshoes from the Jeep. I slid my boots into the bindings and tightened the rawhide cords. Then I started off down the hill.

Larrabee moved pretty fast for a half-drunk man plodding through thigh-deep snow.

The Spragues' house was a little chalet with a steeply pitched metal roof, which allowed heavy loads of snow to fall off. The outside lights were all switched on, bathing the scene in an elfin glow. I saw an old Subaru station wagon hiding against the side of the house, out of the wind, and two new-looking Yamaha sleds—his and hers—parked nearby. There were new tire tracks and a wedge-shaped snowbank that indicated a pickup had recently plowed its way out of the dooryard.

By the time I got to the door, Doc was already standing inside, unlooping the scarf from around his whiskered chin.

A squat little woman was standing beside him, looking back at me with an expression of alarm. She had short hair, dyed a sort of maroonish brown. A rosy line of blood vessels ran from one cheek up over the bridge of her nose to the other cheek. She wore a mint-green sweatshirt with a moose on it and jeans with an elastic waistband.

"Doris, this is Mike Bowditch with the Maine Warden Service," Doc said.

"Thank goodness you're here!"

"Where's your visitor?"

"In Joey's room."

She led Doc into the back of the house while I struggled to escape my snowshoes. I tried kicking off as much of the powder as I could in the mudroom, but a wet white trail followed me down the hall.

The house didn't seem dirty so much as unkempt. On the walls hung amateur oil paintings in the style promoted by those learn-to-paint television shows. But they were all crooked. The odor of an uncleaned litter box drifted from some hidden place.

In a boy's bedroom, Doris Sprague leaned against one wall while Doc bent over a young man stretched on top of a narrow bed. He wore a faded denim jacket with a shearling collar, an untucked flannel shirt, baggy jeans, and motorcycle boots with silver buckles. His wet chestnut hair was plastered over his ears and across his forehead. He might have been handsome once, but now his face was horribly splotched and swollen. Waxy yellow patches of frostbite covered his entire nose and both cheeks. His fingers were bent into steel-gray claws.

"Young man," said Doc. "Can you hear me?"

He snapped open his eyes. The pupils were the size of dimes. "No."

"I'm a doctor," Larrabee said calmly. "I'm going to help you."

Doc had a pretty good bedside manner, considering his patients were mostly cows and horses.

"I'm calling an ambulance," I said.

"Ben already did," said Mrs. Sprague.

"Do you know who this man is?"

"I'm not sure. His face is so . . ." She hugged herself and shivered, as if the man's hypothermia were contagious. "His wallet is over on the table. I tried to cover him with a blanket, but he keeps saying he's hot."

"Press," said the man.

"What's that?" asked Doc. "Press what?"

"Presster," said the man.

"Is that your last name or your first name?" Doc asked.

I opened the wallet and pulled out the driver's license. The picture showed a good-looking version of the disfigured face before us. He had high cheekbones and feathered chestnut hair cut like a disco dancer's from the 1970s.

"His name is John Sewall," I said.

It's snowing wicked hard out tonight. I'm writing this under the covers with the headlamp Aunt Tammi gave me for my birthday.

THIS IS MY <u>LAST</u> WILL & TESTAMENT

I bequeath everything to Ma except my Bruce Lee poster. Give that back to Dad.

And Tammi should get my headlamp, I guess.

I want to be buried at sea or burned like a Viking. Either way is fine.

On my tombstone it should read—

I hear something.
WHISPERING!
It ain't the wind. That's a voice speaking. A woman's voice.
SHE'S HERE!

8

Should I have made the connection between the face on the driver's license and the incident I'd witnessed at McDonald's? It's easy now to say yes. In my defense, I hadn't focused on the smaller of the two men. My attention had been fixated first on the jaw-droppingly beautiful woman behind the counter and later on the tattooed thug. I'd barely noticed the big one's sidekick, and the name Sewall—like Beal, Cates, or Sprague—is common in eastern Maine.

From his knees beside the bed, Doc looked up at Mrs. Sprague. "Doris, I need you to bring me all the blankets and sleeping bags you have in the house."

The solid little woman embraced herself tightly. Her eyes had a glassy sheen. She seemed to be in a trance. "What did you say?"

"We need to wrap this man up in as many warm layers as possible. I'm barely getting a radial pulse."

"Should I run a hot bath?" she asked.

"Christ no. He could have a heart attack from the shock."

She began blinked rapidly. "I'm sorry! I didn't know."

"It's all right, Mrs. Sprague," I said. "Let me help you."

Hypothermia is a decrease in the body's core temperature to the degree where the entire cardiovascular and nervous systems collapse. The only way to treat it is to warm the afflicted person up gradually. Hospitals pump humidified air into the lungs and irrigate body cavities with warm liquids, but these methods were beyond our capabilities in the little Swiss chalet. The best we could do was wrap up Sewall like a burrito in as many layers of insulation as we could find.

I followed the woman from room to room, gathering up every Navajo blanket, down sleeping bag, and cotton sheet in the place. Doris Sprague found a hot-water bottle for me and began to fill it with water from the kitchen tap. We would apply it to Sewall's armpits or his groin, above the femoral artery.

I brought the accumulated bedclothes into the room with the frozen man. It was obviously a teenage boy's bedroom. A bureau held various sports trophies (baseball and basketball) and assorted animal teeth and skulls. There was a picture of the pop singer Katy Perry on one wood-paneled wall; on another was a poster of an airbrushed-looking wolf, which was staring out at the room with the same intensely blue eyes as Ms. Perry's. The poster bore the slogan IN WILDNESS IS THE PRESERVATION OF THE WORLD.

"How's our patient?"

"Not good. He needs to get to a hospital. I don't know how long the EMTs will take to get here—if they can get here—but we have our work cut out for us. At best, he's going to lose some fingers and toes from the frostbite."

"It's the worst case I've seen," I said.

"Can you find some fluids for him?"

I went into the kitchen and found Doris Sprague standing beside the still-running kitchen tap. She wasn't making a sound, but tears were sliding down her cheeks. I turned the faucet off and gently set my hand on the woman's shaking shoulder.

"Do you have any Jell-O?" I asked.

She gazed up at me and her mouth opened. "Are you hungry?"

"No, ma'am. It's for our patient. If we can get him to drink some hot liquid Jell-O, it would help."

"Is raspberry OK?"

"Any flavor is fine."

I looked around the kitchen. There were two dirty plates with chicken bones on the counter beside the sink, two sets of dirty silverware, four empty Moxie cans. In our circuit through the sad rooms of the house, I realized, we hadn't encountered another person—neither this "Joey" nor the man of the house himself.

"Where's your husband, Mrs. Sprague?"

"Out looking for the other one."

"What other one?"

"This one's friend."

I tried to make my voice soft and reassuring. "Mrs. Sprague, can you tell me what happened here tonight? From the beginning."

As she spoke, she seemed to regain her presence of her mind little by little. "Ben and I had finished eating and were listening to the radio when we heard a thud at the front of the house. At first we thought it was snow falling off the roof, but it sounded too heavy for that. So Ben took a look outside and he found the young man collapsed against the window. He'd just stumbled into the glass like a confused bird. Ben got him inside—my husband's not very tall, but he's rugged—and we put him down in the guest room. He was mumbling the whole time, the young man."

"What did he say?"

"Something about a car. We figured he must have gone off the road somewhere. There's a whole maze of logging roads between Bog Pond and the Heath, and none of them is marked, and if he'd gone in before the snow started to fall, he might've gotten turned around pretty easy. So Ben went to call Doc Larrabee, and I covered the boy with a blanket. He kept saying a name. It sounded like 'Kate.' I asked him if he'd been with someone else out there named Kate, and he said, 'In the car.'"

I glanced at the kitchen window, which was spackled with frost. "And your husband went out in the storm to look for this Kate?"

"He took the plow."

"Does he have a phone with him?"

"Yes, but if he's down in the Heath, he won't get reception."

"Can you heat up that Jell-O for me, Mrs. Sprague? I need to speak with Doc Larrabee for a moment."

In the bedroom, Doc had succeeded in swaddling John Sewall in about eight inches of goose down, wool, and linen. We needed to keep the blood moving through his arteries until the EMTs arrived, and then hope he would hang on long enough to reach the hospital in Machias. Every few minutes, Sewall's eyelids would begin to flutter, and Doc would give his shoulder a gentle shake and whisper to him in the same tone I bet he used with skittish horses.

"So I'm thinking I should go out there," I said.

Doc gave me a frown. "The man's delirious, Mike. There's no reason to believe anything he says."

"All the more reason to find Ben Sprague, then."

"Can't Doris just call him?"

"She says there's a dead zone in the Heath."

Doc pulled a wrinkled handkerchief from his shirt pocket and blew his nose forcibly into the cloth. "Well, it's up to you. There's not much you can do here except spell me on bathroom breaks. And I guess you're right to worry about Ben. But I seem to remember that your Jeep's stuck in a snowbank about a hundred yards up the road."

"I was thinking of borrowing one of the Spragues' sleds."

Doc called my bluff. "So who's going to rescue the rescuer?"

"I'll be all right."

"I'm sure that's what Ben told Doris."

"Didn't you say that Kendrick was headed over this way with his dog team?" I said. "Your house is just up the hill and across Bog Pond." He should have beaten us here by nearly half an hour, and Doris hasn't mentioned seeing him."

"Maybe he ran into Sprague out there," said Doc. "I wouldn't worry about Kendrick. This kind of weather is his natural element."

"It's my job to worry, Doc."

I stepped into the TV room to call the state police. "The EMTs are never going to make it down this hill unless they're driving a military half-track," I told the dispatcher in Augusta. "Can you arrange for DOT to send a plow over this way to help out the ambulance?"

"Anything else?"

"Contact Sergeant Rivard and tell him I need assistance searching for a lost person."

Call me chicken, but rousing my surly new sergeant in the middle of this snowstorm wasn't a task I cared to do myself.

* * *

The Spragues' sleds were Yamaha RS Ventures in the same colors: blue and white. They were touring machines, built for long-distance rides along well-manicured trails. Their meticulous Japanese engineers had never intended them to be ridden into the teeth of a full-on blizzard.

At first the snowmobile floated atop the powder. I gave the engine a half handful of throttle and felt myself pulled along as if by actual horses given their head. The tracks bit into the snow and pushed the runners through the scattering spray.

The conditions didn't seem so bad until, going around a curve, I turned the handlebars and everything went wobbly. The sled rolled to the outside and dug into a drift, throwing cold mist up into the visor of my helmet. I stood up, leaned hard against the inside, and pulled the machine level for all of ten seconds before it pitched away from me again. I needed to find my balance quickly or I'd be wallowing in a snowbank with a quarter ton of steel on top of me. The last time something like that had happened, I snapped two bones in my hand. I planted both feet on the outside running board and let my body weight pull against the roll. Soon I was swaying back and forth down the trail.

Doris Sprague had called the frozen swamp behind her house the Heath. There were about a hundred places with that name in my district. Most were raised peat bogs from which, every now and then, someone dug up a tea-stained mammoth tusk. The word *heathen* is derived from these prehistoric wetlands because heaths were home to criminals, outcasts, and lepers. Bogeymen dwelled in bogs. In northern Europe, they were the sites of ritual human sacrifices.

This one was pretty much just a trackless wasteland. No virgins had ever been sacrificed here except by accident. Beneath the blowing snowdrifts, the sphagnum moss was hardened into permafrost. Stunted pines and swamp maples clustered together on islands of rock. Along the edges of the Heath, loggers had carved a rat's maze through the laden evergreens. Every way you turned, there was another trail that dead-ended against a white wall of trees.

Why had John Sewall been lurking in this swamp on a subzero day? And how had he found his way out?

A lost person usually behaves in certain specific ways. Deprived of his bearings, he travels downhill or downstream under the mistaken impression that water always leads to a road (often it only leads to more water). Once he finds a trail, he will typically keep walking in one direction. A lost person moves with conviction and rarely reverses course, which is why wardens find so many of them headed 180 degrees from their intended destinations. The worst ones start bushwhacking and get themselves thoroughly turned around. Without clear visual clues, humans really do wander in circles.

To make matters worse, John Sewall was hypothermic. In addition to the normal panic one experiences upon being lost, he was freezing to death, and his behavior had likely been irrational. The worst-case scenario was that he'd never been in the Heath to begin with; perhaps his car had slid off Route 277, and maybe Kate was the name of his girlfriend back home. But my gut told me the young man really had come from the bog and that someone else was lost out here.

Snow sparkled in my headlights. It was often easier to see the outline of the road overhead than the road itself; the jagged treetops showed dark gray against the lighter gray of the sky.

Where the hell was Kendrick—or Ben Sprague, for that matter? I saw no evidence in the shapes of the drifts of a plow truck having come this way. The wind was blowing so hard that the snowbanks were moving around me like slow-motion waves. I realized Sprague might have pushed his way down this very road fifteen minutes earlier and I'd never know it.

I decided to mark a waypoint. I fumbled in my coat pocket and removed my DeLorme GPS unit. The satellite showed my location as a green arrow near the intersection of two branching tote roads. There were low hills on either side of me, steep enough to have presented a barrier to anyone traveling through deep snow on foot. Farther to the west was Bog Pond. I toggled north and south. If Sewall had come from this direction, the hills would have funneled him to this same spot. The road divided south of me. I needed to pick a direction.

East, I decided.

Out of the brute force of the blizzard, the wind wasn't quite as loud, and I became aware of a distant sound. It was the barking of dogs.

Kendrick.

I twisted the throttle, and a noxious cloud of gasoline fumes rose up beneath my visor. Very quickly, the sound of the engine drowned out the yapping of the malamutes. I prayed my sense of direction wouldn't fail me, or I would shoot right past them.

In a few minutes, as I moved east along the trail, my headlights found the phosphorescent eyes of a dog. It stood, legs planted far apart, barking at me with a curled lip. Behind it were others. Kendrick had lashed his team to a tree.

I cut the engine but left the lights shining, and tilted up the visor on my helmet. Moving at forty-five miles per hour, the windblown snow felt like shards of glass being driven into my face.

"Kendrick!" I shouted.

A shadow staggered out of the darkness.

Because he hadn't bothered to put on the snowshoes he kept strapped to his dogsled, he was floundering, knee-deep, in the drifts.

"Have you seen Sprague?" I asked.

His fur-lined hood and the shoulders of his buckskin parka were crusted with snow. "I met him on the road outside his house. He said there was a car lost out here with a girl in it. I sent him north across Route Two seventy-seven to search."

"Did you find anything?"

He smiled, cracking the ice on his mustache. "Yep."

I jumped off the snowmobile into a deep drift. It was like trying to walk in wet cement.

The light from Kendrick's headlamp bounced along, leading the way. A huge snowbank rose across the trail. The handle of an entrenching tool protruded from the top of it.

I watched Kendrick drop to his hands and knees and begin jabbing

at the snow with the pointed shovel. I saw that he had already exca-
vated a deep hole, exposing a black car. The door had been ajar
when the storm began refilling the crater. Someone had entered or
exited the buried vehicle in the past hours, and it was logical to
think that person had been John Sewall.

Kendrick burrowed deeper into the car. Snow had piled up behind
the steering wheel and spilled over into the passenger side. From my
perspective, standing behind Kendrick, I couldn't see any farther into
the darkened interior.

I dropped to one knee and squinted into the face-lacerating wind.
"Is there anyone inside?"

Kendrick stopped digging. He propped himself on his elbow and
turned to face me. "Not a soul," he said.

Ma shakes my shoulder in the middle of the night. Get up, Lucas! Get up! she says.

It's pitch-black. I'm all groggy.

Prester is on his way to the hospital, she says. He got caught in the snowstorm.

Is he froze to death?

Put your clothes on, she says.

The first time I went to the hospital was when I tripped on the stairs that time. I was so tired, I fell asleep walking up to my bedroom and my bottom teeth bit straight through my lip. The tops of them got stuck on the skin. Ma had to peel them apart and there was blood everywhere.

They gave me NINE stitches. I still have this scar along my bottom lip.

That was when I was four years old.

Aunt Tam is downstairs in her chair. She has her coat in her lap. I want to go with you, she tells Ma.

Tammi, there's a blizzard, Ma says. What if the van gets stuck? I don't know how we would deal with your chair if we had to walk through the snow.

Tammi starts to cry.

Ma bends over her chair and gives her a hug. It's important that you be here in case the hospital calls with news, Ma tells her. You can call me on my cell if there's an update. I'm relying on you, Lil Sis.

Tammi smiles, but she's still kind of crying, too. She used to be a basketball star in high school. In her room Tammi keeps a picture of her team, with her standing next to the other girls. One of them is holding a gold trophy ball.

9

L et me have a look," I told Kendrick.

The musher backed out of the hole on his hands and knees. I grabbed the car door and tried to force it open, but it was stuck fast in the snow. I wriggled my way through the narrow gap.

It took me a moment to realize that everything was pitched at a slight angle. The car had slid halfway off the road before the storm buried it. The halogen glow of my light turned the scene in front of me a bluish white. When I exhaled, my breath sparkled. I felt like I was deep inside the cold heart of a glacier.

Turning my head slowly from side to side, I swept the beam of my headlamp around the inside of the vehicle. A thin layer of hoarfrost, like a dusting of baker's flour, covered the interior. The car was a Pontiac; I saw the arrowhead logo on the steering wheel. Someone had used pieces of duct tape to stitch up a gash in the seat. There was the odor of old cigarettes badly masked by a pine-shaped air freshener suspended from the rearview mirror. There were empty Budweiser cans, some crushed, scattered across the backseat. There was a handful of twelve-gauge shotgun shells in the console. But no shotgun.

I found the auto registration tucked above the driver's sun visor. The car was a 2004 Grand Am, registered to one Randall Scott Cates.

"Holy shit," I said aloud.

The image of a sneering, tattooed face hovered in front of my eyes. And suddenly I realized who the hypothermic, frostbitten man was back at the Sprague house and why his face had seemed vaguely familiar.

"What's the story in there?" Kendrick said over my shoulder.

I braced myself against the steering wheel and climbed awkwardly out into the open air. A blast of icy wind nearly pushed me back. Several of the dogs were yowling.

"I know the person who owns this car. It's not a girl named *Kate;* it's a man named *Cates.* Randall Scott Cates. I saw him this morning at the McDonald's in Machias."

Kendrick didn't speak. I couldn't make out his expression through the blowing snow. "So where is he?"

"I don't know. I don't suppose any of your dogs can run a track."

Kendrick gave a scornful laugh. "They're *sled* dogs."

If Randall Cates was wandering around in this blizzard, the odds were heavily stacked against our finding him before he froze to death. If he was already passed out inside a snowbank, we wouldn't find his body until the April thaw.

Almost a year earlier, I had found a deserted car on a darkened road. For a variety of lame-ass reasons, I hadn't exerted myself to find the missing driver. A woman ended up dead. Maybe she would have died anyway, but I didn't need another what-if question hanging over my pillow.

I found my cell phone and tried to get a signal, but the screen showed only a single bar. I tried the GPS instead. Our location came up as a logging road that dead-ended at Bog Stream. I marked a waypoint and handed Kendrick the receiver.

"What's this for?"

"Go back to the Spragues' house and call the state police," I said. "Tell them where I am and that I need assistance locating a lost person. Give them these coordinates. Make sure they notify Warden Marc Rivard. We need a search dog here." I reached into my shirt pocket and found the auto registration. "The state police should also make sure Randall Cates isn't asleep in his bed back in Machias."

The wind tore Kendrick's breath from his open mouth when he laughed. "I don't need GPS coordinates. I know exactly where we are." He tucked the registration in his parka. "What are you going to do?"

"I'm going to look for him."

"No offense, Bowditch, but I guarantee you that I am better at it than you are. I know this bog like the back of my hand. Go back to the house. I'll search the Heath."

"No offense, Kendrick, but this is my job." I zipped up my parka and raised the hood over my ears. "See if you can find Ben Sprague while you're at it. Tell him to clear the Bog Pond Road with his plow so the ambulance can get to his house."

Kendrick pulled his goggles down over his eyes. "Suit yourself."

I watched him check his team's harnesses, his body illuminated in the shaky beam of my headlamp. The animals' coats were matted with clumps of snow. They looked at their master with bright, enthusiastic eyes. The dogs were eager to run.

Kendrick stepped onto the runners of his sled. Then he gave a single sharp whistle. The lead dogs barked and took off. There was a pause, and then the sled was yanked forward into the night. In no time at all, Kendrick had disappeared through gauzy curtains of snow.

After the last barks of the dogs had faded and all that was left was the howling of the wind in the tops of the cedars, I sat down on the seat of the snowmobile and strapped my snowshoes to the bottoms of my boots. My bare fingers smarted as I secured the buckles. Kendrick was right about the absurdity of my plan: I was alone, at night, in a blizzard in a pathless forest. I was trying to find a lost, perhaps already dead and buried man. And somehow I was going to accomplish this feat without succumbing to hypothermia myself. Where to even begin?

With a spiral search, I decided.

Starting at the driver's door, I began walking in an expanding circle around the car.

If Randall Cates was indeed dead, my best chance of finding him was somewhere near his encased vehicle. I could imagine the tattooed man lurching off into the dark in his panic or confusion and very quickly collapsing from the cold, especially if he had been dressed as inadequately as his companion was.

Perhaps I was reading too much into his incoherent mutterings, but John Sewall had told us that his friend was "in the car," which suggested that Cates had remained in the vehicle while his passenger went for help. Maybe the two men had gotten stuck and then tried to wait out the storm, until finally the subzero temperature drove them to take action.

I could understand the desperation. Waves of powder washed like lines of surf along the frozen road. After fifteen minutes of tromping around, I paused in the shelter of a big hemlock until a sudden gust knocked an enormous clump of snow off the heavy boughs and down onto my head.

I decided to expand my search. Back at the Spragues' snowmobile, I struggled to remove my snowshoes. I could barely see through the ice-painted visor of my helmet. More and more, my fingers were feeling like they'd been carved from sticks of fatwood.

Fortunately, the sled's engine sprang to life with the first turn of the key. Half standing, with one knee resting on the seat, I rode for maybe a hundred yards into the swamp, calling for the lost man the entire time. The headlights showed no footprints or vehicle tracks. The snow was as pure as a newly washed sheet.

After a while, I gave it up and reversed course. By the time I passed the Grand Am again, the storm had nearly filled the hole that Kendrick had shoveled. If Sewall and Cates had been stuck inside their car for hours, they might have run the engine to keep warm until the gas tank was empty. People who try this maneuver often forget to crack their windows and so expire from carbon monoxide poisoning. Or their tailpipe gets plugged with snow and they die that way from the odorless and colorless gas. Had Sewall gone for help after his friend lapsed into unconsciousness? I was convinced that Cates must have been incapacitated in some way when Sewall had set off on his snowblind journey into the void. Why else stay behind?

I was traveling through a landscape as sharp as a black-and-white photograph. The greens of the pines looked black. The shadows beyond my headlights were gray. The only brightness was the white of the blowing snow.

I had entered a world of ghosts.

Along that spectral road, I met no living thing.

Around 2:30 A.M., I decided to return to the car. It had been two hours, give or take, since I had sent Kendrick off on his mission; four hours since I had arrived at the Spragues' house.

With any luck, Ben Sprague had cleared a passage for the ambulance and John Sewall was en route to the hospital in Machias. With any luck, Sergeant Rivard was on his way to my location and searchers were assembling from across the snowbound county to help scour the woods. With any luck, Randall Cates was still alive.

I wasn't feeling all that lucky.

My lungs hurt from shouting and breathing subzero air. My fingers had begun to throb and cramp. There was no sensation in the tip of my nose.

Back in the glade, there was no sign of Randall Cates. No sign of help. I parked the Yamaha beside the car's open door to block the wind and then crawled inside the vehicle. Once again, I snapped on my headlamp and inspected the inside of the four-wheeled igloo.

If I could figure out what Cates and Sewall had been doing in this isolated place, I might have a better chance of finding my missing person. Under the seat, my stiff fingers encountered something that felt like a magazine but turned out to be a battered copy of *The Maine Atlas,* a staple-bound gazetteer that just about everyone I knew kept stashed in their cars or trucks. Maine was a big state, or at least a largely empty one with too many unmarked roads. It was easy to lose your way.

On a hunch, I turned to the page that corresponded to my present location. The topographical map showed vast white expanses that indicated wetlands. Logging roads and jeep trails zigzagged through these empty places. I followed a curving line down from the Spragues' house, about two miles away. A pencil scratch marked the spot where I was sitting. So Sewall and Cates had come to this specific place for a reason? Was it a drug deal? They'd done something here and then gotten stuck trying to drive out on the snowy road.

I tried the glove compartment again, but it was locked.

What about the trunk?

I loosened the latch. Behind me came a click, but the lid was weighted down with snow. I slid out into the biting night and grabbed Kendrick's shovel. It took me five minutes to clear off enough snow to get the trunk open.

I found the shotgun inside. It was a Remington 870 pump. Someone had recently cleaned the barrel—the metal gleamed blue under my headlamp—and carefully rubbed linseed oil into the hardwood stock. The trunk also contained a spare tire, a jack, a few ice-fishing tip-ups, and a blue school gym bag emblazoned with the Whitney High mascot, a stern-faced and politically questionable Indian chief. I unzipped the bag. There must have been five thousand dollars in cash rolled up in rubber bands. Someone had thrown in a loaded Glock 9 for good measure.

There wasn't another car on the road.

The trees were all thrashing around like those evil trees that almost ate the Hobbits. The electric wires kept swinging like jump ropes. I thought maybe one of them would snap. You can't get electrocuted in a car, on account of the rubber wheels, Mr. Mason told us.

I kept expecting to see the White Owl around every corner, perched on a fence post.

Ma had to lean over the steering wheel to see anything.

What happened to Prester? I asked.

The police say he showed up at somebody's house in the middle of the storm.

Whose house?

I don't know. Somebody who lives in Township Nineteen. Way out in the boondooks.

Where does the word boondocks come from?

I have no clue.

Is there a real place called East Gish?

Lucas, she said. Will you PLEASE stop asking questions! I'm trying to concentrate on the road.

Where's Randall, though? He and Prester said they was going coyote hunting, not last night but the night before.

Lucas! I'm freaking out here!

Before she started going to her Don't Drink meetings, back when she was with Randle, she used to get all weird and dopey, but now she's nervous or angry all the time.

We drove over the causeway in the dark. Usually there are cars parked along it, people hanging out—but not during the Storm of the Century.

We passed Helen's and the Bluebird Ranch and they were both closed. Even the gas station was closed. It was like a NUCLEAR BOMB went off and killed everybody or maybe turned them into zombies.

Now we're in the hospital parking lot.

I wonder how many people die at the hospital every year. Probably a lot.

All hospitals must be haunted.

I O

I was inside the Grand Am, shivering, my teeth clenched to keep from chattering. The gym bag lay open beside me on the seat. I was trying to reconstruct in my imagination the drug deal that had taken place in this frozen swamp when I heard a loud scraping sound. I clambered out of the car and stood knee-deep in the snow, watching as powerful lights tore through the storm.

There were two vehicles: a hefty pickup outfitted with a V-shaped plow and a green warden's truck following behind. I hoped the trucks hadn't just flattened the buried body of Randall Cates in an attempt to reach me.

Over the idling engines I heard truck doors bang open. Three silhouettes came toward me through the headlights.

"Bowditch!" It was Rivard, wearing his green warden's parka with the hood up.

Behind him came a shorter, thicker man: the plow driver.

And then another person with a dog.

Kathy Frost? No, she was two hundred miles away tonight in Greenville. It was her protégé from the K-9 team, Cody Devoe. He had been the warden in my old district before being transferred to Washington County at his own request. Devoe is one of those natural woodsmen whose idea of heaven is being stationed in the wildest, least populated outposts imaginable, the kind of warden who spends his vacations fishing for arctic char in Labrador. He is a big bruiser with a perpetual five o'clock shadow even at five o'clock in the

77

morning. His friends call him Fred Flintstone. His German shepherd is named Tomahawk.

The plow driver—I assumed it was Ben Sprague—was a short but solid guy. He had a hooked, beaklike nose and small, rapidly blinking eyes set close together. He wore a blue snowmobile suit covered with iron-on patches from various clubs, and a New England Patriots cap with a fuzzy pom-pom on top.

"So what's going on?" Rivard asked.

"We've got a lost man out here," I said. "It's Randall Cates."

"That's what Kendrick told me. I didn't believe it until I saw Prester Sewall lying in that bed."

"I thought his name was John."

"Everyone calls him Prester."

"I think Cates and Sewall were out here on a drug deal."

"Is that a hunch, or do you have more specific reasons for saying that?"

I showed them the gym bag full of money, and the gun. I told them about the map inside the car with our location marked in pencil. My lips were so numb, I sounded like I had a speech impediment. "I think Cates is lost out here somewhere, wandering around in the dark or collapsed in a snowbank."

"I'm not sure how we're going to find him in this storm," Rivard said.

"I'd like to try running a track." Devoe squatted down beside his dog and adjusted the little orange vest she was wearing. "Tomahawk's pretty good in the snow. We did some avalanche training last winter up at Baxter State Park."

"Christ, it's cold out here." Rivard rubbed his gloved hands together and stamped his feet, first one and then the other. The Grand Am had almost disappeared again inside the white mound of snow.

"How's Sewall doing?" I asked.

"The paramedics were putting him in the ambulance when Devoe and I showed up," said Rivard. "He looked pretty bad to me, but maybe he'll pull through. They won't be able to get him to Bangor in the storm, so they're taking him to Machias to stabilize his condition."

"Where's Kendrick?" I asked.

"I left him at the house," said Rivard. "I told him to direct assistance to our location, and I thought someone should stay with Mrs. Sprague."

Ben Sprague stared hard at me with a trembling lip and a knitted brow, as if I'd just insulted his mother. "My wife's had a terrible shock!"

What was up with this guy? Maybe he was just mad that his pleasant evening at home with the missus had been ruined by this freak occurrence. I couldn't blame him—Doris Sprague had seemed genuinely upset.

"What about Larrabee?" I asked.

"Doc went to the hospital with the EMTs."

"So who else is coming?"

"I wanted to scope things out before calling in the cavalry," said Rivard. "I woke up Bill Day over in Aurora, but he's going to be all night getting here. The Passamaquoddies are sending a dog handler from Princeton, along with one of their tribal wardens." He stomped his feet again in that same methodical manner he'd used before, first the right, then the left. "We might as well let Tomahawk give it a try, but who knows if that dirtbag Cates is even out here."

I understood Rivard's skepticism. Pitch-dark, in the middle of a snowstorm, at a temperature where even the nose of the best-trained SAR dog in the world might as well have been wrapped in a burlap—these were hardly optimal conditions for a search. And yet I couldn't help but feel that my sergeant's lack of confidence was also personal. We hadn't worked together long enough for him to appreciate my abilities, so all he had to go on was my reputation in the service: impulsive, hotheaded, too impressed with my own intelligence, book-smart rather than woods-smart, a discipline problem, not a team player. In other words, a very, very bad bet.

Devoe found a dime-store bandanna in the Grand Am and let his dog have a good whiff of it. Then he let her begin pulling him around on a leash through the snow. Tomahawk made a circle around the car and began working her way outward in a fan-shaped pattern.

Over the past two years, while on stakeouts and patrols, Kathy Frost had given me endless tutorials on the training and use of canines in search and rescue and human-remains recovery. I knew that Tomahawk was searching for a "pool" of human scent wafting through the snowpack. If she found one, she would begin to dig. And maybe, just maybe, she would discover the frozen-solid corpse of Randall Cates. I also knew that Rivard was right when he said the chances of her finding him in these conditions were slim to none.

Rivard wanted to do his own search of the Grand Am.

Ben Sprague said he was returning to his truck to warm up and wait. I decided to be neighborly and join Sprague.

I opened the passenger door and peered up at him. "Do you mind if I get out of the cold for a few minutes?"

"Be my guest."

I slammed the door behind me and instantly felt embraced in warmth. My night in the blizzard had frozen my bones to the marrow. "The snow seems to be letting up."

"Does it?"

He fiddled with the radio and brought up a fuzzy station playing rock and roll from across the New Brunswick border. So much for conversation.

I removed my gloves and warmed my hands over the air vents. At first my fingers were numb; then they began to throb. I rubbed the palms against my cheeks and nose. I made funny faces to loosen the tight skin.

"Hotel California" was playing on the radio. Sprague tapped a beat to the music with his hands on the steering wheel, but more out of impatience than from a sense of rhythm.

"How long have you and Doris lived out here?" I asked.

"What do you mean—in the sticks?"

"In Township Nineteen."

"Too long."

I wasn't sure what he meant, but he didn't seem inclined to clarify the statement. "You two saved that man's life."

He made a snorting sound. "I wouldn't bet on it."

"Had you ever seen him before?"

His face had a lime-green cast from the dashboard lights. "Which one?"

"Either one."

"No."

"Do you know what they were doing out here?"

"Selling drugs. You saw that bag of money."

"But why were they out here in the Heath, of all places?" I asked.

"I'm not a drug dealer. I don't know why they do anything."

Devoe and Tomahawk moved past our vehicles, heading down the logging road. We turned our heads to follow them. I couldn't tell if the dog had found a scent trail or was just ecstatic to be doing what she'd been bred and trained to do.

"A dog can't find someone in weather like this," Sprague said confidently. "You won't find his body until springtime."

"They find people buried by avalanches."

"Not in weather like this."

We heard a garbled shout outside. I saw Rivard stick his head up from the car. He began walking quickly through the snow toward Devoe's position. I grabbed the door handle and hopped out.

At the edge of Rivard's dancing flashlight beam, Cody Devoe crouched in front of a roadside tree. He was down on his knees, holding Tomahawk around the neck. The German shepherd was straining toward a snowdrift piled against a leafless hardwood.

"What have you got?" Rivard asked.

"Something dead."

Rivard knelt over the drift and began sweeping snow away with his gloved hands. Soon we saw matted brown hair, a human head nodding forward, as if a man had fallen asleep against the ash trunk. Rivard brushed the impacted snow off the forehead and shoulders. He gripped the head by the forelock and tilted the tattooed face up at us. The young man's mouth was open and a blue tongue was thrust between the teeth. The eyes were glassy, sight-less.

Ben Sprague came huffing and puffing along behind us. "Is he dead?" the plow driver asked.

Rivard removed a glove and pressed a couple of fingers beneath the man's jawbone. "No pulse."

I glanced back through the wind-whipped snow. "He didn't make it very far."

Rivard wiped the snow off his hands and bent to retrieve his glove. "He must have left the car after his friend went for help. He sat down under the tree to get out of the wind, and that was all she wrote."

"Do you need a shovel to dig him out?" asked Sprague. "I have one in the truck."

"We don't know what went down here," I said. "For all we know, there's a bullet hole in the middle of Cates's chest."

"Mike's right," said Devoe.

"I know he is," said Rivard sourly. "Use my radio to call Dispatch. Tell them to wake up the medical examiner. Make sure he brings his snowshoes."

I was in the hospital last year.

We was having a Barbie Q in the backyard, and Prester was drinking beer. Ma had wheeled Tammi down the ramp and around the side of the house up onto the little hill. Tammi was wearing a cowboy hat Dad brought her from Texas because he was still trying to get back together with Ma even though they are divorced. There were no mosquitoes and the sun was warm before it went down behind the roof.

Ma hadn't met Randle yet, so everybody was happy.

We was eating hamburgers and hot dogs. Prester had an apron that said on it MR. GOOD LOOKIN' IS COOKIN'. I remember he called himself the Iron Chef and did some kung fu moves with the grill fork and the paddle thing you use to flip a burger. Kee-yaa!

Ma said something about how I needed to go out for a sport at school because she wanted me to be a student-athlete. The reason I needed glasses, she said, was because I was always reading comic books and Stephen King and writing in my NOTEBOOK.

You'll develop more if you use your muscles, said Ma. You're too scrawny, Lucas.

I'm the littlest kid in my class. I could maybe be a jockey if someone would teach me how to ride a horse.

Prester said, What about wrestling? That's a sport for little fellers. What do you say, Luke Skywalker, you want me to teach you how to wrestle?

Wrestling is gay, I said. I don't want to touch some kid's boner.

Lucas! Ma said.

Prester got down on all fours and said, Come on. Kneel down beside me and grab my arm.

I didn't have no choice. Prester got me all arranged. I didn't really want to squeeze his belly, but that's part of wrestling, I guess. He had a weird sour smell leaking through his skin from the beer.

Who's going to count to three? Prester asked.

I will, said Tammi. Then she went, One, two, three! wicked quick.

The next thing I knew, Prester was sitting on top of me, belching beer breath in my face. I was gulping for air because he'd knocked the wind out of me.

Two outta three, he said.

This time he made me get down on all fours.

Don't hurt him, Prester, Ma said.

I didn't want to wrestle, so I figured I would just go limp. When Tammi said, One, two, three, Prester just picked me up like I was a doll and flopped me completely over—wham!—against my shoulder blades. Snap! went the bone. Everyone heard it!

Ma went mental after that. She made me wiggle my fingers and toes. You could have broken his neck, she told Prester. You could have paralyzed him!

He was sobbing like a baby. He cupped his hand and held it up to his face because he was embarrassed to be crying. Ma made us all pile into the van and drive into Machias.

Prester held my hand and slobbered all over it. Will you forgive me, Lucas? Please, please, please, forgive me!

Later I got my REVENGE—I sprinkled Tammi's laxative all over his cold pizza.

Prester had the runs for a week.

Ha!

Shortly before dawn, Rivard sent me back to the house on the snowmobile because my cheeks were turning white. The wind had begun to die and the snow was lightening to flurries, but even so, I had trouble finding my way. In the minutes since Ben Sprague's plow had cleared a passage for the trucks, the drifts had thoroughly reclaimed the logging road. In the east, there was a wash of color against the jagged horizon, a brushstroke of gray along the bottom of a black canvas.

I'd expected to find Kendrick's dog team tied up outside the Spragues' house. Instead, I discovered a white Ford Interceptor. On its door was a silver star against a black badge; on its fenders were the words WASHINGTON COUNTY SHERIFF PATROL. The rockers were spackled with salt brine. Because of Maine's perpetually corrosive weather, our abundant potholes and frost heaves, the life expectancy of most new cars was little more than a decade. Less than that for police vehicles.

A balding blond man with broad shoulders and windburned cheeks greeted me at the door. His name was Corbett, and he was the chief deputy at the Washington County Sheriff's Department. We'd met several times over the previous weeks as part of my orientation. He wore blue jeans tucked into L.L.Bean boots and a black fleece emblazoned with the sheriff's department logo on the breast.

"You look like a Popsicle." Corbett had a resonant baritone that made me think he'd missed out on having a lucrative career in radio.

"I feel like a Popsicle."

"I can't believe you spent the night out there. I live just up the road, and it took me forever to get out of my driveway."

I heard a door open and slam shut down the hall. "Is Kendrick here?"

Corbett offered me a quizzical look. "You mean Professor Kendrick from the university?"

"Rivard told him to wait here and direct search units to our location in the Heath."

"He wasn't here when I arrived, and Doris never mentioned him."

That seemed strange. Why would Kendrick have taken off before the first police cruiser arrived? "How's Mrs. Sprague doing? She seemed in a bad way before."

"She's had a rough time of things since their son's accident. The Spragues are good people—Ben and I are in Rotary—but what happened to Joey has really tested their faith. Is Ben on his way back here?"

"He's plowing the road again. Rivard wants to keep it clear so the medical examiner can get down into the Heath." I was curious to learn more about the Spragues' son and his obscure accident, but my brain felt as numb as the rest of me. "So let me get this straight: You weren't here when the EMTs left?"

"No, but I passed them on the road. I asked if they needed an escort to Machias, but they said no." He glanced at his watch, which he wore with the face on the inside of his wrist. "They should be at Down East Community Hospital by now. I haven't heard how Prester's doing."

"I hope he wakes up, just so we can get the story of what really happened."

"I'm not sure it's such a mystery," said Corbett. "Ben and Doris were always reporting seeing suspicious vehicles going by here, heading into the woods. Ben would get really worked up. I even did some of my own patrols down there, but I only scared up a young couple having sex."

"So you think maybe Cates had a regular place he was doing deals out in the Heath?"

Corbett shrugged his wide shoulders. "It's certainly off the beaten track. I go deer hunting down there every November and always get turned around a few times before I find my way out. It's a scary place. I'm surprised you guys found the body at all."

"We figured he wouldn't be far from the car. And we had a well-trained dog helping us." I described the scene to him—the car, the bag of money, the loaded Glock, and then the startled expression on the corpse's rimed face. "Cates didn't look to me like a guy who had passed out in a snowbank. I'll be curious to hear the coroner's report."

"The sheriff will want to speak with you about it. Randall Cates was on her personal most-wanted list."

The longtime Washington County sheriff was a woman, one of only handful of female sheriffs in the state of Maine. Her name was Roberta Rhine. My professional experience working with sheriffs had thus far been hit-and-miss. The chief law-enforcement officer of Somerset County, where my father had committed his crimes, hated my guts, but back on the midcoast, I'd established a cordial relationship with Dudley Baker, the Knox County sheriff.

"Well, she can cross him off her list now," I said, rubbing my tired eyes. "What about the other one—Sewall?"

"Prester?" Corbett grinned and shook his head. "He's one of our favorite people over to the jail. We've had him in for just about everything—drunk and disorderly, B and E, check kiting, receiving stolen property. Nothing violent, though. A lot of these guys like Cates enjoy having a sidekick to tell them what big-time gangsters they are. Prester's actually a nice guy when he sobers up, which is almost never. It's probably all the antifreeze in his system that kept him alive out there."

I remembered how Sewall had skulked around the McDonald's, a small guy trying not to draw attention to himself. "Does his sister work at the McDonald's in Machias?"

"Jamie? Yeah."

"I was actually in there this morning and noticed her."

"She's easy to notice," Corbett said with the sort of smile that didn't belong on the face of a married man.

"Prester and Randall were there, too. They were giving her some grief, and she ended up taking food out to their car."

"You'll want to put that in your report."

Standing in the Spragues' entryway, I found myself leaning against a wall for support. I had been awake for nearly twenty-four hours, and I still had to shovel out my Jeep and drive back to my trailer.

"I should say something to Mrs. Sprague," I said.

"You're probably better off just hitting the road," said Corbett. "The poor woman seems pretty shaken up. When I told her I needed to get an official statement from her, she asked if she could clean Joey's room first."

"I need to give her back her snowmobile keys."

"You can leave them with me."

I shrugged and handed him the keys.

Ben Sprague had plowed a lane past my Jeep, pushing snow up against the tops of the windows. I had to use my cupped hand to scoop out a hole deep enough to get the tailgate open. From there, it was all shovel work. Beneath my layers of polypro, wool, and Gore-Tex, I began to perspire heavily.

Every once in a while, I took a break from my labors, leaned on the shovel, and looked around me at the dawning world. The last clouds that made up the rear guard of the storm were marching away to the northeast. The blizzard was off to punish Nova Scotia next. The wind came up and rustled the loose strips of paper hanging from the birches. Two silent crows bounced along on gusts overhead.

I'd wondered if my tires had sharp-enough studs to claw their way up that hill, but I had no problem getting back on the road.

As I crested the hill, I thought about the snowmobiler who'd played chicken with my Jeep the night before. Who was he? A neighbor of the Spragues out for a midnight ride? Or the man Cates and

Sewall had met down in the swamp? I'd need to make a mention of his phosphorescent green sled and snowsuit in my report. I wondered what make and model of snowmobile Barney Beal rode. According to Rivard, the big kid was a drug addict who frequented this area.

I never knew you could sprain muscles shivering, but I was sore in places I rarely had cause to contemplate. As my cheeks and extremities began to warm, they started to throb rhythmically. I touched the tip of my nose. There was a trace of frostbite, but at least I wasn't going to lose it. If Prester Sewall survived the week, he was going to have a mug like the Phantom of the Opera's.

God, what a couple of days: from a frozen zebra to two frozen drug dealers.

If you ask police officers what they like best about the job, nine out of ten will probably tell you it's the surprises. Going on patrol, you honestly never know what you're going to encounter next: despicable crimes; bloody accidents; cries of despair and rage; displays of the most jaw-dropping perversity; lies so bald-faced, you don't know whether to laugh or vomit; self-destroying bouts of intoxication; every form of abuse and neglect known to man; but also acts of heroism from the most unexpected quarters; generosity, too; and those simple good deeds that are so important and yet so undervalued in this fucked-up world.

Everywhere, every night: the human comedy showing for your viewing pleasure.

By the time I got home, dawn had broken and patches of blue showed between the clouds. A titmouse was calling emphatically from the big beech behind the trailer. *Peer! Peer!* The swaying treetops made moving blue shadows on the snow.

The electric heater had failed again, and no amount of messing with the fuse box was enough to restart it. I'd need to call my landlord in Lubec. In the meantime, I boiled some water on the propane stove and used a hand towel to clean the sweat from my body. It was the least satisfying bath of my life. I'd considered taking a nap before driving into Machias, but with the temperature inside the trailer hovering around the freezing mark, I worried I might never awaken. I shaved, put on my olive-drab uniform, and resigned myself to the fact that this was going to be one of those thirty-six-hour days all wardens experience from time to time.

I dialed the Washington County jail and asked the receptionist if I could speak with Sheriff Rhine.

"The sheriff is having a breakfast meeting with the Maine Drug Enforcement Agency, but she said it would be OK for you go over there."

"Where's the meeting?" I pictured coffee and bagels in the district attorney's office.

"The usual place—McDonald's."

What else should I have expected? A disquieting feeling came over me as I recalled Jamie Sewall's smiling face. Had anyone notified her of her brother's condition? What if I found her behind the counter?

The plows had barely made a dent in the snowpack. At best, they'd shaved a few inches off the top, sprayed some ineffectual salt brine down to melt the slick spots, and scattered pebbles, which now rattled around my truck's chassis. The sun had finally emerged from wherever it had been hiding to pour sterile light down on the blinding roadsides. The morning was as white as a laboratory.

When I entered the McDonald's, I looked for Jamie Sewall, but she was nowhere to be seen, except inside the frame of her Employee of the Month portrait. I exhaled—out of relief or disappointment, I wasn't sure.

I saw Sheriff Rhine at a back booth, sitting with her face to the door, across from a man whose stiff posture and bristly haircut suggested he too worked in law enforcement. The sheriff had a long, handsome face with the profile of a cigar-store Indian, dyed black hair gathered in a ponytail, and strong-looking hands. She wore a navy suit over a light blue roll-neck sweater. Even seated, she appeared to be a tall woman. She caught my gaze and held it, as if she wanted me to approach.

Her companion was in his mid-forties and anonymous-looking

in the way of some law-enforcement officers: dressed in a black ski jacket over a black cotton sweater, sandy hair clipped short.

As I neared the table, I heard him raise his voice.

"All we want is some goddamn cooperation, Roberta," he said. "We're on the same team here."

"Not according to your boss. He says one of my guys is dirty."

The agent heard me and glanced over his shoulder. We made eye contact briefly and he dropped his tone again. "You can't keep going on TV and accusing the MDEA of malfeasance."

"If the shoe fits."

I knew from reading the newspaper that the Washington County Sheriff's Department and the Maine Drug Enforcement Agency—known locally as the MDEA—had a feud that made the tussle between the Hatfields and the McCoys look like a polite disagreement between perfumed gentleman, but no one had yet explained to me the grievances that had fueled the conflict.

"Maybe you think this media crusade of yours is a joke," he said. "But it's going to come back to haunt you at your next election."

"That's what your director told me two years ago. And yet here I am."

The agent stood up suddenly in the booth, bumping the table with his knees. "You'll be hearing from us."

"I'm giddy with anticipation. Have a safe drive back to Augusta."

The agent didn't say good-bye to me, but then he hadn't said hello, either.

"Asshole," said the sheriff as the door closed behind him. "Have a seat, Warden."

I settled down and eyed her half-eaten sausage McGriddle enviously.

"You've probably heard about my beef with the MDEA." Roberta Rhine had a gruff voice.

"I don't know any of the particulars."

"It's a rogue agency, with a director who excuses and covers up misconduct by his agents. Did you know an MDEA agent lost—I repeat, *lost*—three thousand dollars in buy money? And then they have the gall to accuse one of my men—they won't say who—of being on the take from Randall Cates." She sipped from her paper coffee cup. "So you're the one who found him dead, I hear."

"Me and a couple of other wardens. Your chief deputy told me you had some special interest in Cates."

"I certainly do. That tattooed freak killed a student over at the university last year."

"That would be Trinity Raye?"

The sheriff nodded. "Randall Cates sold her some tainted heroin laced with a blood-thinning agent. Her friends said it was her first time smoking the stuff. She was just a hippie chick, experimenting. ODs are pretty common around here, but when it's a nice girl from a nice home, everyone screams bloody murder. We had nothing to connect Cates to her death except about a thousand rumors." She leaned back in the booth. The vinyl made a noise like a hand rubbing a child's balloon. "Speaking of drugs, you look like you could use some caffeine. Why don't you go get yourself a cup of coffee. Then you can tell me what happened last night."

On the sheriff's instructions, I bought myself the largest-size coffee the restaurant served, added three egg McMuffins, and returned to tell my tale. She listened with rapt attention, not interrupting, fiddling with a big turquoise ring on her right hand the whole time I talked.

When I'd finished, she said, "The state police will start with Prester Sewall as their prime suspect."

"I would, too, if I were investigating the case."

"Let's see if Walt Kitteridge can shine any light on the matter." Rhine removed her cell phone from her pocket. Kitteridge was the state's chief medical examiner. She apparently had his number on speed dial, given how quickly the call went through.

"Walt," she said. "It's Roberta Rhine. I bet you know why I'm calling."

She smiled at me while he spoke. Then she moved the phone away from her ear and held a man-size hand over the microphone. "He just got out of the woods, and he sounds wicked pissed about being called out in a storm."

She moved the phone back to her ear. "I understand it's still early, but I need to decide whether to put a guard on that guy in the hospital. If there's a chance he killed Randall Cates, then I owe it to the doctors and nurses to send a deputy over there, don't you think?"

Without hearing the other side of the conversation, I could guess the bone of contention: The medical examiner didn't want to speculate on cause of death until he'd done an autopsy.

"It'll be our little secret," Rhine said. "Cross my heart and hope to die."

Dr. Kitteridge must have relented, because the sheriff fell silent for a full minute while she listened to his preliminary findings.

"Thanks, Walt. I swear I won't tell a soul. Give me a call when it's official."

She grabbed her winter coat from the booth and began working her arms into the sleeves.

"How'd you like to follow me to the hospital, Warden?" she said with a horsey smile. "Kitteridge found contusions on Randall's neck and signs of petechial hemorrhage. It looks like someone held his face down in the snow until he suffocated to death."

The hospital has got a weird smell. Like Dr. Frankenstein's laboratory or something. Creepy!

Ma sits me down in a chair in the waiting room while she talks to some frog-faced woman at a desk.

She says Prester is in the EMERGENCY ROOM and we can't see him until he is STABLE.

Prester has never been stable, Ma says. I think it's supposed to be a joke, but she don't laugh.

She smiles and pats my hand. What do you know, Edgar Allan Poe? she asks me.

Nothing, I say. That's what I always say.

Do you think you'll be all right here on your own for a few minutes? I need to get something out of the van.

A cigarette?

You know I don't smoke anymore, Lucas. It's just something I need right now. She smiles and opens my NOTEBOOK on my lap. Just stay here and write some more stories for a while, she says. No one's going to bother you.

Can I have a Coke? I need one dollar and twenty-five cents.

Lucas, don't think you can trick me just because I'm upset.

When she goes out the automatic door, a cold wind blows in behind her, and the mean lady behind the desk shivers hard.

If Prester is frozen solid, that must mean his willie is frozen, too. What if the doctor accidentally snaps it off like an icicle?

OUCH!

Ma comes back and she has something in her hand. I can't tell what. She's got her eyes closed and she's moving her lips like she's praying, but no words are coming out. She sits down next to me again.

What did you forget, Ma?

She holds out her hand and there's a little green plastic chip. It says UNITY/SERVICE/RECOVERY *in a triangle around the words 3* MONTHS.

What's that? I ask.

My good-luck charm, she says.

Y ou can tell a lot about a town from its hospital. The one in Machias was located on a piney stretch of road, not near anything in particular except an abandoned horse-racing track festooned with NO TRESPASSING signs. Most people would have driven past the building without realizing it was the local medical center. The low-slung brick structure was smaller than my old junior high in Scarborough.

Whoever decorated the interior had gone for a casual down-home effect, sort of like a country inn. The waiting room was painted a canary yellow, with several blue couches and floral-print chairs arranged around an imitation woodstove. A totally bald man who looked like he might have fought in the Battle of the Bulge sat in a robe and slippers, watching old newsreels play in his head. The only other person in the room was an odd-looking boy who had his legs drawn up beneath him in his chair and was scribbling violently in a notebook.

We met a male nurse, a whip-thin guy in green scrubs, coming down the checkerboard hallway that led to the emergency room.

"Hey, Sheriff," the nurse said. "What's up?"

"Who's on duty in the ER this morning, Tommy?"

"Dr. Chatterjee."

"Can I speak with him?"

"He's with a patient—it's a severe hypothermia case."

"Yes, I know," said the sheriff. "The patient's name is Prester Sewall. We have reason to believe he might be dangerous."

The nurse nodded as if he understood—although he clearly didn't—and disappeared down the hall in the direction of the ER.

The last time I'd set foot in a hospital had been a year earlier, when I'd had my skull fractured by the scariest man I'd ever met. He'd beaten me to within an inch of my life, and it was a miracle I'd survived. It was a different hospital, different emergency room, but the memories of that day made the hairs on my neck prickle.

After a few minutes, a doctor in a white coat and scrubs came hurrying along from the ER. He had the darkest skin of anyone I'd met in Washington County, and jet-black hair swept up from his forehead. His plastic-frame glasses didn't hide the shadows under his eyes.

"Is there a problem?" There was a trace of Bangalore in his inflections.

"Not yet," said Rhine.

"I've been up since last night, Sheriff, so I am in no shape for badinage." When he spoke, his Adam's apple bobbed up and down like a walnut caught in his throat.

"I'm stationing one of my deputies in a chair beside Prester Sewall's bed."

Young Dr. Chatterjee gave a high-pitched laugh. "Tell him to bring a good book."

"Now you're the one not being clear, Doc."

The doctor crooked his finger at us. "Follow me."

He led us to the intensive-care unit, or med-surg unit, as they called it at this hospital. It was an open area—loud with beeping machines, buzzing phones, and snatches of conversation among passing people—where a nurse sat at a central desk, facing a row of glass-walled rooms. In one of these rooms lay Prester Sewall.

If anything, he looked even worse than the last time I'd seen him. He was stretched out on a wheeled bed, with a sheet pulled up around his chest and an IV jammed into his freckled arm. Most of his nose and both of his ears had gone completely black. His blistered cheeks were mauve. His hands were wrapped in bandages that made his arms look like soft white clubs.

"We've just moved him here from the ER," said Chatterjee.

"Can he hear us?" Rhine asked.

"We've given him a dopamine infusion, but he's so exhausted, he keeps slipping back into sleep."

"This is the warden who treated him," the sheriff explained.

Chatterjee studied my face. "You did an excellent job of rewarming him. He's not showing any signs of atrial fibrillation."

"So it looks like he's going to make it, then?" Rhine asked.

"His condition is critical but hemodynamically stable," the doctor said.

I sensed movement behind me.

"Prester!"

Jamie Sewall stood in the door. Her hair was a frizzled mess and her eyes were red as beets, but I recognized the high cheekbones, the wide lips.

"How did you get in here?" the doctor asked.

"He's my brother!"

"Miss Sewall, please," implored the sheriff. "You can't be in here right now. His condition isn't stable yet."

"He's my brother!" She seemed to be on the verge of hyperventilating.

Chatterjee stepped between the young woman and the bed, but she nearly knocked him aside.

"Warden, can you help me with this?" asked the sheriff.

"Miss Sewall." I put my hand on her arm, but she threw it off. I tried again with more strength.

"Let go of me!"

"Take her outside," the doctor told me. "There's a room down the hall—number three. Stay with her."

"I want to talk with him!"

"He's sedated," I said softly, trying to calm her down with my voice while I pulled her from the bedside. "He can't speak to you."

"I'll be there in a moment," said Chatterjee.

The woman turned her brown eyes up at me, and I felt her resistance give way. "Why can't I stay here?"

"They're trying to take care of him."

It was the only answer I could muster, but it must have sufficed, because she went willingly with me into the examination room the doctor had indicated.

Inside room number three, I sat her down in a plastic chair and stood with my back against the door in case she grew wild again. She had one hand clenched into a small fist, as if ready to throw a punch with it, and she was shaking and crying at the same time.

"Why won't they let me see him?" She had a smoker's rough voice, although there was no smell of cigarettes on her clothing, just a touch of faded perfume, musky and sweet in the closed room. "They said when he left the ER, I could go in and see him, but now the nurse at the desk says he's not permitted to have visitors. Why is the sheriff here? What's going on?"

"The police are conducting an investigation. Do you know what happened to your brother last night, Miss Sewall?"

"He has hypothermia. The doctor told me he got lost in the storm." She used her sweater hem to dab at her eyes.

"He was in a car that got stuck on a logging road in Township Nineteen. Do you have any idea what he was doing out there?"

She took a while to respond. "No."

"Does he own any property in the Heath?"

Jamie Sewall burst out laughing. "Prester? He doesn't even own a car."

When she smiled, she became again the beautiful young woman I'd met the previous morning. So far, she had shown no signs of recognizing me from McDonald's. I was just another guy in a uniform, as far as she was concerned.

"Where does he live?" I asked.

"With me and my son, Lucas, and my sister, Tammi, in Whitney," she said.

"What does he do for work?"

She laughed again. "Prester doesn't believe in work."

I decided to gauge her candor. "Do you know a man named Randall Cates?"

She sat up in her chair and looked at me coldly. "He used to be my boyfriend. We broke up last year."

"When was the last time you saw him?"

"Yesterday afternoon. He stopped at my house to pick up Prester. Why? What happened to him?"

"Did either of them tell you where they were going or who they might be meeting?"

Her eyes widened. "Randall is dead, isn't he? I can tell by the way you're talking about him."

How had I given myself away? I wasn't supposed to disclose that information until the state police had notified the next of kin. For all the apparent hysteria, Jamie Sewall was a perceptive young woman.

I remained silent.

She slumped in her plastic chair. "Oh my God. It's true." She didn't seemed shocked by the news so much as relieved but unwilling to get her hopes up prematurely. Her topaz irises were shining with new tears. "Please tell me he's really dead."

By all rights, I should have refrained from offering a confirmation. Regulations say you should never disclose a death until the next of kin has been notified. But when Jamie Sewall gazed at me with that pleading expression, I found that I couldn't stop the words from coming out of my mouth.

"Yes," I said. "He's really dead."

She clapped her hands to her face. When she did, an object she'd been clutching dropped to the ground and skidded across the floor. I knelt to pick it up. It was a green poker chip. I recognized it as one of the tokens they hand out in Alcoholics Anonymous meetings to mark the milestones of sobriety.

"Thank you," she said, accepting it from me with an embarrassed smile.

"You're welcome."

We smiled at each other for a while, and then she leaned forward as if to get a closer look at me. "I know you," she said suddenly. "You came into the McDonald's yesterday. You ordered an egg McMuffin and a large coffee."

"That was me."

"I told you about how Lucas is reading that book on rangers."

"Is that your son in the waiting room?"

"The kid with the glasses, writing in the notebook? Yeah, that's my strange little man."

The door opened behind me. It was Dr. Chatterjee. "How is everyone doing in here?"

Jamie rose to her feet. She was nearly a foot shorter than me. "Is Prester going to be OK, Doctor?"

Chatterjee cleared his throat and adjusted his glasses on the bridge of his nose. "Can you give us a moment, Warden?"

I stepped outside the room and closed the door. I stood in the antiseptic-smelling hall, thinking about the enigmatic woman inside. Her brother and ex-boyfriend were drug dealers. I suspected she knew why they had been going to Township Nineteen and whom they'd planned to meet there. And yet the relief she'd showed when I'd let slip the news of Randall's death hadn't been fake. Nor was the gratitude she'd expressed when I'd handed her the sobriety chip.

Who the hell is this woman? I asked myself.

I could hear her voice rising as she spoke with Dr. Chatterjee. Washington County wasn't the most diverse place in the world. What was a young Indian doctor doing in Machias? Another man in exile, I thought.

The door opened and Dr. Chatterjee peered out. "She wants to know if you can check on her son in the waiting room. We're going to visit with her brother now."

"The police need to get a statement from him before he talks to anyone else."

"The sheriff will be there if he wakes up." His tone suggested that the likelihood of Prester Sewall's waking up at present was slim.

The door swung open and the doctor came out, followed by Jamie Sewall. Her model-perfect face was dry now, but she was still clutching the sobriety chip for dear life, and when she passed me in the hall, the smile she gave me was heartbreakingly gorgeous.

God help me, said the voice in my head.

FEBRUARY 14

The last time I was awake all night was when Dad showed up that time outside the house and started yelling for Randle to come out and fight him like a man. Dad could have beat him easy, but Randle went out there in his underwear with his Glock and I thought he might really shoot Dad until Ma ran out, screaming.

After Dad drove off, Randle called the cops and said there was a drunk guy driving on our road, because he wanted them to bust Dad for OPERATING UNDER THE INFLUENCE.

That's what happened, too.

Dad didn't know it was Randle who ratted him out until I told him. He didn't thank me or nothing, though.

13

Lucas Sewall was still seated in the same chair, head bowed, skinny legs drawn up beneath him, lost in his own imaginings.

"Lucas?"

The boy continued to scribble. He was left-handed, so he held the ballpoint pen upside down. His pale little hand was stained with blue ink.

"Lucas?"

The boy stopped and jerked his head up, as if I'd tossed a bucket of cold water on his head. His hair was thin and chestnut-colored like his mom's, and he had the same cleft in his chin. His head seemed two sizes too large for his scrawny body. He was wearing a hooded gray sweatshirt with abundant ink stains, and blue Dickies tucked into snow boots. A puffy orange vest was slung across the next seat. I had no clue whatsoever how old he was.

I'd been nine when my mom left my dad and we began our gypsy period, moving from apartment to rented house, just the two of us, always on the move.

I towered over the boy. "I'm Warden Bowditch. Your mom asked me to see how you were doing."

"Are you a ranger?"

"No, I'm a game warden. Rangers work in parks, helping people camp or watching for forest fires. Wardens are like police officers in the woods."

"Is Prester dead?"

"No," I said. "But he's very sick. Your mom is visiting with him now."

His eyes darted to my holster. "What kind of gun is that?"

"It's a semiautomatic pistol."

"Can I see it?"

"I don't think that would be a good idea. Guns are very dangerous. You should never play with them."

"Did you ever shoot anybody?"

Unfortunately, yes, I wanted to say. Two people, in fact, and both occurrences haunted me in the predawn hours. But I kept my mouth shut. "What are you writing?"

He closed the front cover and tucked the pen over his outsize ear. There was blue ink on his earlobe. "Stories."

"What kind of stories?"

"Do you have a dollar and a quarter for a can of Coke?"

"Maybe we should ask your mom if it's all right."

"She don't mind if I have a Coke if I'm in the hospital. I'm dying of thirst!"

For some reason, I gave Lucas the money. He seemed so pathetic, I couldn't deny him the treat. He leapt in the direction of the nearest soda machine. There was something toadlike about the boy.

Kids had always scared the hell out of me. I had grown up as an only child, more or less. My stepfather had a daughter who was ten years older than I was. She'd been in college when my mom and I went to live in their McMansion, and she'd treated me like an unwelcome interloper until she finally moved away to California after graduation. So young children had never been part of my experience growing up, and the only ones I seemed to encounter these days were those who got lost in the woods and needed rescuing.

Lucas had left the notebook on the chair. It was a spiral-bound one with a canary-yellow cover.

"Don't touch that!"

The boy jumped past me, doing another of his froggish leaps, and grabbed the notebook. He tucked it to his chest. I had a brief mental image of Gollum clutching the Ring of Power.

"I wasn't going to read anything," I said.

He eyed me with mistrust as he settled back in the chair. "What happened to Prester anyhow?"

"He got lost in the blizzard. He was very lucky to find help when he did."

"What about Randall?"

"Randall Cates?"

"Him and Prester said they was going to hunt coyotes. Not last night, but the night before. Then they didn't come home. Ma was pissed."

"Did they say where they were going hunting?"

"Nah, but that was just a lie anyhow. Randall was going to sell drugs, like usual."

I'd begun to wonder if Lucas was older than I'd first guessed. He stared at me through those thick glasses of his with such obvious intelligence. "How do you know that Randall Cates was dealing drugs, Lucas?"

He gave me a broad smile. "I'm a detective."

The automatic door opened across the room. It was Jamie Sewall and the anorexic male nurse we'd met earlier. She shuffled along uneasily until she caught sight of her son. Then she stopped, took a deep breath, as if trying to collect herself for the boy's sake. But her smile wasn't fooling anybody.

"What do you know, Edgar Allan Poe?" she said to Lucas. "I see you met the warden."

"We were just getting acquainted," I said.

Without a word of reply, the boy flipped open his notebook and began writing again.

Jamie looked at me. "He does that all the time. Lucas is going to be a best-selling writer like Stephen King. Isn't that true, Lucas?"

He raised his eyes at us and clenched his lips together, then returned to his scribbling.

"So how are you doing?" I asked.

"I need a cigarette."

The confession disappointed me, but I was in no position to judge her bad habits. "There's no smoking here," I said.

She shook her head. "I don't smoke anymore. I just meant that I'm a wreck and am craving a smoke like you wouldn't believe." She ran both hands through her hair, pushing it back from her face. "This place gives me the heebie-jeebies. If I sit around here, I'm going to go crazy. Maybe I should just go home. They've got Prester pumped full of so many chemicals, he's not waking up till next week."

"Did you speak with the sheriff?" I asked.

"Yeah, I spoke with that sheriff," she said sharply. "I don't understand what the problem is. Prester's the one who's injured, and you're all acting like he's some sort of dangerous criminal."

I realized that the boy was watching us closely.

"The police are just trying to determine what happened in the woods."

"I guess that makes sense." She was fidgeting, swaying back and forth. She reached for her son's orange vest. "This place is going to make me crazy. Come on, Lucas. Tammi's probably worried sick."

"Are you sure you're going to be OK?" I asked.

She looked hard into my eyes. "I can take care of myself."

That was my signal to give them some distance, so I did. I stepped back and watched them bundle up against the cold. As they left the room, the boy looked back at me over his shoulder. Then his mother gave his arm a gentle pull, and they were gone.

It had been ages since I thought of that period in my own childhood: between the time my mom left my dad and the time she married Neil. We'd been so poor. My mother had waitressed in a rough bar down on the Portland waterfront and worked as a temp in offices, hoping to meet a rich lawyer. And, what do you know, she actually did.

I decided to return to the med-surg unit. When I got there, Sheriff Rhine was on her way out. "Where's Little Miss Hot Pants?" she asked.

"She took her son and went home."

"That one is a piece of work. She knows exactly what her brother and boyfriend were up to in the Heath, but she'll never cop to it."

"She told me that she and Cates broke up last year."

"Really? What kind of conversation did you two have, anyway? Somehow she seemed to sense that Randall was no longer among the living."

I tried to keep the guilt from showing on my face. "She stuck me as a perceptive young woman."

"Perceptive young women don't climb into bed with drug dealers."

"She seems like she's trying to get her act together," I said.

"If so, that's a news to me," said the sheriff. "I just spoke with one of my deputies, and he said he'd been at her house a few times last year, mediating various nocturnal disputes."

"So what happens now?"

"As soon as my deputy gets here, I'm going back to the jail. The state police detectives are going to want a statement from you. If you want some motherly advice, I'd suggest you get some sleep. You look like hell."

I had no doubt she was right about my appearance. The adrenaline that had carried me through the night had evaporated from my bloodstream. I would need to dose myself with caffeine just to drive home.

I said good-bye to Sheriff Rhine and then stopped in the cafeteria for a cup of coffee. I decided to call Rivard from my truck and see what was new, but as I left the Skylight Café, I came across an unexpected sight.

Lucas Sewall was waiting outside the admittance desk, and I knew at once that the person he was waiting for was me.

"Mister, can you help my ma?" he asked.

"Sure, Lucas. What's wrong?"

"We're locked out of the van." And then he spun around and marched back through the automatic doors and across the parking lot. Puzzled, I followed him.

Jamie was bent over, looking at the snowy asphalt around a gray Toyota Sienna. A cold wind was ruffling the hair around her face.

"Did you lose something?" I asked.

"I can't find the goddamned key," she said.

"Did you check inside the hospital?"

"Yes, we checked inside the hospital," she said, her voice rising. "We checked inside the waiting room and inside the med-surg unit and inside the ladies' room. We checked all over the goddamned parking lot."

"Take it easy," I said.

Lucas watched his mother. He was silent, but he seemed to grow more visibly distraught as Jamie lost her composure. The boy had his notebook tucked inside his orange vest. I saw the yellow corner protruding from the collar. He wrapped his arms across his chest to hold it in place.

"We just want to go home," she said. "We're cold and tired, and we just want to go home."

"I'll help you look," I said.

But the keys were nowhere to be found. Finally Jamie Sewall began to sob again, and I felt a compulsion to console her. "How about I give you a lift home, Miss Sewall?"

"No, thanks."

"It's no trouble," I said. "I'm off duty anyway."

Jamie looked at Lucas. The boy made a show of shivering, but it was a poor acting job on his part.

"OK," she said hoarsely.

I had to completely rearrange the contents of my patrol truck to make room for passengers. I removed the laptop computer mounted on its adjustable arm in the center console and zipped it into my briefcase, then moved a bunch of extra blankets and a toolbox in which I kept my evidence-collection kit. Somehow I found room for Lucas in the backseat.

His mother sat quietly beside me, looking out the window at the shining landscape. I felt self-conscious. The inside of my truck smelled of stale coffee. I started the engine and idled to the edge of the parking lot.

"So where am I going?" I asked.

"Whitney," she said without meeting my eyes. "The Machias Road. I'll tell you where."

And with that, she fell silent again. She started to chew on a bothersome cuticle. I glanced in the rearview mirror. Lucas was writing in his notebook again.

How could such a bright and alluring woman get involved with a tattooed creep like Randall Cates? Best-case scenario: She was a former addict with lousy taste in men but had sobered up and was seeking to repair her life. Worst-case scenario: She was a pretty little liar who was about five minutes away from a relapse.

We drove for about twenty minutes on greasy back roads until we came to a two-story frame house, set back about a hundred feet from the roadside snowbanks. It had once been white with red shutters, but the clapboards were rotting and the paint had begun to flake. A poorly carpentered ramp—assembled out of two-by-fours, plywood, and asphalt shingles—angled up to the front door. The windows were heavily curtained and dark; they reminded me of an addict's hollow eyes.

The entire place was snowed in. No plow had cleared the drive; no shovel had liberated the door.

"Do you need a hand shoveling out?" I asked.

She unlocked the door and dropped down to the ground. "No, thanks."

"You sure?"

"We don't need anyone's help. Come on, Lucas."

Jamie pushed down the passenger seat and the boy slid through the opening. As he did, he gave me the strangest look, and my immediate thought was: That kid just stole something from my truck. I turned around to see what might be missing as his mother slammed the door.

I watched the two of them labor up the snowy driveway, plodding along through snow as deep as the boy's waist, until they reached the ramp. Then Jamie stopped and looked back at my idling truck. I saw her mutter something to her son and then she came trudging in my direction.

In spite of myself, I felt a buoyant sensation in my chest.

Jamie came around to the driver's side. I rolled down the window.

"I want to apologize," she said. "It's been a bad night. I know you were just trying to be helpful. I'm sorry to be such a royal queen bitch."

I smiled back at her. "When you're a game warden, getting yelled at goes with the job," I said.

"I bet it does."

"If you want to grab your extra car keys, I can take you back into Machias to get your van."

She laughed her pretty laugh. "I've left my sister alone too long as it is. I got a friend who can drive me later. But thanks for the offer. What's your name anyway?"

"Bowditch."

She rolled her eyes. "Your first name."

"Mike," I said.

A game warden came through the hospital door. At first I thought he was a ranger, on account of his uniform, but he says rangers only work in parks. That ain't the way it is in NORTHWEST PASSAGE.

I wonder if the warden's the one who found Uncle P.

The game warden comes up to me and says that Ma asked him to check on me. He is tall and has a crew cut and a scar on his head.

I ask him if I can see his gun, and he gives me a lecture about how guns ain't toys.

He don't know that I got a rifle! It ain't mine really, but it will be now if Prester dies. He showed me how to shoot beer cans from the picnic table once, but Ma made him stop.

I ask the warden for money for a Coke, and he gives me the money. Ha!

Then he starts asking me all these questions about Randle, which means Randle's DEAD, *because he ain't here in the hospital. If he was in jail, they could interrogate him themselves.*

Yes!!!

He asks me how I know Randle is a drug lord, but I don't tell him about the secret stash in the sewing room.

Instead I tell him, "I'm a detective."

Then Ma comes out of the emergency and she's crying and crying because she's seen Uncle Prester.

I guess he ain't dead.

The game warden likes Ma! He's all nervous and stuttering. But she don't seem to notice because she is freaking out. She freaks out a lot now that Randle ain't giving her those pills. She used to get all dopey before and would fall asleep all over the house.

Now she's like a different person.

The warden is giving us a ride home because Ma lost the keys! She used to lose shit all the time.

You can see the warden has a crush on Ma, which is why he offered to give us a ride. He keeps looking over at her when she's looking out the window.

Ma says she and Dad ain't never getting back together—never, ever. Maybe the warden will become her new boyfriend now that Randle's dead. That would be kind of cool, I guess. He could show me how to shoot a pistol and solve crimes and stuff. I could be like his deputy.

His truck is really cool. It's got a shotgun rack and GPS and police radio and everything.

There's some binoculars on the floor.

They'd be good for spying and stuff. I bet I could hide them under my vest if I zip it up good. . . .

14

Lucas didn't realize he'd dropped his notebook when he stole my binoculars, and it took me days to notice they were missing. It took me even longer to unlock the secrets that he kept in his weird journal, although I understood from the start that he was a child used to keeping secrets. Lucas didn't exactly remind me of myself at that age—I'd always been athletic and big enough to scare away bullies— but there was something in his obsessive scribbling and the intensity of his stare that seemed disconcertingly familiar. My parents' violent marriage had also forced me inward in certain ways. Perhaps it was my own sad dreaminess that I saw reflected in Lucas Sewall's eyeglasses.

Or maybe it was just his miserable circumstances.

After leaving my dad, my mother had dated a couple of hardened assholes—a bartender named Rick and a builder (also, unfortunately) named Mike—handsome, confident guys who couldn't disguise their disdain for my existence. I was my mother's baggage and not necessarily worth the high cost of bedding her. Fortunately, my mom chose loneliness over the false comfort of a strong man's arms. But that choice never seem preordained at the time. Instead of marrying an affluent tax attorney, she might easily have ended up with her own Randall Cates, and what would have become of us then?

I drove down the road a ways until I came to a Department of Transportation maintenance lot. Plow trucks had been exiting and entering the facility during the blizzard, reloading with sand and salt brine to spray on the roads, but at the moment all was quiet. I parked beside a snowbank and let my engine idle.

"You'll be all right once you get laid," Kathy Frost had said.

If I closed my eyes, I could picture Jamie Sewall's full lips, and I felt an all-too-familiar stirring. Sarah had been the last woman I'd slept with. There were nights after we'd broken up when I'd thought about going out to bars with some of the other single wardens and cops, but I'd become worried about my growing thirst for alcohol. Then the Maine Warden Service had seen fit to transfer me to the wilds of Washington County, where the term *nightlife* referred to the sorts of creatures that got into your garbage cans at three in the morning.

A couple of years earlier, I had been so reckless—so driven by self-destructive impulses—that I might have called Jamie's house that very instant to ask her on a date. But I had been working hard to keep my emotions under control. Avoiding a romantic entanglement with the ex-girlfriend of the local drug dealer seemed like a good first step in that direction.

Feeling both virtuous and blue-balled, I telephoned Sergeant Rivard and got his voice mail. I left a long-winded message, telling him about my conversation with the sheriff and our visit to the hospital, and asking him to call me with news. Then I started off in the direction of my unheated little trailer. There was a hardware store along the way where I could buy some new fuses for the electrical box, and I needed to get some milk and frozen burritos, too.

I glanced at my wristwatch. It wasn't even ten o'clock yet. I'd been awake and on the go for more than thirty hours. No wonder my brain felt like Muhammad Ali's punching bag.

The date, I noticed, was February 14: Valentine's Day.

There was a four-door pickup, a silver Chevy Avalanche, emblazoned with the logo of the Call of the Wild Guide Service and Game Ranch, parked in my dooryard.

Now what?

Two men were seated inside the cab. I recognized Brogan's fur hat through the window, but the other guy was just a shadow. I put on my sunglasses and stepped outside into the bright and freezing morning.

The passenger door opened and a blond-bearded man unfolded himself from inside the Avalanche. He was about six five, maybe 230, my age more or less, and he glowed like a fallen god out of Norse mythology. His skin was deeply tanned, and he had gathered his blond hair up in a braid, which was draped over one shoulder like a pet snake. He wore a camouflage jacket over a heavy duck-hunting sweater, loose-fitting wool logger's pants, and tall LaCrosse boots. I spotted a big knife in a leather sheath on his belt.

"Hey, Warden," said Billy Cronk.

"What are you guys doing here, Billy?"

A week earlier, I'd busted Cronk for guiding a party of coyote hunters through an old lady's front yard. They'd been running dogs at night with GPS units fastened to their collars, chasing coyotes over hill and dale, until the dogs finally cornered a pup in a streambed, seventy feet from a woman's bedroom. Then one of Cronk's sports had recklessly opened fire with his AR 15, perforating her porch light. I'd watched the whole episode unfold through night-vision goggles; a week later, the sheer stupidity of the act still left me speechless.

"I just want to apologize again."

For all his physical grandeur, Billy's body language was completely lacking in confidence. His head was hanging, his shoulders were slumped, and he couldn't meet my eyes. He reminded me of a little boy whose father had just introduced him to the business side of a belt.

"We've already been through this."

"I'm not trying to make excuses," he said, which meant that he was about to make an excuse. "I totally fucked up. But the sports I was guiding, they were real demanding, you know? They were from Pennsylvania, right? And we'd been at it two nights in a row with no luck, and then one of the guys got overexcited. He'd never been hunting at night before, and he didn't follow my instructions."

Brogan was glowering at us from behind the wheel of the Avalanche.

"You were his guide," I said. "It was your job to make sure everyone followed state law about shooting near a residence."

"You know how some of those out-of-staters are." He raised his head. His eyes were like pale crystals set into a bronze war mask. "These guys were big-time businessmen—insurance agents!—and they kept busting my balls about every little thing."

"The point is that you put that man in a position to take a shot at that animal."

"I know, I know. But I told him not to shoot. I saw the house through the trees. If you was watching, you saw me yell at him to stop."

I had indeed seen Cronk shout at the man before he raised his rifle. But that scarcely excused his negligence as a guide. "I'm sorry, Billy, but I've got to put the summons through. My hands are tied."

In reality, I had all sorts of latitude. No law-enforcement officer is ever compelled to report every petty illegality he happens across. But gonzo coyote hunters had never been my favorite people. Back in Sennebec, I'd busted a father and his three sons for terrorizing the entire town, running their baying dogs through the woods at night like the Wild Hunt.

"Come on, man," he said, looking down at me from his considerable height. "I've got four little kids at home. My wife don't work because she's got to take care of them. I should have been more forceful with those assholes. I shouldn't have let them boss me around that way. But this one mistake is going to fuck up my entire life. The punishment doesn't fit the crime here."

Unlike some of the officers I worked with, I'd never enjoyed the power trip that came with being a cop. Billy Cronk seemed like a good guide who'd had a bad night. I reconsidered letting him go with a warning and was on the verge of doing so, in fact.

Before I could open my mouth, however, the driver's door swung violently open and Joe Brogan hopped out. I didn't know how much he'd heard of the conversation—his truck engine was loud—but he'd come to the conclusion that I wasn't going to cut his guide any slack. His thick brown beard bristled as he said, "So you're just going to be an asshole?"

"Stay out of this, Brogan. You're not persuading me of anything by invading my property this way."

"Billy has a wife and four little kids to feed. Doesn't that mean anything to you?"

"This conversation is over."

I opened my passenger door and grabbed the plastic bag of over-priced groceries I'd purchased at the variety store. On the floor mat in the backseat, a yellow notebook was peeking out. I leaned in to retrieve Lucas Sewall's forgotten journal.

When I tried to walk to my door, Brogan stepped in front of me and crossed his arms. "We know all about you," he said. "Your superiors think you're a fuckup, which is why they transferred you here. Everyone in Augusta is just waiting for you to make a mistake so they can fire your ass."

Brogan spoke as if he were sharing a secret he'd learned from an informant deep inside the Warden Service. My reputation was fairly public, but it wouldn't have surprised me if the ranch owner had had a few buddies in the department, as well. I realized he was trying to goad me into doing something stupid. A voice spoke to me from my days at the Maine Criminal Justice Academy: *If you lose control of yourself, you lose control of the situation.*

"Get out of my way," I said.

"You're going to wish you had a few friends real soon."

"What does that mean?"

Brogan's eyes smoldered like hot black coals. "You'll find out."

The temptation to pop him on the nose was nearly uncontrollable. Instead, I clenched my molars and made a wide circle around his position. Over my shoulder, I said, "Don't come to my house again, or I'm going to bust you for trespassing and threatening a law-enforcement officer."

Loud enough for me to hear, Brogan muttered, "Asshole."

As I fiddled with the keys, I noticed the hole left by the nail in my door. My vandal's identity no longer seemed much of a mystery. It had to have been Brogan or one of his men.

The trailer was cold and dim. I parted the curtains and looked out at my snowy dooryard. I watched as Brogan snarled something and then spat his entire wad of tobacco against the side of my patrol truck. He raised his collar and climbed behind the wheel of the Avalanche.

Cronk remained where he'd been standing, his blond head in his hands.

15

After I heard Brogan and Cronk drive away, I put in another call to Sergeant Rivard. "Were you ever going to call me back?" I asked him.

"What are you all worked up about?"

"Nothing." I sat down hard on the sofa and released all the air from my lungs. "I just had a run-in with Joe Brogan and Billy Cronk. They were waiting for me at my trailer."

Rivard paused, waiting for me to continue. "So what happened?"

"Never mind."

Kathy Frost would have kept nagging me for more details, but my new sergeant seemed relieved to let difficult matters drop.

"How's our buddy Prester doing?" he asked.

"He won't be getting many dates in the future. The doctor says he could still have a heart attack, but the more time that passes, the better chance he has of pulling through. Were you there when the ME examined Cates's body?"

"I took off after the state police evidence technicians showed up. It was too cold out there to hang around drinking coffee and shooting the shit with the troopers. I had to take Gail to her doctor, anyway. This new baby is going to bankrupt me. My advice to you is, never have kids."

"At the moment, that's not an issue. Who's handling the case for the CID?"

"Zanadakis is the primary. He's going to want to talk with you in person. Do yourself a favor, though, and write up your report ASAP."

It was yet another task to finish before I could get some shut-eye. "So what do you really think happened out there between Sewall and Cates?" I asked.

"They got stuck in the snow and had a fight."

"So Prester smothers his buddy, then wanders off to find shelter from the storm? When he arrives at the Spragues' house, he's almost half dead, but the first thing he does is tell them to go help the man he just killed. That makes no sense."

There was a silence on the other end.

"Even if he had the presence of mind to concoct some kind of story—"

"Enough, Mike."

"I'm just trying to piece this together."

"It's not your job to conduct homicide investigations. It's Zanadakis's. If you want to play detective, you should join the state police."

"I'm not *playing* anything."

"Curiosity killed the cat. Did you ever hear that before?"

The message had been delivered, loud and clear. If I'd ever doubted that Sergeant Rivard had been instructed by the brass in Augusta to keep his new cat on a tight leash, I finally had my answer.

"Yes," I said. "I've heard it."

After I got off the phone, I reclined on the sofa and rehashed the various threats I'd experienced since I'd returned home. First, Brogan had showed up to strong-arm me into dropping criminal charges against Cronk, and then Rivard had all but come out and said that he was going to make my life miserable if I didn't stop thinking about the Sewall case. I looked at my BlackBerry, feeling a desire to call Kathy Frost or Charley Stevens, but what did I really have to say to my friends, except that I was feeling lonely and frustrated? There was no point in whining about the situation.

I screwed the new fuses into the box and was relieved when the heater begin making a reassuring ticking sound. After a few minutes, the odor of the electric baseboards—the earthy smell of warming dust—emanated from the four corners of the room. I removed my parka and sat down at my laptop with a glass of milk.

I wrote up my report in the short sentences and strict chronology that the criminal justice system demands:

> *On 2/13 I attended an off-duty social event at the residence of JAMES LARRABEE on Route 277 in NO 19 TWP. I left the residence at approximately 2215. At approximately 2230, I was driving west on Route 277, when I received a call on my personal cell phone from LARRABEE, asking me to return to his residence. He advised me that his neighbors, BEN and DORIS SPRAGUE, of Bog Road, had called him, requesting his emergency medical assistance. (LARRABEE is a veterinarian.) He said that a man, whom I later identified as JOHN SEWALL, of Whitney, had appeared at their door in a state of extreme hypothermia and frostbite. LARRABEE asked that I accompany him to the SPRAGUES' house and assist him in assessing SEWALL'S condition and performing medical assistance as needed.*

I debated whether our game of chicken with the unknown snowmobiler merited inclusion but decided to make note of everything. Detective Zanadakis could decide which incidents warranted further discussion and which did not.

It took me half an hour to finish the report. I reread it twice for omissions, but the words kept blurring on the screen. Eventually I gave up worrying about errors and pressed SEND.

Lucas Sewall's yellow notebook lay in front me on the table, where I'd first put it down. The kid's drawings were positively grotesque. One picture showed an owl with its wings extended and blood dripping from his parted beak; another image was of a scary-looking woman wearing a wimple and gown made entirely of feathers. Lucas must have a strange bird phobia, I decided.

There was some sort of code on the cover:

DORT OSNZ CNAP IOZZ

Usually I enjoyed riddles and thought of myself as having an aptitude for solving all manner of puzzles, but I was too exhausted to play word games. I returned to the couch and unbuttoned the top buttons on my shirt. After a while, I closed my eyes.

The phone woke me. I snapped awake with a start, not knowing where I was. The room had grown almost completely black. How long had I been asleep?

"Hello?"

"Warden Bowditch?" It was a man's voice.

"Yeah. Who's this?"

"Detective Lieutenant Zanadakis of the state police's Criminal Investigation Division. They've given me the Randall Cates mess to clean up. I read your report, and I wondered if you can come into Machias to talk with me about what happened. You've given us the play-by-play, but I'd like to hear the color commentary."

I leaned forward and rubbed my eyes, trying to wake up fast. "Just tell me where and when."

"We're running this investigation out of the sheriff's office. Can you be here at ten o'clock?"

It was nearly 7:00 P.M. now. "Tomorrow?"

"Tonight." He paused. "Is that going to be a problem?"

"No, sir."

"I appreciate the cooperation," he said, and hung up.

At least I had a few hours to take a shower and guzzle coffee. I yawned and stretched my arms above my head, experiencing once more all my exertions of the previous day in my aching joints and sore muscles.

The phone rang again.

I thought it might be the detective calling back, but this time it was a woman. "Mike? This is Jamie Sewall. You gave me and my son a ride home from the hospital."

How had she found me? Had I given her my business card? I couldn't recall.

"Hi, Jamie. How are you doing? Is everything OK?"

"This is going to sound funny, but you know how you offered to drive me back to the hospital? My friend said he can't do it, and it would be like sixty bucks for a taxi from Machias, and I really need my car to go to work in the morning. I hate to ask and all, because you were so nice before, and I feel embarrassed for losing my keys, but can you possibly give me a lift?"

I glanced at my watch again, making quick calculations. If I left in ten minutes, that would give me fifteen minutes to get to her house, half an hour for us to ride into town, some time together at the hospital. Yes, it was totally doable.

"It's no trouble," I said. "I'll be right over."

"You're my hero."

I took the fastest shower of my life and put on the last clean uniform in my closet.

It was a crystal-clear night—the kind you only get far from the light pollution of the big cities. The sky was as hard as an obsidian desert. The Milky Way flowed across it like a river of light.

Someone had done a half-assed job of shoveling a parking spot in the Sewalls' driveway. A narrow path wound through the snow to the house. Above the wheelchair ramp, a weak porch light glowed like a dying star. I stayed in the truck with the engine going until it became clear that Jamie wasn't waiting in the window for me to arrive. I needed to knock, in other words.

The subzero air was bracing as I pulled it into my lungs. I never felt more alive than when I was outdoors on a Maine winter night. The cold made me hyperaware of my existence as a hot-blooded animal, part of and yet apart from the natural world. I pushed the glowing orange doorbell and waited with excitement for an answer.

There was no response.

I tried the bell again, this time with more persistence.

Finally the knob turned and I found myself looking down at a haggard woman in a wheelchair. She had shoulder-length brown hair that looked freshly washed, brown eyes that seemed to have trouble focusing, and a cleft chin I recognized as a Sewall family trait. She wore a faded gray-and-red flannel shirt, stonewashed jeans, and white tennis shoes.

"Hello," I said.

"Wow," she said, giving me a lopsided smile. "Jamie didn't tell me you were a hunk. I'm Tammi. Come on inside."

She wheeled herself in reverse away from the door. I stepped over the threshold.

I knew another woman who lived in a wheelchair; Ora Stevens, the wife of my friend Charley, had broken her spine in a plane crash, but although she could no longer walk, she radiated good health and good cheer. I didn't know Tammi's affliction—multiple sclerosis or cerebral palsy?—but she seemed broken in a way that went beyond malfunctioning nerves and muscles.

Outside, the house looked to be a wreck, but inside there wasn't a hint of dust or disrepair to be seen. The hardwood floors gleamed beneath the overhead light fixture. The air had a pleasant floral smell, as of a scented candle flickering in some distant bathroom. Framed family photos hung neatly on the walls.

"You want a Moxie or something?" Tammi asked me. "We don't have any beer in the house anymore."

"I'm on duty anyway. But no, thank you."

"Jamie says you're the one who found Prester." She twitched her nose like a rabbit. In her hollow lap was a clump of wadded tissues. She dabbed the corner of an eye with one.

"I just helped get him to the hospital," I said.

"Jamie says Randall is dead, too." She framed the sentence as a statement, but I sensed that she'd hung an invisible question mark at the end.

"Yes."

"Good fucking riddance."

Brain injury, I decided. It was the uncensored way Tammi had of speaking aloud every thought that came into her head.

There was a creak at the top of the stairs. I glanced up, expecting to see Jamie, but instead, I caught a glimpse of her son's pasty face poking around a corner. I sensed that he had been watching me in secret since I'd arrived. As soon as we made eye contact, he pulled his head back, like a turtle disappearing into his shell.

"Lucas, what are you doing?" I heard his mother ask him.

His response was muffled, but her reply carried down the drafty staircase. "He's taking me to the hospital to get the van. It has nothing to do with you," she said. "How did you get to be so paranoid?"

I became aware that Tammi was still speaking.

"I'm sorry," I said. "What did you say?"

"I was asking how much you can bench. I used to work at Down East Fitness, and I could always tell whether a guy was really strong or whether he just had balloon muscles. I'm guessing you can bench three hundred pounds."

"It's been a while since I lifted. Mostly I just do push-ups and sit-ups."

"Go to your room, Lucas!" A moment later, Jamie came hurriedly down the stairs, carried along by gravity. "I see you met my sister."

"We were discussing bench presses," I said.

"That's one of Tammi's favorite subjects."

She had taken a shower, and her hair still shined wetly under the overhead light. She wore a pumpkin-toned fleece pullover and burnt ocher corduroys that flattered her legs. Her eyes were luminous. "I really, really, really appreciate this."

"It's no big deal."

"Sir Galahad," said Tammi, and then she gave a throaty laugh, which made her sister smile with closed lips.

"I'll be home in about an hour," Jamie said. "Don't let Lucas eat any more of my Caramel deLites. I found an empty box under his bed yesterday."

"You know he doesn't listen to me."

"Just try to keep an eye on him if he sneaks into the kitchen."

"Nice meeting you," I said to Tammi Sewall.

"Be good, you two," she called after us.

"Sorry about Tammi," Jamie said as I followed her down the narrow walk.

"Do you my mind my asking what's wrong with her?"

Her breath in the cold air reminded me of a dialogue balloon emerging from the mouth of a cartoon character. "Oh, God. Did she proposition you?"

"No."

"Because she does that all the the time with guys. She was in a car accident a few years ago with my folks and had a head injury. They were bringing her home from a basketball game in Jonesport." She touched the side of her head gently. "If you put your hands under her hair, you can feel the scar from the brain surgery. My beautiful little sister became a completely different person. Most days, I don't even recognize her."

"I'm sorry."

"Me, too, but the one you should blame was my dad, who shouldn't have been behind the wheel."

She fell silent, and I could tell that my question had shoved her back into the past, where she was reliving dark days again. I didn't dare ask about her parents, although her tone suggested that they— her father at least—might have died in that same crash.

"What are Caramel deLites?" I had no idea why I asked this.

"Girl Scout cookies. The neighbor kid sold me like twenty bucks' worth of them last month. It's no wonder I didn't get my butt back after Lucas was born. Working at McDonald's doesn't help."

I found myself at a loss for words, but Jamie didn't seem to notice. Sitting beside me in the truck, she fastened her seat belt and resumed her commentary. "I guess hospital visiting hours are until eight, so if

127

we go fast, maybe I can see Prester. Would you mind stopping at the Rite Aid first? I need to pick up some Nicorette. I'm going through serious withdrawal. You don't smoke, do you?"

"No."

"You don't look like a smoker."

"How do I look?"

"I don't know," she said with a grin. "Clean."

In spite of myself, I found myself glancing out of the corner of my eye at her reflection in the passenger window. She caught me looking and smiled.

"I've never sat in the front seat of a cop car until today. Does this qualify as a cop car?"

"Technically."

"Prester practically lived in them," she said. "I worry sometimes that Lucas is going to end up like him. When Prester was a little boy, he was so sweet and loving. That was before he started drinking. Once he got to high school, the cops started bringing him home on Saturday nights, or he would call from the jail, and I would have to go bail him out. Lucas is way smarter than Prester is—he's a genius, I swear—but they have that same mischievous streak. That reminds me—did he leave his notebook in your truck?"

"Yeah, he did," I said. "It's back at my house."

"He was going crazy trying to find it."

"I'll drop it off tomorrow."

The suggestion made her smile, as if a second visit would not be unwelcome. She leaned forward and braced her arms against the dash. "There's the Rite Aid."

I parked under a bright klieg light, which made Jamie's face look bloodless. A Ford Thunderbird with a mismatched driver's door, blue against red, was parked in the adjacent spot. Two teenage boys looked over at my patrol truck and then slunk down in their seats.

"You need anything?" she asked.

"I'm good."

The boys in the T-Bird watched Jamie go inside the store with wolfish grins, which vanished as soon they caught me glaring in their direction.

I sat there in the idling truck, trying to determine whether Jamie was interested me in particular or whether flirtatiousness was just her natural behavior. I'd been in such a hurry to see her again that I'd lost track of the line I'd set for myself, the one separating professional detachment from here-we-go-again impulsiveness. Without meaning to, I'd drifted into oncoming traffic and was headed for another of my usual collisions.

I glanced at the dashboard clock. We'd be cutting it close at the hospital if Jamie hoped to visit her brother. But I should have plenty of time to make my appointment with Zanadakis at ten.

After a few minutes, Jamie returned, scowling. "That woman is such a bitch. I'm in there all the time, and she still cards me." She tore open the cellophane and used a nail to pierce the cardboard. She removed two pieces of nicotine gum and popped them into her mouth.

A hidden cell phone chirped from somewhere on her person. She dug into her pocket and looked at the luminous screen. "I need to take this," she said.

"That's fine."

She swung the door open and stepped out again. I watched her stand, shivering, under the klieg light. She spoke with animation into the phone and then began to pace back and forth, ranging farther and farther away from the door. She leaned against a white box advertising crushed ice and stared at nothing in particular. Finally she flipped the lid of the phone down and climbed back into the warm truck.

"That was my ex," she explained.

"Your ex?" I thought she meant Randall.

"My ex-husband. Lucas's dad. Suddenly he's available to drive me to Machias to pick up the van. That's Mitch in a nutshell, Mr. Dependable."

I didn't know how to respond. I'd understood that Lucas's father wasn't Randall Cates, but it hadn't occurred to me that another man might still be important in her life. Not that it should concern me.

"You must think I'm a piece of work," she said.

"Kind of. Yes."

"I suppose I am, but I'm trying to be a better person. I'm really, really, really trying. I've made so many mistakes in my life. This whole thing seems like my fault, like it's a punishment for everything bad I ever did." Immediately she started to shake and sob. "Poor Prester. I am so scared to see his face again."

She put her head down and cried into her hands.

I sat quietly, afraid to touch her.

16

We arrived at the hospital ten minutes before the end of visiting hours, which meant that Jamie felt obliged to venture into the medical-surgery unit to look upon her brother's ghoulish face, and because she was in such a state of wild grief, I felt obliged to join her. I thought that she might refuse my offer of help. Instead, she looked up at me and said, "Please," and I realized I was deeper into dangerous territory than I'd previously understood.

We found a sheriff's deputy sitting inside the door to Prester's room, reading a dog-eared copy of *American Snowmobiler* he must have pilfered from the waiting room. He was a fresh-faced guy with the neat mustache some rookie cops grow after joining the fraternity, finely boned hands that would be useless breaking up a bar brawl, and an officious tone that started down around his larynx.

"No visitors," he said, barring our way.

"This woman is his sister," I explained.

"The sheriff doesn't want him talking to anyone until we get a statement from him."

"Has he been charged with anything?"

"No."

"Then you can't stop her from visiting his bedside."

"Look, man, I'm just following orders."

"Is he even conscious yet?" I asked.

"Every once and a while, he starts yammering, but then he passes out again."

"I need to see him," Jamie said. "Please."

"What is it with this guy?" he said. "How many times do I have to tell people he can't be disturbed?"

The deputy's nameplate said DUNBAR.

"Jamie, can you just wait outside for a second?" I said.

She removed her ski jacket and folded it over her arm. Dunbar watched her hips jiggle as she paced across the room, past the nurse's desk at the center, hugging herself tightly.

"Why don't you let her look in on her brother for a few minutes?" I said to Dunbar. "If the guy's asleep, there's no harm in her holding his hand."

He gnawed on the edge of his mustache. "Is she your girlfriend or something?"

"I just gave her a ride to the hospital."

His eyes followed her ass closely. "She's the one banging Randall Cates?"

In the interest of helping Jamie see her brother, I resisted the urge to smack him across the chops. "Not anymore."

He rolled the magazine into a tight tube and thwacked it like a nightstick against his open palm a few times. "I need to be in the room."

I motioned to Jamie.

Prester Sewall lay prone on the wheeled bed. Some time over the past hours, the doctor had wrapped white bandages around his face, so that only his closed eyes showed now. He looked small with the sheet pulled up to his narrow chest and his skinny arms extended at his sides. We could hear his labored breathing through the strips of gauze.

"Prester?" Jamie whispered, taking his hand.

His eyes snapped open, bloodred and filled with terror. "Jamie?"

"Oh shit, he's awake," said Dunbar.

"I'm so happy to see you," she said, but her voice cracked.

"What have they done to me, Jamie?"

His sister started to sob and shudder. Reflexively I set my hand on her shoulder.

"You're OK," she said. "Prester, you're OK."

"I'm not OK! They're going to cut off my fingers!"

"Prester . . ." Her folded coat slid off her arm onto the floor.

"They're going to cut off my nose!"

"Prester . . ."

He tried to sit up but didn't have the strength and dropped his head against the pillow. "They won't show me my face. I keep asking for a mirror, but they won't bring me one." He waved his bandaged arms. "What do I look like, Jamie? I look like a freak, don't I?"

She put a hand to her mouth to hide her sobs. "Maybe they can do plastic surgery. Doctors in France gave a woman a new face."

"I don't want a new face! I want my normal face. I'm never going to have sex again in my life!"

"The doctors can repair your face." She looked at me with pleading eyes. "Can't they, Mike?"

"Doctors can do some amazing things," I replied, fully aware of the lameness of this as a response.

"Who's he? What's he doing here?" His crimson gaze turned on the deputy standing behind me. "Why are the cops here, Jamie?"

"This is my friend Mike. He's the warden who found you. He said you and Randall got lost in the snow."

Again the injured man tried sitting up, and again he flopped back against the pillow as if attached to it by a string. "Where's Randall? Is he here in the hospital? Is his chest OK?"

"We'd better cut this off," the deputy whispered in my ear.

Jamie dropped down to one knee and clutched at her brother's freckled arm. "Randall's dead, Prester."

"Jamie," I cautioned.

"He's dead?"

"The cops won't tell me what happened," she said.

"OK, that's enough." Dunbar tapped his rolled magazine against his open hand. The gesture was meant to be intimidating but came across as comic—as if he was really going to club anyone into submission with an old issue of *American Snowmobiler.*

Prester's voice rose to the level of a wail. "Randall's dead?"

If Sewall really did kill his friend, I thought, he's a terrific actor.

"Give me a fucking break," Dunbar muttered.

Prester was breathing heavily through his bandages. His bloody eyes were locked on mine. "What happened to him? Did he freeze to death?"

The deputy had forgotten his own orders to prevent the injured man from having any conversations. "You know exactly what happened."

"Leave him alone," said Jamie. "My brother's an injured person."

"Your brother's a murder suspect."

"Dunbar," I said, my voice heavy with warning.

Prester Sewall had begun to flail his arms and kick his legs. "The cops think I killed Randall?"

"Hey! Hey!" a woman said, stepping into the fray. She wore an unbuttoned sweater over surgical scrubs. She was as lean as a marathon runner and had short sandy hair and a voice like an army bugle. "What's going on here?"

"I'm sorry, Doctor," I said.

"I'm not a doctor. I'm the charge nurse."

"This is Mr. Sewall's sister," I explained.

"I don't care who she is. This man is in serious condition. He's recovering from hypothermia, and he's detoxing off alcohol and opiates. Are you officers trying to give him a heart attack?"

"Everything is under control," Dunbar said.

"The hell it is." She thrust her finger in the direction of the nearest door. "I want you out of here right now."

Prester seemed to be hyperventilating. "The cops think I killed Randall, Jamie."

"No, they don't," she said. "It's got to be some kind of mistake. Isn't it, Mike?"

My silence must not have reassured her because a look came into her widening eyes, as if she'd just guessed the answer to a riddle.

"You all need to leave this instant," said the nurse.

"You heard the nurse," said Dunbar in his "Move along" voice.

"Including you, Deputy," said the nurse.

"I want to wake up now," Prester sobbed. "I'm having a nightmare!"

Jamie grabbed her coat from the floor and said, "I'll be back tomorrow. I'll bring Tammi and Lucas."

"I want to wake up," wailed the injured man.

"If you don't all leave this instant, I'm calling the sheriff," said the nurse.

"We're leaving," I said.

The nurse yanked the drapes shut across the glass windows; it was like a curtain closing at the end of a play.

"You need to calm down, Mr. Sewall," I heard her say. "Take deep breaths."

Jamie stormed down the hall to the admittance desk as if she'd forgotten I was in her company.

I glared one last time at Deputy Dunbar, who looked like a kid who'd just broken a window with a baseball, and followed her out into the stark light of the parking lot.

By the time I caught up with her, she'd beeped open the van and was rummaging around the passenger side for something.

"Jamie?"

She spun around with an ice scraper in her hand and went to work on the layer of frost that had built up across the windshield. Her motions were quick, compact, and violent.

"So when were you planning to tell me?"

"Tell you what?"

She stopped scraping but kept her back to me. "The cops think my brother killed Randall."

"I'm not part of the investigation," I explained.

Jamie turned around. In the cold light of the parking lot, I became aware of the bones beneath her skin. I could easily imagine the shape of her skull. "What does that mean?"

"It means I don't know what theories the state police are pursuing."

"Prester wouldn't hurt anyone," she said.

"Not even if he was provoked?"

The question seemed to catch her off balance, because she took her time answering. "My brother loved Randall. Don't ask me why."

"And you have no idea what they were doing in the Heath?"

"You asked me that before."

"Look, I know this has been a horrible shock." I dug my bare hands into my parka pockets. "But if you want to help your brother, you need to tell me what you know."

"You just said you weren't part of the investigation."

"I'm not, but maybe I can help you."

She let out a sharp laugh. "Because you care so much for my well-being."

"I know we just met," I said. "But I understand what you're going through."

"Oh, you do, do you?"

It was a good question. "Let me buy you a cup of coffee, and I'll try to explain."

"I thought you were different," she said.

"I am different."

"No, you're not. You're just a guy with a stiff dick like all the rest."

I opened my mouth to respond, but really, what was there to say?

17

After Jamie screamed off into the night, I decided to grab a late, lonely dinner and reflect on the absurdity of my day.

I made a circuit of the mom-and-pop restaurants that constituted the Machias dining scene and found that all of them had ceased serving for the night. Eventually I put aside my scruples and returned to the McDonald's on Route 1.

I paused in front of Jamie's portrait on the wall and felt my pulse speed up. Her golden brown eyes looked so clear in the photograph, and her smile seemed so genuine, as if being named Employee of the Month were truly an honor. And maybe it was an honor after all she'd been through: a busted marriage, the death of her parents, caring for a brain-damaged sister, an alcoholic brother, and a weird little boy. I remembered her sobriety chip and her breakdown in my truck, when she'd blamed her past behavior for the calamities that had befallen Prester.

She'd accused me of being no different from all the leering men she met at the restaurant, as if somehow my desire to save her was just a deluded manifestation of lust. Looking at her portrait again, feeling the effect her smile had on my heart and groin, I found I couldn't totally deny the accusation.

My dinner consisted of a rubbery Big Mac, served with some wilted lettuce, too much special sauce, and a side order of oversalted fries. To compensate for the empty calories, I ordered a Diet Coke, as if that would make any difference. I settled down in a corner booth and watched a party of intoxicated young people nervously watching me. A hulking kid with his back to me was wearing a T-shirt with the slogan YOU AIN'T HAVING FUN TILL THEY DIAL 9-1-1.

Was that Barney Beal? I contemplated going over to speak with him. But then one of the giggling girls leaned over to kiss him, and I saw that it was just another pimple-faced lunk.

Poor Prester. I wasn't sure how often he'd been getting laid before—he looked handsome enough on his driver's license—but having a nose was usually the minimum requirement to lure a woman into bed. I needed to remind myself what the sheriff had told me: As pathetic as he now seemed, he and Randall Cates had been dealers in deadly narcotics. At least one person, a young woman, had died from ingesting the poison they'd peddled. Wasn't there poetic justice in the idea of a man who'd traded in snortable drugs losing his nose? The sheriff, I was certain, would say yes.

My brief encounter with Roberta Rhine led me to believe that Dunbar might be headed for an extended stay in the doghouse if the sheriff got wind of what had happened at the hospital. For the first time, I began to wonder how my own sergeant would react when he learned I'd showed up in the med-surg unit with the sister of a murder suspect. And here I'd been so pleased with my professional development as a law-enforcement officer. My old reckless self was still lurking in the shadows, ready to jump out and say "Boo!" as soon as I turned my head.

When we'd first arrived, Dunbar had made a cryptic remark, but in the ensuing chaos I'd forgotten to pursue the matter with him: "What is it with this guy? How many times do I have to tell people he can't be disturbed?" The comment suggested that someone else had shown up, asking after Prester.

What the hell had happened out in the Heath? It seemed impossible for someone so distraught, so emotionally naked, to lie about his innocence with such skill. Unless he'd killed his friend in some sort of irrational state brought on by severe hypothermia and could no longer remember his actions, it meant that someone else had suffocated Cates.

When I was busing my plastic tray, I realized that the drunken teenagers had slipped out without my seeing them. What are the odds, I wondered, of my being summoned in a few short hours to scrape their dead bodies off the road?

Instead, I received a call from Detective Zanadakis. I glanced at the automated clock on the BlackBerry screen. It was 10:30. I was half an hour late for my interview.

"Is there a problem?"

I apologized and told him I was on my way.

The Washington County Sheriff's Department occupied one wing of a sprawling brick building in a neighborhood of handsome houses and venerable maples in downtown Machias. On one side was the county courthouse; on the other was the jail. Yard-long icicles hung from the eaves above the concrete front steps. I eyed them cautiously, thinking about swords hanging over unwitting heads and other metaphors of impending doom.

Whenever I entered the sheriff's office, I had the sensation of having blundered into the sitting room of someone's run-down, albeit historic home. On my first tour of the building, a deputy had told me that in bygone days the sheriff used to live in these very suites and that his wife would cook for the prisoners. The current sheriff lived with her female partner in a fancy house on the water in Machiasport, and the guy who cooked for the prisoners was a taciturn fellow who went by the nickname "Chef" and tended to reduce all solid food to mush because he himself was missing most of his teeth.

Rhine and Zanadakis were waiting for me in a parlor with a bricked-up fireplace and tall windows that dated from Edith Wharton's girlhood. On either side of the mantel stood flags in stands, the Stars and Stripes to the left and the Maine state flag to the right. The sheriff's Nike gym bag was wedged into the bookcase, below a shelfful of heavy legal tomes. A white-muzzled golden retriever sprawled on the hooked rug. The dog snored soundly, drawing deep and even breaths. It reminded me of Doc's old mutt, Duchess.

A man was seated in a black leatherette chair across the desk from the sheriff. He wore a pigeon-gray sport coat over a black button-down shirt and a knotted wool tie. Faded black jeans and scuffed wing tips completed his outfit. His dark hair was tacky from some sort of hair product, and his skin had a bronze glow that, in this season, was either the residue of a Caribbean vacation or a tanning booth.

"We were just talking about you," the sheriff said. "Have you met Lieutenant Zanadakis?"

"No, ma'am," I said.

The detective and I shook hands. He made a point of making steady eye contact the whole time, as if testing whether I would look away. I didn't.

"Thanks for coming in," he said.

"Glad to help."

"Have a seat," said the sheriff. She was wearing an unflattering khaki uniform shirt, which was tucked into black polyester pants. She had clipped her star-shaped badge to her belt. Aside from her signature turquoise ring, the badge was her only fashion accessory.

"We were discussing your report just now," said Zanadakis. "Sounds like you had quite a night."

"It was certainly a long one."

There was a knock at the door behind me. Chief Deputy Corbett, the balding blond officer I'd met at the Sprague house, leaned against the lintel. His jowls were red, and he wore his familiar black fleece vest with the star on the breast. "Mind if I sit in?" he asked the sheriff.

Rhine turned to the detective for his assent. Zanadakis's shrug indicated he didn't have a problem.

Corbett took a step into the room and leaned against the wall. I couldn't see him there when I turned to face the sheriff and the detective, but I felt his presence the way you do in the forest when a crow is watching you from a tree.

"I'm going to take some notes." Zanadakis removed a reporter's notebook and pen from his blazer. "These are just for my own reference."

"Where do you want me to begin?" I asked.

"At the vet's house," said the detective. "You were there for some sort of dinner party. Is that correct?"

"Yes," I said. "Dr. Larrabee had invited me to his house for dinner. We were joined by Professor Kevin Kendrick from the University of Maine."

"I need to ask if you consumed any alcoholic beverages while you were there."

"No," I said. "Just coffee."

The detective made a note of this. "Did Larrabee or Kendrick?"

"Yes. I don't know how much they had before I arrived, but while I was there, they split a bottle of wine and had a couple of glasses of whiskey. They were talking about having cordials when I left. That was one of the reasons Doc—"

Zanadakis looked up. "You mean Larrabee?"

"Sorry, yes. One of the reasons Dr. Larrabee asked me to drive him to the Sprague house was that he felt unfit to operate a motor vehicle."

"Was he impaired?"

"In my judgment, yes."

"What about Kendrick?"

"Possibly. He showed no outward signs of intoxication, but he consumed quite a lot of alcohol in my presence."

"This was the first time you and Kendrick ever met?"

"Yes."

"What was your impression of him?"

Even though Zanadakis was conducting this conversation in the most informal way possible, I was aware that his notes would be entered into evidence at a trial. We could all pretend that this was just a bunch of fellow cops collegially sharing information on a case, but anything I said now might haunt me at cross-examination.

"I found him to be highly intelligent and interesting. It sounds like he has led an adventurous life. When we were together in the Heath, he impressed me as a highly skilled outdoorsman." I decided to stop there and let the detective tease out the rest.

"Did either Kendrick or Larrabee mention Randall Cates or John Sewall at the dinner?"

"No. However, we did discuss Trinity Raye."

The sheriff couldn't stop herself from leaning forward across the desk. "In what context?"

"Sergeant Rivard had been telling me earlier that day about a student who had overdosed. When I learned that Kendrick taught at the university, I asked him if he knew her. He said, 'It's a small school.'"

"Were those his exact words?" Zanadakis asked.

"As I recall them."

"And that was all he said?" The sheriff turned her ring around 360 degrees on her finger.

"Yes," I said. "It made me wonder if she was a student of his."

"She wasn't," the sheriff said flatly, "so you can stop speculating."

That dispensed with one of my theories. "I just realized that there's something else that's not in my report that you should know."

They all waited for me to continue.

"I saw Prester and Randall earlier that day. It was at the McDonald's in Machias. Sergeant Rivard and I were there getting breakfast. They came in and caused a scene."

Zanadakis showed me his bleach-white teeth. "Sergeant Rivard included that information in his own report. It seemed a curious omission from yours."

"I was exhausted when I wrote up my notes." The truth was that I'd been distracted by my confrontation with Brogan and my lingering thoughts of Jamie Sewall.

"You also neglected to mention it to me when we met at that same McDonald's yesterday." Rhine's tone was as sharp as a butcher's knife.

"I was exhausted, as I said."

Zanadakis glanced down at his notebook before reestablishing eye contact. "Describe the 'scene' Cates and Sewall caused."

In my mind's eye, I saw Randall snatch the visor from Jamie's head and the look of pure anger on her face when I asked if she needed help. I worried that if I described her expression, it might sound incriminating in a way I didn't intend. Once again, I felt inexplicable protectiveness toward her.

"They came into the restaurant and hassled Prester's sister, Jamie Sewall," I said. "She works there as a shift manager. I think they were harassing her for free food. She asked them to leave. They waited in the parking lot until she brought them a bag and a couple of coffees. It was how I recognized Cates later, when we discovered his body in the Heath."

"It seems important, don't you think?" the sheriff said. "Your having an encounter with the murdered man?"

I slouched a bit in my chair. "Yes, ma'am."

How was Rhine going to react when she heard from Dunbar that I had accompanied the murder suspect's sister to the hospital a couple of hours ago? I experienced the familiar sensation of watching my career flash in front of my eyes.

"Can I ask a question?" It was Corbett, behind me. He didn't wait for permission. "I'm curious about that snowmobiler you and Larrabee passed on the Bog Road."

I was grateful for the change of subject. "What about him?"

The sheriff glanced down at a piece of paper on her blotter. "In your report, you noted that you encountered a male in a green snowsuit riding a green sled. He was heading toward Route 277 from the direction of the Heath."

"That's correct," I said. "At least I think the rider was a male. We saw him only for a second, and he was wearing a helmet with the visor down. Maybe Larrabee got a better look."

"So you don't think you'd recognize the rider again?" Corbett asked.

I considered the question. "I might recognize the sled—it was a distinctive shade of green. Larrabee and I were in a rush to reach the Sprague residence. At that time, all we knew was that an injured man had appeared at their door suffering from frostbite and hypothermia. We didn't realize a homicide might have taken place."

"Had you met the Spragues before?" Rhine asked.

"Not before last night."

Zanadakis coughed. "I think we're getting off track here. I'd prefer to ask my own questions in my own manner."

In their eagerness, Rhine and Corbett had hijacked his interview.

"How would you like me to proceed?" I asked.

"I want to know everything you did yesterday," the detective said. "Sheriff, can we use your interview room? I'd like to get this on tape."

18

The interview lasted two hours. Now that Zanadakis had learned I was prone to omitting relevant details from my reports, he wanted to cover all the bases again. He made me run through the events of my day from the moment I awoke until the discovery of Randall Cates's body. From the encyclopedic scope of his questions, I couldn't determine what theories the detective might be pursuing. He seemed interested in everything at once and in nothing in particular.

The more I heard myself talk, the more certain I became that the key to the whole mystery was the identity of the person, or persons, Randall and Prester had met in the Heath. If, as Jamie insisted, Prester would never have harmed his friend, then the next suspect had to be the man they'd sold drugs to that snowy day. My suspicion was reinforced by Corbett, who followed me out of the sheriff's office and down the heavily salted front steps.

"Hey, Bowditch," he called. "Hold up."

I waited for him to descend the stairs behind me. A cold wind was howling down the street, and he hadn't even bothered to grab a coat.

"I need to talk with you," he said, already shivering. "You mentioned Barney Beal in there."

"What about him?"

"I'm fixated on that snowmobiler you saw. Any chance it was Beal? I'm wondering if he was the one they were meeting."

I remembered Corbett's saying he lived up the road from the Spragues and that he had staked out the Heath a few times after they'd reported suspicious activity. Was his interest personal or professional?

"Rivard says he's been busting into camps around Bog Pond to get money to buy drugs. Find out if his sled is green."

Corbett wrapped his arm around his broad shoulders for warmth. The breeze was lifting the individual blond hairs from his head and making them dance. I hadn't noticed before, but his neck was suffering from the worst case of razor burn I'd ever seen. "Whoever it was did a number on Cates," he said.

"What do you mean?"

"Haven't you heard what the ME found during the autopsy? Randall's sternum was cracked. That's why he must have stayed behind when Prester went for help. The guy was probably in pain every time he took a breath. I'm surprised he made it even ten steps from his car."

I watched the chief deputy ascend the steps to the sheriff's office, wondering about the significance of that detail and why Corbett had chosen to share it with me. I was still wondering when my cell phone rang. The number that showed on the screen belonged to Rivard.

"What's going on?" I asked.

"I'm back at your house."

"My house?"

"Yeah, I was passing by and decided to stop in."

That was unlike Rivard.

"You'd better get back here," he said.

"What for?"

"Your place has been trashed."

By mid-February, Maine's back roads are as battered and bruised as an old boxer's face. Potholes form yawning craters deep enough to swallow a tractor wheel. Frost heaves create sharp ridges in the asphalt, which, taken at speed, will launch a vehicle clear off the ground. Factor in patches of black ice—slick spots invisible in your headlights—and towering snowbanks that hide driveways from view, and you have the perfect formula for a wrecked car.

I drove home with the gas pedal pressed flat against the floor. The road bounced me up into the air until the shoulder belt drew tight across my chest, then pulled me hard against the seat. Later, I would discover a strap-shaped bruise on my shoulder, but at the time, I didn't feel anything but mindless fury.

Rivard's truck was pulled up in the dooryard beside my snow-covered Jeep. He had the engine running and the headlights blazing, and I saw his darkened profile behind the wheel as I drove up. From the outside, my trailer looked intact. No windows had been broken; no new animals had been crucified on my front door. So why did Rivard think the place had been vandalized?

I got my answer as soon as I opened the truck door. The night air was cold and crisp; in my lungs, it felt as thin as the atmosphere atop Mount Denali. Then the night breeze pushed a sour but unmistakable smell in my direction: skunk.

Sergeant Rivard climbed out of his vehicle. He was wearing a black baseball cap with the embroidered Maine Warden Service logo, a green pine tree with red letters, on it. Despite the hour and the darkness, he had his sunglasses propped atop the bill of the cap, as if he might require their protection from some sudden glare.

"There's a skunk loose in your trailer," he said.

"I can smell it!"

"How did it get inside?"

"I don't know. I didn't put it in there."

My eyes were adjusting to the darkness, and I could see that Rivard was having a hard time containing his amusement; the corners of his mouth kept sneaking up.

"This isn't funny," I said. "Do you know how hard it is to get stunk spray out of things?"

"I own two dogs, remember? I reckon you'll need about a thousand gallons of tomato juice to start."

"Do you think it's still in there?"

"Only one way to find out."

I fetched my flashlight from the truck and approached the front door as quietly as I could, which wasn't very quietly, considering how loud the crunching snow was beneath my boots.

Rivard leaned against the hood of his truck. "I'll wait out here!"

I turned the key in the lock and eased the door open. In an instant, I was enveloped by a vomitous miasma. My eyes began to gush as if they'd been smeared with raw onions, and I had to press my tongue against my teeth to keep from gagging. I shined the light slowly around the living room, knowing that a skunk's retinas are reflective.

The stench was overpowering; I could feel it seeping through my pores.

"Do you see it?"

I glared at Rivard for him to be quiet. Except for the nauseating odor, all my possessions looked exactly the way I'd left them a few hours earlier.

I shined the light under the coffee table and sofa. No green eyes flashed back at me. The room was stuffy from the electric baseboards, but when I straightened up, a draft brushed my face. It seemed to be coming from the kitchenette. I crept in that direction until I could get a good look at the countertops and appliances.

The window over the sink was broken. Someone had shattered the glass in order to undo the lock, then raised the window until the gap was large enough to let in a skunk. George Magoon had paid me another visit in the night. The skin along the back of my neck grew hot as I recalled my confrontation with Brogan and Cronk. I would make them pay for this.

First, I needed to find the skunk.

My next stop was the bathroom. Nothing there but mildew.

The bedroom door was ajar. Gently I pushed it open and swept the flashlight beam around the walls.

The skunk was curled up on my unmade bed. Its fluffy black tail was draped like a sleep mask across its eyes. I saw the fur ripple as it breathed.

What to do? If I shot it, I feared the worst—a total, dying release of stench.

I edged into the room, feeling my heart pause when the floor creaked, and slid the closet door open on its cheap plastic wheels. On the shelf was a gray wool blanket. I spread it open in my arms, extending my wingspan to the widest possible extent. It would be like throwing a minnow net.

A skunk typically won't spray if it can't see. I'd caught many of them over the years in box traps. The trick was to creep up on the trap from the direction of the steel door and then quickly cover the cage with a sheet or blanket. A skunk can still empty its anal scent glands even when it cannot raise its tail, but it is unlikely to do so if it is blind. I reminded myself of these facts as I stepped toward the bed.

I came within a yard of the animal before it opened its eyes. The skunk cocked its tail as if an electric charge had shot through the hair fibers, and it let out a sharp, almost reptilian hiss. I dropped the blanket on top of it. As fast as I could, I gathered the animal into a ball. With the skunk hissing in my arms, I rushed out the front door, nearly tripping over my welcome mat, and threw the bundle from the top of the steps into a snowbank.

"Fire in the hole!" Rivard called, and ducked comically behind his truck.

I stepped back over the threshold and watched the skunk claw its way loose. It emerged, shaken but seemingly uninjured from the blanket, stomping its feet and shaking its fluffy tail: aggrieved and looking for someone to punish. I slammed the door and waited a minute before peeking out again. My last glimpse of the skunk was of its black-and-white derriere as it waddled off into the balsams at the edge of the yard.

Rivard contorted his face muscles to keep from grinning as I went down to meet him.

"Nice work," he said.

"Go to hell. Everything I own is ruined."

"That's really bad luck."

"It has nothing to do with luck. It's that George Magoon bastard fucking around with me again."

Rivard narrowed his eyes. "What makes you say that?"

"Who else is going to set a skunk loose inside my trailer? It didn't just wake up from hibernation and decide to invade my home. The kitchen window was broken."

Rivard reached into his jacket for a tin of snuff and unscrewed the lid. He pinched some tobacco and jammed it down between his cheek and gums. "Was there another note?"

"No, but it had to be that son of a bitch Brogan again. He was just over here this afternoon with his Viking bodyguard."

"I wouldn't jump to conclusions," my sergeant said.

"I want to hear him deny it himself." I sniffed my forearm. I hadn't touched the skunk. I hadn't even spent five minutes inside the mobile home. But I smelled like a stink bomb had exploded in my face.

"You're not going over there."

"The hell I'm not."

"That wasn't a request, Warden."

"You want me to just let this go?"

"No," Rivard said, "I want you to wait here while I pay Brogan a visit. I'll give you a call after he and I have a conversation. If he was behind this, I promise you that we'll make him pay. Understood?"

I spat on the ground, trying to expel some of the bitter skunk taste from my mouth. "Understood."

I watched his taillights disappear into the night, fighting the impulse to wait ten minutes and then follow. My head ached from frustration, pent-up rage, and lack of sleep. How do you de-scent an entire trailer? I'd have to rip out the carpeting and the drapes and probably jettison the furniture, too. In the meantime, I would have to get a motel room at fifty bucks a night, minimum.

Where had Brogan and Cronk found a skunk in mid-February? They must have known where one was hibernating.

A thought came to me.

I took the big Maglite I kept in my backseat and went exploring around my trailer. My feet punched holes in the deep snow as I made my way around to the backyard. I felt the cold snow being jammed up my pants legs against the bare skin.

Beneath the kitchen window, my flashlight showed tracks: a man's snowshoes. They were traditional: trapper-style, oblong-shaped, fash-

ioned of northern white ash in all likelihood. The man who owned them was a traditionalist. No modern aluminum and plastic Tubbs for George Magoon. There was good information in these tracks. Now I knew something about my prankster that I hadn't known before.

I foundered in the snow, following the tracks through the balsam and white spruce. My ears began to tingle, and I thought of Prester Sewall wandering desperately in search of help the night before. The snowshoe trail looped around toward the main drag. Whoever had walked here hadn't been heavy, I decided. The prints of a big man would have been deeper. That ruled out Billy Cronk.

Eventually the tracks emerged from the birch and beech saplings that made up the second-growth timber. They ascended the high snowbank the plow had muscled out of the road. Then they scrambled down the other side of the drift to the salt-white asphalt. I walked up and down the roadside, scanning for distinctive tire prints with my flashlight, but there were too many marks to distinguish anything useful. Something silver and red glittered up ahead. I reached down to pick it up. It was a round metal tin that had been flattened under the wheels of passing traffic. Someone who had passed by this way chewed Red Man tobacco.

19

In Machias, I ended up at a 24/7 gas station, where I purchased a bottle of bleach, two hand-soap dispensers, and four liters of Clamato juice. The clerk behind the register pinched her nose as she took my money.

"Adieu, Pepé Le Pew," she said, to the delight of the tipsy customers behind me in line.

No one would describe midwinter in a remote coastal town with no ski or snowmobiling industries to speak of—almost no industries whatsoever—as peak tourist season. Most motel owners had declared their unconditional surrender, switched off their neon signs, locked their doors and boarded up their plate-glass windows, and departed for warmer climes until after the spring thaw. The few holdouts had begun renting out rooms at weekly rates, becoming flophouses for the shiftless, the addicted, and those criminally minded people who intentionally avoided living with fixed addresses.

After despairing of ever seeing another bed, I found a shabby little motor court with a lighted VACANCY sign on the road to Lubec. The Blueberry Bunch Motel consisted of six peeling cabins arranged in a horseshoe shape around a semicircular driveway. Only one of the cabins had an occupant; the others looked dark and forlorn. But when I pressed the luminous doorbell outside the office, a light went on in the house next door, and presently an old woman came hurrying down the walk.

She stood about four and a half feet tall and looked to be a hundred years old. She had big glasses that covered much of her wrinkled

face, tightly curled hair that reminded me of sheep's wool, and a generous nose. She wore a fuchsia sweater, which she might have knitted herself, flannel pants, and boots she'd probably purchased in the kids' section at L.L.Bean.

"Can I help you, Officer?" She had an accent I couldn't place. Baltimore, maybe?

"Yes, ma'am. I need a room for the night, if you have one."

When she laughed, I saw that her gums were receding from her long yellow teeth. "Young man," she said, "I can't give rooms away this time of year."

She unlocked the door and let me into the office. She stepped up onto a wooden box behind the registration desk, opened a book on the counter, and asked me to sign my name. Bleary-eyed, I filled in the information and handed her my credit card.

"I can give you the government rate," she said.

"Thanks, but I'm not here on government business."

"I won't tell if you won't."

She handed me a key attached to an enormous piece of blue plastic on which someone had painted the number 6 with silver glitter nail polish. "That's the bridal suite," she said with a wink. "Would you like me to show it you?"

"I'm sure it will be fine."

"I'm not going to ask you about the skunk," she said. "But I take it you didn't get the better end of your dispute."

From the driveway, the cabin looked no bigger than a garden shed, but inside, once the hesitant light decided to flicker on, I saw that it was more spacious than I'd imagined. Most of the room was taken up by a full-size bed with a synthetic oak headboard and a coverlet woven out of blue polyester fabric. A small television no bigger than a toaster sat atop a pressed-wood bureau. The view through the front curtains was of the parking lot.

Inside the bathroom was a stained tub with a long pipe that rose to a rusty showerhead. The first thing I did was to strip down to my underwear. I dumped the clothes I'd brought with me into the tub and then doused them all with Clamato juice. Bent over the tub, I worked the tomato juice into the fibers. I let the clothes soak in the bloodred liquid and lay down on the bed. That was when it dawned on me that I would have no way to dry my wet clothing. I could hang a shirt over the creaking radiator, but how long would that take?

After a while, I got up and returned to the bathroom and ran cold water over my clothes. When the last of the juice had swirled down the drain, I pumped hand soap over the laundry to get a good lather going. I rubbed the foam into the fabric and kept rubbing until my shoulders ached. I rinsed the clothes until the water ran clear and free of bubbles. Then I wrung the last drops from every sleeve and pants leg. Done at last, I pressed my green uniform shirt to my nose and sniffed.

It smelled like someone had soaked a gym sock in a Bloody Mary.

In high school, I'd dated a girl who had been born without a sense of smell. I wondered if she was still single.

I went around the bedroom, hanging shirts on hangers from every nail I could find. I draped wet pants over curtain rods and the desk chair. I arranged socks and underwear on the shelf above the radiator.

It was after 3:00 A.M. by the time I finished with my washing. I turned off the bedside lamp and pulled the cold sheet and thin wool blanket across my chest. Falling asleep, I listened to the dripping sound my wet clothes made in the darkness, and I dreamed that I was camping alone in the rain forest and that outside it was raining.

The cell phone's melodic ringtone pulled me up out of my coma. When I opened my dry eyes, I saw cold sunlight streaming into a tiny room decorated with haphazard items from my wardrobe. I knocked my BlackBerry off the nightstand and then nearly fell out of bed reaching to retrieve it from the floor.

My mouth was gummy, lips, teeth, and tongue. "Hello?"

"Warden Bowditch, I think you've got some splaining to do."

"Sheriff Rhine?"

"My deputy has been telling me how you showed up at the hospital last night on the arm of Jamie Sewall."

That prick Dunbar—I should have figured he would throw me under the bus. "I was just giving her a ride," I said in a sleep-thickened voice. "She lost her van keys in the parking lot."

"And somehow this entailed accompanying her into the hospital?"

"I didn't anticipate her brother would be conscious."

"I think I'm beginning to understand why your superiors transferred you Down East. You should expect a call soon from Lieutenant Zanadakis. He's going to be as curious as I am to hear why you neglected to inform us of your relationship with the Sewall family."

After I got off the phone, I went into the bathroom to relieve my bladder and take a shower. My uniform was still musky and damp when I put it on. I decided to pack all of my still-wet clothes into the duffel bag. It appeared that I would be spending my morning at the local Laundromat.

First, I had a stop to make on the other side of town.

Outside, the sunlight bounced off the snowbanks, scalding my eyes. Winter was a season of such sharp contrasts. There were overcast days when the whole world faded to shades of gray. But when the sun was shining, the landscape became as gaudy as an old Technicolor circus movie.

I drove across the causeway, where a dam caused the Sabao River to bulge up before it emptied into the Machias below. The lower river was tidal, so whatever ice formed would shift and buckle twice a day as the sea pushed salt water up the estuary. Pressure ridges formed where the ice had broken apart and then crumpled together again.

But the Sabao, above the sluice, was all fresh. At this time of year, fishermen pulled brown trout, black bass, and pickerel through holes in the ice. State regulations prohibited anyone over the age of sixteen from fishing the Sabao—it was a kiddie fishery, a place where the local youngsters could learn the pleasures of angling without being elbowed off the river by adults—but I never seemed to drive past without having to chase some knucklehead off the ice.

This morning I spotted a tiny figure way out on the ice. Maybe a teenager—he was too far away for me to tell at a glance. But then the clouds moved off and the sun caught him full-on, and I saw a flash of orange clothing.

I hit the brakes so hard, the rear of my truck almost fishtailed. The driver in the car behind me tooted his horn and then zipped past on the left. I swung the truck into the causeway lot and reached behind the passenger seat for my binoculars. My hand roved across the backseat debris like a blind tarantula. But it found nothing. Where had my binoculars gone? I remembered using them two days earlier, when I was working ice fishermen on Gardner Lake.

I leaned forward, shaded my eyes, and squinted into the middle distance, uncertain that I was seeing what I thought I was seeing.

That numbskull out on the ice was wearing an orange life jacket.

If you have to wear a personal flotation device out on the ice, then maybe, just maybe, the conditions are unsafe for fishing.

Did that joker really think a PFD would prevent the river current from pulling him under the ice? The rule of thumb with ice thickness is: It takes a foot of ice to support a medium truck, eight to twelve inches to support a car, five inches to support a snowmobile, and four inches to bear the weight of a person. But those guidelines don't take into account moving water, not just actual rivers like the Sabao but also the inlets and outlets of larger bodies. Most people assume lakes and ponds are still waters; they don't realize that strong currents can move beneath their placid surfaces. And wherever the water is flowing, the ice tends to be thin, even when the temperatures collapse in the middle of February. Countless vehicles and people fall through the ice because they have no appreciation of Mother Nature's treacherous side.

On some other morning, I probably would have ventured across that unsafe surface to box that idiot's ears. Not that he was violating any laws by being out there. Kathy Frost had always reminded me that taking stupid chances isn't illegal. A good thing, too, or else I would already have been serving a life sentence.

20

I felt self-conscious entering a public space, smelling even faintly of skunk. As I pushed through the double doors of the McDonald's, I passed an old geezer on his way out. He gave a noticeable wince, which made me even more nervous than I already was about speaking to Jamie.

It took her a while to notice me in line. She was busy assembling orders, salting hash browns, and bagging breakfast sandwiches. She was dressed in that ridiculous referee uniform with its indoor sun visor, using a radio headset to converse with someone in the drive-through. When she finally spotted me, she paused briefly and then let the teenage boy at the register take my order.

"What can I get you?" The kid had a cowlick that stuck up like the stem on a pumpkin.

"I'd like to speak with the shift leader, please."

"Is there something wrong?"

"Tell her I'll be seated around the corner."

I stepped out of line and made my way to the rear of the narrow restaurant, settling down in one of the booths to wait. The satellite radio broadcasting through the restaurant speakers was playing "Low Rider" by War.

After about five minutes, she appeared, carrying a plastic tray. She had removed the headset but not the visor. It gave her a vaguely sporty look. I noticed the puffy circles beneath her eyes from ten paces away.

"What's this?" I asked as she set the tray down in front of me.

"The usual," she said. It was an egg McMuffin and a large cup of coffee with cream and sugar.

"Please, sit down," I said.

"I'm working."

"Just for a minute so I can apologize."

As she slid partway into the seat across the table from me, her nose twitched. "Did you get sprayed by a skunk?"

"Sort of."

"Shouldn't they all be hibernating?"

I didn't want to get into the whole sordid George Magoon story with her. "They should be. One got into my house and polluted the place."

"That's horrible."

"I had to get a room at the Blueberry Bunch Motel until I can clean everything." I took a breath. "Look, I owe you an apology."

She crossed her arms and glanced toward the frosted window.

"As a warden, I'm not allowed to share information about ongoing police investigations. In the eyes of the attorney general, we're both material witnesses to a homicide. Technically, we shouldn't even be talking."

She started to stand up, but I put my hand on her arm and eased her back down.

"I should never have agreed to take you to the hospital."

"Why did you do it, then?"

"Because I wanted to get to know you. I still do."

"Why? So you can get me to say something that will incriminate Prester? Thanks but no thanks."

"That's not it. You're right that I am attracted to you. Who wouldn't be? But there's more to it than that."

She sensed a truckload of bullshit headed her way. "Like what?"

"My mom was a single mom. She and my dad split up when I was nine. My father was a son of a bitch—worse than Randall. For a few years, it was just the two of us, bouncing around from apartment to apartment in Portland. My mom never worked at McDonald's, but she waited tables at a pub."

"What are you saying—that I remind you of your mother?" A look of disgust appeared on her face.

"Not at all!" I said. "I just remember how difficult those years were for both of us. It must be that way for you and Lucas."

She grew quiet and seemed to settle into the booth, as if the urge to flee had passed.

"In my truck last night, you told me how you were trying to change your life. If I were in your shoes, I'd feel pretty desperate, too."

"You wouldn't have become an alcoholic and a drug addict."

I pictured that tantalizing can of Foster's in my refrigerator. "I don't blame you for not believing me, but I hope you will accept my apology. I wish you and your family the best, Jamie. I really and truly do."

Her posture had softened while I'd been speaking; her shoulders no longer seemed so tense and she was holding my gaze. Finally she said, "Aren't you going to get in trouble for coming in here? The whole town knows I'm bad news."

"Let me worry about that," I said. "I'd like to drop off Lucas's notebook tonight."

"I'm going to try to see Prester later, if they'll let me. Then I have a meeting at seven. My sponsor is already pissed that I missed two days in a row. Come by after eight-thirty. I should be home by then."

"Is there any chance Lucas might have taken a pair of binoculars from my truck?"

She gave a sigh that made me think it wasn't the first time Lucas had stolen something. "There's a one hundred percent chance he did. I'll find them when I get home tonight."

"I'd appreciate it."

"He has this idea of becoming a ranger someday. That's probably why he took them. If you want, you can have dinner with us. I'm sure Lucas would like that. He's sort of infatuated by you."

"Thanks for the invitation, but it's probably best if I just drop off the notebook."

"There will be extra food, if you change your mind. I'm making

American chop suey. Please take a shower before you come over, though. You really do stink."

I smiled and reached for my wallet. "How much do I owe you for breakfast?"

"It's on the house," she said, rising to her feet.

"Are you allowed to do that?"

She gave me the kilowatt version of her usual megawatt smile. "Didn't you see my picture by the door? I'm the Employee of the Month. I can do anything I want in this place."

From McDonald's, I drove downtown to the Wash-O-Mat, where I spent the next two hours watching my clothes do somersaults in the dryer.

There was a college student behind the counter when I entered, jawing into a cell phone about her "lame" professor. I got coins from the machine and various boxes and packets of detergents and softeners, anything with a perfume to mask the stench of my clothes.

I brought my laptop from the patrol truck. After everything I'd learned over the past forty-eight hours, I had plenty of people whose names I wanted to feed into the secure databases that law-enforcement officers can access in the state of Maine.

I typed the name Randall Cates and the date of birth from his car registration into the search fields and brought up his fish and wildlife and motor vehicle records. There was a conviction for night hunting, and another for operating a snowmobile under the influence, citations for speeding and driving unregistered vehicles. Fewer than I'd expected, frankly. Up until someone killed him, he'd been very careful to maintain a Teflon coating around himself.

Not so Prester. The string of Title 12 and driving convictions was as long as Corbett had claimed: practically the entire Maine Criminal Code from A to Z. No violent offenses, however.

Barney Beal had incurred speeding tickets on the road, on the trail, and on the water. I couldn't access his criminal records, but the kid was definitely a speed demon, if nothing else.

Who else? I'd need a date of birth or license number to check Kendrick's records in the database.

I did locate the article about him in the *New York Times Magazine,* and as Doc Larrabee had suggested, the tone was as breathless as a teenage girl posting on her Facebook page about her favorite pop singer:

MAN, OUT OF TIME
By Ariel Evans

Kevin Kendrick is a teacher, an environmental activist, and, he'll tell you, the best woodsman left in America. He believes that the nation's survival depends on relearning forgotten skills, from building a fire with nothing but sticks of wood to making a boat out of sealskins. It might sound far-fetched, but spend a week with him in the wilderness of eastern Maine, which he calls home, and you just might decide he's right.

The article was long but well-written and interesting. It repeated the stories Larrabee had mentioned of Kendrick's amazing adventures living among the headhunters and paddling across the Labrador Sea.

It also laid out his philosophy in depth, of which I'd sensed only the vaguest outline the other evening. It was, verbatim, the credo of Earth First! "The Earth is currently experiencing the fastest mass extinction event in its history and the perpetrators of this holocaust are none other than ourselves, the human race. Much as addicts have no hope of a cure until they admit to themselves that they have a problem, so must we admit to one in our relationship with the Earth."

Kendrick, the article said, had collected an almost cultlike following among young people who came to the University of Machias to study with him or attend his Primitive Ways survival school. I wondered if Trinity Raye had been one of these youthful devotees, but when I searched her name, all I found were some brief news stories in the *Bangor Daily News* and the *Ellsworth American* and an obituary that claimed she had "died unexpectedly" in her dorm room.

I bought a Snickers bar from the vending machine to gnaw on while I folded my clothes. My diet, never great to begin with except when I'd been living with Sarah, had deteriorated in recent weeks. Thinking about her made me melancholy. I wondered what man she'd woken up with this morning while I was stuck in a suffocating Laundromat washing the skunk smell out of my T-shirts.

On my way out the door, I stopped at the counter and was startled to find the teen blabbermouth gone and Ben Sprague, of all people, standing in her place. He wore a starched white shirt, which showed the undershirt beneath it, blue Dickies held up by red suspenders, and an expression of inexplicable hostility.

"What are you doing here?" he asked.

I tried to project good fellowship. "Laundry. I was in town and had an emergency load to do. Is this your Laundromat?"

"We own one in Machias and another in Calais."

"I didn't know."

"Why would you?"

I continued the charm offensive. "That was quite a night we had, wasn't it?"

"Yes."

"How's Doris doing?"

"The same. We heard the other one survived."

"He's still in the medical-surgery ward at the Down East Community Hospital, but the doctors expect him to pull through."

Sprague blinked at me a few more times. "What can I do for you?"

"I have a lot of laundry to do, and I was wondering about wash, dry, and fold service."

"We don't offer that."

Glancing at the wall behind him, I noticed a sign advertising the prices for laundering shirts, dry cleaning, stain removal, and basic tailoring repairs. "The sign says you do."

"We're not currently offering that service. We can't afford the staff."

There were also framed photographs on the wall: pictures of Rotary Club members selling Christmas trees, a studio portrait of Doris and Ben. Several of the pictures included a young man with a beak-like nose wearing a UMaine sweatshirt.

"Is that Joey?" I asked.

Sprague blinked rapidly, started to turn his head, then stopped. "Yes, that's my son."

"He goes to UMaine?"

"No, he's down in Boston now. Is there anything else I can do for you? Because I'm fairly busy here."

The two of us were the only ones in the Laundromat.

I was pushing my duffel bag into the backseat of my patrol truck when I spotted a familiar figure heading in the direction of the Wash-O-Mat. He was wearing a wool sports jacket instead of a buckskin parka, and he was carrying a battered leather briefcase instead of a shovel. But the dashing bearded man was unmistakably someone I knew.

"Hey, Kendrick!"

The dog racer stopped in mid-stride and peered down the street, shading his eyes with his hand. It seemed strange to see him suddenly, having just read at length about his adventures; it was as if I had conjured him up somehow. In his tweedy professorial garb, he looked like a person wearing a costume. He didn't seem to belong in the outfit he had on; he reminded me of one of those old paintings of a Carib Indian, who, having been snatched from the New World, was being presented in pantaloons and a doublet at the court of Queen Elizabeth I.

I slammed the truck door and slid the keys into my still-damp pants pocket. I needed to find a bathroom where I could change into my newly dried clothes. The cold, wet fabric made me shiver now that I was out in the polar air again.

"Laundry day?" Kendrick asked as he came toward me.

"I didn't realize the Spragues own this place."

"Ben and Doris have another one in Calais," he said.

"That's what he was just telling me." I lowered my voice, although there was no one around to hear. "Do you know what the story is with their son? I keep hearing he had an accident, but no one will tell me what happened."

Kendrick straightened up and gave me a piercing look. "Have you considered the possibility that the family is embarrassed that their son tried to kill himself?"

His intention had been to shock me into silence, and he achieved the effect he was after. "That's tragic," I said at last.

"And none of our business, wouldn't you agree?"

I nodded, feeling genuinely ashamed at my own curiosity. "You haven't spoken with Doc lately, have you?"

"No. Why?"

"I haven't heard from him since that night at the Spragues'. I wondered how he was doing."

"He falls into funks these days. Helen's death hit him hard."

"I expected he'd call me or something," I said. "By the time I got back to the Sprague house, you two had taken off."

He waited, unsure if this was supposed to be a question. "Doc caught a ride out with the ambulance. I had my dogs. There wasn't any reason to stay."

"Rivard was expecting you to direct help to our location."

"There was no point. Ben told me you found the other man—Cates—buried inside a snowbank."

"That's right."

"I also heard Sewall is under guard at the hospital. From that, I can infer that the police are regarding the death as suspicious."

"Now you're the one asking inappropriate questions."

"I'll take that as confirmation," he said in the lofty tone that entered his voice every so often. "Has Sewall been talking to the police?"

"You seem to be pretty good at reading me," I said. "I'll let you figure it out."

I could see his quick mind working in the little movements of his eyes. His nostrils flared suddenly. "Did you get sprayed by a skunk?"

There was no point in denying anything; Kendrick was too smart for me to fool. "You remember the prankster I told you about?"

"George Magoon."

"He let a skunk loose in my trailer."

Kendrick laughed so hard, he began to cough. "No wonder you're spending your day off at the Laundromat."

I nodded, my lips pressed together in imitation of a smile.

"You have to admit that was an inspired practical joke," he said.

"No, I don't."

"Well, I think it's pretty hilarious." Without looking at his watch, he said, "I need to get to class. I'll be curious to hear how the Prester Sewall case develops. Those two bastards deserved their miserable fates. If it had been up to me, I would have let them freeze to death out there."

And with that, he walked away. No handshake, no good-bye. I watched him climb into a burgundy 4 X 4 pickup with a kennel setup in the bed, a stack of cages for his malamutes. He started the engine but didn't pull into traffic immediately. I had the strong sensation he was studying me in his side mirror. For a man with a class to teach, he was in no particular hurry to get to campus.

After a minute of this ridiculousness—Kendrick watching me watching him—I returned to my vehicle. Next stop: the hardware store. I wondered how much it would cost to rent a carpet steamer. More money than I had in my checking account probably, but what choice did I have, short of moving out and forfeiting my security deposit?

I needed to call Rivard, too. It was obvious my sergeant was avoiding me, since he hadn't contacted me yet on the Brogan matter.

When I glanced up the street again, I noticed that Kendrick had disappeared while I wasn't paying attention.

21

I had the day off, which meant I could apply myself to the task of cleaning my trailer. How do you remove skunk spray from window curtains? I doubted that the guys at the local hardware store had encountered that particular problem before, but as a matter of fact, they had.

The kindly white-haired man behind the counter recommended I try a special "Skunk-Off" spray, a compound I never knew existed. I rented a carpet cleaner with an upholstery attachment and bought a gallon of the cleaning solution. My shopping list included bleach, agricultural lime, contractor-grade trash bags, and twelve rolls of paper towels. By the time I left Machias, I'd pretty well disposed of all my disposable income for the month.

Seven hours later, after I was done with my labors for the day, I wasn't sure my trailer smelled a whole lot better. By then, my nose was useless; I could no longer discriminate between the actual skunk odor and my suspicion of its lingering presence. I'd worked up a sweat scrubbing the floors and walls, washing countless loads of laundry, and stuffing irrecoverable bedclothes into trash bags. I took a shower and changed into a T-shirt and jeans. Before I left, I decided to prop the windows open to air the place out overnight, which meant packing all my firearms and other valuables into the patrol truck. Fortunately, I owned almost nothing of value.

I found Lucas Sewall's notebook lying open on the kitchen table. Like everything else, the paper had absorbed a musky aroma. I flipped through the lined pages, but the boy's cramped handwriting discouraged me from actually reading any of the dated diary entries. I glanced at my watch. Jamie should be home from her AA meeting, I realized.

The thought of seeing her made me feel like a love-struck teenager. I laughed out loud in embarrassment.

There was an enormous pickup truck—an emerald-green Toyota Tundra—parked beside Jamie's van in the the Sewalls' driveway. I nosed my truck in behind its bumper and prayed that I wouldn't get clipped by a passing car. I tucked Lucas's notebook under my arm and started up the shoveled walk.

As I reached out to press the buzzer, the door sprang open. I found myself looking down at a remarkably small man. His features were fine-boned, and his eyes were overly large and heavily lashed. He had sandy blond hair parted in a heavy bang on one side. He stood no more than five feet two. He wore black snowmobile pants and boots and a T-shirt bearing the dragon logo of a karate school. My first thought was that he must be a boy, because he reminded me of those baby-faced kids in junior high school all the girls had crushes on. It took me a moment to realize that I was staring down at a man older than I was.

"What do you want?" His voice was adenoidal, as if he had ceased the aging process when he turned fourteen.

"Is Jamie here?"

"Who are you?"

Another realization came winging into my head. This man was Lucas's father. The resemblance was uncanny.

"Mike Bowditch. Maine Warden Service."

One small hand tightened into a fist. "Why do you want to see Jamie?"

"Mitch, who's at the door?" It was Jamie's smoke-strained voice.

"Some game warden."

Looking over the man's blond head, I saw her emerge from the kitchen. She had changed out of her zebra uniform and was wearing an apron over a chambray shirt and faded jeans. The overhead light brought out the golden strands in her hair. "Mike?"

"Hey, Jamie," I said.

The boyish man flashed his eyes back and forth from her to me. "You know this guy?"

"He's a friend." She took a step to place her body between us. "Please come in, Mike."

"Thanks," I said.

The house smelled warmly of an apple pie baking in the oven.

"This is my ex-husband, Mitch Munro," she said. "He dropped in *unexpectedly.*"

The emphasis she placed on the last word wasn't lost on Munro. "Why shouldn't I drop in?" he asked. "This is still my house."

"This is my parents' house. You only lived here once, a long time ago. We're divorced, Mitch. Or have you forgotten?"

This statement seemed to be for my benefit, because she rolled her eyes at me when she was done. The look said, Can you believe this guy?

For his part, Munro looked dumbstruck. He started to open his mouth, then shut it fast when he caught me staring. "I haven't forgotten," he said under his breath.

"Are you joining us for dinner?" she asked me.

It was true that I had considered staying, but the appearance of her ex-husband seemed like an ill omen. "I'm afraid I can't. I just wanted to drop off Lucas's notebook."

She frowned and took the dog-eared journal from my hand. "He's been going crazy trying to find this thing. His notebook is like his security blanket. I told him I'd buy him another one, but he said this one has all sorts of important stuff in it." She turned toward the living room, from which canned laughter and music from television advertisements was drifting at intervals. "Lucas! Get your butt out here and thank Warden Bowditch for finding your notebook!"

"I'm also hoping he has my binoculars," I said.

"Oh, shoot," she said. "I forgot all about them."

"What binoculars?" Munro asked.

"Lucas took them from the backseat of Mike's truck when he was giving us a ride home the other night."

"My son isn't a thief."

"You don't know the first thing about your son," Jamie said.

The muscles twitched along Munro's jawline. "I'm telling you, Lucas didn't take his binoculars."

I knew better than to get involved in a domestic dispute, but I didn't like the lip this homunculus was giving Jamie. "I'm pretty sure he did," I said.

"Prove it," he said, puffing up his chest. His breath stank of cigarettes.

"Does he have a place in the house where he hides things?" I asked Jamie.

"I'll go look under his bed."

"I'll do it," said Munro.

Jamie rolled her eyes again. "Mitch," she said.

"I'm his father, goddamn it!"

Before his ex-wife could stop him, the miniature man left the room.

"I'm really sorry about Mitch," Jamie said, shaking her head in a way that suggested she'd apologized for him many times in the past. "Before I started dating Randall, he always took Lucas for granted, but as soon as there was another man in my life, he started acting like he was a loving father with all these legal rights."

"Is that why Lucas has your last name?"

Instead of answering me she decided to change the subject. "This is the first time I've seen you out of uniform."

"Disappointed?"

"Not at all."

Neither of us knew where to take this conversation, so we both fell quiet again. I heard Munro stomping around upstairs.

"Were you able to see Prester?" I asked.

"Yes, but the cop there had to frisk me first. Can you believe that?"

"Was it Dunbar?"

"No, some bald guy with a red face." She began to blink away tears. "Prester kept ranting about how they're going to cut off his fingers and toes."

Those were the least of his worries if the state pressed a murder charge against him. "The nurse said he's going through alcohol and opiate withdrawal. He'll be better once it's out of his system."

Her wet eyes glowed in the overhead light. "He keeps saying he wants to die. I'm afraid he'll try to kill himself."

"He's safe in the hospital."

Heavy footsteps came tumbling down the stairs, two sets. A moment later, Munro stepped into the room, tugging Lucas by one scrawny arm. Seeing father and son together, the resemblance was unmistakable: Both were undersize, delicate, and blond. But whereas Munro was as good-looking as a teen idol, Lucas looked like a poorly done caricature of his old man.

"Where's my notebook?" he said.

"Forget about the notebook," said his father. "Tell him what you just told me."

"I didn't steal no binoculars."

"Come off it, Lucas," said Jamie.

"I looked under his bed," said her ex-husband. "All I found was a *Playboy* magazine and a lighter and some other crap."

"What about the closet shelf? He has other places he hides things."

"Who are you going to believe—this guy or your own son?"

At that moment, Tammi wheeled herself into the foyer from the television room. Something about her frailness reminded me of origami, as if she'd been folded like paper into that chair. "What's going on?"

"It's all right, Tammi," Jamie said.

"Look, Mr. Munro, all I want is to get my binoculars back," I said. "Then I'll be on my way."

"I know you're lying, Lucas," said his mother. "You know you can't fool me."

"Search anywhere!"

"That just means you have a new hiding place," she said.

Lucas readjusted his glasses and bit his lip. The kid was as guilty as sin.

When Munro stepped close to Jamie, I realized they were nearly the same height. "Why are you taking this cop's side? You're his mother. Why don't you start acting like it?"

She shoved him with both hands in the chest, hard enough that he took a stutter step backward. "Get away from me!"

Munro turned to me as if I were a referee. "Did you see what she just did?"

I had, and it had taken me by surprise, too. I kept forgetting that Jamie had a temper. "Everybody needs to calm down here."

"Can I have my notebook?" Lucas asked.

Jamie ignored my advice. "You don't care at all about your son," she snarled at her ex-husband. "You were scared shitless of Randall. Now that he's dead, you've decided you're the man of the house again."

"I *am* the man of the house."

"You aren't half the man Randall was. Literally."

He snorted and shook his head. "After everything I did for you, that's what you to have to say to me? You fucking slut."

"Watch your language in front of the boy," I said.

"What are you? The language police?"

He was so small, it was hard for me to feel threatened, but in my short career I'd learned not to dismiss threats of violence, even when they came from little men. Two of the most dangerous sucker punchers in my previous district were a father and son duo who could have weighed in as jockeys at the Kentucky Derby.

"If you don't calm down, you and I are going to have a problem," I said.

"We already have a problem."

Part of me was wary and watchful. I knew how quickly a situation like this could veer out of control.

Jamie grabbed his biceps with both hands. "Stop it, Mitch. Please, just stop it."

Munro peeled her hands away. He pulled his T-shirt over his head, revealing a muscular abdomen totally lacking in body fat. Across his chest was a large tattooed heart bearing the inscription FOREVER JAMIE. "You see this?" he asked her. "Do you even remember when I got it?"

"I remember," Jamie said in a softer voice than the one she'd been using.

"I don't deserve to be treated like this," Munro said. "Not in front of my own son."

On cue, we all looked at Lucas, who was standing there with an expression of dismay on his pale face. The boy had no idea what was going on here. He and I were in the same boat in that regard.

Jamie crouched down to get closer to eye level with her son. "Here's your notebook, Lucas."

"Thank you."

"Tell the warden."

"Thank you," the boy mumbled.

She tousled his hair, then smoothed it back into shape. "Now are you going to tell us where you hid his binoculars?"

"I didn't steal nothing," the boy said.

"See?" said his father, as if that settled the matter once and for all.

22

Before their divorce, my mom and dad were constantly nipping at each other like two starving dogs. Looking back, I realize it was my mom who bit the hardest. Not that I could blame her. Living with a violent alcoholic, watching him stay out all night or disappear into the woods for an entire weekend, not knowing whether he had run off with another woman or was lying dead in some flooded roadside gully, watching him squander the dollars and cents she'd carefully saved on bottles of whiskey while she and I made two meals out of a single box of macaroni and cheese—was it any wonder she wanted to tear his hair and scratch his face? After ten years of this uncertain life, she had become hardened, desperate, even a bit cold-blooded, you might say; a grim woman faced with a choice: leave this dangerous man once and for all, or lose herself and her son forever.

That was why I was so shocked to learn that she'd maintained sporadic contact with my dad over the years that followed. She talked to him on the phone at night when my stepfather and I were asleep. Maybe they even met a few times. It is not inconceivable that they had sex.

In that light, the spectacle I had witnessed at the Sewall house was not surprising. I could believe that Jamie was both determined to break from her past and incapable of banishing her ex-husband from her affections. Jamie's interest in me might very well be heartfelt, I realized, but mistakes aren't so easily shaken off, especially when they take the form of a twelve-year-old boy.

Having been that child myself, I thought I understood the

contradictions inside a mother's heart. But one of the perils of being naïve is that you cannot identify that particular quality in your personality. You have an outsize sense of your own sophistication.

So when Jamie escorted me to the door and whispered, "I'll call you," I felt confident that she would continue to struggle for a while, feeling affection, pity, and disdain for Mitch, but that eventually her emotions would align and point the way forward. In the meantime, all I had to do was be patient. I considered myself to be a realist. Whatever would be, would be.

On the drive through the streets of Machias, heading to the motel, I passed the Spragues' darkened Laundromat and remembered my icy conversation with Kendrick that morning.

When I got back to my motel room, I decided the time had come to check up on Doc Larrabee myself. I didn't know the veterinarian well, but he struck me as a garrulous and inquisitive man. He liked people, and he liked stories. A few nights ago, he and I had raced into a blizzard to rescue a hypothermic drug dealer. Now a murder investigation was under way. By all rights, Doc should have been chewing my ear off. Something seemed amiss.

The phone rang six times before triggering the voice mail. It was the usual spiel about not being available and leaving a message at the tone. Doc included another number for clients with veterinary emergencies. I hung up when the recording kicked in.

I tried his home number again. On the fifth ring, he finally picked up.

"Hey, Doc," I said. "I hadn't heard from you since the night of the storm. I wanted to see how you were doing."

"Fine."

"Have the state police come to see you?"

"I gave then a statement yesterday. That Detective Zanadakis said I'm not supposed to talk about what happened, even with you." His voice sounded thick, gummy, as if he might have been drinking.

I considered whether this sufficiently explained his distant demeanor. "I ran into Kendrick this morning outside the Spragues' Laundromat."

"Where?" His voice went up a few decibels.

"The Laundromat in Machias. He's a strange character. I don't think he likes me, for some reason."

Doc paused before he spoke. "Kendrick is his own man. He doesn't care what people think of him. He says and does what he believes is right. Damn the consequences."

That description matched the wild-eyed activist I'd read about in the *New York Times.* "I wanted to let you know that I saw Prester Sewall in the hospital. The charge nurse says they're going to transfer him to Eastern Maine Medical so they can deal with his wounds."

"Frostbite in January, amputate in July."

"But it's February."

"It's an old medical saying. It means they'll amputate the gangrenous tissue in six months."

"Thanks to you, it looks like he's going to pull through."

He seemed to chuckle. "Thanks to me."

"Are you OK, Doc? You sound out of sorts."

"I'm an old man, living by himself in a wreck of a farmhouse, a thousand miles from his grandkids. Why shouldn't I be out of sorts?"

I decided to bring the conversation to an end. "Thanks again for dinner the other night," I said. "Julia Child would have been proud."

"Not hardly."

After we'd hung up, I sat on the bed and wondered where Doc's outburst of frustration had originated. I could tell that he was a lonely man who missed his dead wife. Maybe the stress of that night at the Sprague house had undermined his abilities to cope. He was a veterinarian, not a medical doctor, and being thrust into a position where the life of another human being rested in his half-drunk hands must have terrified him. Still, I was surprised he didn't want to hear more about my own experience in the Heath or quiz me about the murder investigation. Doc didn't seem like the sort of straight arrow who would obey a detective's order to refrain from discussing a criminal investigation.

But maybe I was projecting Charley Stevens's rebelliousness on the veterinarian, trying to make the two old men more similar than they actually were. I hadn't spoken with the retired warden pilot in many weeks, and I missed him. Charley and I had become good friends following the manhunt for my father in the mountains around Flagstaff. He had taught me more about being a good warden—about being a good man—than anyone I knew. He'd listened to me recite my romantic troubles with Sarah or describe my latest dustup with the warden colonel without passing judgment; instead, he would set my mind on a healthier course by asking, "Now what other way might you have handled that pree-dicament, do you think?"

It was ironic that we no longer saw each other, since we were living less than an hour apart. Charley and Ora were up around Grand Lake Stream and I was down along the coast. The move had kept them busy, and they'd had a troubled adult daughter, Stacey, living with them for a while. For my part, I had figured that the best way through my current problems was to be a man and tough them out.

To hell with that. I decided to brew myself a cup of coffee and give him a ring.

"Hello there!" said the old pilot.

"Hey, Charley. How's that new house treating you?"

"Just grand. We may be short on a few creature comforts, but we're long on scenery."

"So when are you going to invite me up there to see it?"

"When my moose survey is over. The department has got me hopping like a flea across this country."

I'd gotten a report that the state was conducting an aerial census of moose in District C, but no one had told me the contract had gone to Charley. Although he was officially retired as chief warden pilot, he still did odd jobs that required a fixed-wing aircraft for both IF&W and the U.S. Fish and Wildlife Service. He might be in his late sixties, but there was no better pilot in the state of Maine.

"I'd like to go up with you some time. I'm still getting to know this area, and it always helps to see things from the air."

"How about tomorrow? The forecast calls for snow showers and northwesterly breezes, but I never let a few flurries hold me down."

A woman murmured something in the background. The volume went dead, as if Charley had clapped one of his big hands over the receiver. I had to wait half a minute for him to return to the line.

"I had a bird singing in my ear," he explained. "So I heard about your escapade in last week's blizzard. Got the story from young Devoe, who said it was a drug deal that went off the road, so to speak."

"I suppose you want me to tell you the whole story," I said.

"You know I'm as curious as a tomcat."

Charley and I chatted for the next hour. It had been so long since I'd really opened up to someone. Everything came pouring out: the frozen zebra, the coyote pelt nailed to my door, the note from Magoon, the dinner at Larrabee's farmhouse, the mad rush to the Spragues' chalet, the long hours I'd spent searching in the storm for the lost man, my meeting with Jamie at her brother's bedside, the encounter with Brogan and Cronk, my grilling by the state police, the skunk loose in my trailer, even my recent near-fisticuffs with Mitch Munro.

I hadn't realized, until I'd finally shut up, just how lonely I had been been.

"You can't say your life is boring," Charley offered.

"That's never been my problem."

"Something doesn't smell right about the way that Cates character died."

"Don't mention bad smells. I'm going to be smelling skunk on myself for the rest of my life."

"It's just a little musk. Why, they make French perfume out of the nether glands of weasels! How bad can it be?"

"Pretty bad."

He chuckled. "I'm glad we're having this conversation by telephone."

"I swear to God I'm going to nail Brogan."

"Be methodical about it if you do. Joe has friends in the governor's office."

Which reminded me again that a day had passed and I hadn't heard so much as a peep from Rivard.

"I have a question for you," I said. "When I got my transfer, you said I should introduce myself to Kendrick. What were you thinking? The guy is a world-class egomaniac."

"I didn't mean you should bring him a coffee cake! I meant that he was someone for you to keep an eye on. Kendrick is one of the best woodsmen I've ever met—and I've known a few—but he's got some odd notions about right and wrong. Someone vandalized the logging equipment over on that old International Paper timberland last year. I'll bet you a dollar it was Kendrick or one of his young apprentices."

"In that case, I'd say your instincts were correct," I said, "as usual."

"Where and when should I pick you up in the morning? I've got skis on the Cessna."

We agreed to meet at nine o'clock at the Gardner Lake boat launch in East Machias. I had just hung up when headlights swept across the closed curtains, backlighting the fabric, and tires crunched on the compacted snow outside my cabin. A metal car door opened and shut loudly, and I heard quick footsteps coming up the cabin steps, followed by a knock.

I peeked through the spy hole. "What the hell," I said, opening the door.

Jamie Sewall stood on the little porch, holding a paper bag with both arms. She had arranged her hair and applied lipstick to make her lips shine, eye shadow to deepen her eyes, and liner to darken her lashes. She was wearing my binoculars around her neck.

"May I come in?" she asked.

23

I caught the smell of jasmine and warm vanilla as she stepped past me into the motel room. Sarah rarely wore perfume. I had forgotten how much I liked the right scent on the right woman.

"I wanted to give you these." She meant the binoculars, but the suggestion of other gifts wasn't lost on me.

"How did you know where I was?"

"You told me you were staying here when you came to see me this morning."

She set the bag down on the embroidered doily atop the bureau and looked around with an amused smile. "This is cute!"

I had a dozen good reasons to send her packing, starting with her being the sister of a murder suspect and ending with the irrefutable fact that I needed no more trouble in my life, however beguiling the package it came wrapped inside.

"I appreciate your bringing me my binoculars." The room was so small and the bed took up so much of the available space. "But I think you should probably leave."

"Guess where he hid them." She didn't wait for me to respond. "My dad's old wood shop in the basement. Lucas is terrified of that room, for some reason. He never goes down there. After I searched all the usual places, I tried to imagine where the last place he might go would be. Lucas is crafty. He likes codes and puzzles and things. His favorite writer is Edgar Allan Poe. That's why he keeps that notebook with him all the time. He wants to write books and movies when he grows up. You and Lucas have a lot in common."

I couldn't stop myself from smiling. "I'm not so sure about that."

"You're both big thinkers." She removed a six-pack of beer and a twenty-ounce bottle of Diet Coke from the paper bag. "Does this room have a refrigerator?"

"There's an ice machine outside the office."

"I guess it's cold enough." She offered me one of the Budweisers. "I thought you could use a beer after the day you had."

I accepted the bottle from her. I hadn't expressly stopped drinking or even announced to myself that I might be developing the alcohol problem that had bedeviled my father. But for many months, I had refused glasses of wine and bottles of beer when offered and had walked fast, with eyes turned to the floor, down the liquor aisle of the supermarket. And there was that lonely can of Foster's back in the refrigerator in my trailer.

"And this is for me." She unscrewed the top from the soda bottle and filled a glass to the brim with the fizzing liquid. "I had to wait for Lucas to fall asleep before I could come over here," she said. "Tammi's not much help with him. She forgets things. She almost burned the house down a couple of times because she forgot to turn off the coffeemaker."

"That must be difficult." I felt my hand growing numb from the unopened bottle of beer.

"It's weird, mostly," she said. "According to the state of Maine, she's one of my dependents. I'm her legal guardian." She raised the glass of soda to make a toast. "Here's to family."

She waited for me to open my beer and take a sip. She made eye contact with me the whole time. I felt my heart speeding up.

"Thanks for the beer," I said. "But I don't think your being here is a good idea."

"Why was it a good idea when you came to my house, but I can't come to yours?"

It was a question for which I didn't have an immediate answer. We were standing in the narrow space beside the bed, hyperaware of its presence and everything it implied.

"Can we just have a drink together?" she asked with exasperation. "I just want to have a real conversation with an adult person for once. Sometimes I get coffee with Gloria—she's my sponsor—but all she ever wants to talk about is booze and pills. 'Are you using again, Jamie? You're not using, are you? Keep the plug in the jug!' I'll tell her where to put her plug."

She hadn't meant it as a joke, but when I laughed, she laughed. The beer, I had to admit, tasted very good. "OK. But just one drink."

She smiled and unzipped her ski parka. "I want to apologize for Mitch. He's got that Napoléon syndrome. That's why he learned karate. He works at the Shogun Studio out on Route One in East Machias. When we were married, we couldn't go to the beach or the lake—anywhere with me in a bikini—without him challenging some dude to a fight. I asked if he wanted me to cover up, but he always said no, because he wanted to show off what a man he was despite being so little."

I tried to avoid looking at the bed. "When did you get divorced?"

"A few years back, after the accident. But he's had second thoughts ever since and keeps coming around like a begging dog."

"He seems like the total opposite of Randall."

"On the outside, maybe. But I'm glad you didn't get in a fight with him. Mitch is tougher than he looks. Randall underestimated him, too."

"Can I ask you a question about Randall?"

She narrowed her eyes with playful mock suspicion. "Is this a police question or a friendly question?"

"A friendly question. I'm wondering about that tattoo on his face."

"He got it after I kicked him out."

I felt a sense of relief, for some reason. "I couldn't imagine your being attracted to someone who went around looking like Mike Tyson."

"Yeah, he showed up at my door with it one night. It was all red still and bloody. I think he wanted to scare me into getting back together or something. It made me realize how fucked up I'd been to ever hook up with him."

"Why did you?"

"Because I was an addict—and Randall had all the pills. He was handsome, before he got that tattoo, and he could be pretty charming and funny, but really it was the Oxy I fell in love with. That's the thing about drugs. Once you start using, you'll do anything to stay high, even convince yourself you love the man who's giving the drugs to you."

"I wouldn't know," I said.

"That's why I'm here." She removed her parka and spread it across the coverlet. She wore a tobacco-colored turtleneck, which clung to her in all the right places. She sat down on the bed.

"What do you mean?"

"You're the first good man I've met in a long time."

I thought about the violence inside me, the people who were dead in Rum Pond and Sennebec because of me. "I'm not a good man," I said.

"You pretend to be all tough on the outside, but you're just lying to yourself about who you really are."

"So who am I?"

"Someone who could be a role model for Lucas," she said, nodding as if in agreement with herself. "He needs a real man in his life, someone he can look up to. They say you're not supposed to start a new relationship your first year of sobriety, but I don't see how being lonely and miserable helps you stay clean."

For the past few days, I had fantasized about this moment, but now I felt like things were moving too fast, and I needed to slow them down. Instead of sitting down beside her, I perched myself on the rickety wooden chair at the desk.

"What made you stop using?" I asked.

"Randall did. I used to think I liked bad boys, but there's a difference between bad and evil. Randall was evil."

My bottle was empty. "What do you mean?"

"Did you hear about that girl who died last year?"

"Trinity Raye," I said.

"Randall sold her the heroin that killed her. She was just seven-

teen years old. Prester kept crying and crying when he told me she'd died. You don't know him, but he's wicked softhearted."

Jamie got up and poured herself another Diet Coke. She brought me a second Bud. I opened this one without hesitating.

"When that girl OD'd," she said, "I realized it could have been me. I thought about Lucas and Tammi and even Prester, and I wondered what would happen to them if I died. Who would take care of my family? And then I realized that it was a stupid question, because I hadn't been taking care of them either, not for a long time. I was too busy drinking and drugging, trying to escape from how shitty my life was. Lucas started having these weird nightmares about a white owl, and Tammi seemed to be getting worse and worse. I tried to quit a few times last year, but it didn't work, and then one day it finally did. I still don't know what happened. My sponsor, Gloria, thinks it was my Higher Power telling me I'd finally had enough."

"Maybe she's right," I said.

"I'd like to think so." She put a hand on the back of her neck, pushing up her hair and massaging the skin underneath. "Gloria says I'm stuck on step two. She tells me to 'let go, and let God,' but I don't know. When your parents die in a car crash and your sister gets paralyzed and brain-damaged, and you're already on welfare with a kid, and now you have to take care of your sister, too, instead of opening your own real estate business like you'd always hoped— it's hard to feel like there's a lot of love in the universe. Having your brother get all deformed and accused of murder doesn't help any, either."

I felt the familiar urge to help her. "Prester hasn't been arrested yet. That means the state police are still considering other suspects. You're sure you don't know who they met on the Heath?"

"Randall had a lot of enemies." Her eyes glittered. "Maybe I can talk with Prester and get him to tell me who they met. He'll confide in me. But not if there's a cop in that room. Maybe you can help get that deputy out of there so I can have a private conversation."

"I can't do that," I said, but in my imagination I was plotting how I might be able to make it happen.

Her cheeks flushed. "Didn't you hear what I said before? Prester wouldn't hurt another person, especially Randall."

"We don't know what happened out there," I said. "Prester himself might not even remember."

"What do you mean?"

"The symptoms of hypothermia include confusion and altered judgment. It's possible Prester held Randall's face in the snow without being aware of what he was doing. In his incoherent state, he might have even thought he was helping him breathe."

"That's not what happened." Her eyes had grown wet again. "I'm *sure* that's not what happened. You're a cop. Can't you convince them that Prester is innocent?"

"Jamie, it's not that simple," I said.

"Can't you do something? Can't you do anything?"

"I'm just a game warden."

The words didn't come out the way I'd intended; it sounded shameful, as if I were apologizing for my job instead of making a point about where my authority ended. What I'd meant was that I had no business involving myself in another homicide investigation—as both Rivard and the sheriff had reminded me. But any pretense I had entertained of being a responsible officer of the law had disappeared the moment I let this lovely woman into my motel room.

Jamie raised both hands to her face and began to sob. She bent over so that the hair hid her humiliation. I watched her for a while, and then I got up and moved to the bed and sat down beside her. I placed my hand against her spine, resting it between her shoulder blades.

As soon as I did, she wrapped her arms around my chest.

"It's all right," I said.

One of her hands found the side of my face. She looked up at me with tears streaking her makeup and her lips parted. I bent my head down and kissed her. Her other hand came up, and she gripped my head between both hands. She opened and closed her lips while she held me with real force, and then she thrust her tongue into my mouth. I could taste the sugar water she'd been drinking.

"Wait," I said.

"It doesn't have to mean anything."

"Yes, it does."

"I need to be with someone. Everything's so fucked up, and I'm so lonely. You're lonely, too. I know you are."

I nodded my head, unable to say the word.

"You don't have to be." She framed my face again with her hands and lifted her mouth to kiss me.

Then her hand worked its way up under my T-shirt and she gripped my chest hair with such force that I stopped kissing her. We stared at each other without speaking and then her hand dropped to my crotch. She undid the zipper of my jeans and pushed me back on the bed.

With one hand, I ran my fingers through her chestnut hair, smelling the musky-sweet perfume rising from the warmth of her neck. I found myself whispering her name, the sound of it adding to my arousal, until I was afraid I might lose all control in her mouth. Before I could let go, she stopped and rose to her feet.

She unbuttoned her jeans and dropped them to the floor. She had a tattoo on her hip—a butterfly with blue wings.

"I don't have a condom," I said.

She laughed and went to the bureau and removed a foil packet from inside her purse.

She planned for this to happen, I thought.

She straddled me on the bed. Leaning forward, she guided me inside her. With her turtleneck still on, she began moving back and forth, rocking her hips with a rhythm that suggested she was hearing a sensuous song in her head and was keeping time with the music. We went on like that for a long time, and then she reached over her shoulders and pulled her top off. She unhooked her bra and lifted my hands to her round breasts. She bent forward to mash her lips against mine, her tongue darting, and that was how we both came, the first time.

Hours later, as we lay side by side on the damp sheet, she guided my hand to her hip and used my index finger to trace the outline of her tattoo. "I got this butterfly the day my divorce came through," she said.

"To celebrate?"

"No, it was more like 'Screw you, Mitch. Here's something you're never going to see.' It was like a new beginning for me. That's why I got a butterfly."

She had other tattoos: a ring of thorns around her ankle, a Chinese symbol at the base of one wrist. She said she'd gotten them to mark important events in her life, which was what Sarah had also said when she surprised me after graduation with a delicate birdwing design spreading across the small of her back. I had pretended to be pleased, but in secret I was heartbroken because something that I had loved in its natural state now had an unnatural mark on it.

With Jamie, these images were part of who she was. Even though I didn't find them attractive, her tattoos told stories of personal significance about which I was curious.

"I got this when my folks died." She pressed a red nail against the Chinese character. "It means 'wisdom,' because what happened seemed pretty random, and I was going to need wisdom to handle everything that was coming to me."

"What happened to your parents?"

"Their car hit black ice on the Machiasport Road and they crashed into a telephone pole. They died at the scene. Mitch and I had to move into their house to take care of Tammi. Prester was still living at home because he wasn't working, as usual. I wish the tattoo had brought me wisdom, though I guess I finally did wise up to what a loser Mitch is."

I rolled onto my side and propped myself against the pillow. "It sounds like you've had a rough time."

"It wouldn't be so bad if I didn't have to take care of Tammi and Prester. All I dream about morning, noon, and night is escaping somewhere."

"Where would you go?"

"Someplace warm. The jungle, maybe, like Prester John."

"Who?"

"Prester John." She peered up at the ceiling, as if reaching for an elusive memory. "He was like this white Christian king who lived in Africa with all these natives in a city of gold. My dad was a Holy Roller at the Church of the Living Spirit. He was into all those TV shows about finding Noah's ark on top of mountains and stuff. It was my dad who gave Prester his nickname, because he acted like a little king."

"I never heard of that legend," I said.

"It's probably bullshit, like every other bullshit story," she said. "But someday I'm going to escape from this land of winter. I'm going to take off south, and I'm not going to stop until find my own golden city in the sun."

24

The next morning, I awoke to find myself lying naked across a bed that smelled of perfume, stale beer, and sex. A watery white light was leaking in through the window shades. I heard the toilet flush in the bathroom. I turned my head heavily on the pillow and saw fuzzy red numbers sharpen into focus on the clock face. It was 7:15.

The events of the previous night returned to me in a rush of sounds and images. Jamie and I had slept together. I'd wanted so much for it to happen, but now that it had, my emotions were all tangled and I couldn't pick them apart. I was undeniably happy; the thought of being at the start of a relationship with a stunning, surprising woman filled me with excitement, if not fear. And yet the heedlessness I'd shown troubled me, too. Why couldn't we have waited at least until the murder investigation was behind us? I'd worked so hard to leave my impetuous self in the past. But here he was again.

I hadn't drunk that much, just four beers ultimately, not enough to get drunk in any meaningful sense. Not enough to excuse anything. And Jamie hadn't touched a drop. She'd come to the motel with a six-pack of beer and condoms in her purse. Whatever else she was, she wasn't the emotionally fragile victim of circumstances I'd imagined her to be. This was a woman who made choices. We'd had sex because Jamie Sewall wanted it to happen.

The bathroom door opened, and she came out dressed in her turtleneck and jeans, looking hurried but radiant. Seeing her again in the morning light, with her hair mussed but gleaming, and her tattoos hidden, was like seeing her again for the first time, and all my second thoughts disappeared, replaced by powerful feelings of attraction and affection.

"Oh my God, I am so late for work," she said. "Jim's going to fire me this time for sure. And I have to drive all the way home to get my uniform still."

"I could tell him you hit a moose," I suggested.

"Would you do that? If he gives me any grief, I might need you to give me an alibi."

I clumped the sheet in my lap to cover myself. "You look great," I said.

She smoothed the wrinkled front of her top without making eye contact. "How many beers did you have?"

"I mean it."

She turned and leaned across the bed to kiss me. Because she was so short, she didn't need to lean much. Her breath had the winter-green taste of Nicorette.

"I've really got to run," she said. She zipped up her ski parka and reached into her pocket to check that she had her keys. She must have pressed a button, because I heard the van beep outside in the lot. "Why don't you stop by McDonald's later?"

"I'm supposed to meet a friend, or I would. He's taking me up in his plane."

"Don't crash! That would definitely send me into a permanent binge."

"I'll give you a call when we land."

She smiled and then leaned across the bed to kiss me again. "I'd like that."

After she left, I let my gaze wander happily around the room. Joe Brogan and his skunk had forced me out of my house and into this tiny motel room, but I would always remember it now as the place Jamie and I first made love. The Blueberry Bunch Motel had unexpectedly attained landmark status on my life's crazy road map.

I would need to clean up the place before I checked out. I always wondered what it was like for the maid to clean up a room where two people had enjoyed a debauched night of lovemaking. Five empty beer bottles were arranged in a straight line along the desk, beside Jamie's half-empty soda bottle. Funny, I thought I'd drunk only four.

A gust blew the door open, causing me to shiver. The skin on my arms and legs was covered with goose bumps. Jamie must not have closed it tightly enough. I clamped the sheet to my groin and got up and turned the lock, then wandered into the bathroom.

I stared at my bleary, stubbled reflection, wishing I could reach into the mirror and slap the reckless bastard. Instead, he confounded me with an unspoken question: Do you always have to make things so difficult for me?

I drank three glasses of water from the tap, then shaved and showered. I put on my uniform, but it only made me look more sheepish. I tried tidying up the room, but it was no good. The stained sheets told our illicit story.

I went over to the office with my duffel bag.

The little old woman was standing on her wooden box behind the registration desk, a *Forbes* magazine spread out beneath her withered fingers. "Checking out?" she asked.

"I had company last night," I said.

"Did you?" Of course she had noticed Jamie's van parked in front of my cabin, but I appreciated the feigned ignorance.

"I want to pay for another person, since it was just supposed to be me in there."

"Forget about it," she said. "What happens in Vegas stays in Vegas."

I smiled. "But this isn't Las Vegas."

"That explains the snow."

I stopped at the nearest gas station and bought a quart of Gatorade, which I swallowed in one enormous gulp. I also purchased a cup of coffee and half a dozen granola bars for the plane ride. The snacks Charley usually brought with him were things like smoked bear jerky and pickled eggs—food I could barely stomach, even without a low-grade hangover.

The coffee was too hot to drink until I'd arrived at the Gardner Lake boat launch and was sitting in the plowed lot. There were clusters of ice fishermen out on the frozen surface. One group had driven a big SUV out there—a Chevy Yukon. You had to have a lot of balls, or very little brains, to drive something that heavy onto the ice. People assumed that because it had been so cold lately, the conditions must be safe, but they didn't understand how snow cover could retard ice formation. I rarely felt safe on the ice, no matter how frigid it was, and always wore a float coat in case I fell in.

The sky and the ice were the same hard zinc color this morning, and every few minutes, a gust of flurries would blow through, scattering flakes across my windshield.

I heard the plane before I saw it. The whine of the engine preceded its appearance above the treetops. I saw the people on the ice shade their eyes and point, and I followed the direction of their raised arms until I saw the white-and-blue Cessna 172 come swooping down like a fish hawk through a cloud of snow showers.

The sight brought back the memory of my first ride with Charley, two years earlier. Wanted for murder, my father had escaped into the North Woods. Charley had flown down to the coast to take me to the search area. He'd had a Piper Super Cub then. It was as fragile as a model airplane, and it broke into a thousand pieces when it crashed into Rum Pond, its fuselage pierced with bullet holes.

I got out of the truck and removed the Cap-Stun canister from my belt. If the pepper spray discharged inside the cockpit, it would blind us both, and the plane would fall from the sky. The wind vibrated the wings of the Cessna as it skipped down onto the ice. I raised my hand in greeting and ventured out to meet my friend as he taxied toward the ramp. The ice was slick beneath my boots, making me wish I'd paused a moment to fasten on the cleats I usually wore.

The door popped open—literally popped—and I found myself gazing into the smiling face of Charley Stevens. He looked as craggy as ever, with his sun-browned skin and lantern jaw; his eyes were as clear and green as sea ice. His white hair was longer than I'd seen it

before, and he wore an outfit of heavy wool clothing that his grandfather might have worn half a century earlier, going off on a river
drive.

It took me a second to realize that Charley was seated in the passenger seat and that someone else was behind the controls of the
Cessna.

"Good morning," I said.

"Howdy do!" he replied, hopping down with surprising agility
to shake my hand.

"It's been too long, Charley."

"That it has."

"I've never seen you riding shotgun before."

"I'm just the flight attendant for this trip. You've got the top pilot in the fleet today. Mike Bowditch, meet Stacey Stevens."

A young woman leaned toward the open door, but she remained
seated behind the yoke, the belt drawn across her chest. Her mirrored sunglasses and the awkward headphones clamped down over
her brown hair made it difficult for me to act a good look at her.
I saw high cheekbones and a slightly pronounced chin.

"Hello," I said.

"You two need to stop gabbing and get inside before you frost
up all our windows," she said.

Charley chuckled and clapped me hard on the collarbone. "You
heard her. Captain's orders."

He slid the passenger seat forward so that I could clamber onto
the seat behind him. The Cessna, like the Piper before it, was packed
with all sorts of odds and ends, making my patrol truck look neat
by comparison. Snowshoes, ski poles, an ax, blankets, first-aid and
survival kits, extra parkas and boots, and God knows what else
were stowed in various canvas bags and pack baskets. I leaned forward between the seats to make a joke, but Stacey stopped me before I could speak.

"Use the mic," she said.

I put on the pair of headphones and moved the microphone so
close, I was almost sucking on it. Charley slammed and locked the

door. Stacey stepped on a pedal on the floor to turn the nose of the plane and then pushed a lever forward. We began taxiing toward the wide part of the lake, where we could take off without running over ice fishermen.

"What were you going to say?" Charley asked over the intercom.

"Stacey, your dad didn't tell me you were a pilot."

"Yeah, I'm full of surprises," she said without humor, although the electronics made it difficult to catch subtle intonations.

Now that we were in the clear, she opened up the throttle, and we began to slide faster and faster on the skis. Stacey pulled gradually back on the yoke until I felt the nose of the plane rising, although it looked as if we were still on the ground. Suddenly the ice dropped away beneath us and we were airborne, ascending sharply into a cold headwind.

"I had the devil's time teaching her," said her father. "She was the worst white knuckler I'd ever flown with."

"Watching your parents crash tends to have that effect," she said.

Charley had told me that his daughter blamed him for the flying accident that cost her mother the use of her legs. I hadn't expected to hear that long-standing grudge expressed so soon.

If Charley felt stung by his daughter's words, he didn't show it. "You ever do one of these aerial moose surveys before, young feller?"

"No," I said. "Maybe you can explain to me how this works."

"We fly transects within a random sample of survey plots," Stacey said. She had recently gotten a job as an assistant wildlife biologist, Charley had told me. "We record the number and sex of the moose we spot. The presence of antlers this time of year isn't the best indicator, so we're also looking for the vulval patch on the females. . . . Stop snickering."

"I'm not," I said.

"I was talking to my dad."

She went on to explain that, because of tree cover, it was impossible to see every moose, especially in a fixed-wing aircraft that couldn't hover, so the biologists had developed a model to overcome what she called "visibility bias." I couldn't quite follow the rest, but it had something to do with visual obstruction being a covariate of something or other and bulls being estimated as a ratio of cows to calves seen, or maybe it was the other way around, but she used the term *confidence interval* as if it was a phrase I should have picked up in elementary school. Results would be adjusted for sightability and sampling, she said. "Does that make sense?"

"Sure."

"Just tell me if you see a moose."

She leaned forward to wipe away some frost that was forming on the windshield in front of her. At that moment, a gust grabbed the plane and gave it a shake, the way a cat does with a mouse. Neither Stacey nor Charley seemed alarmed, but the flurries seemed to be gathering into a white vapor around us.

"How are we going to see anything in this snow?" I asked.

"What snow?" asked Charley.

"Those big white flakes falling all around us."

"Oh, that's just a little scud."

I glanced down at the rolling pine forest and snow-covered muskeg beneath us. The ancient history of the landscape showed itself as a series of geological scars. Round kettle lakes, left behind by the last glacier's advance, pockmarked the face of the land. There were undulating moraine ridges, miles long and dotted with boulders the size of houses. There were peaked eskers bisecting sprawling blueberry barrens. There were bleak expanses of frozen swampland, layers of frozen peat piled atop sandy glacial till, through which urinous streams wiggled like worms. One of these swamps might be the Heath that bordered the Sprague property, although, by my reckoning, we were many miles south of that trackless bog.

"I promised Mike we'd do a spy mission for him over that game ranch in Narraguagus," said Charley. "Maybe we should buzz over there first."

"You didn't tell me about that!"

"It's just a quick detour."

"No way."

"Tell Stacey about your zebra," said Charley.

"What zebra?" she asked.

"I knew that would pique her curiosity," her father said.

It was difficult telling the story over the intercom, above the drone of the engine, with the windows of the plane rattling and gusts buffeting us from every direction. But I described the poor animal with its frosted haunches and rictus smile, and that was all I needed to say.

"You mean some idiot imported a zebra to Maine and then released it onto his property in the middle of winter for hunters to shoot?"

"Not just the zebra," I said. "Brogan advertises other exotics. He keeps bison, red deer, and who knows what else."

The plane swung around sharply and accelerated in the direction of Call of the Wild.

Charley turned in his seat and gave me the thumbs-up sign. "I think you got her attention," he said.

25

The longer I spent in the plane with Stacey, the more curious I became to see what she looked like beneath the headset and sunglasses, but I was seated behind her, and she kept her face turned to the window.

I'd wanted to meet Stacey Stevens forever. Charley and Ora were the parents I would have chosen had such a thing been possible, and yet Stacey seemed to have no end of grievances with them. Based on the stories her father told, the younger of their two girls had inherited these qualities from him: an eagerness to take risks that bordered on suicidal recklessness, a capacity for stirring up mischief, and a love of the great outdoors that surpassed his own.

"Fortunately," Charley always added, "she got her looks from her mother."

Ora was quite beautiful.

How ironic it was that I was finally meeting her on the day I'd just started a new relationship with a woman. Nevertheless, I found myself gawking. Her skin was uniformly smooth and pale. There was a small mole beneath her jawline. She wore her brown hair tied in a ponytail, exposing a long neck. Once or twice she may have caught me staring, because she turned her head sharply, and I saw my goofy face reflected in her mirrored glasses.

"How are these game ranches legal?" she asked. "Why come to Maine to kill an elk? Why not just go to Wyoming?"

"Novelty, I guess."

"People will pay to kill anything," said Charley. "The money is part of the turn-on."

We followed the road at an altitude of three hundred feet to avoid the blinking cell-phone towers that jutted periodically from the low hilltops. Traffic crawled along the highway beneath us, headed west to Bangor or east to St. Stephen. I couldn't see the speedometer, but I could mark our velocity by how quickly we outpaced the logging trucks below.

After fifteen minutes, I caught sight of the Call of the Wild sign, and I knew that all of the property to the north of the highway was fenced with barbed wire. I indicated for Stacey to take us down so that I could get a better look. Away from the truck route, the timberland was webbed with access roads to bring hunters into the backcountry. Brogan had logged portions of the ranch heavily. Most big herbivores dislike mature forests; they prefer clearings that have been heavily cut, where alders and striped maple are growing back in low bushes. I guess this forage appealed as much to Sitka elk as it did to Maine moose.

"There goes a pig," said Charley.

Down one white road, a wild boar was jogging. It looked brown and shaggy and fairly well fed. As a creature of northern European forests, it didn't seem to find the temperature oppressively cold, nor did it spook when Stacey descended for a closer look. It glanced at us over one hairy shoulder and then set its head down and charged off into a line of spruces without breaking stride.

Stacey turned the plane back toward Brogan's office and brought it about in a tight circle until we were spiraling over the building at an alarmingly low altitude. After a few minutes, a door swung open and a man stepped out, looking skyward. I saw a blond beard and ponytail.

"That's Billy Cronk," I said. "He's the one I was telling you about."

"The one with the skunk?" asked Charley.

"What skunk?" asked Stacey.

"That feller down there let a skunk loose in Mike's abode."

"Why would he do that?"

"He's mad because I pinched him for discharging a firearm too close to a house, so he's been pulling pranks on me," I said. "He calls himself George Magoon, after a famous poacher who liked to torment game wardens."

"What kind of pranks?"

"First, he nailed a coyote pelt to my door, and then he broke into my trailer and released a skunk, which sprayed all over the place. I've been sleeping in a motel the past two nights."

Other men emerged from the cabins to join Cronk. They watched us with generally perplexed expressions, their heads back.

"Are you sure it was the same person both times?" Charley asked.

"Yeah. Why?"

"You don't want to leap to the wrong conclusion."

It never occurred to me that the incidents might have been unrelated. Now that I thought about it, I realized the skunk had not been accompanied by a note from Magoon. Charley had always warned me against making assumptions in my investigations.

"Can you pass me a bottle of water from the cooler?" asked Stacey.

The tight spirals were making me nauseous. A drink sounded like a good idea, but there was only a single Poland Spring in the little Igloo Cooler. I wiped the moisture off with my sleeve and handed it to Stacey. She untwisted the cap, took a swig, and set it between her thighs. Then, very quickly, she lifted the window. A blast of arctic air tore through the cockpit.

"Stacey," warned her father.

Before I could ask what was going on, she hurled the nearly full bottle straight into the cluster of men beneath us. Cronk leapt nimbly backward, but one of the others, a tubby brown-bearded character, fell flat on his ass in the snow. The plastic bottle struck a patch of rock and exploded like a liquid bomb among them.

"Assholes!" Stacey called out the window before she latched it shut again.

"You could have beaned one of those guides." Charley did his best to suppress a chuckle.

"That was the idea."

"I appreciate the gesture," I said.

"I didn't do it for you. I have no problem with hunting if the animal is taken fairly and doesn't suffer, but turning the Maine woods into a private shooting gallery for lazy jerks who just want to fire their guns and pose with a trophy steams me."

Her feelings were almost exactly my own, although my job prohibited me from saying so too loudly, let alone dropping water bombs on the heads of hunting guides.

"You're going to get Mike in trouble with his superiors," Charley said.

"He's a big boy," she said. "And it's not like it will be the first time, according to Mom."

I wondered what stories Ora had told her daughter about me. I knew that Charley's wife cared deeply for me, but I also suspected she worried that I brought out her husband's daredevil side. Ora didn't blame me for the violence I had brought into their life, but the same couldn't necessarily be said for Stacey.

My cell phone rang on my belt. I barely heard the ringtone over the engine. The number on the display belonged to Sergeant Rivard. I removed the headset.

"Yeah?" I said, holding the phone to one ear and covering the other with my hand. The noise inside the plane was deafening.

"Where are you?" he asked.

"In a plane."

"What?"

"In a plane with Charley Stevens and his daughter. We're flying over Narraguagus."

"Can you head over to Machias? Prester Sewall just escaped from the hospital."

"What?"

"A school bus hit a snowplow. He escaped during the Code 66."

Code 66 is hospital jargon for an all-hands-on-deck emergency, such as a natural disaster or a school-yard shooting. In other words, it means any event requiring every staff member to drop what they are doing, even if they are off duty, and assist with triage. A bus loaded with kids striking a plow definitely qualified. I thought of Jamie's son, Lucas, and felt a surge of worry.

"Can Stevens help with the search?" Rivard shouted.

I held the phone against my leg and rearranged the headset to explain to Charley and Stacey what had happened.

Before I could finish asking for help, Stacey had turned the nose of the Cessna in the direction of the coast and reached for the throttle. The plane banked to the right until we caught sight of the Narraguagus River itself, and then we turned southeast across a no-man's-land of peat bogs and frozen beaver flowages without a house to be seen.

Prester Sewall and Randall Cates had sought out one of these heaths for their drug deal. They'd wanted isolation and had found it in spades. Now Cates was dead, and Sewall was on the run. An escape attempt would be interpreted by the court as an admission of guilt. It surprised me that Prester had been capable of flight in his condition. Unless he'd found a ride—a difficult task to accomplish when you had a mug like that of the walking dead—he wouldn't get far.

Snow streaked by the windows, and Charley scraped off frozen condensation from the windshield with the heel of his hand.

"So much for counting moose today," he said.

"I should have figured something like this would happen," said Stacey.

I raised my binoculars at an angle to the window. Peering through the scud, I could make out hills forested with leafless trees that made me think of thinning hair on a balding man. Every once in a while, a black rooftop would pop into view along a gray line of asphalt.

Stacey picked up the half-frozen Machias River and followed it downstream through the impoverished little village of Whitneyville, where Route 1 crossed over the new bridge. I saw the conjoined roofs of the hospital, steam rushing up out of stacks from the power plant inside. The parking lot looked like pandemonium: cars everywhere, police cruisers arranged at checkpoints, blue lights flashing in the snowy morning.

I called Rivard back and had another shouted conversation with him above the Cessna's engine. He wanted us to scout across the road, in the wooded area between Sylvan Park and the riverbank. There was an oval harness-racing track there, long abandoned, bordered by evergreens that bore a resemblance, from above, to a thick shag carpet. A man could hide from view handily in all that greenery.

"Cody Devoe is here with Tomahawk," Rivard said. "He's trying to find the scent."

"What should we do?"

"Look for tracks."

There were plenty of those, crisscrossing the snow-covered fields. The high school was just down the road, and kids no doubt sneaked into the woods to smoke pot and make out on a daily basis, no matter how cold it got. A deceptive coating of ice covered the slow water above the park; from the air, you could see how wafer-thin it was and how the crust broke apart as the river approached the rapids. Eventually, you came to a place where there was no ice at all. There were white streaks in the tea-stained water where the current tumbled over submerged boulders and dropped down hidden cascades before it picked up serious speed above Bad Little Falls.

I wondered if anyone had contacted Jamie. The panic I knew she'd feel when she heard the news was like a punch to the heart.

The phone rang again. "He's headed for the river!" Rivard said. "Bowditch, do you see him?"

Not on my side of the plane. I unstrapped myself and leaned across the cabin. In the open fields to the north, searchers were converging and moving en masse toward the water's edge. With my binoculars, I scanned the ragged tree line, trying to draw a bead.

"There!" said Stacey.

Prester Sewall staggered out from beneath the cover of the evergreens. He lurched through the snow like a wounded soldier. Another man—this one in uniform—was thirty yards behind and closing fast.

The pursuer had Prester trapped against the frozen river, with nowhere left to run.

The other man must have called something to him, causing Prester to pause for a moment along the stony riverbank. They seemed to be having a shouted conversation across the space between them. The police officer raised his hands in a gesture of peacefulness. Prester swayed uncertainly, hugging himself against the biting wind.

And then, as we watched helplessly from above, he turned and took a tentative step onto the ice.

26

During the Code 66, when doctors, nurses, and techs had been scrambling to meet the bus carrying the injured children, and the deputy who was guarding the ward had slipped away to help, Prester Sewall had pulled the IV from his arm and stumbled on wounded feet out of the med-surg unit. How exactly he had escaped detection, no one could say. With his bandaged nose and wine-colored cheeks, he was hardly inconspicuous. Someone suggested he might have found a stray coat to pull on over his pajamas.

Given that it was snowing at a rate of half an inch an hour and the temperature was in the low twenties, Sergeant Rivard calculated that Prester couldn't have gotten far. To Rivard, who had conducted a fair share of searches for escaped prisoners in his time, this line of thought led irresistibly across Route 1A into the locked and abandoned grounds of the old Sylvan Park racetrack.

The hospital staff had provided Warden Devoe's K-9 assistant, Tomahawk, with a hearty whiff of Prester's bedclothes, and sure enough, it took only a few minutes of patrolling along the roadside snowbank before the dog indicated. She nearly pulled her handler over as she took off into the woods.

The searchers found a trail staggering off into the trees. Rivard said the prints were unmistakably those of a man wearing small-size hospital slippers. All available units—wardens, troopers, and deputies—converged on the overgrown park.

Prester had cut across the windy field where horses had once raced, making a beeline for the birch and pine forest to the south. The falling snow hadn't yet obscured his footprints, and the dog was hard on the scent. Excitement built as the wardens and police closed in on the fugitive. Devoe and Rivard heard the Machias River before they saw it. The tracks made straight for the ice-clotted riverbank and then veered east, paralleling the channel as it rushed downstream into town.

The searchers were amazed at Prester's endurance, having forgotten the tremendous survival instinct he had shown the night of the blizzard. The wardens radioed for police cruisers to cordon off Water Street, blocking Prester's escape into the small riverfront neighborhood above Bad Little Falls. Rivard said that you could read his mounting desperation in the meandering tracks. He was in a panic and didn't know where to go.

A call went out over the air: Corbett had cut him off at the river. Moving independently of the other searchers, the chief deputy had found his man by taking a different vector on the Machias, closing off any escape. According to Corbett's written report on the matter, which I later read, he had shouted at Prester to stop. The fugitive had paused at the riverbank and responded inaudibly.

"Suspect seemed to be on the verge of giving up," the chief deputy had written.

Which is why we were all caught off guard when the escaped prisoner decided instead to step to his death.

It happened so slowly, like a movie playing at half speed. When Prester first set foot on the ice, I didn't believe what I was seeing. From aloft, you could see how thin the ice was. Even at ground level, he must have recognized that the crust was nothing but a lie.

Then he took a second step.

"What's he doing?" Stacey asked over the intercom. "Is he nuts?"

Three more steps, and Prester broke through. It reminded me of a horror movie in which an actor is crossing a cemetery and skeletal arms reach up from the ground to pull him down into the grave. He disappeared just like that. His head jerked back, and his bandaged arms went flying skyward—for a moment he seemed to be looking right at us—and then he was gone. A hole in the ice, brown with churning water, was all that was left of him.

My first thought was of Jamie.

Instinctively, Stacey turned the plane downriver. We hoped to see his head pop up in the open water below Sylvan Park, thought we might spot his green pajamas bobbing along. But we never did.

Rivard returned to the line, asking me what I could see.

"Nothing" was my answer.

Nevertheless, we kept looking—and followed the river to Bad Little Falls. As it cascaded into the bay, the Machias was such a raging torrent—with so many plunging waterfalls and swirling eddies capable of sucking entire logs to the bottom without a trace—it seemed futile even to hope. Eventually, I stopped trying. I lowered my binoculars and buckled myself back into my seat.

"Do you think it was a suicide?" I asked Rivard. "Or did he have some crazy idea about getting across?"

"We'll never know."

After I hung up, I put on the headset and told Stacey to set me down near my truck at the Gardner Lake boat launch.

"You mean that's it?" she asked. "Shouldn't we keep looking?"

"If we haven't seen him now, it means he's probably stuck on something beneath the surface, or the hydrodynamics of the falls are keeping him submerged."

"The wardens will recover the body," said Charley. "You can't send divers anywhere near those falls, though, so that's going to complicate things. The river's tidal below the waterfall. They might have to look all the way down the bay before they find him."

At least I knew what I would be doing for the near future: scouting the river for a corpse.

"It seems anticlimactic," said Stacey.

"Not everything has a neat ending," I replied.

Where is Jamie at this moment? I wondered. Does she know? Has anyone told her? It felt very urgent and important for me to be the one to break the news.

Stacey brought the plane around for an approach on Gardner

Lake. Once again, the ice fishermen all paused in their chitchatting to watch the Cessna drop down out of the white sky and skate across the frozen pond. The propeller roared as we slid to a stop just yards from the boat ramp.

Both Charley and Stacey got out of the plane to bid me good-bye.

Stacey, I discovered, was taller than her father, nearly six feet, and slender. Her legs were long and her shoulders were broad for a woman. Physically and, I suspected, in most other ways, she was the opposite of shapely little Jamie Sewall.

Charley clapped one hand on my shoulder and patted my chest with the other. "This was a sad day, so let's make plans for a happier one. Ora will be heartbroken if you don't join us for supper soon. We could go ice fishing for some of those big salmon we've got up at West Grand Lake."

Stacey folded her arms above her breasts and studied us. She had propped her sunglasses atop her head. I finally had a good look at her face. Her eyes were almond-shaped and as green as Chinese jade. Those are the greenest eyes I've ever seen, I thought with some discomfort.

"I'm sorry I dragged you into this," I said.

"Just let me know when you recover his body."

"Your father will hear about it first," I said. "Somehow he gets all the news before anyone else in the Warden Service."

"That's because he's the biggest gossip in the North Woods."

Charley lifted his chin and grunted. I don't think he cherished his daughter's relentless teasing.

In preparation for takeoff, she lowered her glasses back to the bridge of her nose. Until that moment, I hadn't noticed the engagement ring on her finger. The diamond was the size of a pea.

I extended my right hand to Stacey. "Thanks for the plane ride."

She had her father's iron grip. "Good luck," she said.

I saw my dopey reflection again in her mirrored sunglasses.

In my truck, I tried to decide what to do about Jamie. Should I call her on my cell? And tell her what? If she hadn't yet heard, then I couldn't very well inform her over the phone that her beloved brother was now dead. My sixth sense told me she had already rushed to the scene. Machias was such a small town. News of a dangerous prisoner escaping from the hospital was the sort of information that moved from person to person with the speed of electrical impulses flashing between neurons.

My phone rang, settling the question. It was Rivard, asking me to meet him where Sylvan Street dead-ended. It was a little riverside neighborhood, near the spot where Prester had disappeared.

As I drove into town, it dawned on me that, in all likelihood, Zanadakis would be closing his case now. Prester's flight from the hospital seemed a self-incriminating act. Why run if he wasn't guilty of killing Randall Cates? Then there was the manner of Prester's death. Whether or not you could brand his actions as suicidal, at the very least they suggested the mind-set of a man who would prefer drowning over a lifetime spent behind bars.

The whole episode flew in the face of everything Jamie believed. She had been so vehement about her brother's innocence. How would she process the information that he was, in fact, (a) a murderer and (b) dead? I was having trouble accepting these realities myself, and I barely knew the guy. The twin bombshells would blow Jamie to pieces.

By the time I arrived at the end of Sylvan Street, there were only a few police vehicles left: Rivard's patrol truck, the sheriff's Crown Vic, and two white cruisers with the Washington County star on the door. Deputy Dunbar stood in the street with his hands raised, indicating I should stop.

I rolled down my window. "Any news?"

"I'm looking for a new job," he said. "Does that count?"

"Seriously?"

"How the hell was I supposed to know he was strong enough to run away? I was just trying to help the kids who got hurt in that school bus."

I didn't particularly like Dunbar, but I sympathized with his plight. In his shoes, with the hospital in such a state of chaos and everyone focused on the injured children, I probably would have left Prester unguarded, as well.

"Have you seen Jamie Sewall?"

He sneered at me. "I thought that was your department."

I found my capacity for sympathy diminishing rapidly. "Just tell me, Dunbar."

He made a hitchhiking motion over his shoulder. "Why don't you ask the sheriff?"

Dunbar stepped away to avoid being clipped by the door of my truck. I brushed past him and headed down the unplowed street. I found Rivard, Sheriff Rhine, and Chief Deputy Corbett standing in a snow-covered yard fifty feet from the river. A few snowflakes drifted past on the breeze.

"Just the person we were talking about," said the sheriff.

"Where's Jamie?"

"She showed up at the hospital during the search," Rhine said. "I had a deputy escort her home."

Jamie didn't strike me as the sort of person who would follow police orders, especially when they involved separating her from someone she loved. "How did you accomplish that feat?"

"We told her he might try to call home," Corbett said.

Rhine fiddled with her turquoise ring. "I'm headed over to her house now."

"And you want me to go with you," I said.

"How'd you guess?"

Rivard moved a wad of tobacco around in his cheek. "You didn't tell me you were dating the suspect's sister, Bowditch."

"I'm not dating her." Technically, this was not a lie.

"Whatever you want to call it," said the sheriff, "I'd like you to come with me to break the news."

"Thank you," I said.

"I'm not doing it for you, I'm doing it for *her*. This kind of news is always better coming from someone you trust."

Rivard tried to work some stiffness out of his neck by moving his head around. "When you're done with the sheriff, give me a call, and we'll talk about the recovery efforts. I need to talk with the dive team and airboat guys. I have no clue how they're going to tackle this one."

"Maybe they should just string a net at the base of the falls," said the sheriff.

"Crazier ideas have been tried," replied Rivard.

I stared past them at the frozen river. The opposite shore seemed deceptively close at this stretch, and the light was dull enough that you couldn't see the treacherousness of the ice. Beneath its thin coating of windblown snow, it looked solid. Maybe Prester really had expected to get across. It was confusing that he could have shown such a determination to live when he was lost in that snowstorm and then have decided to end his life just days later.

"Throwing yourself into a waterfall is a hell of way to commit suicide," I said. "I don't think he intended to die."

"You didn't see the look on his face," said Corbett. His own face was blazing red from the cold wind.

Until that moment, I hadn't realized it was the chief deputy who had pursued Prester out onto the ice. "From the plane, he looked like he was taking tentative steps," I said. "He didn't appear to be racing headlong to his death."

Rivard started in on his sore neck with both palms. "Does it make any difference?"

It will to Jamie, I thought.

"It was a suicide," Corbett said, his voice rising. "I don't know why it's such a difficult concept to accept. The guy was maimed for life. He was in agony from the detox. And he was headed to jail on a murder rap. Those are three good reasons to end it all, if you ask me."

I remained unconvinced, but Rhine pursed her lips, as if she could see the logic.

Rivard just didn't seem to give a shit.

The sheriff motioned me to follow her to our vehicles. "Come on, Bowditch. Let's get this over with."

I gave one last look at the river and dug my hands into my parka pockets. Rhine didn't speak to Dunbar as she strode past, but she fixed him with a withering stare, which caused the woeful deputy to examine his boots.

I'd scarcely gotten behind the wheel before the sheriff took off at warp speed. It was fortunate Roberta Rhine was the chief law-enforcement officer, or she would have racked up more speeding tickets than anyone in Washington County. I started the engine and turned around in hot pursuit.

27

The sheriff arrived at the Sewall house before I did and took the only parking space in the largely unshoveled driveway, pulling into the slot beside Jamie's van.

I turned off the engine and studied the house. What a wreck it was on the outside. The asphalt shingles were flaking away from the rooftop like dead skin from a dry scalp. A rusted washing machine rose from a snowbank in the lawn like a weird garden sculpture. Jamie had hung some laundry to dry on a clothesline in the front yard—bedsheets and towels—but the hyperborean temperatures had frozen them solid.

I knew that she killed herself trying to keep everything spick-and-span inside. She mopped and vacuumed and dusted every surface. I had the sense it was a recovery thing: literally getting her house in order. But the face the house showed the street was drawn and haggard, a reflection of its owner's recent afflictions and a reminder how tenuous a hold she had on sobriety.

Jamie had shown up at my motel door with beer, which seemed unwise for someone in AA, even if she was drinking Diet Coke, and then there were the five empty bottles this morning, when I recalled consuming only four. But maybe I was mistaken. And maybe the Higher Power she couldn't quite believe was real would assert itself now and stand between the sucker punch headed her way and the seemingly inevitable fall that would result.

I joined Rhine at the foot of the walkway. Fat snowflakes drifted like falling cherry blossoms on the breeze. The beauty of it seemed jarring, given our morbid task.

I'd participated in only one death notification so far, visiting the family of a young man who'd crashed his snowmobile into a tree, but I'd had with me the Reverend Deborah Davies, who served as one of the Warden Service's two female chaplains. Her presence proved a great help when the mother collapsed to the floor, insensible from the shock.

"I hate this part of the job," Rhine said.

"I'm surprised you didn't bring a chaplain along."

"I wouldn't be much of a sheriff if I didn't do my own dirty work."

The more time I spent with Rhine, the more I respected her. She was notorious in law-enforcement circles, known for her Pocahontas hairstyle, her public feud with state bureaucrats, and the landslide elections that kept returning her to office. When you picture a Maine county sheriff, the first image that springs to mind isn't a gimlet-eyed lesbian, and yet Roberta Rhine had won the job and made it her own in a part of the world not known for its open-mindedness. I was beginning to understand why.

I followed her up the snow-dusted wheelchair ramp.

Lucas answered when the doorbell rang. He blinked at us silently through thick glasses. His hair was wet and smeared across his bulbous forehead. He wore pants rolled at the cuffs to fit his stunted legs and a long-sleeved sweatshirt decorated with the leering face of Batman's archnemesis, the Joker.

"Hello, Lucas," I said. "Is your mom at home?"

"I didn't do nothing!"

"We're here to see your mother," explained the sheriff.

He spun away from us. "Ma!"

A woman's voice croaked from a distant room. "Who's at the door?"

"The cops!"

And then he took off up the stairs. I remembered what Jamie had said to me the night before, how I reminded her of Lucas. The comparison left me baffled and disturbed. All I could conclude was that she hoped I might take a paternal interest in the kid. Having met his father and uncle, I could understand why Lucas might require another male role model.

The house smelled of cigarettes. What I'd first taken to be wood smoke from the stove was, in fact, burning tobacco. A bubble of fear unlike anything I had felt before formed in my stomach.

I am about to cause someone great pain, I realized.

Jamie emerged from the living room, still dressed in her McDonald's uniform. She usually pinned up her hair to work, but she must have lost a barrette during the day, because a strand of hair hung in her eyes, which were already bloodshot from crying or smoking. She hung in the doorway as if barred from approaching by an invisible force field.

"Where is he?" The question was directed at me, as if we were alone in the motel room again.

"May we come in, Jamie?" the sheriff asked.

"Tell me first."

The cold tickled the hairs along my neck, but I stopped myself from shivering. Stillness seemed important at this moment. I wasn't sure how to begin.

Fearing that I wasn't up to the task, the sheriff threw herself into the breach. "This afternoon, your brother escaped from Down East Community Hospital," she said.

"How could he just escape? I thought someone was watching him."

"Prester walked out of the med-surg unit while the doctors and nurses were distracted with a bus accident. We followed his footprints across Route 1A into the woods behind Sylvan Park. He tried to elude our searchers by crossing the Machias River, just west of town."

The sheriff paused. She wanted the import to sink in without having to say certain words. She hoped Jamie would take her meaning.

"And?"

I knew the next line belonged to me: "Prester is dead, Jamie."

Her lip began to tremble. "What?"

"He fell through the ice."

"No."

"We're very sorry for your loss," Rhine said.

Jamie didn't speak. The news about her brother's death seemed to have left in her a nearly catatonic state. With some people, hearing about a death can have that effect. Others become wailing banshees.

Her wet eyes met mine. "Where is he, Mike? Where is he right now?"

"We don't know."

"The Warden Service has begun operations to recover his body from the river," offered the sheriff.

This seemed to be a cue for me to say something. "We're going to bring him back to you, Jamie, I promise." My words made it sound as if her brother's corpse were a lost puppy, a *living* puppy.

"No," she said again.

She began to wobble. Looking across the foyer, I could see her knees going weak. She put a hand out to steady herself against the lintel but miscalculated the distance. I barely got there in time to catch her.

We were together on the floor, with me down on one knee, supporting her slumped, shaking body. I smelled her faded perfume and the cigarettes she'd been smoking. I stroked her chestnut hair.

"Jamie?"

"No, no, no, no, no, no, no."

"I'm here," I said.

She was sobbing uncontrollably, great wrenching sobs that seemed to be coming from someplace deeper than her heart.

"No, no, no, no, no, no, no."

"What's wrong?" Tammi appeared in her wheelchair. She'd crept out to the edge of the foyer like a shy animal at the edge of a field. "Is it Prester?"

The sound of her sister's voice seemed to affect Jamie instantly. She squirmed loose of my arms and struggled to her knees. She threw herself between her sister and me, as if her body could be a shield.

"Something's happened," she said in a sniffly voice.

"He's dead, isn't he? The sheriff wouldn't be here otherwise."

No censor between brain and mouth—that was the way I understood brain injuries, some of them anyway.

"He fell through the ice," Jamie said. She turned her head at me, red eyes half closed with confusion. "How did he fall through the ice?"

"He was trying to get away from the police," I said.

"Warden." The sheriff's tone was stern with warning.

"You mean you were *chasing* him?"

"Not me. I wasn't there." I didn't mean this to sound defensive, only explanatory.

"Where were you, Mike?"

I climbed to my feet. "In a plane."

Another unsatisfactory answer. "Who chased him?"

"It doesn't matter," said Rhine.

"It does too matter! I wanted to know what happened to my brother."

"We're still trying to determine how he escaped from the hospital," said the sheriff.

"I don't care about that," said Jamie. "I want to know who was chasing him. Who was he trying to get away from?"

"Jamie," I said.

"You told me he'd be safe in the hospital. You told me he'd be safe."

I felt utterly helpless, afraid to speak lest I make the situation even worse. "I know how hard this is."

"No, you don't."

"Is there someone we can call for you?" the sheriff asked.

"Gloria," I said, thinking of her AA sponsor "Do you want me to call Gloria?"

She sprang to her feet. "I want you to tell me who chased him onto the ice."

"Your brother escaped police custody, Miss Sewall," the sheriff said. "That was his decision."

"Get out of here," Jamie said with a snarl. "I want you to leave my house."

"I think we should call your sponsor," I said softly.

"Will you shut up about Gloria?"

"We'll be on our way, then," the sheriff said. "We'll be in touch when we have more information."

"I'd like to stay," I told Rhine.

"I don't think that's a good idea." The sheriff was afraid that if I remained there, I would tell Jamie it was Corbett who had pursued her brother across the frozen river. It was a legitimate worry.

"No," said Jamie. "I want you to go, too."

"What?"

"I can't look at you right now."

"I want to help you, Jamie," I said.

"I don't want your help! I don't need your help!"

The words hit me like a slap across the face.

Rhine put her hand on my shoulder. "Let's leave them in peace," she whispered in my ear. Then she looked at Jamie and said, "You have our condolences."

I raised my eyes and saw a face peering out of the shadows from the upstairs landing. Lucas Sewall had been eavesdropping on our entire conversation. He made no effort to disappear this time. We stared at each other, and I was struck by the look of utter betrayal on his face. Like his mother, he blamed me for what had happened to Prester.

Neither Rhine nor I spoke until we had returned to our vehicles. The snow was falling thickly in the cedars across the road. The scene was as quiet as a Japanese woodblock print.

"People can't be held responsible for what they say in those situations," the sheriff said.

"I guess not."

Rhine gazed up at the house. "I'd forgotten the sister was in a wheelchair. That explains a lot."

"How so?"

"People with lots of prescriptions are real popular around here.

For someone like Randall Cates, living in the same house with Tammi Sewall would have been like having his own in-house pharmacy. It might even have been why Cates cozied up to her sister in the first place."

An image came to me of Jamie naked in my bed. "I doubt that was the reason."

"I guess you would know," Rhine said. "Should I even bother giving you advice, or are you just going to ignore it again?"

The question was obviously rhetorical, so I let her continue.

"Leave the Sewalls alone for a while. Otherwise, you might find yourself named in the wrongful-death lawsuit she'll probably bring against the hospital, the county, and God only knows who else."

"Jamie wouldn't do something like that."

"How sure are you of that?"

Not very, I realized.

Rhine climbed behind the wheel of the Crown Vic. "Call me if you hear anything."

I backed my truck into the road so she could pull out. She snapped on her headlights and hit the gas hard. I watched the sheriff rocket down the road toward Machias.

When I glanced back at the house, I saw a parted curtain in an upstairs window. Lucas Sewall was still watching me.

28

People can't be held responsible for what they say in those situations.* I hoped the sheriff was right, but I could't deny that Jamie's outburst worried me. It reminded me of the bitter comments that my dad used to spit out at me when he was drinking hard: "Be a man for once. Stop acting like such a fucking pussy." Grief, like alcohol, seemed to facilitate the expression of a person's true feelings.

Jamie was already smoking again; how soon before she took a drink? And then what? A trip down to the Machias causeway to score some Oxy? If only she would let me help her, I thought. Then I remembered the nickname Tammi had bestowed upon me when we'd first met: Sir Galahad.

I felt more like a fool than a knight. How had I come to think I could save Jamie from herself? I needed to have faith that she would reconsider my offer of help before she did something rash. Beyond that, I could only hope.

Driving seemed easier than sitting alone in my stinking trailer. Rivard still hadn't told me about his conversation with Brogan. Had he even spoken to the outfitter? I remembered my sergeant standing on the frozen riverbank with Rhine and Corbett, chewing his disgusting tobacco. I remembered the redness of Corbett's face, as if it had been scalded with boiling water. The sheriff didn't want to identify her chief deputy as the man who'd pursued Prester onto the ice, and for good reason: It would only suggest that a police officer had been to blame for another man's suicidal decision. Her department didn't need the bad publicity or the lawsuit.

What was the extent of Corbett's involvement in this case? He had been the first on the scene at the Spragues' house because he lived up the road. He'd even patrolled the Heath on his own the previous summer after Ben and Doris had reported suspicious activity. I remembered the way the chief deputy had inserted himself into my interview with Zanadakis. And how he'd come running after me to ask if I might be able to positively identify the snowmobiler as Barney Beal. When Prester had escaped, Corbett had been the pursuing officer who chased him to his death.

The Maine Drug Enforcement Agency believed that Randall Cates had had a mole in the Washington County Sheriff's Department, someone who tipped him off to busts. What if it was Corbett?

A sharp turn in the road loomed ahead. When I braked, I nearly lost control of the vehicle. Without meaning to, I had been pushing harder and harder on the gas pedal. Someday I was going to kill myself doing that.

My cell phone rang on the way home to my trailer. My heart did a little leap in my chest until I saw that the number wasn't Jamie's.

"Bowditch? It's Mack McQuarrie."

He was the warden in an adjoining district, the one that included the border city of Calais and the Moosehorn National Wildlife Refuge. McQuarrie was a big, bluff veteran who'd worked for three decades in the woods and didn't much cotton to the changes that had swept through the Warden Service since he'd earned his red jacket—all those female wardens and high-tech gadgets. He was always teasing me about my effete Colby College education. In McQuarrie's mind, the only school a Maine warden should have graduated from was the school of hard knocks.

"Hey, Mack. What's up?"

"Heard about your swimmer." His voice was raspy from a lifetime of chewing tobacco and sipping scotch. "If he went into the river above the falls, he's probably halfway out to sea by now. One of those scallop draggers will probably pull him up in its nets."

My windshield wipers smeared snowmelt across the glass. "You never know."

"I just got off the phone with Charley Stevens," McQuarrie said, dispensing with the small talk. "He told me you were looking for a sledder you saw out on the Heath the night of that big blizzard. Guy on a green sled, dressed all in green."

Leave it to Charley to stick that Roman nose of his into my business again.

"That sledder nearly ran me down on the Bog Road."

"Well, I busted a guy for playing chicken with other sledders last month over by Meddybemps Lake. He was this little asshole with a great big mouth. A real pint-size piece of shit."

"Did he have a green sled?"

"Yep. Green Arctic Cat ProCross turbo." McQuarrie coughed away from the receiver. "Anyway, after I finished gabbing with Charley—Jay-sus, that old bird likes to talk—I checked my laptop for his name and address. You want it?"

"What do you think?"

"Name's Mitchell Munro. He lives over on Wyman Hill in Township Nineteen."

It's a wonder I didn't careen off the road into a telephone pole. Jamie's ex-husband, Lucas's father, had been the man we'd seen the night Randall Cates was murdered. It couldn't have been a coincidence.

"Do you have his street address?" I asked.

"You're welcome. Happy to help."

I took the hint. "Thanks, Mack."

McQuarrie couldn't resist giving me the pickle one last time before we got off the phone. "Didn't they teach you manners in that fancy finishing school where you matriculated?"

I couldn't help but smile. If McQuarrie knew the word *matriculate,* he wasn't quite the proud Neanderthal he made himself out to be.

I stopped my truck at the nearest safe spot and hit my hazard lights. I turned on my computer and read the information that

Mack had e-mailed me about Munro. It took a while for his criminal record to come up. He had two convictions for driving to endanger, three for simple assault, one for soliciting a prostitute, and an aggravated drunk-driving conviction. He had been found guilty of misdemeanor drug possession, harassment, criminal trespass, and public intoxication. In short, he was a choirboy.

Had Prester and Randall gone to the Heath to sell drugs to Mitch Munro? I had trouble picturing Jamie's ex-husband doing business with her ex-boyfriend, but stranger things happened in the woods of Washington County. And it wouldn't have taken much for such a truce to be broken. Munro was a violent little man, and he had a reason to resent the thug sleeping with his former wife. What if Jamie's ex-husband had killed Cates? It would explain Prester's reluctance to name the man they'd met in the Heath, if it meant fingering Lucas's father.

I didn't even want to contemplate the possibility that Jamie might have known all along.

I considered telephoning Zanadakis, but would he even care at this point about the identity of my asshole snowmobiler? Prester was dead. For all I knew, the state police considered the case closed. Besides, all I had to back up my theory was McQuarrie's report about Munro's owning a green sled. Until I saw the snowmobile myself, I felt reluctant to open my mouth.

My better judgment, such as it was, cautioned me against any further involvement in the investigation. At the same time, the memory of that runt insulting Jamie in front of their little boy brought my blood to a simmer. If Munro had let Prester take the rap for him, he deserved punishment beyond anything I could inflict with my own fists. Besides, what else do I have to do? I thought. Rivard would wait until first light to begin the recovery efforts for Prester Sewall's remains.

The snow had begun to let up, but the roads felt slick beneath my tires. The digital thermometer on the dashboard told me that the temperature had climbed since morning, rising into the mid-twenties. By the standards of mid-February in Down East Maine, that was close to balmy, especially after the extended stretch of subzero days we'd just endured. I passed a reflective yellow-and-red sign that showed the outline of a leaping deer. CAUTION. HIGH HIT RATE.

After I crossed the line into Township Nineteen, I fiddled with the GPS to bring up the map of local streets and goat paths. The screen of the DeLorme showed Wyman Hill Road branching off from the north side of Route 277. It didn't look like much of a thoroughfare.

Nor was it, in fact. The road was poorly marked and hadn't received a visit from a plow truck in days. My pickup climbed a steep hill through ankle-deep snow. Halfway up, my headlights illuminated a snowshoe hare, as white as the wintertime, bounding from one row of pines to the other.

The road emerged from dense evergreens into a pale landscape of rock walls and snow-covered fields. The top of the hill had been razed for blueberries. I passed one lighted farmhouse and then another before I began to descend again into a copse of paper birches. A low-slung ranch house sat back in the trees. It had tattered gray clapboards and a gray shingled roof that seemed to sag under the weight of the accumulated snow. The GPS told me that I'd reached my destination.

I surveyed the house. The dark windows reminded me of the eye sockets of a skull.

From the road, I saw no vehicles, no cars or trucks, no green snowmobiles. I parked at the end of the drive and waited for a light to come on in a window or outside the front door. None did. The question was whether someone was watching me through the curtains with a loaded shotgun. In my line of work, you always approach a house after dark with extreme caution. Just because a property isn't posted doesn't mean the owner won't unload a burst of buckshot in your face. You have to put yourself in the place of the paranoid home owner. In a stretch of wild country plagued by poverty and infested with drug addicts, home invasions are all too frequent occurrences.

I reached down to touch the grip of my .357 SIG. The holster came equipped with a self-locking hood that required me to release a special catch in order to draw my weapon. The gadget was designed to prevent someone from overpowering me, pulling my sidearm loose, and shooting me through the heart with it. An assailant might eventually succeed in getting my pistol away from me in a wrestling match, but it wouldn't be easy.

Gray clouds billowed over the hilltop as the line of snow showers passed away into the Bay of Fundy. I blew out my breath and watched the vapor dissolve in the cold air. The paper birches rustled in the darkness. I started up the drive.

Immediately, a dog began barking. It sounded big; it sounded mean. I dropped my hand to my canister of Cap-Stun pepper spray, but no hellhound came charging out of the shadows. The dog was locked inside the house. And the windows remained dark.

I stopped at the side door and rapped my knuckles hard against the aluminum. I heard the clawing of the dog as it came racing down the hall and heard its heavy body collide against the locked door. It leapt up at the window, snapping its jaws and growling. I couldn't see what breed it was, but I was glad there was a barrier of wood and metal between its fangs and my face.

No lights, no answer.

I stepped away from the door and circled around behind the building.

The snowmobile was parked behind the woodpile. McQuarrie had been right. It was a goblin-green Arctic Cat ProCross turbo: a racing sled, the speed demon's choice. The very machine I'd seen coming straight at my grille the night of the blizzard.

I dug my camera out of my jacket pocket and took a picture. The flash created a burst of light, like an exploding firecracker. I snapped a shot from every angle. I wanted Doc Larrabee to remember this snowmobile. I wanted to convince the state police to bring Mitch Munro in for questioning. I wanted that son of a bitch out of Jamie Sewall's life forever.

I wanted her to myself.

29

In my mind, I began preparing my bullshit story: *No, Detective, I had no intention of meddling in the official investigation. I simply went to Township Nineteen to clear up some personal loose ends about the night of the blizzard. It was only after I positively identified Mitch Munro's Arctic Cat ProCross turbo that it occurred to me he'd had the means, motive, and opportunity to kill Randall Cates. . . . No, sir, I'm not putting forth my own theory. I just wanted to provide you with information in case you chose to follow up.*

Given my reputation, would anyone believe this line of crap? It would definitely help to have Doc Larrabee corroborate that the snowmobile we'd seen belonged to Munro. I decided to stop at his farmhouse and show him the photographs and then tell Zanadakis what I'd happened to find.

Night hadn't yet fallen, but as I pulled into Doc's driveway, I was startled to find lights burning in almost every window. You might have thought he was having another party.

Doc took his time answering the door, and even then he felt compelled to peel back the curtain in the window to get a good look at me. His Amish beard was poorly trimmed, and he looked as baggy-eyed as an insomniac. "What are you doing here?"

"I'd be lying if I said it was a social call. Can I come in? I want to show you something."

He squinted over my shoulder into the gloom with what seemed like real nervousness. "What is it?"

I tried to put him at ease with a smile. "Some photos."

"Does this have something to do with Prester Sewall? I heard he killed himself today."

Despite my best efforts, Doc seemed intent on having this conversation on his freezing doorstep. "This morning, a plow truck hit a school bus, and a bunch of kids went to the hospital with minor injuries. During the confusion, Prester slipped out of the ambulance bay and took off into the woods. The police tracked him to the river. He tried to cross on the ice but went through and was swept under by the current. I'm sorry, Doc. You worked so hard to save his life."

"So it was definitely suicide?"

I pictured Corbett standing on the riverbank, staring down at the hole in the ice. "I think it's premature to conclude anything one way or another."

"No one helped him to escape?"

"What do you mean?"

"I wondered if he'd had any visitors at the hospital."

"Just his sister and me."

"*You* visited him?"

I nodded and rubbed my hands together. "You don't have any coffee, do you? It's kind of chilly out here."

Doc took hold of the doorknob again, blocking my way. It was as if the jovial, wisecracking guy who had accompanied me to Brogan's ranch had been replaced with some sort of pod person. "You'd better not come in. I've been sick with the flu."

He certainly looked ill, but unless he was treating himself with Maker's Mark, I would have suspected first that he was intoxicated. I reached into my pocket for the digital camera. "Do you remember on the night of the blizzard how a crazy snowmobiler almost rammed my Jeep as we were driving down to the Sprague house? I think I've found out who it was, and I'm hoping you might recognize the sled."

"What does it matter now?" he asked in a scratchy voice. "If Prester murdered Cates and then killed himself, isn't that the end of the investigation?"

"I'm just trying to tie up some loose ends."

"The state police were clear about my not discussing that night with anyone, especially you."

I turned on the camera, and the picture of Munro's sled showed on the stamp-size screen. "Come on, Doc. Do me a favor. You won't get in trouble. Just tell me if this is the snowmobile you saw on the Bog Road."

His watery eyes remained focused on mine. "Whose sled is it?"

"I don't want to prejudice you."

His gaze darted to the screen. "Sorry."

"What about these?" I clicked through the series of pictures I had taken.

"No."

I couldn't keep the frustration out of my voice. "You're positive?"

"I don't understand why this is important. Are you planning on charging the driver with reckless driving or something?"

"It would help if you would corroborate that this was the sled that almost hit us."

"I'm sorry, Mike." His voice softened and he seemed genuinely apologetic, more like the kindly old man who'd invited me to dinner. "My eyes aren't any good anymore."

"OK. Thanks."

He called after me, "So what will happen now?"

I stopped short. "With what?"

"With the murder investigation?"

"I guess it depends how interested the investigators are in what I have to show them."

A gust kicked up, and he shivered noticeably. "You're not going to tell me whose sled that is?"

"As you said, I'm not sure it matters. Have a good evening, Doc. Sorry to disturb you."

He smiled sadly and seemed to be on the verge of offering a comment, but he caught himself and closed the door. As the porch light was snuffed out, I found myself again in the dark. Everyone I had met in recent weeks seemed to be a cipher, and I didn't know whether it was a characteristic of the people of Washington County or a reflection of my woeful inability to see clearly into the heart of another human being.

I decided to e-mail the photos of Munro's Arctic Cat to Detective Lieutenant Zanadakis and Sheriff Rhine and leave it to them to follow up with me. Under most circumstances, the word of a game warden testifying that he recognized a vehicle was good enough for investigators to pursue, but my history of making imaginative leaps—as the sheriff might say—combined with my ill-considered sexual involvement with Jamie Sewall was likely to weigh against my credibility.

Some days—most days—I wondered whether I was really cut out for my job.

I suspected my superiors thought the same thing.

The wet snow had whitewashed all the fixtures in my dooryard: my ATV beneath its tarp, my Ski-Doo on its trailer, my overturned canoe, my rusting Jeep. I made a quick sweep around the property, looking for new tire tracks or footprints. There were none.

A sour smell greeted me as I opened the door. The odor was definitely fainter than it had been, and masked somewhat by the chemical freshness of the industrial cleaners I had used on the carpets and walls, but the place still reeked to high heaven. I dragged my duffel bag inside and flung it on the floor. I would just need to resign myself to smelling like roadkill for the indefinite future. It seemed to be a message from the universe that I was truly meant to live alone.

I microwaved three burritos and sat down at the table. The mushy beans scalded my tongue on the first bite, and I rushed to fill a coffee mug with cold water. I remembered the can of beer in my refrigerator and figured that, after last night, I might as well drink it now. The beer made me think of Jamie. How much time needed to pass before I could safely call her?

After I'd finished eating, I plugged my camera into my laptop computer and downloaded the pictures of Munro's snowmobile. The phosphorescent paint job was unmistakable. It puzzled me that Doc hadn't made the identification instantly. I tried to conjure up the look he'd given me when I showed him the photos. In my mind's eye, I saw his mouth widen and the side of his face jerk with an uncontrollable tic.

Doc Larrabee had been lying when he'd said he didn't recognize the sled. I was 100 percent certain of it now. But why? What reason would the veterinarian have had to cover for Mitch Munro, of all people?

I composed an e-mail, recounting the tip I'd gotten from Mack MacQuarrie and my subsequent visit to Munro's residence. I reaffirmed my eagerness to speak with the state police, the sheriff's office, or Maine Drug Enforcement agents should they find this information of interest. I attached the pictures as JPEG files, CC'd Sergeant Rivard, and sent off my message in a virtual bottle.

Then I went to take a long, hot shower.

After I got out of the bathroom, I made myself a cup of coffee and checked my mailbox for new e-mail. Zanadakis hadn't responded, but there was a new message from an address that got my heart pumping: georgemagoon@anonemail.com.

At first I marveled at how he'd tracked me down. Then I remembered that all Maine government e-mail addresses follow the same formatting, based upon the state employee's full name, followed by @maine.gov. My own address was also printed at the bottom of the business card I handed out all the time.

The message was short and to the point:

> *Good evening, Warden.*
>
> *You need to keep a closer eye on your prisoners! You shouldn't let them wander off into rivers.*
>
> *Did you like the sweet-smelling present I left for you?*
>
> *I've enjoyed playing with you, but I'm beginning to get bored. My crystal ball says you're headed for a bad end*

sooner than you think. Will it happen tomorrow? I won-
der. Wait and see.

Sincerely,
Your Friend George

30

That night I slept like the proverbial dead. The next morning, I printed out Magoon's e-mail. On its surface, nothing in the message seemed to rise to the level of criminal threatening, but that decision belonged to the district attorney.

Rivard called while I was wolfing down a bowl of Cheerios. He was all business, in a hurry. He said the Division C airboat and dive teams would lead the recovery effort for Prester Sewall's body. Teams of searchers from local law enforcement, fire, and rescue, members of the Coast Guard station in Jonesport, and community volunteers would scour both banks of the Machias downstream of the point where Prester had gone into the water. I would help coordinate the search along the shore. Rivard didn't mention the e-mailed photos I'd sent to the sheriff, and I didn't bring up the subject, knowing that his mind was appropriately elsewhere.

There were no messages from Rhine or Zanadakis, either. They, too, had more pressing subjects on which to focus than Mitch Munro's snowmobile.

The sky was blue-black, almost indigo, and there was again the feeling of imminent snow in the air. Some early chickadees were whistling in the pines across the right-of-way as I backed out of the drive and headed toward Machias. Rivard had told me to meet him at the little park on the eastern side of Bad Little Falls.

By the time I arrived, a cluster of patrol trucks was already jammed into the tiny lot. A woman in a bathrobe was standing on the doorstep of a clapboard house across the street, smoking a ciga-

rette and watching the show. I spotted Sergeant Rivard, Cody Devoe, and Mack McQuarrie out on the pedestrian bridge that
stretches across the waterfall. I made a beeline for my colleagues.

The bridge is normally barred in the wintertime, but Rivard had
arranged for the gate to be opened. He was pointing at a deep-
looking plunge pool beneath one of the falls. "See that eddy there?"
His voice was loud above the roar of the river. "We need to drop a
sonar head into that pocket."

"Probably full of dead trees," said McQuarrie.

Devoe nodded. "And God knows what else. Dead deer, dead
moose."

They raised their eyes from the water as I stepped onto the icy
bridge. "Gentleman," I said, touching the brim of my cap.

"Good morning, sunshine!" McQuarrie turned his head and spit
a brown stream of tobacco juice over the railing. He was barrel-
chested, with a shock of white hair you could see from a distance,
like the tail of a deer. "How nice of you to join us."

"I take it Prester didn't wash up overnight," I said.

"No such luck," said Devoe. He had probably shaved an hour
ago, but already there was a blue shadow along his caveman's jaw.

"So what's the plan?"

"This one is going to be a bitch," Rivard said. "There's a chance
he got stuck upriver—snagged in a tree or wedged behind a
boulder—but the current's pretty powerful, so I figure no. That
would be a good thing. We can't put divers in above the falls, and
we can't put them into those pools because of the hydraulics and
debris. Let's hope he made it all the way down to the bottom. With
any luck, we'll find him stuck in the mud down there."

I cast my gaze downriver and breathed in the fetid smell of the
tidal flats. Dawn was breaking above the humped eastern shoreline,
and I saw gulls bobbing in the dirty foam line of the river, where the
freshwater met the salt.

"I just got off the horn with Petey," said McQuarrie. "He said
the airboat's on the way."

"That'll wake up the neighborhood," said Rivard with a laugh.

I pointed at the woman in her bathrobe across the street. "The neighborhood's already awake."

The prop-powered airboats we used were identical to the ones that skim along the Everglades. They made such an ungodly racket, you needed to wear protective headphones in order to have a conversation on board. Hearing loss is an occupational hazard in the Maine Warden Service. Hours of exposure to airplane engines, outboard motors, snowmobile and ATV four-strokes, and the occasional shotgun or pistol blast do a number on the eardrums.

"Let's go find the dead guy," Rivard said.

McQuarrie clapped me hard on the shoulders. "Ain't this the greatest job in the world?"

I followed Mack to his patrol truck. The snow in the park was already dirty and beaten down with boot prints. Beer bottles and cigarette butts littered the banks.

"Thanks for the tip about that snowmobile," I said. "You were right about Munro being my guy."

McQuarrie grunted. "Little prick. You wouldn't believe the crap he gave me. 'Yes, sir. I always obey the speed limit. No, sir, I never drink or take drugs when I'm riding. Thank you, sir, for giving me this ticket.' I wanted to slap the smile off his pretty little face."

"Was he with any buddies?"

"No, but he had a girl on the back of the sled."

I found myself breathing more quickly. "Did you get her name?"

"If she'd mouthed off, I would have, but she knew enough to keep her mouth shut. She was just some chick with a show-off boyfriend. It's the ones who chime in who're the worst."

"What did she look like?"

"She didn't take her helmet off. She seemed pissed at him, though, judging from the body language. She was short." He cupped his hands around imaginary breasts and winked at me. "But big in other ways, if you know what I mean."

Unfortunately, I did.

* * *

Rivard hurried past on his way to confer with the state police dive team guys who had just arrived. He strode with a sense of purpose, which made him seem taller than usual. The division lieutenant would become the officer in charge, or OIC, once he arrived from Bangor, but at the moment, my sorehead sergeant was glorying in his position of responsibility.

"Hey, Marc. Can I talk with you?"

He glanced at his wristwatch. "Make it fast."

"Did you get that e-mail I sent? The one with the pictures of the snowmobile?'

He gave me a frown. "I don't have time for your conspiracy theories right now, Bowditch. I need you upriver to direct the search along the banks."

"Understood," I said. "But there's something else you should hear. I received a threatening e-mail from Brogan last night. I think I should show it to the DA."

The mention of the district attorney caught his attention. "Threatening, how?"

"He took responsibility for putting the skunk in my trailer. He said he'd been watching me and that I was headed for a bad end. He sent the message from one of those anonymous e-mail addresses, but he signed it 'George Magoon.' I know it was Brogan."

"He did what?"

"He signed it 'George Magoon.' That means he was also responsible for nailing that coyote pelt to my door. The note establishes a pattern. I think there might be enough for a stalking or criminal-threatening charge."

Rivard rubbed his face with his gloved hand. "Jesus Christ. Why can't you just give it a rest?"

"Give what a rest?"

"*I'm* George Magoon, not Brogan."

"What?"

"I found that coyote skin in an abandoned trapper's cabin and nailed it to your door as a joke. You're so paranoid. I knew it would drive you crazy trying to figure out who put it there."

"Why would you do that?"

"You were so gung ho to bust Billy Cronk. I wanted to teach you a lesson about how wardens are viewed Down East before some poacher shot you in the head."

"What about the skunk?" I asked, feeling the blood rush to my cheeks.

"That wasn't me."

"Who was it, then?"

"Brogan, probably. The fucking idiot. I keep meaning to knock some sense into him. But right now, we've got something more important to do."

Charley had cautioned me against connecting the two pranks; he'd observed that with the skunk, there had been no note left with Magoon's signature. But if Rivard had been behind the coyote skin, and Brogan had let the skunk loose, then who had sent the threatening e-mail?

"You're an asshole, Rivard."

"And you're an arrogant fuckup who thinks he's the smartest guy in the Warden Service. So, do you want to stand here and trade insults all day, or do you want to help us find Prester Sewall before he floats off to Nova Scotia?"

"Warden Bowditch!"

Roberta Rhine slammed the door of her Crown Victoria and started up the steep road in our direction. She wore a black Gore-Tex parka and black chinos tucked into rubber-bottomed boots. She had arranged her long braid so that it protruded through the hole in the back of her sheriff's baseball cap. Her lips were thin, red, and unsmiling.

"Sheriff Rhine," Rivard said.

"Am I interrupting something?" she asked.

My sergeant dropped his voice a couple of octaves. "I was just telling Warden Bowditch that we have a search and recovery operation to begin."

"Indeed you do." She smiled at me without any warmth. Her lipstick had left a crimson smear on one of her front teeth. "But first I need to speak with Warden Bowditch. I got the e-mail he sent me last night. I'm not sure what you hoped to accomplish by sending it."

"I assumed Lieutenant Zanadakis might want to interview Mitch Munro about his whereabouts at the time of Randall Cates's death."

"That's very conscientious of you. It's not often that a warden offers his assistance to a homicide investigator in such a determined fashion. Your efforts to absolve Prester Sewall of responsibility are quite heroic. You'd think it was because you had a personal interest in this case. Did you ever see your girlfriend last night, by the way?"

"No, ma'am."

"So you didn't confer with her about the new 'evidence' you unearthed at the home of her ex-husband?"

I couldn't guess what garden path Rhine was trying to lead me along; there was clearly some ulterior motive behind this line of questioning. "I haven't talked with Jamie Sewall since you and I left her house last night."

"And you don't know how she spent the rest of the evening?"

"Come off it, Sheriff." I said. "What's going on? Did something happened to Jamie?"

"As a matter of fact, yes."

A lump in my throat made it hard to speak. "Is she OK?"

"That depends on your definition," Rhine said. "Your girlfriend had quite a night after she kicked us out of her house. I just came from seeing her. She's my guest in the fishbowl over at the jail."

31

"Trooper Belanger picked her up around three A.M.," the sheriff explained. "She was driving back to Whitney from somewhere in Machias. Her van was weaving across the center line. When he pulled her over, he detected a strong smell of alcohol on her breath. She refused to take a field sobriety test. He found a vial of Adderall in her pocket. We're holding her at the jail on drunk-driving and drug-possession charges."

The sensation was of all the blood in my body draining down out of my head and heart and pooling down around my ankles. I was devastated by what she'd done to herself. Depending upon the quantity of the drugs in her possession, she might be facing mandatory jail time. If Jamie went to prison now, who would care for Tammi? Who would look after Lucas?

I felt heartsick and culpable, but the sheriff used another adjective to describe my bloodless expression.

"You look shell-shocked," she said.

"Disappointed is more like it," I said. "Her brother just committed suicide, and I was worried she was going to fall off the wagon."

"I'd say she leapt off the wagon—with both feet. She wasn't particularly coherent when Belanger brought her in. Still isn't, in fact."

I wanted to rush over to the jail anyway, wanted to see her myself. I figured that even if she was totally wasted, the enormity of the crime she'd committed and the implications about what it might mean for her family must already be sinking in. If the Department of Health and Human Service removed Lucas from the house, Jamie would destroy herself for sure.

"I'd like to see her," I said.

"No dice," said Rivard. "I need you here."

"Prester will still be dead an hour from now."

Rivard moved the tobacco wad around in his mouth, causing his cheek to bulge out as if he'd tucked a golf ball in there. "Bowditch, I've had it up to here with you. OK? We've got a bunch of people ready to search. We need to find the stiff before it starts snowing again. You have a job to do, and I expect you to do it."

I stared across Bad Little Falls at the road that curved around the corner storefronts in Machias and climbed through a neighborhood of neat houses and yards to the courthouse and the jail. It was beyond my power to rescue Jamie from the fate she'd brought upon herself. But at least I could find her brother.

"What do you need me to do?" I asked Rivard.

Cody Devoe and Tomahawk took the northern bank of the river with one group of searchers while I led another team along the southern shore above the falls.

Devoe had brought along a cork lobster buoy. While we watched, he dropped it into the channel below the spot where Prester had fallen in, and we watched the buoy bob along in the current. It bounced off a couple of ice-crusted rocks and lingered amid foaming eddies. Eventually it found its way into the rapids and was swept quickly downstream, where it was lost from our view over the falls. A man's body is significantly heavier than a lobster buoy, but Devoe's science experiment gave us a better understanding of the river's specific hydrodynamics. We made notes of the places where Prester's cadaver might have gotten stuck beneath the surface.

Drowned corpses will usually sink before they rise. Once water has flooded the lungs and filled the gastrointestinal organs, a human body will submerge and drift down to the bottom of a lake or river. Eventually, if it stays there long enough, the decomposition process will begin, and methane and other gases will cause the cadaver to swell. In time, it will rise like a volleyball that you've held beneath the surface of the water with the palm of your hand. Watching your first bloated corpse ascend from the depths is a special moment in a young warden's education.

I led a team of four firefighters who had been trained extensively in search and recovery techniques. They were a no-nonsense bunch of guys who made my job considerably easier by actually shutting up and paying attention. Some volunteers will leap into a search with real enthusiasm, but once the hours stretch on without the subject being located, their concentration flags. My guys seemed untroubled by the bitter temperature and overcast skies.

The circuitous path taken by the lobster buoy suggested that Prester should have fetched up on the north side of the river—since there was no chance that he had swum even ten strokes before the cold and current overpowered his best efforts—but there was a slim possibility he might have lodged against one of the boulders midstream, so we turned our binoculars on every square inch of the Machias, recording our findings on maps and GPS, watching our counterparts on the opposite shore do the same.

I kept expecting to hear Tomahawk begin barking, indicating she'd found our drowned fugitive, but the only sound was the constant rush of water and occasionally a shout when someone spotted some bright shard of plastic or a flesh-colored branch. After a time, and despite all my willpower, my own mind began to wander. I couldn't keep out the distractions.

I tried to keep my mind off Jamie—the thought of her in jail was too damned heartbreaking—so instead my thoughts drifted toward George Magoon.

If Rivard had left the coyote skin and the note on my door, then who had sent me that threatening e-mail? To the best of my knowledge, Brogan was unaware that a prankster calling himself George Magoon was harassing me. Leaving that skunk in my trailer was an independent act of vandalism on his part. So who else knew about

Magoon? I'd recounted the incident to Kathy Frost and Charley Stevens. I might have mentioned the name Magoon to Jamie at some point, but I didn't think so. That left Doc Larrabee and Kendrick. But what reason would they have had to send me a harassing note? Doc had a definite alcohol problem, and Kendrick seemed like a merry prankster in the Earth First! sense. It was possible one of them had sent the message. I had a hollow feeling in my stomach that I was overlooking some detail that might prove significant.

The search dragged on until my team had studied every square foot of water and shoreline between Grove Street and the Route 1A bridges. A Forest Service helicopter appeared over the horizon at one point. It hovered low above the river, its rotors whipping cold water at those of us gathered along the banks, while, inside the chopper, our lieutenant directed a spotlight down at the channel. The lieutenant spent a long time inspecting the pile piers in the center of the stream, but eventually he gave up and the copter moved down below the falls.

As the afternoon progressed—or failed to progress—I found myself growing increasingly angry. I was mad at Prester for falling through the ice, mad at Corbett for chasing him there, mad at Munro for whatever the hell he was doing on the Heath, mad at Rhine and Zanadakis for not taking the matter seriously, mad at Jamie for getting busted, mad at Rivard for being a dick, mad at Brogan and Cronk and Kendrick and even that sourpuss Ben Sprague for making my life so damned difficult when all I'd wanted was to do my job quietly for once. Mostly I was mad at myself.

Rivard was right: I really was an arrogant fuckup who thought he was the smartest guy in the Warden Service. And look at all the good my attitude did me. This emotion no longer felt like self-pity, but, rather, an accurate assessment of my questionable fitness to do the job I'd been hired to do.

I'd just emerged from the Salvation Army trailer that had showed up to feed the assembled searchers, balancing a bowl of chili in one hand and a Styrofoam cup of coffee in the other, when my cell rang.

For some reason, I knew it was the sheriff. Rhine had spent a couple of foot-stomping, hand-rubbing hours on the scene before she'd decided to seek warmth back at her office.

"How's the search going?" she asked.

"We haven't found him yet, if that's what you're asking."

"There's a line of snow squalls moving through Bangor. You probably have another hour before they get here."

Even light snow would ground our chopper, meaning that unless the guys below the falls got lucky, we would be forced to suspend the search until conditions improved.

Rhine hadn't called to give me the weather report. "What can I do for you, Sheriff? I'm kind of busy."

"How well do you know Jamie Sewall's son?"

"Not very well. He's a weird little kid, as you saw for yourself."

I watched searchers in reflective vests milling in the parking lot. Steam rose from their open mouths and white coffee cups.

"Well, it seems he's run away," said the sheriff. "The sister, Tammi, called us, saying she was scared because Jamie hadn't come home. Given her brain injury, I asked DHHS to send a social worker to break the news about Jamie's arrest and assess the situation. I know Tammi's not competent to care for a child, so I figured DHHS might need to find temporary placement for them both."

If possible, the Department of Health and Human Services was even more widely disliked in Down East Maine than the Maine Warden Service. My fears about Jamie potentially forfeiting custody of both her sister and her son acquired a new intensity. Losing Lucas, especially, would be her worst nightmare.

"So what happened?"

"The social worker—her name is Magda Mueller and I've worked with her before, a real pro—shows up and the boy immediately freaks out. He won't listen to the aunt. Instead, he locks himself in the basement and won't come out. The aunt says there might be a gun down there, so Mueller does the smart thing and gets them both out of the building. I send an officer out to have a look—"

"Not Dunbar?"

"No," she said. "Corbett."

If anything, that choice seemed worse to me, given my misgivings about the chief deputy.

"So what happened next?"

"By the time Corbett got there, he found the bulkhead door open. He said there were new tracks leading from the basement off into the trees. He wanted to pursue, but I told him to stay put until I called you."

"You want me to go over there?"

"I have more confidence in your finding him. My guys aren't trained to look for a kid in the woods. Besides, you already have a relationship with the boy. Just remember, he may be armed."

"I need to ask Rivard."

"With the snow coming, he's about ready to suspend the search. He thinks you would be better off looking for the boy."

I felt like a prehistoric animal that had fallen into a tar pit. No matter how much I struggled, I couldn't extricate myself from the mess the Sewalls had created. "I need to stop by the jail first," I said.

The suspicion in Rhine's voice came through the receiver. "Why?"

"To talk with Jamie. Something tells me that she might know where Lucas went."

The opportunity to see her again was no small incentive, either.

32

From the outside, you might have mistaken the Washington County jail for a new building, but inside, the ceilings hung low and the air had the stuffy chill of a mausoleum. The brick walls were the color of curdled cream and showed signs of having been painted innumerable times for the sole purpose of keeping inmates busy. Men had died in this building, and it didn't take much of an imagination to sense their presence in the flickering lights and the sudden drafts that moved through the halls.

The grizzled captain who ran the jail met me at the door, along with a couple of slack-jawed guards who seemed to have nothing better to do. The sheriff had a meeting with the Maine Drug Enforcement Agency, the captain said in a tone that suggested the discussion would be an unpleasant event for everyone involved.

Jails tend to be loud, clanging places filled with shouts, echoes, and the slamming of metal doors. The guards made me secure my service weapon in a wall-mounted lockbox before they led me into the visitation room. The room smelled of disinfectant sprayed over every possible surface. A Plexiglas barrier running down the center of a table divided the inmates' side from the visitors'. There was an intercom-type contraption in the glass to speak through.

"No sign of Prester?" the captain said.

"Not yet."

"First the brother, now the sister." He gave me that familiar world-weary expression that all law-enforcement officers eventually adopt. "Quite the family, them Sewalls."

"Quite the family," I agreed.

A lock clicked loudly, and the door opened on the visitors' side of the barrier. A stout blond woman in a khaki uniform led Jamie into the room. She was wearing a jumpsuit the color of a moldering tangerine. The guard guided her, not ungently, into a chair facing me through the glass.

Jamie's eyes were threaded with veins, her skin looked bleached, and her hair was a rat's nest.

I recalled the seductive woman who had shown up at my motel door, the one with the soft curves who had curled against me in bed and confessed her desire to escape her depressing life for some tropical paradise. She was nearly unrecognizable as the suffering person seated across from me, and I was left to wonder what, if anything, had been real between us.

"Fancy meeting you here." Her voice sounded like she'd been gargling with sand.

"You look like you've had a hard night."

"Gee. Do you think?"

"If you'd needed a ride, you should have called me rather than driving drunk."

"I wasn't drunk."

"The trooper who arrested you says you were."

"I was buzzed."

Her hands were trembling—either from nervousness or withdrawal from substances unknown. I realized I could smell the alcohol on her breath through the holes in the glass.

"What about the Adderall the trooper found in your purse?" I asked. "Did that get in there by accident?"

"Those were Tammi's. She has a prescription. I picked them up for her at Rite Aid." She lifted her cleft chin and showed her teeth to the assembled deputies. "Can we have some privacy here?"

I nodded to give my consent, and the men filed out.

I motioned to the wall-mounted camera above my head. "They can still see us, you know."

"Just as long as I don't have to look into their stupid faces." She pushed a strand of greasy hair back over her ear. "You don't have to be such an asshole, you know? I didn't do anything to hurt you. You shouldn't treat me like I did."

"I'm sorry."

Her voice quavered. "Have you found Prester yet?"

"We're still looking."

"Let me know when you do, please."

I felt sorry for her in her intoxication and her grief and that pathetic jumpsuit, but I was still angry. "If you didn't want to talk with me, couldn't you have just gone to a meeting or called your sponsor last night?"

"Why? So she could talk me out of it? I *wanted* to get drunk. I *wanted* to get high. Is that so fucking hard to understand?"

I wasn't entirely sure where to begin. "Jamie, you're in serious trouble."

She began to blink back tears. "Don't you think I know that!"

"If you're found guilty and sent to prison, the state is going to remove Tammi and Lucas from your house."

"They can't do that!" Her voice broke as she spoke the words.

"They can, and they will." I needed to tell her that Lucas had run away, needed to find out where the boy might have gone, but one unanswered question kept pushing its way to the front of my brain. "If I'm going to help you," I said, "I need to know the truth about something."

She narrowed her eyes. "What?"

"I went to Wyman Hill last night, over in Township Nineteen. Do you remember how I told you I saw a snowmobile out on the Heath the night Randall was murdered? I know whose sled it was now."

She brought her hands together in a praying motion but remained silent.

I leaned forward. "Mitch was the one Prester and Randall were meeting on the afternoon of the blizzard, wasn't it? He was buying drugs from them."

She looked up suddenly. "That's not what happened."

"So tell me the truth."

"I can't."

"Do you want Prester to be remembered as a murderer? Is that what you want for your brother?"

"Mitch is Lucas's father."

"That won't stop me from taking him down."

"Mitch didn't kill Randall. I swear to God he didn't." Tears streamed down her face. "This is all my fault. Everything that happened is all my fault."

She had said these same words before, and I had assumed she meant it in the sense of bad karma plaguing her for past misdeeds. "What happened?"

She wasn't so stoned that she didn't give a glance at the wall-mounted camera. "Randall beat up Lucas. He knocked him to the ground and bruised the whole side of his face. I thought he might have broken his arm, too. I asked Prester to do something about it—be a man for once—but he wouldn't because he was too afraid of Randall. So I said, 'Couldn't you just lure him somewhere where Mitch could kick the shit out of him?' He knows karate, and if he took Randall by surprise . . . I just wanted Mitch to beat Randall up."

The medical examiner said that Cates had suffered a cracked sternum in the hours before his death. The injury had rendered him immobile, which was why Prester had been the one to seek help after their car got stuck. But what if Munro had lied to Jamie? What if he had returned to the stranded Grand Am later to finish the job?

"Do you know where Mitch is now?" I asked her.

"He wasn't at his house?"

"No." A door slammed shut down the hall, and I remembered why the sheriff had called me in the first place. "Is it possible he could be with Lucas?"

"Lucas is at home with Tammi."

"No, he isn't. Lucas ran away, Jamie."

"What are you saying?"

"The sheriff sent someone from DHHS to look in on Tammi and Lucas," I said. "When the social worker showed up, Lucas locked himself in the basement."

"He's afraid of the basement. There's something down there that scares him. He won't tell me what it is." She raised her fingers to her lips as if to chew on her nails but then stopped herself. "But you said he ran away. I don't understand."

"The sheriff decided to send one of her deputies over there, too, because she was concerned for everyone's safety. The deputy found tracks leading from the bulkhead into the forest behind your house."

"Deputy? Which deputy?"

"Chief Deputy Corbett"

"He's the one Randall used to talk about!"

"Talk about how?"

"I don't know—he just mentioned his name sometimes. Then he and Prester would laugh. Oh my God. Was he the guy who frisked me at the hospital? The blond guy with a red face?"

I didn't answer, but suddenly the Maine Drug Enforcement Agency's accusation that Rhine had a dirty cop in her department seemed less and less far-fetched. And to what lengths would a man like Corbett go to avoid exposure? Might he have killed Randall Cates and driven Prester Sewall to his death? Might he even harm Lucas if he suspected the boy knew the truth?

Jamie sat bolt upright in her chair. "You need to go over there, Mike! You need to make sure Lucas is safe!"

"I need to ask you some questions first."

"What kinds of questions?"

"First, would Lucas have access to a firearm? He told me he did."

"Prester had a twenty-two he used to shoot squirrels and wood-chucks. It was my dad's."

"Where did he keep it?"

"In the basement."

My heart sank. "Is it loaded? Does Lucas know how to fire it?"

"Prester took him out back to shoot cans one day when I was at work."

I pictured Lucas fleeing into the snowy woods. Was he afraid of Corbett, and that's why he fled? There was also the father to consider. I couldn't even begin to guess how Mitch Munro might fit into this particular puzzle, if he even did. Maybe the boy had decided to cross the Heath to reach his father's house.

"Does Lucas have some favorite place to hide—like a tree house or a cellar hole? Maybe a cave?"

"Prester used to have an old fort my dad built him in the woods. I think Lucas goes there sometimes."

"Can you tell me where it is?"

"I've never been there. He draws maps of the woods in his notebooks. There's a stack of them under his bed."

"What about friends?"

"My son doesn't have a friend in the world."

I wasn't sure I'd heard a sadder statement in my life, but she said it with such frankness, I knew it was the truth.

"You need to find him, Mike," she said. "Please!"

"That's my job," I said. "Finding lost kids is what I do."

It sounded like a boast, but I hadn't meant it that way. I wanted her to understand that on this one thing at least she could trust me. I was a Maine game warden, and I wouldn't rest until I found her child.

She pressed her hands flat against the Plexiglas. "I can't afford to lose him, too, Mike."

"I know."

"I'm sorry I've been so horrible. You don't deserve this shit. You're a sweet guy. You should find yourself a sweet girl."

Down the hall, another iron door slammed. "I don't want a sweet girl. I want you."

She wasn't sober, not by any means, but when she spoke again, her voice was clear and even. "No, you don't. You want some fantasy version of me. You want the employee of the fucking month." She gestured at her prison jumpsuit. "*This* is the real me. It always has been and always will be."

"I don't believe that."

"That's what makes you so sweet. Good-bye, Mike. Please let me know when you find Lucas."

I nodded, unable to muster a full sentence. I knocked on the door, and one of the guards let me out. Then I went to retrieve my service weapon from the lockbox. When I stepped outside, there was a dusting of snow on my patrol truck.

33

I needed to tell the state police about Mitch Munro so that they could bring the snowmobiler in for questioning, at the very least. The medical examiner had found evidence of a cracked sternum. The injury had been inflicted hours before Cates died. Circumstantial evidence pointed to Munro as the attacker. The problem was Jamie. It was doubtful she would repeat the story she'd told me to a courtroom—not unless she was allowed to retain custody of her sister and son.

As I drove through the falling darkness, I wondered whether I could help broker a deal between Jamie and the prosecutors. If she could deliver Munro, would that be enough to waive the drunk-driving and possession charges? Might she be permitted by the DHHS to keep Lucas?

Of course I would have to find the boy first. I needed to focus on the challenge at hand before I worried about convincing detectives and prosecutors to make deals they would have zero interest in making.

When I arrived at the Sewall house, I found a Volvo V70 station wagon parked in the shoveled section of the dooryard. Beside it was the familiar Ford Interceptor I'd first seen outside the Sprague house so many nights ago: Chief Deputy Corbett's cruiser.

A woman leapt out of the Volvo as if it had burst into flames. "What took you so long?" she said.

The social worker, Magda Mueller, had a wide, flat face and

tightly curled red hair that reminded me of the coats of certain exotic breeds of water dogs. Her charcoal-colored coat hung to her knees, and I saw that she was wearing faded blue jeans and no-nonsense snow boots.

"I stopped by the jail to get some information from the mother."

"Like what?"

"Whether the boy has access to a loaded firearm." I spotted Tammi Sewall sitting meekly in the Volvo's passenger seat, listening to Inca music on the stereo. She gave me a broad smile and a friendly wave, as if she had no idea how dire her family's situation was. "Where's Chief Deputy Corbett?" I asked.

"He said he was going to scope things out."

"He's inside the building?"

"As far as I know. He might have gone out the basement door if he decided to pursue the boy into the woods."

The last thing I needed was Corbett blundering around, disturbing Lucas's footprints. The snow was drifting down at a steady clip. I was going to have a devil of a time tracking the boy as dusk fell.

"Can you tell me what happened?"

"I arrived to check on the aunt and the boy. The aunt let us into the house, but when the boy found out I worked for DHHS, he became agitated. He ran down into the basement while I was trying to deal with the disabled woman."

"You didn't follow him?"

She crossed her arms. "I have a policy of not chasing troubled kids into dark holes."

I couldn't question her wisdom there. "So you evacuated Tammi from the building and called the sheriff?"

"The next thing I knew, Corbett showed up. He told me to wait outside here while he checked the premises. A little later, he came out and said there were tracks heading off through the backyard into the woods. I called the sheriff, and she told me a game warden was on the way. That was, like, an hour ago."

I lowered my voice. "What are you going to do with Tammi?"

"There's a foster-care home in Lubec where she can stay for a few days."

"And the boy?"

"Corbett says the father is a convicted felon, which isn't ideal. I know a family in Calais that will take him temporarily."

"You mean you're going to split up Tammi and Lucas?"

"Just for the time being. The department will need to do an assessment. Maybe there's some extended family we can place them with. That's usually preferable to a foster situation or a group home."

"What happens when the mother gets out of jail?"

"Shouldn't you be more worried about finding the kid? I'm freezing my ass off out here."

I took her point.

The front door of the house was ajar. A wedge of light streamed through the crack. I kicked snow off my boots and pushed the door open. "Corbett? It's Bowditch." My words seemed to bounce off the entryway's walls.

There was no reply.

The light in the foyer was burning, but the other rooms were dark. The home had seemed so warm and welcoming the first time I'd visited. Now a chill was blowing through some open door or window, and the faint odor of Jamie's cigarettes hung in the air.

It troubled me how the chief deputy kept appearing around the Sewalls. I didn't want to feel suspicious and unsafe, but my hand kept drifting down to my sidearm.

The floor creaked beneath my feet. "Corbett?"

The answer came from above my head. "Up here."

There was a single narrow staircase leading up to the second floor. The house was old and, like many nineteenth-century New England farmhouses, seemed to have been built for a race of ascetic pygmies. I had to duck my head to keep from knocking my brow against an oak beam.

There were three small bedrooms and a single bath on the second floor. The first room was Jamie's. It had a queen-size mattress beneath a quilt that looked like a family heirloom. The walls had been freshly painted—a soothing lavender—and there was a vase of grocery-store flowers on the bureau, but there were telltale signs of disarrangement if you looked closely. The carnations were beginning to wilt, and the bed was unmade. I hung in the doorway for a moment, breathing in the familiar smell of her perfume and feeling a pang at the thought that I would never share this bed with her.

I found Corbett in the next room, sitting on Prester's Sewall's narrow bed. In his hands he was holding a quart-size Ziploc bag filled with dried herbs. His high, scarlet forehead was furrowed, but the turn of his lips suggested amusement.

"What have you got there?" I asked.

"It ain't oregano," said Corbett.

Unlike Jamie's, this room was a mess. It seemed more like the sanctuary of a hormone-crazed teenager than that of a man in his mid-twenties. Posters showing women in bikinis, cupping their heavy naked breasts in their hands, beckoned from the walls. Empty cans of Milwaukee's Best, a plate with congealed grease in the shape of a pizza slice, a pile of dirty jeans and undershirts on a chair—these were the dead man's personal effects, all that he had left behind.

"So you just found that lying in the open?" I asked, half wondering if he'd planted the pot for reasons I couldn't guess at the moment.

"Exigent circumstances," he said. "I was looking for the boy."

"In Prester's bureau?"

"Kid could have been hiding anywhere."

"Jesus, Corbett. The guy's already dead. What do you plan on doing, busting his corpse for intent to distribute?"

"No, but I'm sure the sheriff is going to have some pointed questions for the sister."

"This is her brother's room!"

"But it's her house."

I couldn't bring myself to argue with him. The entire situation was more than I could wrap my head around. "I take it you didn't find Lucas."

Corbett tilted his razor-burned chin toward the window. "His footprints lead off into the trees. Unless the snow picks up, you shouldn't have any trouble following them."

I exhaled loudly, trying to dispel the depression from my soul. "I need to look in his room first."

"Why? What for?"

I didn't answer. Lucas's room was at the end of the hall. It was nearly as dirty as his uncle's, although not quite, thanks to the ministrations of his mother, no doubt. The poster on his wall showed Bruce Lee flexing every muscle in his fat-free body. Books were scattered everywhere: detective novels and comics, science fiction and strange histories of Stonehenge and the Loch Ness monster.

I lifted the bedspread from the floor and discovered the stash of notebooks his mother had mentioned. There were at least a dozen of various colors and styles: Some were big and spiral-bound; others reminded me of old college exam booklets. I recognized the most recent notebook immediately, with its lemon cover and violent illustrations.

Corbett stood in the doorway. "What are you looking for?"

I didn't feel like explaining myself. Jamie had mentioned that her son wrote constantly in his notebooks and that if he had a secret hideout, I might find evidence inside. Standing over his bed, I read the kid's most recent entry. It was dated that morning:

Mom never came home for the second night in a row!
  It's all my fault.
  I can't believe Uncle Prester is DEAD.
  What if they never find his body?
  What if Ma never comes home AT ALL?
  What if the social lady takes Tammi to some mental home and Dad decides he don't want me to come live with hiim?
  I will be all ALONE!

I hadn't realized that the notebook contained Lucas's diary. When I had looked at it before, I'd focused only on the disturbing drawings and assumed the rest were imaginary stories or schoolwork. Now I understood that the odd little boy had been keeping a journal, and I wondered if some of the answers I was seeking—about Jamie and Mitch, Randall and Prester—might be found inside. I'd had this notebook in my possession for days without realizing what it was.

"What is that?" Corbett asked, showing more interest than usual.

"The kid's diary," I said. "I am hoping it will lead me to him."

I leafed through the pages and happened on a map that showed what looked like the forest behind the house. It was stylishly rendered—Lucas had a talent for drawing—and showed a few of landmarks linked by a single dotted line that must have been a trail. The path crossed a stream labeled "Injun Brook" and detoured around a tangle of fallen trees besides which he'd scrawled "Widow-makers." It ended at a cartoonish-looking building he called "Fort Knox."

I wasn't certain if the map was purely fanciful or whether it would be of help locating the boy, but I decided to take the note-

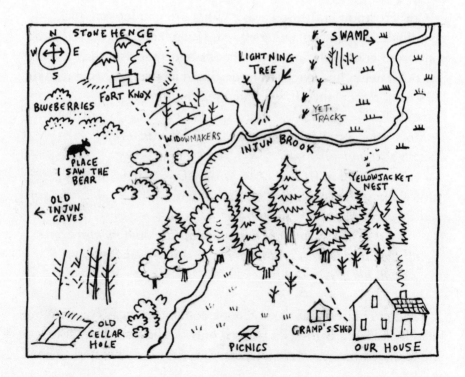

book with me in case I wanted to refer to it again during the search. I spent a moment inspecting the strange images inked on the cover— the demonic owl, the feathered woman—and shook my head sadly. Lucas, I decided, was a deeply troubled kid, and why shouldn't he be, an intelligent and imaginative child growing up in a rancid drug den?

"What kind of diary does a twelve-year-old keep? Is it like a re-cord of how many times he jerks off in a day?" Corbett's tone was light, but I could sense that he wanted to have a look for himself.

I unbuttoned my shirt and tucked the notebook against my bal-listic vest. It seemed the only way to carry it securely.

I clicked off the light and went downstairs. Corbett took the hint and followed.

In the entryway, I nearly had a heart attack when the social worker stepped through the front door.

"I take it you haven't found him yet," she said.

"I thought you were going to wait outside."

"I got tired of sitting in the car."

"It would be better if you did," said Corbett.

Snow had accumulated atop her hair, as if someone had sprin-kled her with powdered sugar. "Do you think the boy is danger-ous?"

"If he's scared, he might be dangerous," I said.

"Look," she said. "I can't keep the engine running, or I'm going to run out of gas. I'm going to take Tammi over to Lubec to that foster home I mentioned. I can't just wait around all evening for you to find the boy. Why are you looking in the house? I thought the kid ran off into the woods."

"I want to have a look in the basement," I said.

"Can't you just follow his tracks? I thought you game wardens were supposed to be expert trackers."

"I'm just gathering some information." I didn't feel like explain-ing my search techniques to this woman, or to Corbett, for that matter. "When I find Lucas, what would you like me to do?"

"If he's been outside this whole time, take him to the hospital.

The poor kid could have frostbite or hypothermia. Isn't a lost kid supposed to be like a super high-level priority?"

"There's a difference between lost and hiding," I said.

"Hiding from what?" Corbett asked.

I focused on the social worker. "If you give me your phone number, I'll call you when I find him. To be on the safe side, I'll take him to the hospital. Please just take care of Tammi."

Mueller gave me her cell number. Muttering to herself, she wandered outside.

Standing at the mudroom door, I took a look at the backyard. In the twilight, the snow outside appeared a luminous blue. I could just make out the footprints staggering away into a hedgelike row of small pines that were about the size of Christmas trees. Beyond it were taller evergreens and birches. I would need my snowshoes, I decided.

"I've got to agree with the lady," said Corbett. "You don't seem like you're in much of hurry."

"I know this kid," I said. "He's not the type to go running off in a panic. I have a good idea where he is from the map he made in his notebook. What I don't know is whether he took his grandfather's rifle with him. Now, if you'll excuse me for a second, I'm going to look in the basement."

"I'll go with you."

"If you need something to do, call the sheriff and tell her about that pot you found. I'm sure that'll make her day. You certainly have a nose for the stuff. The psychic connection you have with these drug dealers is uncanny. It defies all belief."

Corbett tightened his mouth, not quite sure what to make of my veiled accusation. The truth was that I would never be able to prove that the chief deputy had been on the take from Randall Cates. Everyone who could testify to that effect was conveniently deceased.

The cellar was pitch-black, and the light switch didn't seem to do anything when I gave it a try. Probably there was some sort of naked bulb with a pull cord down there. I trained my flashlight on the steps and carefully descended.

The air felt damp but not as cold somehow. I crouched down and shined the light around the corners of the room. There were boxes everywhere, plus a tool bench, a dusty old television, a girl's bicycle, a brace of canoe paddles—the usual detritus of a family's life. An ancient oil tank squatted against the fieldstone wall, an open box of rat poison beside it.

I couldn't stand up without knocking my head against a pine rafter or getting a faceful of cobwebs. Hunched forward slightly, I picked my way through the junk to have a look at the door that opened onto the bulkhead steps. On the dirt floor there was a small drift of snow that must have tumbled in when Lucas turned the doorknob and took off into the wild.

The next question was whether he had taken his dead grandfather's .22 with him. Dusty tools hung from a Peg-Board over a wooden workbench. I saw a hammer, various wrenches, an electric drill—all dusty, and some showing signs of rust—and I had the feeling somehow that none of these tools had been used since the death of the Sewall parents.

I saw an antique advertisement hanging on the mossy fieldstone wall in the corner above the workbench. Someone must have clipped it from an old magazine and stuck it inside a picture frame. It showed an attractive woman in a strange white outfit made of feathers. She wore a sort of cowl that hid her hair from view, and she had her finger extended straight at the viewer, in imitation of the famous recruiting poster featuring Uncle Sam. Her eyes were heavily made up in 1960s fashion, but there was nothing alluring, or even friendly, about them in the least. Beneath her picture, the poster said I WANT YOU FOR THE DIPLOMAT CORPS.

Below the command, or the threat, or whatever it was, was some explanatory fine print about the corps, along with a picture of an open cigar box.

It was an ad for White Owl cigars.

The scary drawings on the covers of Lucas's notebook made a certain sense now. He'd been terrified of this poster above his dead grandfather's tool bench. The image had entered into his nightmares in that inexplicable way that things do when you are a child—or an adult.

"You and Lucas have a lot in common," Jamie had said. I'd rejected the suggestion as absurd at the time, but now I could begin to understand what she'd meant.

My moment of empathy didn't last long. It ended the second my flashlight beam picked out the open box of Winchester .22 long-rifle ammunition on the pallet. Lucas Sewall was armed.

34

When a child disappears in the forest in the winter, especially after dark, you don't want to waste time, since hypothermia can take hold so quickly. But my sixth sense told me Lucas Sewall was in no immediate danger. As I'd said to the social worker, there is a difference between lost and hiding.

"His mother said he has a tree fort about half a mile from here," I told Corbett as we returned to our vehicles. I needed a pair of snowshoes if I was going to wade out into that snowy forest. "There's a map of it in his diary. I think that's where he went."

"What else is in that diary?"

"Kid stuff," I said.

The chief deputy raised the collar on his parka against the chill. "I want to go with you."

The last thing I needed was a man I didn't trust trailing after me through snowdrifts and deepening shadows. "Do you have snowshoes in your vehicle?"

"No."

"Then you'll just slow me down."

"The kid doesn't have them, either."

"Do me a favor," I said, "and just wait here until I get back. Call the sheriff for me and ask her if anyone's questioned Mitch Munro about what he was doing on the Heath the night Cates was murdered."

Corbett gave me a sad shake of the head. "You won't let that one go, will you?"

"Call it a character defect," I said. "Excuse me for a minute. I've got to talk to my sergeant."

Rivard sounded dog-tired on the phone, but he would have mobilized the entire division if I had requested assistance. I had a hard time dissuading him from doing so, in fact. That's the standard operating procedure for a child who goes missing on a snowy evening.

"I know where the kid is," I said with confidence I had no right to feel. "His mom told me he has a tree fort behind the house. That's where his trail goes. I just need to get in there and bring him back. It'll just take a few minutes." I withheld the tidbit that the kid I was chasing was armed with a .22 rifle.

"I take it Prester never washed up," I said.

"I would have notified you if he had." His mouth sounded dry from the cold air and chewing tobacco.

"What time are we getting started again with the search?"

"That depends on this snow. The forecast calls for it to end just after dark."

I flicked my wipers to push the accumulating snow off my windshield. "It's still snowing here."

"It's still snowing everywhere."

Then he hung up.

I found a halogen headlamp in the glove compartment and snugged it down over my baseball cap so that the light would follow my eyes whenever I turned my head. I removed my snowshoes from the bed of my pickup and strapped the bindings to my boots. The shoes had been fashioned out of white ash and rawhide by a Penobscot Indian craftsman up in Old Town. The modified bear-paw design was oblong in shape, not too long, which made the pair ideal for working in dense cover.

Corbett inspected me from head to foot. "What do you plan on doing if you find him?"

"Mueller wants me to take him into the hospital to get checked out for frostbite and hypothermia. After that, I don't know. I guess she'll hand him over to a foster family until his mom gets out of jail."

"It can't be any worse than that house."

I was in no mood to debate. For all of Jamie's problems—her addictions and self-loathing—I knew she tried to be a good mother. She *was* a good mother, albeit in ways the bureaucrats at the Department of Health and Human Services would never believe. Lucas was an odd little specimen, but she clearly doted on him and encouraged his preoccupation with writing. Jamie was right to worry that her son might slip from her grip now and tumble into the maw of the state.

I knew people like Magda Mueller did important work. They rescued innocent children from nightmarish situations of abuse and neglect. I also knew that certain bureaucrats considered being poor to be a form of child abuse, no matter how desperately the parents wanted something better for their children. In my experience, multigenerational poverty was a kind of inheritance, impervious to state mandates or meddling, as impossible to change as the color of one's eyes. My mom had taken advantage of opportunities in the classroom to get her GED and associate's degree—although mostly she owed her salvation to being beautiful enough to eventually marry a rich man. Then again, she hadn't fallen into addiction the way Jamie Sewall had.

"See you in a few," I told Corbett.

"Happy trails," he replied.

I made my way around the house to the open bulkhead. Snow had tumbled down the concrete steps leading to the basement door. In the blue-white light of my headlamp, I saw the boy's trail leading across the open yard, past a wood and tar-paper shed that was listing to the right, as if pushed that way by the wind. The light snow had begun to fill in the tracks, but I could see from the jagged treads that Lucas was wearing sneakers.

I removed the notebook from inside my shirt and searched for the map I'd seen earlier. There were no distances marked, but if I remained still, I could hear moving water ahead, so I knew "Injun Brook" wasn't far.

I tucked the notebook against my chest and followed the tracks. The trail led into a copse of second-growth birch trees that were about as thick around as baseball bats. Snowshoe hares had nibbled the low-hanging buds.

Beyond the shed, the hill sloped steadily, and I could tell from Lucas's treads—deeper in the heels than in the toes—that he had descended at breakneck speed, nearly losing his balance a couple of times. He'd snapped a dead branch off a decaying tree at one point to keep from falling. I angled my snowshoes to sidestep my way down after him.

The trees grew taller as I approached the hidden stream: a mixed grove of white pines, yellow birches, and northern white cedar. The evergreen boughs had blocked the snow, making it easier to read the trail. The brook at the bottom was about ten feet wide at its narrowest point. It was a gurgling little creek, ice-crusted along the edges, with water that looked like flowing ink in the light of my headlamp and smelled, very faintly—because cold dulls the sense of smell—of the rotting pine needles clumped along the streambed.

Lucas had tried hopping his way across from one rock to the next, but the dislodged snow on one of the boulders showed where he'd lost his footing. His feet would be wet now, which increased the likelihood of frostbite. I needed to find him quickly, before his feet froze.

My snowshoes weren't made for jumping, so I had to untie them and prop them over my shoulder as I waded across. My boots were waterproof, but the iciness of the creek pierced the leather uppers like repeated jabs from a needle.

When I reached the far side, I shined the lamp along the stream, looking for the point where Lucas had continued on, but I found no other tracks. It took me a few seconds to understand what I was seeing—or rather, what I *wasn't* seeing—and then I laughed out loud. The boy had used the stream to disguise his passage. He had waded either up- or downstream.

Upstream, I guessed, and I was correct, although not in the way I'd expected. I rediscovered Lucas's trail, but it was now on the opposite side of the bank. It looped back toward his house, then stopped suddenly halfway up the hill. You might almost have concluded that a passing UFO had teleported him from the ground into space.

I knelt down, and again I started smiling at my own stupidity. I'd been in such a rush, I hadn't noticed what should have been plainly obvious to even a rookie warden: Lucas had retraced his steps. The boy had walked backward in his own tracks down to the creek.

This kid is really clever, I said to myself. I'd better read *Northwest Passage* again.

I located the tracks again on the far side of the brook, even farther upstream. As I snowshoed my way up the bank, I came across a spectacular pine that had been blasted apart; the bark was deeply scarred, torn open to the heartwood down the length of the trunk. Lucas's map, I remembered, included a "Lightning Tree." I expected this was it.

According to the notebook, the boy's fort should have been nearby. I decided to remove my snowshoes to make myself more agile, even if it meant that I would flounder in the deep drifts. I tied the laces together and draped the knot across my left shoulder.

My headlamp had a green lens that I could snap over the bulb. The green light had been designed to protect a hunter or fisherman's night vision, so that if you switched it off suddenly, you wouldn't be left completely blind. The lens gave an eerie cast to the trail in the snow.

The footprints dived headfirst into a dense mass of deadfall. The boy was leading me through his own private obstacle course. Fallen and half-fallen trees now formed a barrier to my passage. I peered under the first widowmaker and considered dropping down on my hands and knees to follow, but then I thought better of risking my neck by placing it under a heavy, spiked trunk. I would have to go around, I decided, until I regained his trail.

I crept clockwise around the blowdowns, pushing my way through some low evergreens, which gave me a faceful of snow when the boughs sprang back. It was slow going without the snowshoes. Each step had me sinking down to my knees, if not my thighs.

I stopped several times to listen, but the only sound was the wind rustling through the treetops.

Eventually I located Lucas's path again. The clues to his ordeal showed in the snow. After wriggling through the blowdowns, he'd scrambled on his forearms and knees up out of a hollow beneath a broken tree. I noticed a wet green dot on the snow. It was a drop of blood turned the color of seaweed by the fairy light. The boy had knocked his head or scraped a limb against one of those cruel spikes. So now he was wet and injured, as well as armed.

The wind shifted, and I smelled wood smoke. There was just a hint of bitterness on the air before it drifted away. I moved cautiously upwind, noting that the prints were headed in the same direction, feeling certain that Lucas had lit a campfire. Glancing ahead, I saw a snowy knoll where two huge boulders, bigger than bulldozers, had been dropped by a passing glacier. At the foot of one was a flickering yellow light.

I shut off the headlamp and waited for my pupils to expand. As I drew closer, the boulders gained gigantic proportions. They reminded me of ancient monoliths from the barrow downs of England. At their base, I could make out a boxy shadow wedged in the crack between the glacial erratics. The campfire light leaked out from between the planks, and a spiral of pine-flavored smoke—light gray against the darker gray of the evening—corkscrewed up into the sky.

Lucas was inside.

The question was how to pry him out. He had nowhere to run. The fort was pressed tightly into the vee formed by the leaning rocks. The structure seemed to be about the size of an ice-fishing shack, turned on its side and reinforced with plywood and Typar siding.

Then I remembered the backtracking footprints and the maze of deadfall, and I recalled something Jamie had told me about her son: "Lucas loves puzzles and riddles and secret codes." On a hunch, I decided to creep around the boulders and have a look at them from behind.

In the nearly pitch-darkness, I almost speared my eye on a sharp branch. Every sound I made seemed amplified to my ears. I worried that my awkward movement through the snow might alert him to my presence.

After a while I came through the birch saplings and the hedge of cedars on the far side of the rise. As I had expected, there was a receding shadow between the boulders: the fort's secret back door. I moved to one side of the opening and flattened myself against the cold granite.

I lifted my snowshoes gently off my shoulder and pressed them together in my left hand. Then, with all my strength, I hurled them up over the tops of the boulders. I heard the wood frames clatter off something—maybe the rock, maybe the fort—and then a hurried movement that reminded me of a squirrel in an attic.

Faster than I would have dreamed, a rifle emerged from the crack between the two boulders beside me. As soon as I saw it, I grabbed the barrel and gave it a yank, dragging the boy out from the hole. He sprawled forward, landing on his scrawny chest. His glasses fell into the snow and disappeared beneath the surface powder. Half blind, he flipped himself over, waving his arms and kicking out his legs and screaming something unintelligible. It might have been a plea for mercy.

"Relax, Lucas," I said. "No one's going to hurt you."

But he kept screaming.

35

Once I had gotten him to stop howling, I unloaded the .22 and put the cartridges in my pocket. Then I flicked on my headlamp and helped him dig for his Coke-bottle glasses. He rubbed the lenses with his thumbs before he put them on again. He blinked at me through the wet plastic, blinded by the halogen glow emanating from my forehead.

"Lucas, why did you run off like that?"

"That lady was going to confiscate me."

Where did he come up with that word? I wondered. "She was just going to take care of you until your mom comes homes."

"That lady told Tammi that Ma's in jail."

I considered my response. "That's right. She is in jail."

"What did she do?"

I felt very reluctant to offer him any information. It wasn't just my usual uneasiness communicating with children; there were legal issues involved. I figured my best bet would be to hand him over to the DHHS woman before I said something that would get me into trouble in Augusta. "She drove a car when she shouldn't have."

"How long is she going to be there?"

"That's for the judge to decide."

I lifted the .22 by the sling. It was attached to the barrel and screwed into the wooden stock. "You shouldn't be playing with firearms, Lucas. You could have shot yourself—or me."

"I know what I'm doing."

"Have you taken a gun safety course?"

"No."

"Well, you shouldn't touch this rifle again until you've had some instruction in how to use it safely."

"That's my grandpa's gun. I inherited it."

The boy was dressed in a camo green sweatshirt and wet jeans. He wasn't wearing a coat, gloves, or a hat. All at once he started to shiver.

"Where did you cut yourself?" I asked. "I saw blood on the snow."

He pressed a hand to his hairline, beneath a long, loose bang. "It ain't nothing."

"Let me have a look." I reached out my hand, but he recoiled from my touch. "Stand still."

I lifted the flap of wet hair. There was a cut there, but it was nothing worse than the kind of scrape that kids got on the playground every day.

"Do I need stitches?" he asked.

"Just a Band-Aid. But I'm thinking a doctor should have a look at you anyway."

He repositioned his glasses on the bridge of his nose. "What for?"

"Well, your feet are wet, so you might be getting frostbite in your toes."

"Are they going to amputate?"

"I highly doubt it. Let's get you back to the house and into some dry clothes." The smell of smoke drifted past. "First, though, we need to put out that fire."

We circled the two boulders. I made Lucas walk in front in case he decided to take off again, but in truth, he didn't look like he had the energy. I found my snowshoes on the tar-paper roof of the fort. As I inspected the structure, I realized that it was indeed an old ice-fishing shack that someone had remodeled into a boy's playhouse.

Smoke billowed out through the plywood door when I gave it a tug. Inside, there was a hibachi grill under a piece of PVC piping that angled through the side wall. Lucas had lighted a small fire in the grill out of broken twigs, birch bark, and wadded newspaper. I was surprised he hadn't expired from carbon monoxide poisoning, but I decided that I had already given him enough lectures.

There were stacks of water-warped paperbacks in one corner—the Conan books and Stephen King—and a moldy sleeping bag. It reminded me of a fort I had built the year we'd lived in North Anson, before my mom and dad split up that last time. I decorated it with the skulls of animals—raccoons and crows—I'd scavenged from the leaf litter. Every night I'd begged my parents to let me sleep out, where I would read myself to sleep by candlelight, until finally the snow began to fall and my mother decided that I might freeze to death.

I found an empty Maxwell House coffee can and told Lucas to fill it with snow. When I dumped it on the fire, a puff of steam exploded into the air, followed by a sizzling sound. I used a stick to stir the coals until they were cold and damp enough to touch with my bare hand. Then I backed out of the sideways shack.

"Who built this fort?" I asked.

"Me."

"It's very impressive."

"My grandpa helped a little."

I bent down to strap on my showshoes again.

Lucas watched me with fascination. "How did you find me?" he asked.

"It's my job to find people in the woods. You were challenging to track, though. It was very clever how you used the stream to disguise your direction, and you almost fooled me backtracking in your own footprints. You would have confused lots of people who aren't professional trackers like me."

He grinned, almost literally from ear to ear. The expression made him look even more than usual like a species of large-mouthed amphibian. "Thanks!"

"You're welcome." I straightened up and repositioned the sling across my chest. The leather pressed against my hidden ballistic vest.

"Are you sure you ain't a ranger?" he asked.

* * *

As is usually the case, the return journey seemed shorter because I knew where I was going this time and didn't need to scout for tracks.

I held Lucas's hand going across the stream again. He pouted and told me he could do it on his own, but I distrusted the footing and grabbed his wrist to steady his balance on the snow-slick rocks. As soon as we were across, he shook me loose and started fiercely up the hill.

Corbett's cruiser was gone. I checked my pager and cell phone but there were no messages. His unexpected absence unnerved me.

We entered the house through the basement. I wanted to return the rifle to its place above the tool bench, but Lucas hung back, shivering. It wasn't until I spotted the framed White Owl advertisement that I remembered his strange phobia about the feathered woman. He went leaping up the stairs as soon as I gave him leave to do so.

I followed him up to the bathroom so I could have a look at the scrape on his forehead under the 100-watt lightbulb. I soaked a wad of toilet tissue in hydrogen peroxide and blotted the wound. Lucas squirmed and moaned as if being tortured while the disinfectant bubbled down his brow.

I sat him down on the edge of the bathtub and untied his wet sneakers. His feet were as pale as thin-skinned subterranean animals that lived in total darkness. None of his toes or fingers were blue, which was a healthy sign, but he complained of sharp pain when I tried to massage blood back into the epidermis.

"Ouch! Ouch!"

"I'm sorry," I said.

"I don't like people touching me."

"This is not the highlight of my evening, either."

I found dry clothes for him in his bureau and let him change in private. While he was getting dressed, I put a phone call into the Washington County jail and asked to speak to the matron on duty. I waited a long time for one to be fetched, wondering whether Lucas might have something problematic hidden inside his bedroom, a bazooka or crossbow or God only knew what.

"Yeah?" said a woman with a deep voice.

"This is Warden Bowditch," I said. "I was in there earlier tonight. The sheriff wanted me to speak with Jamie Sewall. Can you give her a message for me?"

"I'm not supposed to do stuff like that."

"Just tell her I found her son and that he's safe."

"I'm not supposed to do stuff like that."

"Her son ran away. She's been worrying that he might have fallen through the ice. Imagine if it was your child."

"I don't have kids." She fell silent, and I worried we'd lost the connection, but then she added, "OK. I'll let her know."

My next call was to the social worker, Magda Mueller.

"This is Warden Bowditch," I said. "I wanted to let you know that I found Lucas Sewall."

"How is he?"

"Cold but otherwise fine, I think. He got a cut on his forehead from running into a tree branch, and his feet showed signs of frost-nip, but they seem better now that he's warmed up a bit."

"You should take him to the ER as a precautionary measure. How about I meet you at the Calais Regional Hospital?"

The city of Calais, on the Canadian border, was nearly an hour's drive away. "Why not Machias?"

"The foster family lives in Calais."

I heard the bedroom door open. When I spoke again into the phone, I dropped my voice. "What's going to happen to him now?"

"I've been trying to reach the father all evening, but there's been no answer. I have questions about placing the boy with him even temporarily, based on his criminal record, but I'm required to exercise due diligence. Unless I can track down a family member who isn't incarcerated, Lucas will stay with a foster family until a judge can schedule a hearing. We have seventy-two hours."

"What if his mother is still in jail at the time of the hearing?" Given the drug charges against her, it didn't seem likely she'd get out in time.

"I'd rather not speculate on the outcome."

Lucas emerged from his bedroom, shoulders sagging. He had

made a clumsy attempt at combing his own hair. He looked tired and sad and resigned to his unhappy fate.

"Should I pack a bag for him?" I asked Mueller.

"That would be a good idea."

After we hung up, I saw that I'd received two missed calls from Doc Larrabee. He'd tried to reach me while I'd been on the line with the jail matron and then again while I was speaking with the DHHS caseworker. Neither time had he left a voice mail. Maybe he'd had a change of heart and could testify to having seen Mitch Munro's sled on the Heath. I thought about how curt and unhelpful he'd been the last time we'd spoken—letting me freeze on the doorstep—and decided to ignore him for the moment.

"Where's Tammi?" Lucas asked.

"That woman who was here before took her to stay at a guest-house until your mom gets home." It felt like a lie to say the words aloud.

"So she got 'confiscated,' too."

"It's just temporary," I said. "Do you have a gym bag or back-pack?"

"What for?"

"We need to take along some socks and clean underwear for the trip."

"Where are we going?"

"First, I'm going to take you to a hospital so a doctor can make sure your fingers and toes are OK, and then I'll take you someplace where you can spend the night."

His eyes widened behind the plastic glasses. "Am I going to jail?"

"Of course not," I said.

"Why can't we just stay here? I thought you were Ma's new boy-friend."

I was no longer sure what I was, but I was fairly certain it wasn't Jamie Sewall's boyfriend. Before I could formulate an answer suit-able for a twelve-year-old, my phone vibrated in its belt holster. It was Doc Larrabee calling for a third time. I let it go to voice mail. Once again, he chose not to leave a message.

36

I waited until we were on the road to give Lucas his notebook. He snatched it out of my hand without so much as a thank-you.

"Did you read it?"

I decided to tell a fib. "Why would I?"

"You better not have."

The plow hadn't passed along this stretch of winding country road in hours. As I crested hills and rounded curves, heading toward Route 277, I felt the tires slide on the new coating of snow. I had a vision of my pickup bouncing like a pinball from one snowbank to another if I didn't watch my speed.

Lucas began rummaging around the console between the front seats. "Do you got a pen?"

The inside of my truck cab was as dimly lit as a dive bar. "We can't drive with the overhead light on."

"Why not?"

"It makes it harder for me to see the road, and besides, it's against the law."

"That's a stupid law," he said. "Do you got a pen anyway?"

I removed the ballpoint I kept in my uniform pocket. "What are you going to do, write in the dark?"

He produced a child-sized headlamp from his overstuffed backpack. He yanked it down over his stocking cap and switched on the beam. It needed new batteries, but the grayish illumination was enough for him to begin scribbling.

His empty stomach made a liquid gurgling noise, like water being pulled down a drain.

"If you're hungry," I said, "there's a Ziploc bag with some beef jerky in that pack basket."

"Is it made out of bear meat?"

"No."

"Moose meat?"

"No, it's just regular meat. I bought it at a gas station."

"I don't like regular jerky."

"What do you think Rogers's Rangers used to eat?"

Lucas swung around toward me, and I was nearly blinded by his headlamp. "You did read my notebook!"

I raised my elbow to shield my eyes. "Just the part about the Ranger Code."

"That's how you found my fort, You followed the map that I drew." His voice was heavy with disappointment, as if using a map was cheating. A real ranger would rely on footprints alone.

I had been feeling that I was gaining Lucas's trust, but now I saw how fragile the bond between us was. Not that I could blame him for being suspicious, given the men he'd grown up around.

I decided to make a fresh attempt at conversation. "My dad was a real-life army ranger, just like the men in *Northwest Passage*. He fought in the Vietnam War. That's near China."

"I know where Vietnam is," he said.

The police radio crackled and popped. The dispatcher wanted to know my location. "Twenty-two fifty-eight," I said into the mic, giving my call number. "I'm ten-twenty on the New County Road."

There was some additional chatter, and I heard Corbett identify himself. It sounded as if he was on the scene of a fender bender near Bog Pond. At least his whereabouts were accounted for.

I waited for Dispatch to come back: "Twenty-two fifty-eight, disregard."

A false alarm, evidently. It happened from time to time.

"Speaking of rangers," I said, "here's something you might find interesting. In Vietnam, the rangers called the jungle 'Indian Country.' "

"Why?"

"Because it was the area controlled by the enemy."

"Were there Indians living there?'

"No. It was a metaphor. Do you know what a metaphor is?"

He crossed his scrawny arms over his chest and slumped as far away from me as he could into the shadows. "It's a word that don't mean what you think it means."

I decided not to quibble with his definition.

Once I dropped Lucas with the social worker, there was a chance I might never see him again. If his mother was sentenced to prison and his father was denied custody, if the aunt vanished into some state custodial institution in Bangor or Augusta, this would be our last conversation, and I'd barely gotten to know him at all. It seemed one more sad thing dropped onto a mountainous pile of sad things.

"Lucas, why did you steal my binoculars before?"

"I didn't mean to."

"You're telling me that you accidentally stole them?"

"I was just looking at them. I put them on my neck and I forgot to take them off. That's what happened. If you don't believe me, too bad."

"I don't believe you," I said. "And a judge wouldn't believe you, either."

He sat up abruptly. "You said you weren't taking me to jail!"

The boy was certainly paranoid on that score. "I'm just trying to explain that you shouldn't steal things. Right now, you're just a kid, so you think the worst thing that will happen is you'll have to apologize if you get caught. But if you steal something expensive, they send you to a detention facility until you turn eighteen."

After I'd finished, I realized how much I'd sounded like Sergeant Rivard when he was trying to put the fear of God into Barney Beal, and I regretted bringing up the subject. I wasn't going to change Lucas Sewall's destiny in one interaction.

"What happens if a kid kills somebody?" he asked.

I tried to lighten my tone. "Who exactly are you planning on knocking off?"

My cell phone vibrated. I didn't have to look at the screen to know it was Larrabee again.

"It's just a question," said the boy.

"Hold on a second, Lucas." I brought the cell to my ear. "Hey, Doc."

"I've been trying to reach you all night." His words were slip-sliding into one another in a way that suggested he'd been drinking.

"I've been on duty." I didn't feel I owed him any further explanation. "What's the emergency?"

"I have a dead animal here!"

"What animal?"

"Duchess! My dog!"

"What happened to her?"

"It's my fault; it's my fault. I should have—when you asked me—you need to get over here immediately."

To do what, bury the dog in a snowdrift? The veterinarian wasn't making any sense. "Explain to me what's going on."

He sounded exasperated. "I can't explain—not over the phone. I did something I shouldn't have. I violated my oath. Do you understand?"

I could feel Lucas watching me through those heavy glasses. "How much have you had to drink tonight?'

"Not enough." He made a wet throaty noise that might or might not have been laughter. "How far away are you? When can you be here?"

A stop sign glowed red in my headlights. "I'm coming into Township Nineteen now."

"Good!"

"But I'm not going to be able to get to your house for at least a couple of hours. I'm taking a little boy to the hospital in Calais."

"Is he all right?" he asked, slurring.

"He's fine."

"Then you can stop on the way. My house is right on the road to Calais."

"I can't just take the boy with me to your house."

"My dog is dead! Don't you understand what that means?"

"Are you saying someone killed it?"

He must have dropped the phone. I heard a jarring, breaking noise that sure sounded like a receiver striking hardwood and then the signal cut out. It didn't stutter or fizzle; it just ended.

"Doc? Doc?"

After a long interval of not hearing a response, I tucked the cell in the cup holder.

"Who was that?" Lucas asked.

"A friend of mine." It seemed easier to characterize our problematic relationship in these terms than explain what a pain in my ass the old veterinarian had become.

"What got killed?"

"His dog passed away."

"You said someone killed it."

Despite his affected lack of interest, the boy had been listening closely. "I don't know what happened to the dog."

"You're going to his house?"

"After I drop you off."

"Can I go with you? I want to see the dead dog."

"No way."

But sure enough, as I left the shelter of the birches and white pines and came out into the windswept blueberry barrens, my conscience began to gnaw at me. I thought about the abrupt manner in which Doc's call to me had ended. He'd sounded pretty wasted before, and despite his generally good health, I needed to remember that he was an elderly man. He was definitely intoxicated. What if he had fallen and injured himself? I tried his number again and got no answer. I tried his cell and got voice mail.

Doc Larrabee's farm was just a few miles up the road. What if the old man was bleeding to death from a head wound? I took my foot off the gas and hit my blinker.

"Where are we going?" asked Lucas.

"To check on my friend."

"The one with the dead dog?"

"Yeah," I said. "That one."

37

A line of kids on snowmobiles crossed the road just before we reached the farmhouse. I counted five of them, all going too fast. I watched them shoot away into the night, their lights growing dim as they followed the groomed trail across the barrens.

Atop its low hill, beneath the leafless elms that had somehow survived a century-long blight, sat the farmhouse. The porch light was turned off, but a yellow glow showed in the mudroom window, and I saw Doc's pickup parked outside the yawning barn. I unbuckled my chest belt. Lucas fiddled with his, but I caught his arm.

"Stay here," I said. "I'll be right back."

"I want to see the dead dog."

"No way."

I swung open the driver's door and a strong gust of wind nearly pushed it closed on my leg before I could get out. I braced the door with my arm. "Don't fool around with anything in my truck, please. I'll know if something's missing."

He didn't say anything in response, just reached inside his backpack and drew out his notebook.

As I trudged through the snow up to the farmhouse, I felt the hairs in my nostrils begin to bristle from the cold. The temperature was plunging again, headed back below zero, but at least the clouds were breaking. Every now and again, the moon showed its pale, pock-marked face before ducking out of sight. The last time I'd visited this farm, the blizzard had hidden most of the surroundings from view. Now I saw snow-covered blueberry barrens tumbling down the rocky hillside toward Bog Pond. In the moonlight, I spotted a couple of shadowy shapes that must have been ice-fishing shacks on the frozen lake.

I rapped with my knuckles on the old door, hearing the glass windows rattle in the wood frame, then resorted to my fist when no one answered. Maybe the old guy really had passed out. I gave a glance down the drive and saw Lucas's headlamp flickering inside my truck.

The door opened when I twisted the knob. Given the near panic in Doc's voice earlier, I was surprised to find it unlocked.

The house was cold, and it smelled bad—not just that mustiness that I remembered from the night of the dinner party but the reek of food scraps beginning to rot in the garbage, and a sharp vinegar odor that made me think of spilled wine.

"Doc?"

A moan came from the interior. I switched on the hall light and made my way down the cramped passage to the living room. Doc was slumped across the horsehair sofa in the dark. I flicked the switch. He squeezed his eyes shut and jerked his head away, as if he couldn't bear the brightness.

There were several empty bottles on the side tables and the window seat—wine bottles, a bottle of Maker's Mark, and even some bottles of fancy liqueurs I associated with his late wife. It was as if the old widower had raided his cabinets, looking for every last remaining intoxicant in the house. Was all this chaos over a dead dog?

I folded my arms across my chest, pressing the armored vest I wore beneath my shirt against my rib cage. "What the hell happened to you?"

"I must have tripped." He tried to prop himself up on the couch arm but seemed to lack the strength. When he turned his head to me, I saw that his lip was swollen.

"Your phone went dead while we were talking."

He glanced around at the floor, looking for his cordless phone. "It's around here somewhere."

"I was worried about you. What's so important that you had me rush over here?"

"I made a mistake. I should have told you before."

"Told me what?"

"What really happened."

"You're not making any sense, Doc."

There was dried blood and food in his beard. "You were right about Prester Sewall. He didn't kill his friend."

I felt my beating heart push against my sternum. "How do you know that?"

Doc sat up and reached for the nearest liquor bottle. He tilted it over his open mouth, but nothing dripped out. "I just know."

"You have to stop drinking and tell me what happened."

"The night of the blizzard . . ."

"Yes?"

"I didn't know who he was," he said. "Not at first. His face was too swollen, and I didn't recognize his name from the license; none of us did."

"Are you talking about Prester Sewall?"

He nodded. "After they came back to the house—you were still out there in the Heath—Kendrick told me who the frozen man was."

"Kendrick?"

"I told him I couldn't do it. I'm just an old vet, but I was a medic in the army, and I took an oath!" He coughed into his closed fist. "You should have seen him, the look on his face. He would have done it himself. He tried to push me aside. But then the ambulance arrived, and it was too late."

I could feel my pulse throbbing in my neck. "Why would Kendrick want you to kill Prester Sewall?"

"He wanted them both dead."

"Both of them? Are you saying Kendrick was the one who murdered Cates?"

In my mind's eye I saw the sled-dog racer coming across Randall in the storm—hypothermic, stumbling, unable to defend himself—then holding Randall's face down in the snow until he could no longer breathe.

Doc Larrabee nodded his whiskered chin. "Kendrick said they deserved to die." He began to shake, as if on the verge of tears. "But I kept dreaming about Helen. She wouldn't have wanted me to lie. 'You can't let them convict the wrong man,' she told me, 'no matter what those men did to those young people.'"

The wind howled outside the house. It sounded like a living thing now, some sort of choral voice of animal spirits.

"So you told Kendrick you were going to the police?"

"I tried to convince him. I tried everything to reason with him, but he wouldn't listen. It was poetic justice, he said. The police already had their suspect. Then he heard that you were asking questions."

"What did you tell him?"

"That you showed me a picture of a snowmobile. I said you didn't believe it was Prester who killed his friend. He got really worried. He knows about your history."

I remembered running into Kendrick outside the Spragues' Laundromat, how inquisitive he'd been. And later, during the search for Prester's body, I'd thought I spotted his pickup parked near the Machias River.

"Did Kendrick have something to do with Prester's disappearance from the hospital?"

He hung his head. "I don't know."

"Think!"

"He didn't tell me. But I know what he did to Duchess!"

"Kendrick killed your dog?"

"I let her outside today, same as I always do, and she didn't come back. Then I found her body in the road, like she'd been hit by a car. She *never* went in the road! Kendrick did it—as a warning to keep my mouth shut." He started sobbing. "She was Helen's dog—my last link to Helen."

Thoughts were darting around my head like quick-moving birds. Doc was rambling and nearly incoherent, but his condition seemed to vouch for his troubled conscience. He sounded like a man haunted by a past misdeed. The problem was that I was missing a key piece of information, without which everything Larrabee had told me was just useless hearsay.

A dog was howling. At first I thought it was the wind again. Then I realized there was a mournful undertone that could only have come from a living creature. I stepped to the nearest window, parted the dusty curtains, and looked out. The light from inside the room made it impossible to see anything but my own troubled expression.

"What's wrong?" Doc asked. "Is someone out there?"

Ever since I'd arrived in Washington County, people had been invoking the name of poor dead Trinity Raye. Even I had wondered if she'd been one of Kendrick's favorite students, but the sheriff had said she wasn't even in his class. Would the professor really have committed one murder, and attempted a second, to avenge the death of a girl he barely knew? It was possible, but as an explanation it seemed insufficient.

The phone rang. The sound—shrill and insistent—seemed to be coming from Doc himself. He turned his head, slowly and stupidly, and patted the cushions.

I bent down on one knee and reached beneath the couch. My blind hand found the cordless receiver embedded in an inch of dog fur and dust.

"Hello?"

"Warden Bowditch! What a surprise."

"Kendrick?"

"Hell no. It's your old buddy George Magoon." The reception had that slightly overloud distortion that indicates the person on the other end is speaking from a cell phone. "Is Doc there?"

"You know he's here, Kendrick." Doc was staring at me with wide, glassy eyes, and I could see that he was genuinely afraid. "Where are you?"

"Here and there. I tend to move around a lot." There was a rustling on the line that sounded like wind. "Doc has been telling you some of his crazy stories, I imagine."

"He thinks you killed Duchess."

"He must be drinking again. Why would I kill my good friend's dog?"

"As a warning to keep quiet."

"Keep quiet about what?"

"He says you've been lying about what happened the night of the blizzard. He says you killed Randall Cates out in the storm and wanted him to kill Prester Sewall before the EMTs arrived."

"That's quite a story! His imagination really runs wild when he's hammered."

"You're saying it's a lie?"

"I've never killed anyone in my life. Besides, the state police have already determined that Prester Sewall murdered Cates."

"The police haven't determined anything."

"Sewall's suicide suggests he had a guilty conscience."

"I'm not so sure he committed suicide."

"Now you're the one with the hyperactive imagination. Tell me this: Why would I want to kill two men I'd never even met?"

"Because they were drug dealers."

"So are a lot of people in this godforsaken country. I'd have my hands full if I decided to kill all of them."

"Because Cates and Sewall sold contaminated heroin to a student named Trinity Raye, who died as a result."

"Go check at the university. Trinity Raye wasn't even my student. You're just grasping at straws now—just like you've done in the past. Isn't it enough that your career is in tatters?"

"Since when have you taken an interest in my career, Kendrick?"

"I'm a teacher," he said. "I believe in doing my homework. Let me see if I've got this straight. You're saying that while embarked on a selfless mission to rescue a lost man, I spontaneously decided to kill him?"

It did sound ridiculous when he put it that way. "You didn't know it was Randall Cates lost out there until you came upon him in the snow and saw that crazy tattoo."

"It might surprise you to learn that I don't have an encyclopedic knowledge of drug dealers and their tattoos. Your entire story is absurd."

"I'll make a deal with you, Kendrick," I said. "Why don't the three of us pay a visit to the state police—you, me, and Doc—and we'll let them decide whose story sounds the most absurd."

"Sorry, I've got a prior commitment."

"You should clear your calendar. Detective Zanadakis will want to talk with you after he hears what Doc and I have to say."

"Now who's the one issuing threats? We both know our mutual friend was intoxicated the night of the blizzard and that he's been self-medicating ever since his lovely wife passed away."

"What about the Spragues? They were there in the house."

He gave a laugh. "They're the last people who are going to say anything."

"What does that mean?"

He took a long time to answer. "What is it going to take to make you drop this absurd inquiry? How can I persuade you that you're making a terrible, terrible mistake?"

"It won't be the first mistake I've made."

"But it might be the last," said Kendrick. "My crystal ball says you're headed for a bad end, Warden."

Just then a dog barked. I heard it over the telephone line but also through the window.

There was a click and then nothing.

I pressed *69 on the keypad. No one picked up, but eventually an automated voice answered. It was my own cell phone.

38

Maybe Kendrick had heard me give away my location over the police scanner and rushed over on his dogsled. Or maybe he'd arrived independently, planning to confront Doc again, and just happened to see me drive up in my patrol truck. In any case, he'd been watching the farmhouse.

He had seen me leave Lucas behind in the cold cab with his notebook and his headlamp glowing. As soon as I was inside, he had slid quietly up to my vehicle. What he'd said to the boy, I didn't know, but it was hardly surprising that Lucas, of all kids, would be enchanted by a man driving a real-life dogsled. Had Kendrick simply asked to borrow the cell phone, which I had left in the cup holder? That was quite the ballsy move: threatening me on my own Black-Berry.

I rushed to the nearest light switch and plunged the room into darkness.

Doc rose unsteadily from the sofa. "What are you doing?"

"Trying to see my truck."

"Kendrick's outside the house?"

"Yes." How could I have been so stupid as to leave Lucas alone? "Does he usually carry a gun?"

"He has a big Smith & Wesson revolver."

I parted the curtains carefully. My eyes needed time to adjust, but slowly the snow-covered landscape sharpened into focus. I saw the periwinkle drifts piled against the stone wall and the gray trunks of the elms. Farther down the hill was the dark silhouette of my patrol truck. I squinted but couldn't make out the glimmer of Lucas's head-lamp.

Stepping away from the window, I dialed the state police dispatcher in Augusta, gave my call numbers, and reported a possible ten thirty-two, which is the code for man with a gun. "Suspect is a white male, five eleven, one hundred and seventy pounds, approximately forty years of age. His name is Kevin Kendrick, of Township Nineteen. He may be accompanied by a twelve-year-old boy and driving a dogsled."

It wouldn't have surprised me if the dispatcher thought I was pulling her leg. Instead, she asked if I had any identifying information on the boy. I described Lucas to her as best I could.

I handed Doc his cordless phone. "Stay away from the windows," I said. "If you hear gunfire, tell the dispatcher an officer is down."

Through force of will, Doc Larrabee was trying to restore himself to sobriety. He worked the muscles around his mouth like a person trying to wake up from a deep sleep. "Mike, what the hell is happening?"

"Kendrick just called me on my own cell phone from the end of your driveway. A twelve-year-old boy is in my truck down there, and I believe he's in danger."

"Why would Kendrick?— He has no reason to harm a child."

"If he really did murder Randall Cates, and he's afraid of being caught, then he's going to do what he needs to do to defend himself, even if it means holding Lucas Sewall as a hostage."

I drew the heavy SIG from its holster and reached for the door-knob.

"I'm so sorry, Mike."

"Now's not the time for apologies," I said. "Tell the dispatcher if something happens to me."

Taking a deep breath, I swung the door open and sprang down the steps, throwing myself so hard against the base of the nearest elm, I bruised my shoulder.

I listened but heard nothing. No voices, no barking dogs, no gun-shots. Just the sighing of the wind through the leafless branches over my head. I rose to my knees, pressed my hand against the scaly bark, and peered down the hill at the snowbank piled along the road. The night sky was a patchwork of stars and clouds. Every few minutes, the moon would appear, almost like a flare going off, lighting up the blueberry barrens that trailed down to Bog Pond.

I rose to a crouching position, getting ready to run in a zigzag pattern to the nearest snowbank, where I hoped to get a view of my truck, when I heard the sound of barking and saw a flash of light. It was the briefest wink, as if someone had turned on a flashlight and then quickly switched it off again. A shadow was moving across the white field behind the farmhouse.

The dogsled.

Kendrick was headed down to Bog Pond. Once he crossed the frozen expanse of ice, he would be at the edge of the Heath again. We would need a plane with a night-vision camera and thermal imaging system to find him in that maze of beaver ponds and tote roads.

The sled was moving rapidly. I heard the happy baying of the dogs as they gave their full effort. On foot, there was no way I could catch Kendrick.

I thrust my pistol into its holster and scrambled up the snowbank on hands and knees. When I saw the passenger door of the truck standing open, I realized that the flash of light I'd seen had been Lucas's headlamp. Kendrick had taken the boy with him.

By the time I reached the truck, I was breathing heavily and sweating under the arms. I reached across the passenger seat and pulled the door shut. I pushed the gearshift on the steering column into reverse and stepped on the gas. It was only when I hit the plowed asphalt again that I realized something was wrong.

Kendrick had slashed one of my tires.

The *thump-thump-thump* of my rapidly flattening tire sounded like a drumbeat. At this rate, I'd be driving on the metal rim in no time. I'd be lucky to make it to the base of the hill. Below the slanting blueberry fields was a ramp the local ice fishermen used to drive their pickups and four-wheelers onto the frozen pond.

Somewhere in the darkness, a dogsled was racing along on a parallel course. If something were to happen to a child placed in my care . . . That was it, I realized. Kendrick knew that my desperation to rescue Lucas would compel me to take foolish risks. He was betting on my reputation for heedlessness, gambling I would make another stupid mistake.

Ahead, at the fuzzy edge of the beams, the sign for the boat launch parking lot came into view. If I turned, I could drive onto the ice and maybe cut him off before he crossed the lake. I grabbed the radio mic and hit the push-to-talk button. "Twenty-two fifty-eight, I have a ten-thirty-three on Route 277 and the Bog Road. Suspect is driving a dogsled across Bog Pond. He has a twelve-year-old boy with him, and he may be armed. Request immediate assistance at the Route 277 boat launch."

Dispatch copied me. Units were on the way.

The turn approached. I braked hard, feeling a shudder go through me as the bad tire ripped loose, bounced in pieces against the undercarriage, and tumbled away in my brake lights. The shriek of the steel rim on the asphalt pierced me like a dentist's drill.

I bumped into the empty parking lot and rolled down onto the snow-covered ice, forcing myself to go slowly. Hit it too hard, too fast, and no matter how thick the ice was, I could go through. My high beams fanned out across the pond, finding the rectangular shapes of vacant fishing shacks in the distance. I scanned for movement but saw nothing.

Had Kendrick pulled a U-turn and gone back up the hill?

No.

Instead of heading straight across the open expanse, Kendrick was moving parallel to the shore, following the ragged edge of trees and brush. I could catch him easily if I accelerated now.

I was turning the wheel to follow his trail when a warning went off in my brain. Rivard had cautioned me there were glacial boulders in the shallows of this lake, some as big as boxcars. In places, the tops of the huge rocks bulged through the snowpack, looking like pressure ridges in the ice or harmless mounds of snow that a vehicle could easily plow through. The edge of the pond was studded with those hidden traps, and if I struck one, even at thirty miles an hour, I would crash headlong across—and probably through—the lake ice.

Kendrick was deliberately leading me through an obstacle course. He was "the best woodsman left in America," according to the *New York Times*. He knew this country so much better than I did; he had every advantage. What could I remember about Bog Pond? What knowledge could I possibly use against my brilliant and experienced adversary without endangering Lucas?

Kendrick's goal was to lose himself in the maze of alder thickets and beaver bogs on the western side of the lake. If he kept following the shoreline, he would skirt a cliff that would be impossible for his dogs to climb. Beyond that cliff was the outlet to Bog Stream, the creek that spilled out of the pond and fell in a series of gradual waterfalls down into the Heath.

Moving water, I thought. Thin ice.

If I cut across the lake sharply, I could pin Kendrick against that cliff, forcing him to make a choice: either turn back in the direction of the boat landing, where police cruisers would soon be assembling (I hoped) or skate across the questionable ice near the Bog Stream outlet. With my truck blocking escape to the center of the pond, he would have no other options.

The problem was that he would easily guess my intentions the moment he saw my headlights turn toward the cliff. I realized I had only a single plan of attack. I pointed the nose of the truck toward the center of the lake, filled my lungs with air, and switched off my headlights.

The world went instantly dark.

I was as blind as if I had fallen into a deep cave. The intermittent moonlight that had seemed so bright outside Doc's farmhouse barely registered on my optic nerves.

Please, God, I prayed. Let there be none of those boulders in this part of the lake.

Leaning forward over the wheel, I stepped on the gas pedal and shot on an intercept course for the cliff. Within a matter of seconds, my front wheels hit a pressure ridge that jolted me against my seat belt. When I came back down, my teeth smashed together on the edge of my tongue. I tasted blood.

My eyes strained to adjust to the black-and-white universe into which I suddenly found myself. I saw a blurry line form far ahead: gray above, black below. I floored the gas and watched the line sharpen until I knew I was getting close to the cliff.

Between the engine and the wrecked wheel, my truck was making enough of a racket that he could hear me coming. But I could still throw some surprises his way. I hit everything I had in succession: blue lights, high beams, spotlight, and siren.

Bingo.

The sled was a hundred yards ahead, moving from right to left against the cliff face. I saw the dogs break stride, startled by the cacophonous noise and illumination. I saw Kendrick, standing on the runners, snap his head in my direction. And I saw Lucas seated on the sled: his pale white face the only part visible.

Be smart, Kendrick. Stop now.

Instead, he shook the leads and shouted at his dogs to leap forward. The sled shot off again, straight for the Bog Stream outlet. He had to know it was an act of madness.

The sled broke through the ice from back to front.

The weight of Kendrick and Lucas dragged the dogs in scrambling pairs backward into the collapsing hole. Over the siren, I couldn't hear their howls, but I saw the animals clawing desperately against the harness that was pulling them inexorably to their deaths. Kendrick had loaded the sled with bricks, he'd told me, to build his dogs' endurance.

I slammed on my brakes, but the truck kept sliding. The end fishtailed as I pulled the parking brake in a last-ditch attempt to avoid the thin ice. My truck spun completely around, once, twice, before it came to a halt. When it did, I found myself facing the center of the lake.

My God, I thought. *Lucas.*

Dazed, head spinning, my mouth bloody from the bite I'd taken out of my tongue, I fumbled with the seat-belt latch and pushed open the door. When I hit the ice, my boots slipped out from under me, and I fell face-first onto my chest in the snow. I pushed myself up onto my knees and then, slipping and sliding, onto my feet.

My vehicle had come to rest with the lights pointed in the wrong direction. In the near dark, I had trouble making out what was happening. I saw heads floating, limbs thrashing; heard animal wails and a boy's cry for help.

"Lucas!"

I slid around to the open door and began madly groping at the junk in the backseat. Where was my rope? In a coil in the pack basket. My personal flotation devices? Wedged under the seat. Where the hell was my float coat? I couldn't find it anywhere. Keep calm, said a voice in my head. Don't panic.

I tied a bowline around the trailer hitch and ran the rope forward toward the hole in the ice, trying to secure another knot to the PFD while I did so.

The dogs were all gone now, pulled down by the brick-laden weight of the sled. But I saw Lucas's head bobbing: glasses gone, a look of utter terror on his stricken white face. And farther out, Kendrick was calmly treading water.

"Kendrick!"

The musher didn't answer me.

Lucas disappeared beneath the surface before I could throw him the PFD.

"Kendrick! Help him, for God's sake!"

Deliberately, he turned away and began paddling for the edge of the ice on the other side of the hole.

I dropped my gun belt on the ice and, without even removing my boots, ran toward the open water. I heard an explosive crack and felt myself dropping as if through a trapdoor. With the PFD tucked under my arm, I didn't go completely under, but the sudden, almost total immersion in freezing water blew the air entirely out of my lungs, as if I'd been hit by a two-by-four between the ribs.

My voice came out as a gasp. "Lucas!"

The shock of going into the water was worse than I'd expected. I could feel my muscles tightening and heard my pulse beating faster and faster in my water-filled ears. I gulped down a breath, let go of the PFD, and let myself sink beneath the surface. I thrust my arms around me like a blind man trying to feel his way out of an unfamiliar room.

My fingers touched something. At first, I thought it might be the boy's hair, and then I realized it was fur—one of Kendrick's lifeless malamutes passing in the dark current.

I shot back up to the surface for another breath.

I'd drifted several yards from the floating life jacket. If I went under again, would I even have the strength to grab it?

Keep calm, keep calm, keep calm.

Again, I filled my lungs with air, and again, I dived down into the gelid waters of the lake.

We collided with each other, literally knocked heads.

I was so startled, I recoiled at first, then understood what had happened. My fingers were so frozen, they could barely close around his arm.

I gave a strong kick and pulled with all my might.

My face broke the surface just long enough to see that the moon was out. Then I went under again. Unless I could summon strength from some unknown reserve, the boy and I would sink to the bottom. Tomorrow the Warden Service divers will retrieve our bodies, I thought.

An image flashed into my head of myself underwater, two years earlier. I'd thought I was going to die when my canoe overturned at Rum Pond. Instead, I had fought for my life. Now I needed to fight for Lucas Sewall's life as well.

I scissored my legs and felt the cold air hit my face. I blinked and thrashed, tugging Lucas along after me, flexing my biceps to pull his head above the surface. Where was the PFD? My eyes were half blind from the lake water.

I kicked hard toward the jagged edge of the ice and saw something orange ahead. It seemed so far away. I could barely breathe. Even if I reached the life jacket, how was I going to pull myself out?

I heard coughing behind me. Lucas was flailing about with his arms. Amazingly, he was back from the dead. I tried to yank him toward the PFD.

"Lucas," I sputtered. "The life jacket."

I didn't think he'd heard me, let alone understood what I'd meant, but the next thing I knew, I felt us surge forward. He was kicking his legs. I gave one last push and reached out with my stiff arm. I brought it down on the PFD. I squeezed the flotation device against my side and felt its buoyancy lift me from the current. I nearly dislocated Lucas's shoulder as I pulled him up beside me.

I heard voices in the dark. People were shouting.

Suddenly we began to move. Someone was tugging on the rope. I had no idea who it was, but I saw lights and heard engines.

"Hang on, dude!" someone said.

I felt my body being reeled in like a fish. Without having to exert myself at all, Lucas and I were suddenly lying on the snow-dusted ice, shivering violently and gasping for air.

"Are you guys OK?"

Above us loomed several people in snowmobile suits. The one who'd spoken to me had taken his helmet off. He was a hulking kid with a flattop haircut and a wide oval face.

"I know you," I sputtered.

"You came to my school," said Barney Beal.

39

My heart felt like a lump of ice in my chest. I couldn't feel my feet.

The boys helped us into the truck, where I could run the heater and call for an ambulance. I found a wool blanket to wrap Lucas in, and another one for myself. I left the blue lights spinning so the responding units would have an easier time finding our location out on the lake.

The boys giggled at my chattering teeth, proving they were as stoned and drunk as I had suspected when I first saw them speeding in front of Doc Larrabee's house. Later, I would need to talk to them about the inadvisability of snowmobiling under the influence. But not now.

Barney Beal brought me my gun belt without my asking for it. The snaps were all open on the leather holsters, so I knew he'd been looking at the secret things inside, the spare magazines and handcuffs.

"That fucker is heavy," he said. "How much does it weigh?"

"Forty pounds." I was having a hard time getting the words past my spastic tongue. "Did you guys see anyone else . . . when you . . . rode up?"

"Like who?"

"Older guy . . . with a beard. Went into the water, too."

"Shit, he must have drowned."

I wasn't so sure. My last sight of Kendrick was of him swimming confidently to the edge of the hole. Maybe he had been unable to climb out and had slipped beneath the surface while I was fighting for my life. Or maybe he had staggered away into the night. One way or another the Maine Warden Service would find him. At the moment I was having a hard time caring if it was alive or dead.

After a few minutes, the teenagers grew bored listening to my castanet teeth and wandered off to sit on their snowmobiles and smoke cigarettes. I saw the orange tips floating in the darkness like fireflies surprised from their hibernation.

Lucas closed his eyes and his head lolled. I felt his pulse beneath his chin. It was scarily slow. I pushed his wet hair back off his forehead and wrapped the blanket more tightly around him, and I put my arm around his shoulders, trying to share some of my own negligible body heat.

What would happen to him now? It would depend on his mother's court case. If she was convicted on the drug charge, then she'd be given a mandatory sentence of not less than two years. Despite Munro's criminal history, a softhearted judge might feel obliged to award him custody. I thought of this weird, intelligent boy in my arms growing up with a violent felon for a father, and I wondered if he would be as lucky as I had been and would somehow escape his doom.

Emergency vehicles rolled across the ice; their lights flashed red and blue.

I squeezed his shoulders. "Lucas?"

His eyes fluttered open. "Am I dead?"

"No," I said. "You're not."

The first officer I talked to was a state trooper. Like most of his brethren, he stood about seven feet tall and had a jaw carved from solid marble. Trooper Belanger listened attentively as I unspooled my story, staring from beneath the shadowed brim of his Smokey the Bear hat.

"Someone needs to check in on Doc Larrabee." I had the blanket wrapped around my shoulders, but it wasn't doing much against the chill of the night.

"You got it."

"I don't know what happened to Kendrick. He might have gone

under, but I think he got himself out of the hole. We'll need a dog to track him if he went into the Heath. I'm not sure how far he can run if he's as cold and wet as I am. But I believe he's carrying at least one firearm, so whoever's tracking him needs to treat him as dangerous. He already killed one man and kidnapped a child."

"Understood."

"We should get those dead dogs out of the water. It doesn't seem right to leave them down there."

"Anything else?"

"No, I can brief Rivard and the sheriff when they get here."

"Can I make a suggestion?"

"Sure."

"Get your ass to the hospital. You're shivering like a half-drowned rat."

For once, I took somebody else's advice. I rode in the back of the ambulance with Lucas. The emergency medical technicians had him lie down atop the folding stretcher and covered him with blankets. He responded with just grunts and nods to the questions the female EMT asked him.

"Do your fingers and toes hurt?" she asked.

"No."

"Can you wiggle them for me?"

"No."

"No because you can't, or no because you don't want to?"

"Wiggle your fingers, Lucas," I said.

He did as I asked. He had lost his glasses in the lake, so he was forced to squint constantly. I don't think his unfocused gaze left me once during the entire trip. It was as if he feared I might vanish like a genie into a puff of smoke if he looked away.

"Did Kendrick force you onto the sled?" I asked.

"Who?"

"The man with the dogs."

Suddenly this boy whom I had never seen cry burst into sobs. "He said he would let me drive them."

I clutched his hand and held on tight.

After he approached the truck, Kendrick must have seen my cell phone in the cup holder and decided to use it to call Doc. Then, when he realized he needed to lure me onto the ice, he had promised the boy a ride.

I replayed the telephone conversation I'd had with Kendrick, searching for answers. There had to have been a connection between Randall Cates and the professor. If it wasn't the dead girl, Trinity Raye, then what was it?

At the hospital, I climbed stiffly out of the ambulance and asked the EMT if I could borrow her cell phone. My energy was beginning to sag as my adrenal glands decided they had done their work for the evening and needed a two-week vacation. The EMTs carried Lucas on the stretcher. He squinted ahead into the brightly lit ambulance bay, his features contorted in alarm, as if he expected to discover a vivisectionist's laboratory behind the secured door.

"Don't be afraid, Lucas."

"Will you come with me?"

"I'll see you inside," I promised him.

His expression said he didn't believe me. He was right not to.

Those were the last words I would speak to Lucas Sewall, although I didn't know it at the time.

I dialed Sheriff Rhine's mobile phone. I caught her on the road to Bog Pond.

"I'm at Down East Community Hospital," I said. "I didn't want to leave the poor kid alone. I also thought it would be a good idea for a doctor to sign off on my fitness for duty after going into the water like that."

"That's uncharacteristically prudent of you."

"I don't want anyone complaining that I refused to follow protocol. My personnel file is thick enough already." My whole body felt like it had been pummeled by a sadistic Swedish masseuse. "I think you should send one of your deputies to the Spragues' house."

"What for?"

"If Kendrick is alive, I'm guessing he might be heading to Ben and Doris for help. Their house isn't far from the lake, and I'm wondering if, somehow, they might be the key to this whole thing. Can you think of any link between the Sprague family and Randall Cates?"

Her voice couldn't cover her skepticism. "Like being drug customers of his? They're both Jehovah's Witnesses, for crying out loud. Ben and his son, Joey, knocked on my door once with a pamphlet."

I remembered that bedroom in the Spragues' house where we had ministered to Prester—there had been a vacant feel to it, as if its teenaged occupant had long since died or moved away—and then something Doc said earlier came back to me. "You can't let them convict the wrong man," his dead wife's ghost had told him, "no matter what those men did to those young people."

Those young people.

For a moment, I felt like the fog was lifting and I was beginning to see things clearly for the first time. Kendrick had told me that they were the last ones who would say anything against him. They must have a reason to keep quiet, I realized.

"Where is the Spragues' son now?"

"Massachusetts. At some sort of long-term care unit, I think. He's still in a coma, the last I heard."

"Was it a drug overdose?"

"Gunshot wound to the head. He tried to kill himself last summer."

Just like that, the fog closed in again. "What? Why?"

"He was an unhappy teenager. I don't know the particulars."

"You need to find out," I said. "I'm betting that there's a connection between him and Cates. Or a connection between him and Kendrick."

The sheriff fell silent.

"What is it?" I asked.

Rhine said, "Joey Sprague was a freshman at the University of Maine at Machias."

My adrenal glands woke up. "Was he one of Kendrick's students?"

"I'll find out."

"See if he was a friend of Trinity Raye's, too."

"Can I put you on hold?" said the sheriff. "I'm thinking it might be a good idea for me to send one of my deputies to the Sprague house."

Ben and Doris Sprague's little chalet was dark and the curtains were drawn when Chief Deputy Corbett arrived outside their door. The fire road had been recently plowed, and Ben's truck was gone. Corbett phoned in, asking what to do. He wanted to head over to Bog Pond, where all the excitement was.

Sheriff Rhine told him to suck it up and wait.

The chief deputy was still waiting two hours later when Warden Cody Devoe and Tomahawk followed the scent trail from the hole in the ice, along the edge of the Heath, straight to the Spragues' doorstep.

By then, it was already too late to alert the Canada Border Services Agency and request that its agents detain a blue GMC with a Fisher snowplow should it attempt to cross from Calais, Maine, into St. Stephen, New Brunswick. Later, the Canadian guards would verify that such a vehicle, carrying a middle-aged man and woman and another man, had been waved through without a search. Like most Washington County residents, the Spragues traveled frequently across the border to go grocery shopping or catch a movie, and they were well known to the Canadian guards on duty. No one suspected that the friendly little couple's companion was a fugitive from justice.

But the next day, after the U.S. Immigration and Customs Enforcement agents picked them up, the Spragues claimed they didn't even know Kendrick was a fugitive.

"Kevin didn't tell us he was on the run," Doris Sprague told the men at the Houlton checkpoint, nearly one hundred miles from Calais. "He showed up at our house, saying he needed a ride over to New Brunswick."

"Why?" asked one of the agents.

"He said a Canadian friend of his had been badly injured in an accident," said Ben.

"Why not drive himself, then?"

"His truck had a blown head gasket."

"So then what happened?"

"We drove him across the bridge into St. Stephen," said Ben. "He told us to drop him outside Charlotte County Hospital."

"And that was the last time you saw him?"

"Yes."

"So why did you wait six hours before returning across the border?"

"We decided to take a moonlight drive."

When asked by the ICE agents and the Maine State Police detectives why they would perform such a charitable service for a man they barely knew, the Spragues admitted that Professor Kendrick wasn't a total stranger. He had been their son Joey's favorite teacher at the university, but they continued to profess their ignorance of any crimes he might have committed. While it was true that their son had known Trinity Raye, his suicide attempt had nothing to with drugs, they insisted. Joey suffered from depression but he would never have taken heroin. Neither of the Spragues had ever seen Randall Cates or Prester Sewall before the night of the blizzard. They had no prior relationships with the dead men, in other words, although they would not mourn their passing. They didn't know why God, in His wisdom, had chosen to deliver those evildoers to their doorstep in that blizzard, but they swore they had nothing to do with what had happened to Randall Cates out in the Heath.

Prester Sewall had obviously murdered his friend, and then he had killed himself. The facts spoke for themselves.

40

That's horseshit," I told Sergeant Rivard.

We were standing on the south bank of the Machias River in Machiasport the following afternoon. A housewife had glanced out her frosted window, and a beam of weak midwinter sunlight had touched something red in the tidal flats below. It was a bloody, bandaged foot sticking up out of the tacky mud.

Rivard called for the airboat team to extract the body of Prester Sewall from the stinking mire where it had become wedged. Now the two of us, along with about fifty other onlookers—some fellow officers and SAR volunteers, the rest just garden-variety voyeurs— were watching Warden Mack McQuarrie lean over the side of the boat and tug with all his might at the dead man's leg.

Prester didn't want to come out.

Rivard tucked a fresh wad of Red Man chewing tobacco in his cheek. "What's horseshit?" he asked.

"The Spragues' story."

Sheriff Rhine had been phoning me with recaps all day. She must have figured it was the least she could do, given that my crackpot theories about Randall Cates's death hadn't proven so cracked after all. She'd given me a detailed account of the state police interrogation of the Spragues in Houlton, and she'd listened patiently as I vented my frustration at the roadblock investigators faced, at least until the Mounties hunted down Kevin Kendrick on their side of the border, if they ever managed to hunt him down. She'd even offered to buy me breakfast at McDonald's some morning.

"Ben and Doris Sprague are lying," I told Rivard. "They knew damn well that Kendrick was on the run last night, and they knew why. They should be charged with aiding and abetting."

"How's the AG going to prove that, exactly?"

It was the same question Rhine had asked me, and I still had no good answer.

"Their son, Joey, was friends with Trinity Raye," I said. "Both kids had been good students at UMaine Machias, but their grades had gotten worse and worse. That screams drug abuse. Then the Raye girl dies, and a few months later, Joey Sprague tries to commit suicide. What does that suggest to you?"

I answered my own question before he could. "It suggests guilt," I said. "Maybe Joey bought the heroin from Cates and gave it to Trinity. For all we know, Randall and Prester might have done their deals in the Heath all the time. They might have driven past the Spragues' house regularly on the Bog Road. Maybe that's how Joey became one of their customers."

Rivard was wearing his sunglasses, as always, so I couldn't see his eyes, but he seemed focused on Mack McQuarrie and the activity around the airboat.

I continued thinking out loud. "I still think it was dumb luck that they got stranded there in the storm. And I don't think the Spragues recognized Prester when he showed up on their doorstep. His driver's license says his name is John, and his face was disfigured. That was why they called Doc for help. It was only later, when they came upon Randall in the Heath, that they realized he was the man responsible for one girl's death and for their own son's turning himself into a vegetable. You're a father, Marc. What would you have done in that situation? You could kill the bastard—and no one would ever know."

I wasn't sure if my sergeant had been listening until he turned his head. "What are you suggesting?"

"I think Ben Sprague was the one who really killed Randall Cates. He had the means, motive, and opportunity. Or maybe he and Kendrick did it together. I could see Kendrick goading him into doing it. He can be quite persuasive. If the two men were mutually involved, that would explain what happened back at the house."

"What happened back at the house?"

"After Kendrick and Ben came back, they wanted to kill Prester, too. Or at least Kendrick did. He tried to persuade Doc that it would be for the greater good if he put a pillow over Prester's face. But Doc wouldn't do it. He's a veterinarian, but he sees himself as a medical man, the Hippocratic oath and all that. It was only the fact that the EMTs showed up that stopped things from getting violent."

Rivard spat a stream of tobacco juice on the crusted snow. "That's quite a story."

"It's the only interpretation of events that makes sense."

"Good luck convincing the attorney general."

With Kendrick on the lam in Canada, suspicion had naturally fallen on the fugitive dogsled racer. He was the one who had told Doc to let Prester die. He was the one who had threatened me via e-mail and killed Doc's dog as a warning to keep his mouth shut. He was the one who kidnapped Lucas Sewall and nearly sent us all to the bottom of Bog Pond. Just as the investigators had focused on Prester, to the exclusion of other suspects earlier, now they had shifted their attention to Kendrick.

"The state police need to keep leaning on the Spragues," I said. "If they do, the truth will come out."

"Not necessarily," said my sergeant. "If you haven't figured it out by now, Bowditch, some people are wicked good liars."

There was a shout, and then the crowd groaned. Out on the airboat, Mack McQuarrie had managed to muscle Prester Sewall's naked body loose. I saw him wrestle the pale, mud-streaked corpse on board. The bloodless color of the skin reminded me of the underbelly of a frog.

Instantly I found myself thinking of Lucas.

Some people are wicked good liars.

Rivard had been talking about the Spragues, but his remark

seemed to be a broader statement about the untrustworthiness of human beings in general. I'd known from my first meeting with Lucas Sewall that he was prone to wild exaggerations. His own mother had called him a liar.

But even I hadn't taken him for a killer.

The confession came in his notebook, which I discovered a few days later under the passenger seat of my truck as I was vacuuming it out. I had wanted to visit the boy in the hospital, but Rivard cautioned me against having any conversations with him until after the state police got a formal statement. It was enough to hear that he was going to make a full recovery.

I'd also heard from the sheriff that Jamie was out of jail. Mitch Munro had ponied up the bail money by selling his prize snowmobile. The karate champ was still denying he had been on the Heath during the blizzard, the sheriff told me, and so far, Jamie had refused to repeat the story she'd told me about how her ex-husband had waylaid Randall Cates. While it was almost certain that Jamie would be convicted of driving under the influence, the drug case against her was falling apart fast. The Adderall found in the van had indeed belonged to her sister, Tammi, as Jamie had stated all along. Even a mediocre defense lawyer could argue that the pills had fallen into her purse in the course of driving her invalid sister to physical therapy (or wherever). The marijuana Corbett had found in her brother's room made it Prester's property when Jamie produced a canceled check in the amount of one dollar for "rent."

As for Jamie and her ex-husband's rekindled relationship (if that was what it was), I realized it was none of my business. Word around town was that they were hitting the bars together again. She'd lost her job at McDonald's. I couldn't bring myself to drive past her house, lest I see Munro's Tundra out front.

I did have a keen interest in knowing whether Mitch was indeed the man Randall and Prester had gone to meet in the Heath that snowy day, as seemed likely. But trying to factor Munro into a murderous equation that already included Kendrick and the Spragues was a leap even my own overly active imagination refused to make.

But it was an equation, of sorts, that revealed the truth about Trinity Raye. More like a code, actually. After I found Lucas's notebook, I took it back inside my malodorous trailer and sat down at my kitchen table and began flipping through the pages.

I'd made myself a cup of instant coffee, but it tasted, like everything in the damned house, like skunk. Rivard had told me that Joe Brogan had fired Billy Cronk because he'd been gossiping too much about what his employer had done to my living quarters. Rivard thought I might be able to wangle a trade out of Cronk: testimony about how Brogan had released a live skunk into my trailer in exchange for my dropping the firearm charge against the gentle Viking.

It was a deal I would make, I decided.

Picking up Lucas's notebook, I stopped on a jumbled series of letters that I had noticed before on the cover. I hadn't given them any attention then, but after everything I had subsequently learned about Lucas's big brain, I now found my curiosity engaged.

DORT OSNZ CNAP IOZZ

It took me a few minutes to realize that what looked like gibberish was actually a simple cipher of the kind that had fascinated me when I'd read the Hardy Boys books as a kid.

I turned on my computer with the familiar sense of anticipation that now greeted me every time the screen lit up. But there was no new message from George Magoon, and perhaps there would never be another one. I went looking for "secret codes" in the Google search menu.

I found the key quickly enough:

DORT OSNZ
CNAP IOZZ

Reading the first letter of the top word, followed by the first letter of the bottom word, followed by the second letter of the top word, followed by the second letter of the bottom word, and so on in a zigzag pattern, I ended with this:

DCON RAT POISON ZZZ

I put down my pen and stared at the words. Then I began reading carefully through the pages, looking for an actual confession. But Lucas had been coy throughout.

He didn't know what I did to the pills, neither . . . and wasn't he in for a wicked surprise when someone swallowed one of them Oxycottons?

What had he done to the OxyContin pills? Sprayed them with some chemical? What had he done with the rat poison? I thought back to my search for the boy in the Sewall house. Down in the cellar, I remembered a rusted oil tank with an open box of d-Con rat poison on the dirt floor beside it.

Trinity Raye had died from snorting heroin cut with baking powder and brodifacoum. People called it an overdose, but in truth the girl had also suffered an esophageal hemorrhage, causing her to bleed out. The active ingredient in d-Con is brodifacoum.

"What happens if a kid kills somebody?" Lucas had asked me.

The boy knew what he'd done. That was why he'd asked the sheriff if we were there to arrest him the night Rhine and I delivered Prester's death notification. It was the reason he kept asking if I was taking him to jail. No wonder he was being chased in his nightmares by an avenging angel dressed like a white owl.

I grabbed the notebook and hurried out to my truck. What was I going to say to Lucas? What would I tell Jamie? I'd been so worried about seeing her lose custody. Now I found myself in possession of circumstantial evidence that linked her son to the accidental death of a young woman. But who would believe me if I turned it in? Everyone knew about Mike Bowditch and his wild imagination.

Lucas had contaminated Randall Cates's stash of drugs to get even for the pain the dealer was inflicting on his mother. Maybe he hoped someone would get sick, so the blame would fall on Randall.

With the boyfriend out of the picture, his mother and father might finally reunite, as had seemingly happened. Had he expected someone to die? I hoped to God he hadn't.

If Lucas hadn't tampered with the heroin, Trinity Raye might still be alive, and if so, Joey Sprague would not have pressed a handgun against his temple and flinched at the moment he pulled the trigger. Kendrick and Ben Sprague would never have had a reason to kill Randall Cates. Prester might not have committed suicide. The whole chain of fatal events, I realized, began with a brilliant, bitter boy who just wanted his daddy back.

You and Lucas have a lot in common.

The drive was a blur. One poor old geezer nearly went off the road when I zoomed past his puttering Buick.

My cell phone rang in my pocket. I dug it out and looked at the number.

"Charley," I said. "I'm in the middle of something."

"Hot pursuit?"

"In a manner of speaking."

"I was just calling to invite you up to the Ponderosa for Saturday dinner," he said. "The Boss said it was past time I offered you a formal invitation."

It had been too long since I'd eaten Ora Stevens's fresh-baked bread or shared a hot cup of coffee with Charley while he told me one far-fetched but invariably true yarn after another. And maybe my wise old friend could advise me what to do about Lucas and his notebook. Should I turn it over to the state police with my unprovable suspicions, and if so, to what end? So that the boy would be shunted off into some facility for troubled children? More than ever, I realized, I wanted the benefit of Charley's considerable wisdom.

The only hesitancy I felt in saying yes to his invitation came when I remembered those jade-green eyes, the most beautiful I'd ever seen.

Charley, as always, was three steps ahead of me. "Stacey will be joining us."

"What about her fiancé? Will he be there, too?"

I could hear the smile in my friend's voice. "No, I believe Matt is working that night."

"I'll be there," I said, cresting a hill. "But I've really got to go. I'll explain why on Saturday."

"You damn well better!"

I tucked the cell phone into my shirt pocket, feeling unreasonably hopeful. Stacey might have a fiancé, but who knew what was truly possible and impossible?

I braked when I came around the corner, and I braked even harder when I saw the FOR SALE sign in the yard outside Jamie's house. My patrol truck slid on its brand-new wheels and tires across a sanded stretch of asphalt before it came to rest in front of the driveway.

In the past, Jamie had barely bothered to shovel out a space to park her van, but someone had plowed out a vast expanse of the dooryard to make way for whatever big truck had hauled away her furniture and other possessions. You could tell from the dark, curtainless windows that the Sewall family was long gone. Jamie had sworn to me she'd do anything to hold on to her troubled son, even if it meant spiriting him away in the dead of night. What reason did they have to stay in that haunted house anyway? Who wouldn't want to escape from this snowbound wasteland?

I tried to remember the story Jamie had told me when we were lying in bed in the motel, the one about Prester John and his legendary African kingdom: "But someday I'm going to take off south, and I'm not going to stop until I find my own golden city in the sun."

I wondered if she would find it.

Does anyone ever?

AUTHOR'S NOTE

Bad Little Falls is a real waterfall in the town of Machias. For the purposes of this story, however, I have taken liberties in describing it and certain other locations around eastern Washington County. There is no Sabao River, for instance; no game ranch in the fictional town of Narraguagus. The Down East Community Hospital occupies an actual hillside on the Bangor Road, but it employs no doctors named Chatterjee. Similarly, there is a McDonald's Cafe on Route 1, but no Jamie Sewalls have ever worked there, as far as I know. Any resemblance between the characters in this book and any persons, living or dead, is entirely accidental.

It's true that George Magoon was an actual poacher who lived from 1851 to 1929. To those who would read more about his exploits, I highly recommend Edward Ives's excellent *George Magoon and the Down East Game War: History, Folklore, and the Law.* The murder of two Maine game wardens, Lyman O. Hill and Charles W. Niles, in 1886 remains unsolved and bears remembering. No law-enforcement organization in Maine has suffered more deaths in the line of duty than the Warden Service.

As always, I am grateful to those who assisted me in the researching of this book: Corporal John MacDonald of the Maine Warden Service, for answering my blunt questions about search and rescue procedures and other protocols; Donna Maritato, RN, of Penobscot Bay Medical Center, for teaching me about the medical treatment of frostbite and hypothermia; Ron Joseph, formerly of the U.S. Fish and Wildlife Service, for sharing with me his unmatched knowledge of Maine's flora and fauna; and Lieutenant Colonel Hugh Tillman, USMC (Ret.), for putting me behind the controls of a Cessna 172 Skyhawk. Any factual errors in the text are the result of my failure to absorb the information they so patiently aimed to provide. Ben Thomas, author of *Code Breaker,* showed me the cipher Lucas Sewall uses in his notebook.

I am grateful to my colleagues at *Down East: The Magazine of Maine* for the support they have given to the writing of these novels. I owe a debt to the readers of my early drafts for their expert editorial advice: Cindy Anderson and Monica Wood. Thank you to my agent, Ann Rittenberg, who is so smart about so many things, and to all the people at Minotaur, especially my wonderful editor, Charlie Spicer, publicist Hector DeJean, and publisher Andrew Martin.

My family continues to be a source of strength and solace in my life. Thank you, everyone. And to my wife, Kristen, this and everything for you.